John Wainwright's writing career as a novelist began in 1965 with the publication of *Death in a Sleeping City*. He is perhaps best known as an exponent of the police procedural, but his books embrace a wide variety of plot and subject, from the psychological thriller, to espionage, to the classic puzzle. He has also published his wartime autobiography, *Tail-End Charlie*, which is a vivid and sobering account of life as a rear-gunner in Lancaster bombers.

He and his wife, Avis, both born and bred in Yorkshire, now live in Lancashire.

John Wainwright

WAINWRIGHT'S BEAT

Twenty years with the West Yorkshire Police Force

Futura

This book is for Avis, my wife. It is a poor return
for what she has given me but without her it could
never have been written because without her this
life could never have been lived.

A **Futura** Book

Copyright © John and Avis Wainwright, 1987
First published in the UK in 1987 by Macmillan London Limited
This edition published in 1989 by Futura Publications,
a Division of Macdonald & Co (Publishers) Ltd
London & Sydney

Printed and bound in Great Britain by
Collins, Glasgow

Futura Publications
A Division of
Macdonald & Co (Publishers) Ltd
66–73 Shoe Lane
London EC4P 4AB

A member of Maxwell Pergamon Publishing Corporation plc

Contents

If what you are about to read pleases you I would ask that you acknowledge the four supports that hold it in place. They are memories, enthusiasm, encouragement and guidance. I provided the memories and the enthusiasm. My editor, Hilary Hale, provided the encouragement and guidance.

JW

and asked about the possibility of becoming a
man. The inspector had been remarkably polite.
even offered me tea and biscuits while he weighed
d measured me and filled in the forms.

ew days later a uniformed sergeant from Hudders-
Borough Police had called at our home at Birchen-
e (where we were living with Avis's parents, Avis
g my wife of a few years' standing) to check that I
d my bills regularly, wasn't given to beating my wife
often and always washed behind the ears. Having
sfied himself on these points, he promptly urged me
have second thoughts and join the Huddersfield
rough Police.

Poaching potential law-enforcement fodder was very
ommon in those days. The war had made it necessary
or men to stay in the force long after retiring age, and a
air slice of the younger coppers had volunteered for the
rmed forces and hadn't come back. Every force was
understaffed. Bobbies were thin on the ground because
men were now retiring by the cart-load and (because
recruiting had been suspended during the war years) the
British Police Service had a distinctly geriatric look.

I resisted the temptation, and stayed with the West
Riding.

Then had come my first visit to Wakefield Headquarters for The Medical. Four of us stripped to the buff while
the police surgeon tapped and listened with approval to
three of us. The fourth lad worried him. He had a testicle
missing. Otherwise, he was quite OK and the medic was
fascinated to learn that despite this shortage of equip
ment the lad functioned on all cylinders. No matter, he
was pronounced 'unfit'. Obviously, to be a bobby it was
vital to have a full quota of balls.

After that had come my second visit to Wakefield
Headquarters for the bibs and bobs. To be measured for
a uniform. To fill in a questionnaire concerning sports,
interests and hobbies. Sport (other than as a very
occasional spectator) interested me not at all and I was
worried that, if I listed any of the normal exertions, I
might find myself in a team wishing to hell I'd kept my
mouth shut. Which is why, under the heading 'Favourite

Prologue

In *The Vicar of Wakefield* Oliver Goldsmith wrote, 'A book
may be amusing with numerous errors, or it may be very
dull without a single absurdity.' Very neatly put, and a
wise observation made by a first-class novelist. Simple
gumption, therefore, insists that I'd be both stupid and
churlish not to take heed.

However many mistakes I may make in the following
pages – mistakes of memory, of opinions, even of fact – it
will not be dull. On the other hand, I will make no
deliberate mistakes or twist the truth to suit my own
purpose.

A couple of times in the past I have dipped a tentative
toe into the frothy waters of non-fiction, and each time I
have rather enjoyed the experience. I found it a pleasant
and exhilarating change. I *enjoyed* myself . . . and that's
what I'm going to do this time.

I start with a confession and a promise.

If what follows is about me (and, rest assured, it is most
certainly going to *be* about me) it must have certain
biographical overtones. I have no choice. The tenets and
the persuasions are mine. The scepticisms and the
dissensions are mine. The lunacies and the biases are
mine. To that extent, then, it is autobiographical.

Nevertheless, I will spare you as much as possible the
monumental boredom attached to the average biogra-
phy; the weariness of my parentage, the unimportant
drivel of my schooldays and the tedious naïvety of my
pubertal years.

Let us as writer and reader make a pact.

I have arrived, unannounced, on your doorstep. I have

goods to offer. Taste them then; if you dislike them, send me away. Close the book and, in so doing, close the door in my face.

As always, the choice is yours.

Embryo

A few months previously I'd walked away from centre and away from the RAF. I still had the cl suit, the shirt and the shoes. I'd passed the ou trilby and the equally outrageous tie to my fath (who happily wore them both for years) and, as I' the RAF battledress away in moth balls, I'd s solemn oath:

Never again. Not even the Salvation Army. If I li be a thousand, nobody would *ever* again lumber me a bloody uniform.

Yet here I was. One of a dozen brand new copper freshly kitted out, complete with high-neck, 'cho collar' uniforms and, from the various permutations fruit salad on every chest, we'd all made our differe ways through Hitler's War.

At a guess, we'd all made that same silent declaration as we'd left our respective demob centres.

We were in the billiard room of the old West Riding of Yorkshire Constabulary Headquarters at Wakefield. And, if this billiard room was a yardstick of the efficiency of that constabulary, we'd joined an uncommonly tatty force. The cloth on the solitary table was stained and ripped. The pockets were torn and the cushions were knackered. The balls were chipped and faded and the few cues still in the racks were all tipless and warped. From a pre-war wireless set in one corner of the room came the sound of Sid Phillips playing his own brand of old-fashioned jazz. It was very reassuring. As long as 'That's a-Plenty' could be swung in that gentle, easy rhythm, some degree of sanity was still around.

Some weeks before, I'd walked into Todmorden Police

Sport', I wrote 'Throwing the Hammer'; it being a reasonable assumption that hammer throwing was not a pastime over-organised out Pen-y-Ghent way.

The last call had been to the chief constable's office; the first of the three times I saw the demigod sitting in the top chair throughout twenty years of service. He was a knight of something-or-the-other, and there, looking very lonely on the vast expanse of the desk-surface, were the first few documents of what would, eventually, become a hefty Personal File.

He glanced through them, raised aristocratic eyebrows, then looked at me. 'Throwing the hammer?'

'Yes, sir.' I kept a straight face, but inside I quaked. From the 'off' I was going to be earmarked as a fly-boy; as a creep who chanced his arm and tried to get away with things.

I'd over-estimated the opposition. The man believed what he wanted to believe, and he seemed strangely delighted at the prospect of having a hammer-thrower in his force.

He nodded slowly and smiled. 'Of course. That accounts for your extraordinary chest expansion.'

That, I fear, was when my faith in chief constables took its first knock.

* * *

But that was past, and now (having held Bibles in our hands and chanted the Constabulary Oath in unison) we were in a tatty billiard room, chest deep in equipment.

In fairness, they hadn't been mean. Four tunics, four pairs of trousers, three helmets, two greatcoats, two capes, a storm-proof mac and a pair of storm-proof leggings, plus odds and ends like truncheons, handcuffs, button-sticks, leather belts and leather 'lamp-plates' (to protect the uniform from the heat given off by bullseye lanterns none of us were ever going to use).

We'd been required to provide two pairs of our own boots. Standard, army-style, heavy chrome-leather. We also had our personal belongings; toilet requirements and our bundled-up civilian clothes.

Memories of the RAF. Memories of rough-fibred underclothes nobody had the courage to wear; of bits and pieces of webbing belting nobody could find a place for; of heaving piles of useless junk from Point A to Point B and losing bits and pieces on route and having to pay for replacements. But at least the RAF had provided kitbags and shoulder-packs in which to carry the damn stuff. The West Riding mob had merely handed it over. Shifting it was *your* problem.

Along with all this gummage, the West Riding Constabulary Stores had presented each of us with a collection of booklets. None of them were new. They were all dog-eared and grubby and looked as though coppers galore had pored over them for years; but this I doubt. 'Fingerprints' assured the reader that everybody *had* fingerprints, and that every fingerprint was unique; it took almost forty pages of dreary prose to impart this information. 'West Riding By-laws' listed footpaths upon which bicycling was prohibited and assured the reader that 'night soil' must not be allowed to carpet the pavement. 'What to Do and When To Do It' dealt with exotica like fowl-pest, swine-fever and sheep-scab. But the gem was 'Force Standing Instructions': 'No officer is allowed to borrow money from an officer of a lower rank than himself. No officer is allowed to lend money to an officer of a higher rank than himself.' And the masterpiece that gave me a clue to the age of the publication was 'Cutlasses will be kept polished and sharpened at all times.'

In the background Sid Phillips changed gear, moved to piano and swung into barrel-house tempo. It was nice. It was comforting.

I doubt if I was the only man in that room wondering what the hell would come next.

*　　　*　　　*

What came next was a glorified lorry that transported all twelve of us, plus our belongings, all the way to Mansfield and a police training college.

It was, we discovered, a three-by-three arrangement. The Initial Training Course lasted three months. Three intakes were worked through the forensic sausage-machine at the same time, a course ending and a new course starting every month. Each intake was, in turn, divided into three classes. Even the exams came in threes; one at the end of both the first and second months, with the Final Exam and the Passing Out Parade at the end of the course.

Monday, 8 September, 1947. That was the day it started, and it lasted until Friday, 1 July, 1966. Almost two decades of bobbying and, although I didn't know it at the time, enough 'background material' to allow me to write police procedural novels and make enough money to alllow Avis and me to live out our lives in comparative luxury.

The strange thing is that I joined the Police Service for an understandable but wrong reason. I joined to get a house. In 1947 the morality of law-enforcement had no bearing upon my decision; I was prepared to wear one more uniform in order to be able to set up home.

By 1966, when I put the uniform aside and took to the typewriter for my living, I didn't *need* the uniform. The job had worked its magic on me. I'd be a 'copper' for the rest of my life.

* * *

I think our intake were very fortunate in that Mansfield wasn't a one-force college. About sixty of us were dumped there that day, and we represented provincial forces from all points of the compass; the West Riding, Derby, Oldham, Leeds, Nottinghamshire and others that have since slipped my memory.

I think we were equally fortunate in that we'd all trudged our respective ways through World War II and this equated with the comradeship of war, without its attendant horrors. Not too long ago, the best in the business had tried to hammer us into the ground: chief petty officers, sergeant majors and station warrant officers. We'd heard it all before and we could not merely take it . . . we actually *enjoyed* taking it. It was something we'd missed for the last few months.

We were allowed what remained of that first day to get ourselves sorted out, foddered and bedded down in various dormitories. We formed friendships that evening, and some of those friendships lasted throughout the rest of our police lives. That was the day I met Buster and Lofty.

5

Buster had fought his war up the leg of Italy, Lofty had soldiered in India and Burma, and I'd looked down on the Third Reich from the rear turret of a Lancaster too many times for comfort. We were a great trio. Between us, we knew all the gags.

That evening the new intake enjoyed a quiet, communal booze-up in the college bar. I banged away like crazy on the piano and we sang the dirty ditties of all three branches of HM Armed Forces at the top of our voices. I have a suspicion that for a few hours Mansfield Police Training College wondered what the hell it had let itself in for.

The next day set the pace. The official moonshine we all knew and recognised had us assembling in the main lecture hall for a welcoming pep talk by the camp commandant, followed by an introduction to our respective tutors.

In truth, I felt a little sorry for that commandant. He was not a man with natural panache, and he was stage-centre facing more than half a hundred of us, all sporting war medals. A very lonely Defence Medal ribbon (a gong given to Boy Scouts) was all he was entitled to wear. He was outclassed, and he knew it before he even rose to his feet.

Every man in the room knew why he was commandant, and why he held the substantive rank of superintendent and the acting rank of chief superintendent. Because of the war. Because of *our* war. Every police force had been stretched to breaking point in the war years, and finding men worthy of promotion hadn't been easy. Those due for retirement immediately after the war had been non-starters. The high-flyers, by their very nature, had left to join the armed forces. Few of those left had been of solid gold. Few had even been gold-plated.

He mumbled a set-piece welcome, handed us over to the assistant commandant, then disappeared into a distant haze. We never saw him again.

The assistant commandant was a chief inspector, acting superintendent and he matched most of us, gong-for-gong. We later learned he'd left his force for war as a sergeant, and having been commissioned in the Army, returned as an inspector, been promoted chief inspector; then, finally, he'd taken what he recognised as a cushy number as acting superintendent and assistant commandant at Mansfield.

He didn't even *try* to kid anybody, and that made him one of us. He talked our language, used a phraseology we all knew and understood and, from the start, we took him to our hearts, accepted his friendship and took his advice.

'You're here to get the feel of the uniform,' he said. 'When you leave, you won't be coppers. You'll be capable of being *made* into coppers. And that's *all* you'll be. . . . You'll know more Criminal Law than most of the lawyers you'll meet in court. You'll forget a hell of a lot of what you've been taught, but that doesn't matter. What slops out isn't important. What *remains* will be the working basis for doing your job. . . . You're public servants. You're *not* public skivvies. . . . You're not "civilians" any more. What opinions you hold, you keep to yourselves. If, for example, you attend a fire, your job is to control onlookers and keep an eye open for pickpockets. If the water pressure isn't what it should be, you're *not* there to upset the Fire Service by suggesting you could piss faster . . .'

*   *   *

I make no apology for admitting that in September 1947 our intake had more than a passing interest in war-service and medals. We were all ex-servicemen. A particularly nasty war was a mere two years behind us. Food rationing, clothes rationing and petrol rationing were all still part of everyday life. In effect, the fighting had ended, but wartime conditions still prevailed.

In the idiom of the day, there was a great gulf between we who had 'gone' and those who had 'stayed at home', but we had sympathy galore for those who had genuinely tried, yet for whatever reason had been unable to get in. We were not heroes and, in fairness, none of us counted himself as a hero, but, nevertheless, we still measured a man of appropriate years by what he had done (or, at the very least, what he had *tried* to do) to put the skids under Adolf Hitler. Those of us who had messed about with the more explosive aspects of warfare knew the meaning of fear, and it was a fear far beyond anything likely to be found in the streets. Ergo the spivs, the black-marketeers and the column-dodgers were targets for our unqualified contempt.

I suspect now that our pride bordered upon arrogance. It is certain that threats were wasted on us. For these reasons, we were prepared to be led . . . but the hell we were prepared to be *driven*.

There was also the business of age. Not merely the subtle ageing process of war, but also actual age.

Officially, we were all a little too old to be recruited into the Police Service, but because we'd spent what might be called our formative years in the armed forces, the higher age-limit had been eased in order to allow us to become policemen.

This, plus our varied service on recent war fronts, made us at least 'different' – 1947 was one of our very personal years of wine and roses – and those who were not of our number were wise enough to handle us with care.

Credit must, however, be given to whoever chose our instructors. He knew his onions.

The intake was divided into Classes A, B and C. Classes B and C had sergeant instructors. Class A had the Inspector, and Buster, Lofty and myself were part of Class A.

The Inspector was a Geordie who'd tried for the Army but was a mite too old for square-bashing. His forte was deadpan humour, delivered in a brisk, authoritative tone.

'Gentlemen, when I enter the classroom you will rise to your feet and stand to attention. Not because of who I am, but because of *what* I am, and because I'll be wearing full uniform. It will also enable me to note which of you haven't yet wiped the egg-stains of breakfast from your uniforms.'

For three months he dragged us kicking and struggling through the thick undergrowth of Criminal Law and Police Law.

From Road Traffic Law . . . 'Under the Road Traffic Act of 1930, a dog is an "animal". A cat is *not*. Don't

8

argue. If you're feline-orientated accept the fact that our lords and masters of the Legislature and the Judiciary live in a world of their own.' . . . To Treason . . . 'Under the Statute of Treasons, 1351, it is treason to violate the king's consort. This, I need hardly remind you, was Henry VIII's favourite Act of Parliament.'

The drolleries spiced the sometimes heavy mix of Statute Law, Case Law and Common Law. Thanks to the skill of the Inspector some of us began to love the law. Its certainty and uncertainty, its logic and contradictions, its simplicity and monumental intricacies all blended and became a complex but fascinating pattern.

About halfway through the course we had the Dirty Week. A whole week covering sexual offences, ranging from rape to indecent exposure. Presumably the powers-that-be figured that a surfeit might sicken us and remove for us the titillation of pornography. I think it worked.

And yet . . .

'Incest is defined as a man having carnal knowledge of his grand-daughter, daughter, sister or mother, or a woman having carnal knowledge of her grandfather, father, brother or son. Which leaves you free to have it off with your grandmother, if you both feel so inclined.'

It was a less enlightened age, and homosexuality was a felony. On one occasion during the Dirty Week the Inspector marched briskly into the classroom and, as we sat down, said, 'Gentlemen, for the next hour we will devote ourselves to the legal niceties of a pastime favoured by members of the Royal Navy.'

There was a clatter as one of our number straightened his back and got to his feet.

'Sir, I wish to object to that remark.'

'A man from the wardroom, I presume.' The Inspector almost smiled. 'A man more used to wine, women and song. My apologies, Constable. I had the mess-decks in mind. Rum, bums and concertinas.'

The Inspector taught us to be coppers. He taught us to use our eyes, and never more so than in the Observation Game. The game started within five minutes of our first meeting.

'Wainwright!'

'Sir.' I stood up at my desk.

'Under that tunic, you have a shirt.'

'Yes, sir.'

'How many buttons?'

'Sir?'

'You put the thing on this morning. You buttoned it up. How many buttons?'

I made a guess, and I was wrong.

'Sit down, Wainwright.' Then, to the rest of the class, he said, 'It's called the Observation Game. The others don't play the game. We do. Before each session I ask a question. I pick anybody I choose. No trick questions. A simple matter of observation. As of now, anybody who can't answer correctly pays a forfeit. He writes out the definition of whatever subject we're discussing, fifty times before the next morning.'

Talk about keeping us on our toes!

How many windows in the dining hall? There's a strange car parked alongside the main entrance; what's its make? What's its registration number? What brand of cigarettes does the assistant commandant usually smoke?

In those three months we were asked hundreds – perhaps thousands – of questions and, because we were often caught napping, we wrote out hundreds of legal definitions. By the end of the course we not only knew law, we also knew how to *notice* things.

Some evenings a group of us would go into town and, occasionally, the Inspector would join us. At those times he was an equal among equals, and a charming companion. And on one of those trips he taught us another aspect of bobbying.

The stranger walking towards us was middle aged and well dressed. He looked like a member of the professional class and, as we neared, he smiled a welcome at the Inspector.

'Good evening, Inspector.'

'Good evening.'

That was all. Very pleasant and very civilised. But when we were well out of earshot the Inspector explained.

'That, gentlemen, was a murderer. A double-murderer. His wife and his daughter. For the insurance money. They were both cremated, and he got away with it. That's not guesswork, gentlemen. We *know*. He *knows* we know. He also knows we'll never be able to prove it.' A tight half-smile came and went. 'Accept it as an object lesson. They don't *all* look like Bill Sikes.'

Towards the end of the course there was much revision, but never enough for the Inspector; nor, indeed, was it ever enough for us. We'd become a single unit, and Class A was something very special. The top half-dozen places in that intake belonged to us – belonged to the Inspector – and none of the rabble from Classes B and C were going to be allowed to pip us at the post. We worked like beavers, and the Inspector made sure we had elbow room.

In the last week of the course the syllabus called for an hour-long session on 'The Care of Feet'.

'Revision, gentlemen. If anybody here thinks I'm going to gaze at the sweaty monstrosities you have hidden away in those boots, he's out of his mind.'

Nor was that the only unimportant session we leapfrogged for the purpose of revision.

If the Inspector made us potential coppers, the Drill Pig and the Muscle Man provided necessary light relief, because we treated neither of them seriously.

We were happy to let the drill sergeant – the Drill Pig – have a personal ball. Indeed, we encouraged him. Nobody was going to run home to mummy with tears in his eyes, and his carryings-on on the parade ground brought a warm feeling of not-too-long-ago nostalgia.

'I will tell you where you stand with me,' he said. 'Perfection is not quite good enough. And that means you will *always* be a shambles. But not *quite* the bloody shambles you are today.'

He'd been a sergeant in one of the guards regiments and was the definitive regimental sergeant major and, because of what we were, we loved him like a long-lost father returned to the bosom of his family. Pride of place on a double row of medal ribbons was a tiny, rose-pink rectangle, edged with pearl and with a vertical pearl stripe in the centre. The OBE (Military Division) is not delivered with NAAFI rations, and rumour had it that this creature of leather lungs and imaginative terminology had earned it at Dunkirk.

None of us were strangers to a drill square, but drill movements differed in each branch of HM Forces.

'You – you – you – and you. The hairnet mob. You call that an about turn? No wonder they gave you bloody aeroplanes. You *need* aeroplanes to get out of that contorted ballet movement.'

And the first time an ex-matelot saluted: 'Holy Mother of God! You're saluting, lad. *Saluting!* . . . Not waving goodbye.'

It was a game, played to fixed and long-established rules. We all played it, we all enjoyed playing it, and in the evenings the Drill Pig was as good a bar-companion as you could wish for.

He even brought the parade-ground 'one–pause–two–pause–three' approach to teaching first-aid. He shared that chore with an elderly local doctor, whose dreary and uinspired manner was monumentally soporific. When the medic taught us first-aid it was universally known as the Twilight Hour. But when the Drill Pig lectured, nobody slept. He lifted it, almost word for word, from the manual and bawled it at us from a tiny rostrum: 'The brachial artery divides into the radial artery and the ulna artery. Two pressure points, see? If I want to put pressure on those points, I take a cork. Like this one. A vino cork. I cut it in two halves, lengthwise . . . so. Now, Wainwright, what do I have?'

'I don't know, Sergeant.'

'I have two halves of a bloody vino cork. Are you listening to what I'm saying, lad? I'm not performing this song-and-dance act for my own benefit, you know. I'm not completely off my crust.'

But if we tolerated, and even respected, the Drill Pig we had little but contempt for the Muscle Man. Again, it was a legacy from the war. Nobody had liked PT instructors, and this one came from the same dreary matrix. Bulging muscles, flashing teeth, convex chest and far too fit and clean-living to be believed. From our first meeting there was an unspoken agreement to break his heart . . . and we did.

12

In the gym he'd bawl, 'One–two–three. *Hup*–two–three' – bouncing around, flinging limbs in all directions – while we took things *very* gently. Sweat would run in rivers down his exaggerated neck muscles, while the PT class moved rhythmically, but very little.

With monotonous regularity we almost killed the fool on the weekly, two-mile cross-country run. We walked when he wasn't watching and broke out into a token jog when he was. Within the first ten minutes we would be strung out in a long, lackadaisical line and he would be racing like a demented yo-yo, from front to rear, in an attempt to keep the forward motion continuous. By the time we were all safely past the finishing line he would be on the point of collapse. We'd made him *run* the best part of ten miles . . . and we wouldn't even be breathless!

And this ridiculous man thought he was getting *us* fit.

Even when he introduced us to judo he dropped the clanger to end all clangers: 'Judo is one of the Japanese martial arts. It enables an unarmed man to deal with an armed attacker. Let's assume that this is a knife.' He lifted a ruler he'd brought into the gym for demonstration purposes. He looked us over with that slightly supercilious stare of PT instructors we'd all met in the past. 'Who'll volunteer to be the "victim"? Then I'll show you how the man with the knife *could* have been handled, with a knowledge of judo.' One of us stepped forward. He was a quiet, unassuming chap who knew nothing about judo. But he knew a lot about unarmed combat; he'd been a trained commando in one of the top groups.

The Muscle Man twisted his face into what he fondly believed was a look of fury, raised the ruler above his head and rushed forward. The ex-commando took careful aim and kicked him expertly in the crotch. Fortunately we were all wearing plimsolls, otherwise the Muscle Man would have sung castrato for the rest of his life.

When he'd straightened and was again able to speak, the Muscle Man gasped, 'Damn it, man, you can't do *that*. If you kick somebody in the goolies when you're on the beat you'll be in serious trouble.'

'Not compared with the silly bugger who comes at me

13

with a knife. He'll be in *real* trouble,' retorted the ex-commando.

Without doubt, the Muscle Man grew to hate our intake. To be charitable, I don't blame him. At various times during our three months we all repaid some of the debts owed to a succession of his kind who in the past had made our lives miserable. This being so, who could blame him for evening things up a little, via Constable Wainwright?

I couldn't swim. I had never been able to, and I still can't. In the RAF I'd discovered that I was completely non-buoyant. At dinghy drill I'd always been the mutt floating around in a 'Mae West', gasping and flapping his arms while waiting anxiously to be 'rescued'. And, despite weekly sessions at the police training college, I remained as aquatic as a brick.

The others were busy earning themselves bronze medals, silver medals and God knows what other life-saving awards. I couldn't even dog-paddle. Each week I would obligingly lower myself into the water and, clinging to the edge of the swimming pool, ease my way towards the deep end. The Muscle Man (who hadn't even undressed) would stroll along the coconut matting, giving false assurances that my body-weight was much lighter than its volume of water-displacement.

'Let yourself float, Wainwright,' he'd urge. 'Push yourself away from the side and relax. You *can't* sink.' And as always – and as so very many times previously – I'd take a deep breath, clench my teeth, force myself to release my hold . . . and sink like a stone.

I was not a complete mug though. Lofty was by far the best swimmer in Class A, and he had very firm instructions from me to be on hand, in the water. Every week, without fail, he saved me from drowning.

Furthermore, that damn fool of a PT instructor will go to his grave believing that I was doing it on purpose. With his dying breath he will assure people that human beings all have a close affinity to a duck.

One evening in the last week of the course I could have made a decision which might have changed my life.

14

There'd been a certain amount of end-of-term horse-play in the lounge, and one of the intake had cracked his forehead open just above the eye. I hadn't been part of the ruckus, but I'd volunteered to go with him to the sick bay and give moral support. There it was decided that he needed stitching together and a medic had been asked to visit. This in turn meant the admin office had to be notified.

The assistant commandant arrived and, while the wounded warrior was being treated, he and I waited in the outer room.

I must explain that I have an exceptionally deep voice. I tend to rumble rather than speak. If, colour-wise, the average voice is the shade of weak tea, what comes from my larynx is the colour of newly hewn coal. The assistant commandant himself was an enthusiastic amateur musi-cian, and the love of his life was a male voice choir he'd formed from instructors and civilian staff employed at the college. As we waited, he opened a packet of cigarettes, offered me one and, when we were con-tentedly puffing away, out came the gentle, man-to-man routine.

'Do you sing, Wainwright?'

'No, sir.'

'You have an unusual voice. A natural bass.'

'I find it an embarrassment sometimes.'

'Not at all. A bit of practice, and you'd be an asset to any choir.'

We smoked in silence for a few moments.

'You *are* musical, of course?'

'Yes, sir. The piano. I like music generally.'

'I've heard you play. Well above average, in my opinion.'

'I was taught well and for a long time. The war got in the way, otherwise . . .'

I didn't end the sentence. I wasn't even sure I wasn't kidding myself. But I knew what musical talent I'd once had had been one of the minor casualties of the war.

Again, there were a few moments of smoke-filled silence.

'Your instructor tells me you learn quickly.'

'That's nice to know.'

'Better than most.'

'That's a relief.'

He drew deeply on the cigarette, then murmured, 'You could stay on here as an instructor.'

I recall, quite clearly, that he wasn't looking at me when he made the suggestion. It was a softly-spoken, throw-away remark.

'Eh?' I think my eyes tended to bulge.

'Acting sergeant . . . that sort of thing.'

'I – er – that's pushing things a bit,isn't it?'

'Comparatively easy,' he said airily. 'Wheels within wheels. A little bit of string-pulling. It wouldn't be *too* difficult.'

'Good God!' Then, when I'd recovered slightly, 'But this voice of mine. It's not *made* for instructing. It's not . . .'

'It's the voice that's prompted me to make the offer.'

I said I'd think about it, and I *did* think about it, but not for long. Of course I was tempted. Stripes, within three months? I was certainly human enough to be tempted.

But, dammit, I'd joined a police force. I hadn't joined a male voice choir.

Nor was I too keen to bring Avis down to join me in the cloister-like environs of a police training college, and I sure as hell wasn't going to live there without her. It was a false world. A world of over-shiny boots and never-ending salute-slamming. A world hemmed in by petty irritations and childish restrictions. And for what? To help create something I'd know damn-all about.

Equally, it would be untrue to deny that past experience had no bearing on the decision. Once before, in the RAF, my passion for music had for a time prevented me from doing what I *wanted* to do. I was wary. I was even suspicious.

Politely but firmly I turned the offer down. I don't think the assistant commandant was too surprised, and I'm sure he thought no less of me.

Thereafter, it was all rush and push. Class A grabbed the first half-dozen places in the final exam. Avis and Buster's wife came down for the Passing Out Parade, and we marched, wheeled and generally performed in a torrential downpour. The end-of-course dance saw a great get-together of budding bobbies, their wives and girlfriends. Then we all moved off to our respective postings.

Within the next two years we were all required to attend two month-long refresher courses, but the same crowd never came together again. I, for one, didn't return to Mansfield. It wasn't the same. That whiff of wartime camaraderie never returned.

Elland Mark I

Today, Elland is lost beneath the curve of a high-level dual-carriageway. You're in, out and away; speeding towards Halifax from Huddersfield, without a glance at the grubby little township below, on the left, or the scatter of broken-down hen runs, up on the right. The tumble of houses and factories are a passing smudge, hardly worth noticing as you speed by.

But that's where it all began, and it wasn't like that in 1947.

*   *   *

Vic was my first section sergeant, and the first copper I met, uniform-to-uniform, outside the police college. I reported at the architectural monstrosity which was part-police-station, part-section-sergeant-living-quarters at 9 a.m. on the Monday after leaving Mansfield.

Vic, of the mane of silver hair. A stocky, quietly spoken man, eternally disappointed that for some reason unknown to himself he wasn't able to join the Freemasons, and convinced that because of this he would never make inspector.

He never did.

The truth was that he was a moderately good sergeant but would have been a very mediocre inspector. But I didn't realise that on my first day.

He guided me to a wall-map of the section and pointed. 'That's your beat, Constable. Upper Edge Beat. Four telephone kiosks. One at Upper Edge, one at Lower Edge, one at Ainley Top, one at Blackley. Those are your points. Be there five minutes before point-time, stay there until five minutes after point-time.' He opened a desk drawer and handed me a dog-eared piece of paper. 'That's your shift-card.'

Instructions were brief. Explanations weren't offered, because it was taken for granted that all coppers were fully conversant with police verbal shorthand. 'Point' was short for 'appointment place' and, because exotica like the walkie-talkie was a thing of the future, a point equated with a telephone. Usually a telephone kiosk. You 'made a point' every hour, arrived five minutes before the required time and hung around until five minutes after the required time. In order to fox the enemy, the points were never referred to by name. Always by a letter, and their sequence was juggled as the section sergeant saw fit.

Upper Edge was an outside beat – police lingo for a village beat – and in order to flummox the opposition even more the shift-card system was operated.

These cards had seven columns, each representing a day of the week, and five lines, each representing a week. Thirty-five little oblongs and, in each oblong, the shift to be worked. Never a full eight hours; always two four-hour stints. Anything up to four hours between each stint. Thirty-five different split-shifts, over a five-week period, and then you started at square one again. The sixth day was your Weekly Rest Day and, when your Weekly Rest Day fell on a Saturday, you took the Sunday with it, in order to do a double-shuffle and catch up with what they owed you.

The consensus of opinion was that whoever had worked out *that* system must have had cross-eyed, Chinese grandparents.

* * *

Vic threw me in at the deep end.

'There's a couple of post-mortems due to start at ten.' He lifted a large key from a row of hooks. 'Nip round to the public morgue and give the pathologist a hand.'

Hell's teeth, that morgue.

It was little more than a brick-walled box-room, and the slab was narrower than the average bunk-bed. It was made of rough-surfaced concrete, stained to blazes with what had gone before. No windows to the place; just a single, low-watt, unshaded bulb hanging from a length of frayed flex.

On the slab there was an elderly gentleman and an

19

elderly lady, squeezed together, head-to-toe, both completely starkers and both as stiff as boards.

I suffered through that double post-mortem. During the war years I'd seen odd incidents of carnage, but this was something very different. The most disgusting morgue I've ever seen, with little light and ventilation. The opening up, the taking out of the bits and pieces, the slicing of the various organs, and all on the foul surface of that slab. That, plus the fact that we had to lift one body down while the pathologist worked on the other; had to step over the elderly gentleman while we examined the elderly lady, and vice versa.

At regular intervals I sought the open air, found a quiet corner and brought my heart up. At a guess, I lost the last three meals I'd eaten.

It ended. The bodies were sewn up, washed down and made as presentable as possible, ready for collection by the undertaker.

Vic accepted the key of the mortuary on my return with a knowing smile.

'That's it,' he said. '*Now* you can attend a bad road accident without turning a hair.'

*   *   *

Elland was and still is a sooty little township, in a basin at the foot of the Pennines. These were pre-TV days, and it boasted two tiny cinemas. One of the perks of the job was that, off duty, you and your wife could visit either of these cinemas without paying. Any seat you fancied. The usherette guided you, then let the manager know where you were. If trouble brewed, and he wanted a bobby in a hurry, he had one on tap.

The town was a place of brickworks and small foundries; of textile mills and engineering works. If it shoved out grime the chances were it was represented in that Elland of 1947.

Some clowns claimed that it could boast more millionaires per head of population than anywhere in the United Kingdom. I wouldn't know. *I* never met any. More than that, if you *were* a millionaire, you'd have to be more than mildly dotty to live in a dump like that.

I was lucky. Upper Edge Beat ran in a semi-circle along

the very rim of the basin. We lived at Upper Edge. To the west was Lower Edge and to the east was Ainley Top. East of Ainley Top was Blackley. Four pokey little holes, each with a telephone kiosk and each between two and three miles from the next. It was a foot-patrol beat, and for one very good reason. With a bicycle I'd have been either pushing the damn thing or free-wheeling with the brakes full on. I doubt if, in the whole of that beat, there were a hundred yards of level road.

And from my half-moon-shaped kingdom I could gaze across the perpetual smog of Elland to where the Pennines rose above the industrial haze. I couldn't actually *see* them. Good, clean air was unavailable within fifteen miles of Elland Town Hall.

Nevertheless, at Elland I encountered Sam, and Sam was the first copper I met who was a genuine character and at the same time a born bobby.

Sam scared the hell out of the ungodly. His helmet was always worn at a slight tilt. Somehow, his cape invariably had a certain swashbuckling swing. He'd been a copper pre-war, left to join one of the guards regiments, and now was back at full throttle. Whenever Vic had a day off, or was on leave, Sam was acting sergeant (known, officially, as 'PC i/c') and Sam didn't merely accept trouble, he sought it out.

He took me under his wing, and couldn't rest until he'd lumbered me with a first court appearance.

We were together when Sam pointed to an oncoming lorry, and said, 'That one. Stop it.'

The driver of the lorry was as rough as his vehicle, and he didn't like the idea of being picked at random.

'What's the bloody game?'

'Checking your log book,' I explained, with all the firm politeness instilled into me at the police college.

'It's a pity you've sod-all better to do.'

'I'm sorry, but . . .'

'I'll take things from here.' Sam elbowed me gently aside and faced the glaring driver. 'Right, lad. Let's have you out of that cab for a start. And bring all the documents you have with you.'

'Why? What the hell for?'

'You might have nicked it.'

'You *what*?'

'If you haven't nicked it, you're in real trouble. It's falling apart at the seams.'

I was given an on-the-spot demonstration of practical policing. How to take a would-be hard-man and reduce him to a sweating, apologetic wreck in a matter of minutes. That originally very stroppy lorry driver collected seventeen summonses. Seventeen! By which time he was almost pleading with Sam not to push things any farther.

The Road Traffic Acts, the Construction and Use Regulations, the Defence Regulations – they were still in force at the time – Sam pushed his arm, elbow-deep, into more Acts and Sections than I thought possible for one, solitary motor lorry.

'Had enough?' he asked, at last.

The driver nodded. I don't think he could trust himself to say anything.

'Good.' Sam jerked his head. 'On your way. The next time you come through Elland, remember. We don't like being told how to do our job, right?'

When we reached the police station, Sam said, 'I'll do this one. I'll show you as witness.'

'At least I now know how to do it,' I said ruefully.

'No. You know how *not* to do it. You apologised for doing your job. Don't, *ever*. His Nibs would have finished up at his local tonight, with a skinful of ale, swanking about how he'd browbeaten a copper. He won't *now*. Now he'll be telling everybody what bad bastards we are. It's a damn sight better than the other thing.'

Sam was no fool. He knew what I very soon learned; that in those faraway days bobbying was as near to piece-work as the powers-that-be could make it.

'Don't tell me you can walk about for eight hours and not see somebody doing *something* you can book 'em for.'

That was the standard remark from on high if you didn't make a weekly court-appearance, and it was always made on pay-day.

We were paid by the week, and Friday was pay-day. Every Friday, at three o'clock on the button, the divisional chief inspector would arrive at Elland Police Station, and all the coppers of that section would be there, waiting. The loot was in tiny brown-paper packets, neatly stacked in a wooden tray which the chief inspector would carry into the office.

But first, the 'Number Four Book'. The Section Offence Book. I never discovered why it was called the 'Number Four Book', but inside its pages every summons and every arrest was carefully noted. The officer responsible, the clown who'd misbehaved, the when, the where and the final result. All neatly catalogued.

Before those wage packets were even touched, the 'Number Four Book' was fine-tooth-combed and then, as your name was called and you stepped forward, saluted and held out a hand for your weekly pittance, would come the standard spiel.

'Only two cases this week, Wainwright? Don't tell me you can walk about for eight hours . . .' etc., etc.

Court-appearances really were the yardstick used to measure efficiency. Nor was it the fault of the chief inspector. It wasn't *his* fault. He was merely the mouthpiece for a damn fool system that refused to accept that people weren't forever spitting on pavements, riding bicycles without lights and keeping dogs without licences. It was a crazy way of looking at things, and something left over from before the war. Something on a par with keeping cutlasses polished and sharpened at all times. It took almost a decade for that monumentally absurd valuation to die out. It took some thick-headed lunatic all that time to realise the obvious: that the presence of a copper *prevented* these fiddling offences from happening, and that 'prevention' was the real name of the game, not the hauling of a required quota of defendants to the Magistrates' Court each week.

There was another crazy swings-and-roundabouts system that also took years to taper off into obscurity. It was built around 'crime statistics'.

In those days all offences were classed as felonies, misdemeanours or summary offences. That in itself was a big enough tangle, but the police itemisation made things both more simple and more complicated. To the coppers

23

only *two* divisions mattered: 'Crime' or 'Petty Offence'. And every felony and misdemeanour was, *ipso facto*, a crime.

Nor was crime subjected to any scale of degree. A crime was a crime . . . period – from murder all the way to the most trivial act of vandalism covered by the Malicious Damage Act of 1861, and that statute seemed to cover just about everything.

If, for instance, a house was broken into and some contents were stolen, it was obviously a crime, and treated as such. The investigation would be pushed as hard and as far as possible. But if, after a fortnight, that house-breaking was still classified as 'undetected', something had to be done to make the crime statistics look healthier. So, if you then saw a youngster using a catapult against the glass of the streetlighting, you would book him. Not merely because he was doing something wrong, but also because that, too, was a 'crime' and the broken glass of the street-lamp countered the housebreaking: one 'unde-tected' balanced by one 'detected'. On the graph – on every graph all the way up to the top office – these were merely 'crimes'. A stolen milk bottle was no less important than an office-breaking; wilful damage to a flower-bed could compensate on paper for a rape.

In those days, as today, figures could be used to prove or disprove just about anything.

In retrospect, we of that massive, 1945–50, ex-HMF intake found ourselves part of an ancient and creaking law-enforcement edifice well beyond our comprehension. Far too many frightened bullies held positions of power; they were terrified of those in authority over them and they, in turn, tried to terrify their subordinates.

To relax, to talk man-to-man, even to officers who held the same rank as themselves, was to them a sign of weakness.

And, moreover, the various local Freemason Lodges *had* power. Vic was quite right. Superintendents, chief inspectors and inspectors *were* Freemasons, and made no secret of the fact. To report a Freemason for anything less than a major Road Traffic offence was a waste of time and effort. The report form was conveniently 'lost' or, at best, the offender received a written 'Caution' from the Divisional Office.

What I think grieved us most of all was the childish simplicity of the uniformed clowns who played this game of you-scratch-my-back, I'll-scratch-yours. They lacked the gumption to realise that, had they *not* been ranking coppers – had they *not* been in a position to ward off petty inconveniences of the law – they wouldn't have been allowed within a thousand miles of a Masonic Lodge.

That was the force we joined.

That was the force we were to change over the next decade or so. We changed it from inside. Albeit slowly and, perhaps, unconsciously . . . but we *did* change it.

* * *

Meanwhile, I was learning the basics of my new craft at Elland and, in the process thereof, rather enjoying myself.

One Sunday morning in high summer, the first summer of my police service, I had been pulled in from Upper Edge to cover the town and (as always) that cover had meant a ten-to-six night patrol. I'd reached the tag end of the night shift and at that moment, even in Elland, it was one of those bright, newly laundered days with the dawn only about an hour behind.

Like a good little copper I'd tried all the knobs on all the lock-up shops and checked all the unoccupied property listed in the Unoccupied Property Book. In less than an hour I was going to crawl into bed, happy in the knowledge that I'd left Elland neatly tied up in pink ribbon and in no way sullied by the grubby paws of the ungodly.

I strolled along, content with my lot and alone in my world. Helmet shoved back from my forehead. Pipe drawing perfectly. Hands in my pockets. Knowing that august beings like chief inspectors and the like were all tucked up between sheets and very unlikely to suddenly confront PC718 Wainwright who, at that moment, figured life to be a nice, easy number.

One more mill needed checking before I wended a gentle way back to the nick and knocking-off-time. The short cut to the main, wooden gates of the mill led between two blocks of terraced houses, along a narrow passageway known in Yorkshire as a ginnel or sometimes a snicket. As I reached the end of the ginnel, I saw His Nibs. His bicycle was leaning against the grimy brickwork alongside the gates, and he himself had his back to me, facing the gates themselves. A whippet of a man. Cloth cap, cheap jacket and cycle clips. He was having a quiet slash against the mill gates. Nothing serious. A mildly unhygienic way of emptying his bladder, but nothing to get excited about. The thick rubber soles of my boots made no noise, and he didn't hear me until I was almost alongside his left shoulder and murmuring gentle reproach at this misuse of other people's property.

The hell he was having a slash! I saw the crowbar a split-second before it landed. I don't remember going down. I was out, but not for long. When I re-focused my eyes the first thing I saw was my pipe, still smouldering away on the pavement, so I knew my absence from this world could be measured in seconds. But it was long enough. His Nibs and his bicycle had vanished.

I needed assistance, but walkie-talkies were a thing of the far distant future. I had a whistle, of course, but that wasn't much of a boost to morale. The nearest fellow-coppers were either at Halifax or Huddersfield, each about five miles away. I could, of course, have tottered to the nearest telephone kiosk, but that was over a mile distant. Equally, I could have weaved my way back to the nick, but that was almost as far and when I'd arrived there it would have meant telephoning DHQ at Halifax.

I required sympathy. I desired compassion. I had the grandfather and grandmother of all headaches. Avis wasn't too far away, and she had a ready and loving shoulder upon which to weep . . . and, anyway, there was a telephone *there*, too. Not to put too fine a point on it, I picked up my pipe and my helmet and, very groggily, went home. Avis put a cold compress on the pigeon's-egg-sized lump above the right eyebrow of her personal wounded warrior, then I telephoned Halifax and started the flap.

I wasn't a hero. Oh, my word, no. I was a mug, and treated as such. At Elland Police Station an admittedly sympathetic Vic stood aside while a particularly irritated chief inspector who'd had his Sunday-morning lie-in interrupted snarled his displeasure.

'What the hell did you think he was doing, Wainwright?'

'I thought he was having a pee, sir.'

'What do you think he hit you with? His prick?'

'If it was, he'd a hell of a hard-on.'

That little sally damn near slapped me on a Misconduct Form for insolence. The 'incident' was circulated to all surrounding divisions, then I was carted off to the local police surgeon. When *that* worthy had finished huffing and puffing, I'd had God knows what pumped into my arm and my head had enough bandaging to make me look like something from *Ney's Last Stand*. But they never found the runt responsible.

As Vic said, prior to my leaving for forty-eight hours' sick leave, 'So now you know, lad. Either hit 'em first, or stay far enough away to make sure they don't hit *you* first.'

I seem to have made this particular chief inspector sound like a complete bastard. He wasn't, really. In many ways he was a cracking good copper and, after the first few years – when I knew *him* better and he knew *me* better – we developed a genuine mutual respect. He could rant and rave like the best but, having cleared his chest of all the dirty water, he never bore a grudge. He was 'Tosh' – short for Tommy – and he backed his men to the limit when the chips were down. But he was also part of a system.

*   *   *

In those days, the system demanded that every report submitted began with the words 'Superintendent X, sir, I beg to report . . .' and ended with the words, 'I have the honour to be, sir, your obedient servant . . .' It was pure officialese, heavily impregnated with lickspittle. You never saw anything, you 'observed' things. You never walked and you certainly never ran. You 'proceeded'. You didn't even arrest. You 'apprehended'.

If you rebelled, and didn't use the approved words, the report was returned with the offending expression ringed with red ink, and the whole report had to be re-typed.

On one magnificent occasion Harry and I turned the system back on itself and scored a small victory.

Harry was of my generation and, like me, new to the job. He was ex-Navy, perhaps slightly more easy-going than myself, but a great one for singing bawdy service ditties, while I thumped the piano, whenever he and his wife visited, or when Avis and I were asked for the evening to their place. We saw less of each other than either of us might have wished, simply because he worked Elland Town, and I worked Upper Edge; Vic obviously wasn't madly keen on having *two* greenhorns on the street at the same time.

But on this afternoon we were together in the Section Office. It must be understood that here *everything* was 'official issue'. From the lino to the typewriter, from the pencils to the light bulbs, from the wall-clock to the ink. Everything. Even the toilet-rolls.

Harry ambled back from the bog carrying a piece of toilet-paper and, printed in bold green letters on this sheet – as on every sheet – were the words PLEASE WASH YOUR HANDS AFTER USE. He dropped the sheet on the desk top, eyed me, grinned, then said, 'Shall we?'

It was a glorious gag and irresistible.

I threaded the sheet of bum-paper into the typewriter and, under the po-faced instructions, typed,

Superintendent Lambert, sir,
    I beg to report that the above instructions have been complied with.
    I have the honour to be, sir, your obedient servant,
                    (signed) John Wainwright. PC718

We slipped the sheet into the manila envelope, with the other daily documents to be collected and taken to Halifax DHQ, then we waited.

Two days later, the sheet of toilet paper was returned with

(2)
Noted
(signed) F. Lambert, Supt.

added to the mock report.

Both Harry and I thought we'd been blessed with a divisional officer with a sense of humour, but not so. A few years later, in another division where *Mr* Lambert had retired, I met up with him and reminded him of the incident. He hadn't even noticed the bum-wiper.

'You see, Wainwright,' he explained, 'in those days I never *read* the rubbish they dumped in my tray for signature. I just scrawled my name under whatever the clerk had typed.'

*   *   *

Ernest also worked Elland Town, and Ernest was a gentle giant. That, of course, is a cliché description, but it's the only description that fits. He topped the six-foot mark by a good three inches but as he walked towards you, or from a distance, he looked almost squat. Such was his breadth. Yet he never raised his voice, and he never lost his temper. With that weight of muscle, he didn't have to.

I saw him in action only once, but it was an eye-opener. I'd arrived at Elland nick to cover the town beat for yet another night shift and, at ten minutes after ten, a nine–nine–nine call came through. Bowes was going berserk.

Bowes was the hard-nut of Elland. Myths and legends had been built up around how many coppers it needed to bring him in, and now he'd had a skinful and was wrecking one of the less reputable pubs of the town. The landlord had flashed the triple-niner and, if *he* was screaming 'Copper!', it meant Bowes was really on the warpath.

I think the expression on my face, as I took the call, gave the game away.

'What is it, Jack?'

'Bowes is running wild.'

'You might need a hand.'

'From what I've been told, I need the Brigade of Guards.'

'He'll come,' smiled Ernest.

We strolled to the boozer at a very sedate pace. I'd already learned that much. In this sort of situation, the trick was to let like knock as much hell as possible out of like before *you* arrived; to let Bowes tire himself out, and take as much reciprocal punishment as possible. It was easier all round. Our speed, therefore, was a steady, constabulary saunter.

As we neared the epicentre we could hear the rumpus. Mrs Bowes' wayward son had certainly built up a fine head of steam. I hooked a thumb through the thong of my truncheon, took a few deep breaths and, as near as possible, because of the little space available, entered the swing-doors shoulder-to-shoulder with Ernest.

Bowes had been having a ball. Customers were standing on side-benches. Wounded troops littered the corners. Broken glass crunched underfoot and there was an immediate impression of blood and guts having been hurled in all directions.

He saw us, from the other side of the room. Policemen were, obviously, the good, red meat he'd been waiting for. He let loose with a yell of unbridled rage, lowered his head and charged. Ernest stooped slightly and, almost offhandedly, lifted a table. A centre-stemmed, scrolled-ironwork table with a round marble top. He timed it to perfection. Quite unhurriedly, he straightened his arm and met the oncoming Bowes with the edge of the marble top . . . and peace descended, like a dove from on high.

We each draped an arm of the dazed Bowes over our shoulders, waltzed him to the nick and allowed him to settle gently on a cell bed. Then, being the fine fellow he was, Ernest began to steer me through the intricacies of the Arrest Form, the Report Form and the eventual Bail Form.

That was when our prisoner realised he *was* a prisoner and, possibly, that he'd been arrested without spilling one drop of his captors' blood. It was, very obviously, something at odds with every religious and political principle held dear by friend Bowes. All hell erupted from the direction of the cell area.

Ernest pursed his lips in a silent whistle of disapproval, and murmured, 'Vic won't like that. His bedroom's directly above.'

We returned to the cell and, squinting through the peephole, I saw Bowes quite deliberately charging the cell door. A door, almost three inches thick, and lined on the

30

inside with steel plate. God in His glory knew what the lunatic expected to achieve, other than to kick up an almighty din.

'Bring the key,' sighed Ernest.

And, having been handed the keys, he quietly unlocked the cell door, turned the handle, placed the underside of a size twelve boot against the door surface and watched through the peephole.

The truth is, I felt rather sorry for Bowes. He'd already had it horizontally from the pub table and, as he charged the length of the cell, he received a second helping, vertically, from a steel-lined door. That he was a tough nut was never in doubt. Anybody capable of sleeping off a skinful of booze, plus the results of those two wallops, had to have a head like granite and a face like teak. On the other hand, Ernie knew his own strength and (or so it seemed) exactly how much clout Bowes could take before he became a hospital case.

*   *   *

Bowes was the first of many. Every copper with service on the streets meets them with gruesome regularity. In the main, they are not crooks although occasionally they are recruited as 'heavies' in some mob-handed escapade. Beyond the influence of the bent brigade, they are not even trouble-makers in the real sense of the word. They merely cause trouble in their everlasting, booze-sodden determination to uphold a super-macho image.

Sober, they are harmless enough oafs. They eff and blind all over the place, and to them every policeman is a 'rozzer' because in comic strips (which are their main source of literary education) that is what policemen are called. Their brawn is phenomenal but what brain they have seems to be embedded in reinforced concrete. It is always their loud-mouthed boast that, when 'pissed', it takes x-number of rozzers to haul them to the nearest cell.

Many of them fringe the lower rungs of the boxing world. About once a fortnight, at local tournaments, they climb into the ring to have what few brain cells they possess shaken around and made even less stable.

What they can never understand is that, even if it takes

31

the whole force to frog-march them to the wrong side of a cell door, once they are arrested the only machinery available to '*un*-arrest' them is the bail procedure. Muscle-power doesn't come into it. Nor is it a matter of who is the 'best man'. When the chips are down, the police rule-book gets trodden underfoot because the copper has to come out on top; . . . otherwise the rule of law takes second place to the rule of fighting-beer.

However, while it is occasionally necessary (as with Bowes and Ernest) to trade thump for thump, ninety percent of the time it is not worth the shoe leather a copper wears out to lay a finger on these child-like apes. The trick is to stop them before their alcohol intake reaches a dangerous level; while they're a public nuisance, but not yet a public menace.

At that point, talk is all that is necessary; talk, plus the ability to remain calm and realise that you're conversing with a raving maniac.

He can then be kidded into trotting off home with his less belligerent pals. Conversely, he can be conned into strolling, albeit rather noisily, to the nearest nick where, when the penny finally drops, the chances are he will grin shamefacedly before meekly removing footwear, tie, braces and belt prior to being led to the awaiting cell bed.

The point is that you have not degraded him in front of his cronies. Within the privacy of the police station he can tacitly admit defeat, knowing that in some mysterious way he's ended up inside the enemy camp. You, in turn, have not allowed him to air his muscles in public.

As always, I return to those immediate post-war intakes.

We knew the trick. We'd done it scores of times in HM Forces. These same men, in service uniform, had been damn good soldiers, sailors and airmen. They'd been the battering-ram with which Rommel and Rundstedt had been splattered all over the continents of Africa and Europe. They were entitled to wear the same medal ribbons we wore and they, in turn, recognised those medal ribbons. In the war years, when they'd drunk themselves stupid, *we* had steered them past waiting military policemen and dumped them safely on to their own bed spaces. We *still* knew how to handle them. And *they* recognised us as being, in part at least, of their breed, but being soft in the head we'd opted for a quieter life.

There was a neat, reciprocal amiability which lasted for about ten years ... until the non-service roughnecks came of age.

It was not, however, all blood and/or kidology.

Town duty at Elland meant, among other things, escorting school kids across a fairly busy road. The youngsters got to know you. They even got to like you. God alone knows how many horrible drawings I 'admired'. How many 'secrets' I had whispered to me.

Those were the days long before such exotic creatures as School-Crossing Patrols, and the kids chattered away like so many sparrows at whichever copper had the job of seeing them through the traffic. I learned which teacher was a 'softie' and which was a 'nasty old thing'. I was told exactly how Miss So-and-So timed things to perfection in order that Mister Such-and-Such might offer her a lift home in his car.

And yet there was more innocence then and less graffiti.

I recall the local builder who having threaded his way through the miles of red tape required in those days at last received permission to build a short street of houses. He was a philanthropically minded type. He offered a prize to whichever pupil came up with an appropriate name for the new street. One young hopeful was highly indignant when his suggestion of 'Dead Man's Gulch' didn't meet with unqualified approval.

*   *   *

Meanwhile, we new recruits horsed around with first-aid and occasionally had the opportunity to make use of the training.

Vic, the section sergeant, was the divisional star turn as far as first-aid was concerned. He knew the bones, he knew the pressure points, and he could perform minor miracles with a triangular bandage. He could quite literally quote page after page of the St John's Ambulance first-aid manual.

He joined me one day at the school crossing alongside

33

the entrance to Elland Town Hall.

The town hall had long ago ceased to *be* a town hall. It was now a cinema and, because of its external appearance, a most imposing little cinema. It had a pillared entrance atop a long and broad flight of shallow steps. At each side of the entrance were the glass-fronted cases showing 'stills' of the picture being shown at the time.

An elderly lady had trudged up the steps to examine the 'stills', lost her footing at the top and, with much screaming and shouting, she purled her way down to the pavement. She was obviously in pain. Indeed, by the row she was making, she sounded as if she'd broken her neck.

Vic did a long-distance diagnosis. 'Her ankle's gone. Get a chair from one of the shops, then come and give me a hand at carrying her.'

I got the chair. I placed it on the pavement, then hurried to where Vic was performing his expertise. In retrospect, we were both great guys at first-aid, but neither of us had the gumption to take the chair *to* the 'injured party'!

'Get your arm under her left armpit.' Thus spoke the oracle. 'I'll get mine under her right, then we can take all the weight from her feet.' And to the elderly lady who was still screaming the place down, 'You're all right, luv. We'll get you to the chair. Don't put any weight on your ankle. Let it all rest on our arms.'

We carried her to the chair and sat her down. I rushed to the nearest kiosk and telephoned for an ambulance. Meanwhile the lady was, literally, weeping with pain.

At the Halifax infirmary the professionals took over. Vic's diagnosis had been a little out. Not a broken ankle, after all, but a broken collarbone . . . and, in effect, that's what we'd been lifting her with.

Small wonder the poor old dear had wept with pain.

Another part of the first-aid training involved visits to the local swimming baths where I piled proof upon proof that I'd never be able to swim. I continued to sink like a block of granite, but that was kept a dark secret and when Tommy, the Permanent Office Reserve, sent me to one of the mill dams to rescue some youngster who'd fallen in and was floating on the surface, face downwards, I wished then, with all my heart, that I *could* swim . . . for everybody's sake.

A mill dam (at least *this* mill dam) is a foul and stinking stretch of water, deep enough to drown an elephant and dirty enough to send a skunk running for cover and there, almost submerged beneath the green surface-scum, was a young boy.

I'd grabbed a clothes-prop on my way to the scene – God knows why. It was possibly some deep-rooted sense of self-preservation; the certain knowledge that, without *something*, there'd be *two* corpses to be fished from the dam.

Among the group of gawpers at the dam side was a Flash Youth. Padded shoulders, two-tone shoes, slicked-back hair and sideburns. I poked one end of the clothes-prop in his direction.

'Hang on to that, son. Hang on for dear life.'

I had sense enough to knock my helmet off before I took a deep breath and went in. How many times I went under I don't know but, by gripping the other end of the clothes-prop and extending both arms, I could get a hold on the boy's coat. Thereafter, it was a simple matter of being hauled ashore.

Then came the artificial respiration. In those days we used the old-fashioned Schafer method. None of the modern mouth-to-mouth stuff. I did it right too. I cleared the gunge from the mouth, then started kneading the ribs. After five minutes I was sweating, but when the muck left his lungs in a rush and the first gurgling breaths came . . . I think God must have had the same feeling on the Seventh Day, when he relaxed and checked up on what he'd done.

The ambulance arrived and the kid was carted off to hospital for a once-over. The Flash Youth handed me back the clothes-prop. *That* was when the berk mentioned that he held medals for life-saving, but hadn't wanted to get his clothes messed up. To be honest, I was too knackered to sling *him* into the dam, but in part I was compensated. That was the first time the local rag carried my name. The tiny headline read 'Clothes-Prop Rescue' and, although it sounded a bit daft, who cared? Avis was quite proud of me.

The truth is I was quite proud of *myself*.

*   *   *

I think every copper looks upon his first .posting as something special. The men. who were his first fellow-officers. The mannerisms of those he recognised as being the best in that particular section, and if, like me, he had an outside beat, that beat, too, takes upon itself an evergrowing nostalgia out of all proportion to the truth.

Upper Edge Beat was *my* beat. The wasteland between Upper Edge and Lower Edge remains in my memory; the night it caught the full blast of a gale howling in from the Pennines and the wind caught me off-balance, lifted my heels six inches from the ground, and slammed me in an untidy heap at the foot of a dry-stone wall.

The hen-runs and the brickworks between Upper Edge and Ainley Top. The roadsters – men and women – who sought warmth in the empty and still-cooling kilns; occasionally a well-educated man who, for some private reason, had opted out of the rat-race. The annual 'fowl-thieves' look-out; forgetting regulations, and taking Snogger, our golden cocker spaniel, on the evening shift and sending him scurrying around the wire, knowing he'd bark a warning if anybody was about.

The sheer, blind isolation of Blackley. It wasn't big enough to merit the description 'village', but neither was it 'country'. A spooky place whose inhabitants all seemed sour-faced and secretive.

The places and the incidents are vivid memories but perhaps most vivid of all are the men: Sam, Ernest, Tommy . . .

From Sam I learned the basics of interviewing. The *real* basics, as opposed to the 'theory' that had been hinted at at Mansfield. The simple trick of not telling a suspect more than he needs to know, and thereafter listening; merely urging him on, and when he lies pretending to believe the lie and allowing him to spin his own cage of untruths until, by proving the one lie you prove a dozen. Of knowing that, even when there are only the two of you, it isn't one-to-one. That if you've found the man you're looking for, his knowledge of his guilt is a factor to be taken into consideration. That even the hardest of cases has a weak spot through which can be reached something approximating a conscience.

From Ernest I learned patience. The patience of a good copper which, when refined and concentrated upon one specific task, can be an awesome weapon against whoever it is directed.

Vic gave me a yardstick by which to measure other section officers. Some I found to be better, but many I found to be worse. He was a sad man – a disappointed man – but to his credit his disappointment didn't make him vindictive. He was (as I now know) resigned to the fact that he'd never make inspector, and was free-wheeling his way, with as little fuss as possible, to Pension Day.

From Tommy . . .

From Tommy I learned absolutely nothing! And yet Tommy deserves a few paragraphs all to himself.

Tommy was old and miserable, gaunt and without humour. For some misdeed, never disclosed, he had earned the job of Permanent Office Reserve. From nine in the morning until five in the afternoon a civilian clerk sat in the Charge Office and answered the telephone; when she packed away her knitting at five o'clock, Tommy took over and was there until 1 a.m.

It was one hell of a shift. One hell of a punishment for whatever it was he'd done. 5 p.m. until 1 a.m. for the rest of his working life. Other than on his Rest Day he could forget social life. He could forget the cinema, or radio or even going to the pub for a quiet drink. He was well and truly *nailed*.

His complaints were beyond count and everlasting. At exactly five o'clock he'd totter into the office and lean, panting, against the table-desk. 'That bloody hill knackers me.'

Then would come the rigmarole of settling a stained and battered beret over the few wisps of hair still clinging to his narrow skull. 'The bloody draughts in this place. For what good they are we needn't have windows and doors.' The Charge Office boasted an open fire and, if the scuttle wasn't filled to overflowing with coal, there was

37

a foul-mouthed tirade about 'nobody giving a bugger about keeping the place warm'.

If the 'In' tray held papers the moan was that the 'idle bitch' had been 'sitting on her arse' all day. If it was empty, she'd obviously had an easy time. 'But, you'll see,' he'd say. 'Some sod from motor patrol will fetch a bloody great pile of the stuff in between now and ten.'

Poor old Tommy. He had a never-ending series of habits that did nothing to endear him to the rest of us. He had a perpetually dribbling nose, but I never saw him use a handkerchief or a tissue; instead he would periodically squeeze his narrow nostrils between thumb and first finger, then flick the muck towards the hearth. Similarly with the phlegm that accompanied the rattling cough he lived with; he would turn in his chair and spit great gobs of the stuff at the blazing coals.

The cleaning lady, who came in at 6.30 a.m. each day, hated Tommy. Her job included cleaning away the ashes and black-leading the grate. And Tommy had always left dried up patterns on the ironwork; like snail-trails, delivered from some part of his guts, and needing to be scraped away before the brushing and polishing could be started.

A strange man, Tommy. He was married and had three children, and God alone knows how his suffering wife tolerated him. He broke wind every fifteen minutes or so, and it was a subtle form of agony to share the Charge Office with him whenever paperwork was called for. I was there when Sam lost his temper. The three of us had shared the Charge Office for about two hours, and the stench was on a par with a Peruvian brothel. Tommy dropped a beaut and Sam leaped from his chair and shoved his face to within twelve inches of Tommy's.

'You dirty old sod,' he snarled. 'One more fart and I'll put a match to your bum and blast you through the ceiling.'

And yet Tommy – even Tommy – hinted at a Police Service I'd never known. A Police Service almost beyond belief.

I was knocking off one evening at ten o'clock and, probably because I'd ended a weary day, I said, 'Goodnight, Tommy', as I opened the Charge Office door to leave.

'Hey, young 'un!' There was near panic in his tone.

'Yes?'

'Take that back.'

'What?' I didn't know what the hell he was talking about.

'What you just said.'

'I said "Goodnight" . . . that's all.'

'*Take it back!*'

'What the deuce . . .?'

'Never say that to a copper.' The old lunatic was deadly serious. 'Never say "Goodnight", "Good morning" or "Good afternoon" to a copper. Haven't you learned *owt* yet?'

'I was being polite,' I explained. 'I was being friendly.'

'It's bad luck,' he moaned. 'Say those things to a fellow-copper, and it puts the jinx on him. He'll have more trouble than he can handle.'

'Good.' All my previous friendliness had evaporated. As I closed the door behind me, I deliberately called, 'Goodnight, Tommy. Have a *very* good night.'

*　　*　　*

But that was Elland. Part of Elland and part of Upper Edge Beat . . . and when I left I felt a little sad.

Court Procedure

In one respect at least it can be said I was the world's worst copper. I thoroughly enjoyed the 'chase', but with equal passion I loathed the 'kill'. I still feel the same. I have seen far too many scoundrels and scallywags step jauntily from the dock, to face a few months or a few years in moderate comfort and without responsibility, leaving their womenfolk and their kids to fend for themselves as best they can.

To that sort of man prison is no real deterrent. What he misses he can do without, and occasionally the nick is a distinct improvement on his normal home life.

On the other hand, some of them – even some of the recidivists – should never have seen the inside of prison in the first place. Apart from their contorted sense of propriety, they were nice enough chaps. Good husbands. Loving fathers. The good Lord simply cursed them with sticky fingers. With this kind, prison was an emotional hell. Thieving to them was a disease, and slamming a cell door behind them was no cure. They'd come back into circulation haggard with worry about those from whom they'd been parted . . . but within a year or two they'd be back inside.

The terrible thing was that in those days the hanging-shed was still in use. And that worried me.

I was on the periphery of a few murder enquiries (to which I'll come later) and every time I had a niggling feeling of 'wrongness'. The machine of which I was a part was hunting a man to death. And true enough the man we were after had killed . . . but I never quite squared it with my conscience that that, of itself, was reason enough for *another* killing.

To put it another way . . .

I respect the right of everybody to hold a personal opinion. But those in favour of the noose shouldn't sit back and pass the final buck to people like Pierrepoint. They should be prepared to stand up and be counted; have their names listed, much like those likely to be called for jury service, and know that the appropriate authority can call upon *them* to personally spring the trap.

All this, of course, has little or nothing to do with the service of a common-or-garden copper, other than that the 'chase', if successful, ends up in court, and courts of various size and description were part of my life.

In those days, and in ascending order of both importance and pomposity, we had Magistrates' Courts, Courts of Quarter Session and Assize Courts. Coroners' Courts fitted in there somewhere. *They* figured themselves top of the list. *We* counted them as something of a nuisance and a throw-back to the days of Robin Hood and Dick Turpin.

'Court Day' meant hours of boredom almost every week, fannying around the local Magistrates' Court.

Stipendiary magistrates were very much of a novelty in those days and so we were invariably lumbered with a bench of local JPs. And Justices of the Peace were odd and unpredictable creatures given to bending both law and evidence to suit themselves when necessary.

The office goes back to around 1195, and the appointment of a JP involves all manner of high and mighty people, including the Lord Lieutenant of the County, the Lord Chancellor and a vague and mysterious body known as an 'advisory committee'. Thus, according to the book of words.

Politics always pokes its inquisitive nose into things. Every bench of lay magistrates I ever gave evidence before seemed to be split down the middle; half of them were roaring Tories, while the other half were fire-eating Socialists. Few had any sense of proportion and, depending on the make-up of the bench, the occupation and social status of the accused and the way he dressed, every copper in that courtroom could make an educated guess about the outcome of the case, the size of the fine, and

41

whether or not he might be slapped inside for a few weeks.

Two extreme cases will illustrate what I mean.

The chairman of one bench was a landlord of local renown. He had an unbending lord-of-the-manor mentality, and seemed to own just about half the county. Once in the dim and distant past some clown had nicked a few chickens from one of his farms and the culprit had never been traced. Shove a suspected fowl thief in front of *him* and he didn't even bother *listening* to the evidence. Before the Clerk to the Magistrates had finished reading out the charge, the chairman was jotting figures down on his copy of the Court Sheet. That lad was going down, nothing surer! The theory was that eventually, and taking into account the law of averages, the unknown berk who'd pinched the chairman's hens would end up in court for the same offence. And he wasn't going to miss him *this* time.

Another chairman had a deep and pathological hatred of policemen. On one magnificent occasion I actually witnessed what could have been a fatal road accident. One of the local bloods tore out of a side-street, past a 'Halt' sign and smashed into a sedately driven motor car which was going quietly and lawfully along the main road. Nobody was seriously injured, but both vehicles were severely bent. I'd *seen* the thing happen, therefore the Road Traffic Offence was cut and dried. I didn't need witnesses. It was there, steaming hot and ready to be served up on a plate.

The charge was dismissed, and the chairman gave me hell. The damned accident was *my* fault. I was there. Ergo, had I been doing my job properly, I should have raised my hand and stopped the offending vehicle.

I plaintively explained – at least six times – that I was a good fifty yards from the blasted junction; but that made not a scrap of difference.

Then, of course, there was the chairwoman of one particular Juvenile Court. She lived alone and unsullied in Cloud-Cuckoo-Land. She was elderly, unmarried, and had a figure like that of a Belsen inmate. She wore wide-brimmed hats of glorious floral design and (or so it

42

seemed) rarely washed her face and neck. Instead she plastered make-up about her features with the wild abandon of an unskilled navvy spreading concrete. She'd figured out her own brand of child psychology, and her two companions on the bench were wispy, tired-looking gentlemen whose sole purpose was to nod agreement to whatever utterance she came out with.

The fourteen-year-old I'd brought to court was, very obviously, destined to make a name for himself in the ranks of the ungodly. He'd broken into a car showroom and without much effort had done ten thousand quid's worth of damage to new and unused vehicles. Windows, windscreens, headlamps, bodywork – the lot – he'd had an uninterrupted beano with a jack-handle.

He came from a poor, basically dishonest family and his parents sat in the well of the court looking worried and, no doubt, wondering exactly what ten thousand pounds looked like in one bundle.

The owner of the showroom had given evidence. I'd given evidence. Now it was the turn of the young tearaway to make what excuses he could think up on the spur of the moment.

The chairwoman asked him to step forward.

She leaned forward and asked, 'How much pocket-money do you get a week?'

The fourteen-year-old told her.

'What do you spend it on?'

'Ice-lollies.'

She smiled a motherly smile, then said, 'Do you know how many ice-lollies you can buy for ten thousand pounds?'

At the back of the court I made a grab for the arm of the showroom's owner. There was murder in his eyes and it would have been either the youth or the chair-woman . . . probably both.

*　　*　　*

Twenty years as a working copper teaches you many things, and one of the things you learn on your journey through a multiplicity of courts is that for every solicitor who's a born 'court man' there are at least a dozen who haven't much of a clue and that, for every barrister sporting a wig and gown who might be a second Patrick Hastings, a hundred are there for the ride.

Agreed, the first time you visit a court higher than the local magistrates' set-up – the first time you clap eyes on that small army of imposing-looking gentlemen, and some ladies, who scurry in and out of doors and along corridors, with gowns flying and wigs askew – your knees tend to tremble slightly. This (you tell yourself) is THE LAW. What's it all about. This is the forensic equivalent of heart-surgery expertise, whereas all *you've* done so far is empty bed-pans.

You soon learn.

The first rumour of a Dock Brief weeds them out.

In those days, any accused person up for trial at Assize or Quarter Sessions could, if he so desired, stand in the dock and point to any barrister whom he wished to defend him. He was not allowed to choose the barrister by name, but the barrister pointed to could not refuse his services. And whatever the legal standing of the chosen barrister his fee remained the same. £2.4s.6d.

But barristers have clerks and solicitors and general dogsbodies on hand and, without fail, the hint of a possible Dock Brief saw a mass exodus from the court of all but the odds and sods. The news always got around. And because he could only *point* – and not name – the poor old accused was lumbered with choosing from a beautiful bunch of unripe bananas.

We, of the fuzz, had other ways of identifying those who might give us a rough time in the witness box.

Wigs, for example. I have a sneaking suspicion that barristers buy only *one* wig (when they are first called to the bar) and thereafter – possibly for superstitious reasons – never buy another. A bright and sparkling wig, regardless of how old the man wearing it, put the mind at rest; the cross-examination would be a walk-over. If, on the other hand, the wig was very much off-white and tattered around the edges ... watch out for those sly, throwaway questions.

We learned other pointers, too.

If the wig and gown were carried in a blue bag, that usually meant a fairly easy ride. If the bag was red, then

44

that meant that on at least one occasion in the past the guy had pulled a sizzler. Barristers are not allowed to buy their own red bag. It remains blue, pending the presentation of a red one as a token of regard from some leading QC to whom that 'stuff barrister' has rendered sterling service in court.

We learned these signs. These subtleties. We learned them and remembered them.

Even the way in which barristers behave in the well of the court. Get some pontificating goofball throwing back his head and gripping the lapels of his gown in the approved motion-picture manner, and you could relax. The man to worry about was the one with his gown thrown back at the hips, and with his hands deep in the pockets of his trousers; the one who didn't seem to be giving much notice to what was going on or what was being said. *That* one had marbles, and to spare.

Judges, too. They tended to live in a world of their own, but sometimes that was a deliberate put-on. They had their likes and dislikes. They rode their personal hobby-horses, and still do. Some judges loathed barristers, and with them you knew the witness-box was never going to be a substitute torture chamber. Some loathed coppers, and with *them* . . . boy, you'd better get it right! Some put damage to personal property ahead of personal injury. Some figured a black eye or a bloody nose was of itself sufficient reason for surrounding the culprit with granite for a few years. And some, be it clearly understood, were quite convinced that rape was utterly impossible without, at the very least, the passive co-operation of the victim.

Goddard rarely came on circuit but, when he did, everybody knew he'd arrived. He was Lord Chief Justice, and nobody knew that better than he did. He came up to Leeds when, in 1952, Alfred Moore was accused of killing Inspector Fraser and Police Constable Jagger. We had the right guy. Nobody on the case had a shadow of doubt about Moore's guilt. But, equally, nobody had any doubt about the verdict, with Goddard sitting in the high chair.

Mr Justice F. was my own favourite. He had a delightfully droll sense of humour and, with a deadpan expression, could debunk anybody who went over the top.

As a perfect example, on one occasion the defending barrister was one given to over-emphasis and wild histrionics. His closing speech was pure ham and, to drive home one particular point, he banged the table with the ball of his fist. Mr Justice F. summed up, as always, with scrupulous fairness. Without a change of tone, he said, 'We now come to the part where defending counsel saw fit to knock the furniture about . . .'

All this, of course, happened many years ago, while I was still innocent enough to believe in the certainty of the jury system. Before I left the force. More importantly, before I was called to *sit* on a jury years beyond the day I left the force. . . .

Let me start by saying that the jury system (in one form or another) is not new. It started long before one of Norman William's archers hit double-top in Harold's eye. It was even the 'done thing' when Ethelred the Unready enacted the Law of Wantage and, in the idiom of the day, said, 'Let a moot be held in every Wapentake, let twelve senior thegns go out, and a reeve with them, and let them swear on a relic that they will accuse no innocent man nor conceal any guilty man'.

That was in the eleventh century – give or take a few months – which means it's been around for some time. In other words, the kinks should have been ironed out by now.

You'd be surprised.

Fortunately (*very* fortunately) my first experience on a jury wasn't a Tower of London job. Just some twit who'd been on the booze, had driven a motor car and had been stopped by a brace of enthusiastic coppers. He'd been asked to blow into the bag and the crystals had turned the wrong colour. Just.

There hadn't been an accident. No Road Traffic offence had been committed. There had been no immediate danger to other road users. Indeed, there'd been no real reason for flagging him down other than (and here I speak as an ex-copper) a desire to relieve boredom. Which means that the bag-blowing routine had been what was technically called a 'random check'. Fine, except that at that time 'random checks' weren't allowed.

They weren't lawful. They are now, but they weren't then. That they should have been I do not dispute, but it was a hole in the drink-and-drive law, and a hole that had not yet been plugged.

Technically, therefore, this meant that His Nibs *had* to be innocent.

I sat in that jury box and squirmed as I listened to two of my ex-colleagues being hammered dizzy by a mock-indignant defence barrister for doing what he knew they'd *had* to do. They'd had to make an arrest. What else? The booze count had been above the permitted amount, therefore the clown was driving a car with excess alcohol sloshing around in his bloodstream. They'd either *had* to arrest him or condone a criminal offence.

They were over a barrel and, to their eternal credit, they didn't try to duck the issue. They told a straight yarn and claimed to be morally right (which indeed they were) but, with equal honesty, admitted that the court dealt with 'law' not 'morals'.

They knew damn well the man *had* to be acquitted.

So did I as we trooped into the jury-room; the judge had left nobody in any doubt about the verdict he expected. The jury was made up of eleven men and one woman. And I (for some mysterious reason) had been elevated to the grand position of 'Foreman'.

The door was closed firmly behind us, and I looked enquiringly at my companions.

'Right! Let's get him sent down, and get off home. I've some sheep to see to.' That was the opening remark, from a grizzled hill farmer to whom the day had been a complete waste of time.

One of the other men said, 'Nay, damn! Let's have a sit down and a smoke before we go back.'

(I recalled the words of one magnificent constitutional lawyer, Sir W. Ivor Jennings: 'The one advantage of the jury system, if advantage it be, is that it secures the opinion of twelve people of the most orthodox class in the community.') I figured it was about time I touted for those opinions. It seemed a sensible idea to have a round-up of views.

The lady said, 'I'll go along with the rest of you, of

course.'

One man said, 'Well, it could have been any one of us, couldn't it?'

Another man fiddled with his hearing-aid and muttered, 'It's on the blink, you see. It's not the batteries. I had them *new* before I set out. It's the earpiece, I think. I haven't heard half of what's been said.'

I may have been unlucky. I wouldn't know. The only thing of which I was certain was that when Lord Loughborough had insisted, 'Take away trial by jury and the whole fabric of the law will soon moulder into dust,' he hadn't encountered the sort of people *I'd* led from the jury-box.

I truly loved the law, and I therefore worked like crazy to make these people understand and accept their responsibilities. It took an hour and a half of argument and simple explanation. We weren't there to slap a man inside because somebody else had almost ridden us down. It didn't matter that the man in the dock might have been stoned out of his mind in the past, or that he might be stoned out of his mind at some time in the future . . . We were there to consider one specific occasion, plus a silly but important technicality of the law.

Perry Mason couldn't have done it better and, by the time I'd got it over to them – that we were there, trying *this* man for *this* alleged offence, and that all decisions should be based upon fact and law, and not personal bias plus a natural desire to call it a day and get back home – I was both hoarse and sweating.

We reached a majority verdict. Not guilty.

One man stood out. He wasn't a fool, and he took his job very seriously. But come hell or high water – against every argument under the sun – he wasn't going to let the police down. Legal niceties could go chase themselves down the nearest drain. 'Random checks' could take a flying jump as far as *he* was concerned. The accused had been carrying too much booze while driving a motor car on the Queen's highway . . . period. The defendant was as guilty as sin. He was a most stubborn man, and he was wrong. But I admired him. Of all the people in that jury-room, he was the one person who saved my faith in human nature ... even though my faith in the jury system went for a complete Burton.

*   *   *

But back to the days of pavement-bashing and the almost weekly trip to the local Magistrates' Court. There, and unless the case was merely a committal hearing due to go up the line, the Prosecuting Officer was always a copper. Sometimes a sergeant, more frequently an inspector, but more often than not the chief inspector of the sub-division. 'Tosh' in other words.

Tosh had worked his way up the ranks the hard way. No fancy Senior Officers' Course for him. He knew all the tricks in the book – indeed, the impression was that he'd *written* the book – and I never met a barrister or a solicitor who knew more ploys of 'unofficial' courtroom antics than he did.

He'd present the case, then sit down and wait for the defending solicitor to cross-examine. During the cross-examination he'd suck sweets. Sweets individually wrapped in stiff Cellophane. Never have I known such noisy Cellophane. The rustling and the crinkling could be heard all over the court-room and, if the defending solicitor risked a quick frown of annoyance, Tosh's attention would always seem to be focused on some far corner of the ceiling. Come some particularly *awkward* question, and immediately a freshly laundered handkerchief would appear; it would be shaken out prior to Tosh suffering a very convenient sneezing bout. That, or a book would mysteriously slip from the table. Or Tosh would unwind himself from his chair, turn and wave weird and wonderful instructions to the gaggle of coppers bunched at the rear of the room.

No defending solicitor ever had a free and uninterrupted ride when Tosh was the Prosecuting Officer.

But all this rigmarole of fidgeting was a mere prelude to what was to come when the Defence went in to bat.

Previous convictions are not of course given until the accused has been found guilty of whatever offence he's charged with. A prior knowledge that the guy in the dock was a regular visitor to criminal courts might sway the magistrates in their decision. But, needless to say, Tosh

49

had all the papers relating to the offence there in front of him, including the Previous Conviction Card. And all the papers were white, except the Previous Conviction Card which was an eye-catching yellow. We all knew this. Certainly the bench knew it; they'd seen similar cards scores of times when in the past 'previous cons' had been read out.

Once the Prosecution had had its say, that yellow card took pride of place on top of all Tosh's other papers. Indeed, he was given to playing with it idly, vaguely lifting it up and down . . . just to make sure everybody saw it. If the poor guy *had* previous convictions, that at least was not left in doubt.

And if the accused was placed in the witness box and gave evidence on his own behalf, what was Tosh's opening move in the cross-examination?

'The court might be interested to know who, in this case, you think might have most to gain by lying? You or the police officer?'

'I object!' would counter the defending solicitor, puce with indignation as he jumped to his feet. 'The chief inspector's question is tantamount to accusing my client of committing perjury.'

'Perjury?' Tosh's look of innocent puzzlement must have taken hours of rehearsal. Then, with a pleading look at the magistrates, 'I asked for an opinion, your worships. That's all.'

'Your worships, my client can't possibly be expected to . . .'

Tosh would sigh, and murmur, 'I withdraw the question, if my friend so wishes.'

Withdraw the question! The question had already been *asked*, and there was only one real answer. That, plus the yellow card, cooked the goose to a turn.

Without Tosh in the driving seat things tended to be rather dull. But I recall one occasion in the Court, when my case – some petty Road Traffic Law offence – had been the last to be heard. I'd given my evidence in my usual rumble, the guy had been dutifully fined and now everybody relaxed. Stiff limbs were eased. Fags and pipes were lighted. The books and papers were being collected.

One of the magistrates leaned forward and spoke to me.

'Y'know, whenever you give evidence, Constable Wainwright, it reminds me of Chaliapin.'

The fussy little inspector who'd been Prosecuting Officer beckoned me towards him.

'Why,' he asked anxiously, 'should *you* remind him of Charlie Chaplin?'

Without such highlights of idiocy life would be very wearisome.

*   *   *

Even in those days – the days long ago when the lower courts in particular were a regular part of my working life – I wasn't happy. I wasn't satisfied. There was a slight element of 'fiddle' and, without being bumptious, without claiming to be one jot more noble than the next man, it worried me occasionally. At first I figured it as a possible backlash of the old 'Police Court' days, but eventually even that excuse wore too thin. It was something else and, moreover, it was something I'd lived with for a very long time.

In my early schooldays (which is going back one hell of a long way) I had an uncle. He wasn't a *real* uncle. He was one of those distant relations all kids had to suffer in those long-past days and, because nobody knew what the deuce else to call these distant offshoots of the family, they were all made honorary 'uncles' and 'aunts'.

He is now dead. Long dead. Whatever his ultimate destination, he has long ago arrived and even *he* has had ample time to settle down, no doubt after the initial long-winded argument about the size of the shovel or the fit of the wings.

I can therefore now speak of him not only with hindsight but also with honesty.

This uncle of mine was many things. He was pompous, he was narrow-minded, he was self-opinionated and he was very bad-tempered. He was always right. *Always.* If he said black was white, black *was* indeed white . . . by virtue of him saying so.

He was well known and greatly admired within the wider circle of the family. *Because he was a lay magistrate.*

He was consulted about everything, from birth-pangs to bunions, and he always knew the answer. Long before I joined the Police Service I had reached my own conclusion about this fatuous uncle of mine; that the day he kicked his clogs one magisterial bench would be vastly improved.

Now, as any copper with twenty years of active service tucked under his belt will tell you, lay magistrates come in all sizes and various flavours; long, short and medium; male, female and your-guess-is-as-good-as-mine. They are all there. The average are just that – average. The bad are a disgrace to the British legal system. The good are outstanding, if only because they are so few.

Stripped of all his glamour, the lay magistrate is a part-time amateur trying to control a court bulging with highly trained professionals. He is given authority which is often far beyond his capability and miles beyond his understanding. Shyster lawyers (*and* crafty old codgers like Tosh) can work rings round him. The Clerk of the Court (a badly paid official at the best of times) is there merely to keep the train on its legal rails and to proffer asked-for advice; and that advice can be, and often is, ignored in favour of out-and-out bias.

Conversely, the lay magistrate may 'like the look of' some solicitor. Or a witness. Or even a defendant. It's a dead ringer he knows the sergeants, inspectors and chief inspectors whose responsibility it is to keep the court running smoothly.

And from this pasticcio of likes and dislikes – this weekly get-together of boozing pals, complete strangers and in-betweens – an untrained man is expected to make sure that 'justice is not only done, but is also manifestly *seen* to be done'.

From some of my past experiences I could say, 'That'll be the day'. Instead, and in all honesty, I'll say this. That justice so often *is* done is a near-miracle. But justice shouldn't *depend* upon near-miracles.

Nor, indeed, am I blaming the lay justice for these weaknesses. He wanted the job, otherwise he would have refused. But from the off, and however hard he tries, he is playing against a stacked deck.

The argument in favour of lay justices is ancient. It goes back to 1362 and revolves around the beautiful theory of like sitting in judgment upon like. It is also argued that a lay magistrate has, in the final analysis, very small power.

So be it, if you accept that the authority to send somebody to the slammer for six months is 'small power', but small power exercised anything up to thirty times every week adds up to a very big power. And predisposition, multiplied by the same number, soon becomes a predominance.

The sad thing is that the *real* Judiciary recognise all these weaknesses. A handful of Royal Commissions have already delivered judgement on the selection of lay magistrates and, *always*, there has been unanimous agreement that too much attention in the appointment of a JP is paid to his political opinions.

It makes you think.

It makes *me* think that the office of lay magistrate should be scrapped. That every petty sessional court should have its stipendiary magistrate; a trained lawyer, expert in that most difficult of all attitudes of mind . . . objectivity.

Strong politics and justice don't mix. The former makes for pre-judgement and defeats the latter. And (going back to my childhood then forward to my police years) far too many times I saw 'Uncle' glaring down from the bench, anxious to get the time-wasting rigmarole of listening to the evidence out of the way.

Finally, a few words about Coroners' Courts.

* * *

Coroners — or 'Crown's Men' as they think they were originally called — have been under our feet since 1194. Originally, they were very big wheels indeed. Now, they only *think* they're big, whereas they are actually fairly insignificant cogs in the legal set-up. Other than fooling around with treasure trove, their job is to hold an inquest on violent, unnatural or sudden deaths where the cause of death is unknown. Consequently, a Coroner's Court is rarely a jovial gathering and, in the main, coroners take this into consideration.

The coroner *I* remember (and whom everybody on duty at his court remembers) didn't. He was an out-and-out. A one-off job. An absolute ringtailer. Let some newly widowed woman allow a single tear to fill her eye, and he'd bark, 'Woman! I will not allow exhibitionism in *my* court.' Let a barrister be there as a legal representative, and he'd glare, then snarl, 'In this court you will be allowed to ask questions of which *I* approve.'

He was, quite simply, an impossible man to please. If the weather was icily cold and the windows were closed, he'd complain about the stuffiness. If it was boiling hot outside and you'd opened the windows there'd always be a draught he wanted stopping. If you put a cushion in his chair it was too high. If you *didn't* put the cushion there, it was too low. His tantrums were a byword and his ill-temper taken for granted.

The only people who liked him were the local publicans. Not that he was a tippler. Simply that he *always* held his inquests at 2.30 p.m., and he *always* demanded a jury. And at that time in the afternoon landlords had a few hours to spare. We had about fifteen on tap. Come a Sudden Death, the minute we knew the day of the case at the Coroner's Court we telephoned a dozen of our tame publicans and they obligingly rolled up, settled in their seats, said what old Misery Guts told them to say, drew their pittance and (if it was summer) pushed off and spent the rest of the afternoon playing bowls.

But there was one day when there had been a Sudden Death that was Sam's case; he was therefore Coroner's Officer. Upon him the axe would fall if *anything* unto-ward should happen. He'd checked the witnesses, he'd checked the jury, he'd checked the seat and the windows, seen that the blotting-pad was new and unsullied, threatened the local press with dire consequences should they mutter among themselves or try for a quiet drag. He'd done everything. All I'd done was fix the forms and generally get in the way.

We were waiting for the coroner.

I wandered across the room and glanced at the shelf of the witness-box.

No Testament!

I almost ran to Sam and whispered, 'There's no Testament.'

'Eh?'

'The Testament. It isn't there.'

'It's on the shelf of the –'

'It isn't *there*!'

'Where the hell *is* it?' Even Sam looked on the point of panic. 'The old sod's due any minute. If we don't have a Bible for the oath he'll have our balls fried for tomorrow's breakfast.'

'I'm sorry, but –'

'For Christ's sake, don't stand there being "sorry". *Do* something.'

I scurried around the room and into adjoining rooms, opening cupboards and drawers and, just in time, I found what I was looking for.

The rest of the inquest went off without a hitch. Sam ushered in the various witnesses and I guided them through the oath-taking. The jury of publicans dozed in their seats before bringing the verdict recommended by the coroner.

When it was all over, when everybody had left and the coroner had been safely escorted to his waiting car, Sam collapsed into one of the chairs and took a few deep breaths.

'God, that was close,' he sighed.

'You don't know how close.'

He looked puzzled.

I picked the black volume from the shelf of the witness-box, turned it and shared my secret. The witnesses had all solemnly sworn to 'tell the truth, the whole truth and nothing but the truth' with their hand resting on the back cover of a copy of the St John's Ambulance handbook *First Aid to the Injured*.

Sam nodded, approvingly.

'You'll do it yet,' he grinned.

'What?'

'Make a fair-to-middling copper.'

Brighouse

Not too long ago I drove through Brighouse and was completely flummoxed. I, who once knew every road, every street and every back-alley in the place, was hopelessly lost. I was driving a Mini and, God alone knows how, I ended up in a strange car-park with, beyond the bollards there to prevent an exit, a road I vaguely recognised. With less than an inch to spare on each side, I eased the Mini between the bollards and reached safe ground.

I was quite unreasonably angry. Brighouse – *my* Brighouse – had been messed around with. The West Riding force had never boasted police boxes but, at Brighouse, we'd had police *pillars*; chest-high, cast-iron posts with a locked compartment on top, in which there was a telephone with a direct line to the police station. All the police pillars had been removed. The police station was no longer where it had been . . . although the street was still called Police Street. Brighouse had been ruined. The main cinema was a bingo hall and the town itself was a dog's dinner of one-way streets and traffic roundabouts.

Dammit . . . it wasn't *Brighouse* any more.

*   *   *

The Brighouse force of 1949 was a police section like Elland, complete with town beats and outside beats; but it was also a sub-divisional headquarters, which meant Tosh had his office there. And Tosh *was* Brighouse. Other than when he was on court duty, he rarely wore uniform, but the uniform wasn't necessary. He was the chief inspector. The Gaffer. The terror of the shirkers, but a man prepared to go out on the slenderest of limbs for any copper under his control. Periodically, an

56

inspector arrived to 'assist' Tosh in his multiplicity of duties. Assist! He was allowed in Tosh's office only when Tosh wasn't around. He was superfluous, and Tosh was the guy to make him *feel* superfluous. The inspectors came, lasted a few miserable months, then left for destinations unknown, but Tosh had apparently been there since the first turf had been cut, and was going to remain there till doom cracked. When Lambert retired the division had a new superintendent who had, years before, been a sergeant under Tosh. As far as Tosh was concerned, he was *still* a sergeant and such was the sheer weight of Tosh's personality that, at Brighouse, he *acted* like a sergeant.

We boasted two section sergeants – Frank and Percy – and, as so often happens, the willing horse was regularly given the heavier load. They split the twenty-four hour day into two shifts. 6 a.m. until 6 p.m. and 6 p.m. until 6 a.m. and, within the twelve-hour period, they worked out their own eight hours of 'on duty' time. Offhand, I can't remember Percy ever completing a full week of 'nights'.

Percy had an undiagnosed but highly convenient stomach complaint. It was a very regular ailment. It became worse every alternate week – when his was the 6 p.m. until 6 a.m. stint – and it *always* necessitated him having a couple of nights off duty. This meant bringing in one of the floating sergeants of the division at short notice, or Frank covering for a double-session, or putting the senior copper in charge which in turn meant re-shifting men to cover that man's beat.

In short, everybody was horsed around generally. Everybody, that is, except Percy. Percy and his stomach enjoyed a good night's sleep.

Percy was not the most popular man in the section.

Frank, on the other hand, was a copper everybody enjoyed working with. In many ways he was the NCO equivalent to Tosh. He made the Law work, but without being nasty about it. He had an answer to everything . . . and sometimes the answer was so damn simple.

The Trolley Bus Incident will illustrate what I mean. A trolley bus service ran between Brighouse and Huddersfield and Saturday night was fireworks night. The drunks from both Huddersfield and Halifax seemed to make for Brighouse and the Astoria Ballroom and, come the last trolley, the fighting-beer ensured pockets of bedlam throughout the town. And, always, some drunken clown had to be slung off the trolley.

The trolley bus pulled up alongside me as I strolled the main street. The conductor told his weary tale of woe with, as background effects, the drunken lunatic bawling obscenities at the bare suggestion that he wasn't a fit and proper person to ride on a public transport vehicle. We hauled him kicking and struggling to the boarding platform, but there he grabbed the upright rail and, short of breaking his fingers, *nothing* was going to make him break his grip.

Then along came Frank.

'Trouble?' he asked, cheerfully.

'The usual.'

Then to the drunk, 'One time of asking, lad. Get off that trolley.'

The drunk suggested that Frank do what is both physically and biologically impossible.

'Grab a leg, Jack. Tuck it under your arm, then dig your heels in.'

I did as I was told. Frank took the other leg and, because the boozed-up clown clung like grim death to the boarding rail, he was held in a horizontal position.

Frank nodded to the conductor, and called, 'OK. Ring off.'

The trolley bus started forward, Frank and I took the strain and, at a guess, the drunk's body stretched about six inches before his fingers left the boarding rail and he landed on the road surface.

When he hauled himself unsteadily to his feet, he was a long way towards being sober. He gaped down at the blood gushing from his nose, then turned questioningly to Frank.

'What happened?'

'You fell.' Frank's voice was as deadpan as his expression. 'You've had a few jars too many. You fell off a trolley bus. We'd better give you a bed for the night in the nick.'

58

That was Frank and the way he worked. He never hurried, he rarely lost his temper and he was a joy to work with. He was the perfect balance to the puffings and panic of Percy.

In retrospect, if the Police Training College was my kindergarten and Elland was my secondary school, Brighouse was my university and Frank was one of the better tutors. That sardonic drollery which is the rock foundation to all good policing was part of his natural makeup. Unlike Vic, he'd reached as far as he wanted to go, therefore he was prepared to chance his arm. He was a vital part of my Brighouse of the 1940s and '50s.

For most people Brighouse equates with Rastrick and a particularly fine brass band. But there's more to Brighouse than that. It stands south of Bradford, east of Halifax and north of Huddersfield. It is (or was) Elland multiplied five or six times; a muck-and-brass town plumb in the centre of the woollen industry. It had just about everything, from moderately flash houses on its outskirts to rows of back-to-back slums tucked away in its dark corners.

It was the perfect spot in which to learn down-to-earth policing.

My own personal beat – as an outside beat man, or village bobby, whichever term you prefer – was Clifton. A beat that took in Clifton itself, plus Cooper Bridge and Kirklees Estate, and that linked up with Hartshead Beat in the adjoining division. It was different from Upper Edge Beat in that it was a bicycle beat, it was more 'countryfied' and poachers were fairly frequent visitors to Kirklees Estate.

But because much activity centred around the town itself, I was just about half-and-half. I worked Clifton when cover wasn't needed in Brighouse itself . . . and cover was often needed.

It suited me. I was young, I was full to the brim with vim and vigour and I had gumption enough to realise that bobbying, if done well and in good company, was a great way to earn a living.

And had I not worked Brighouse town beats I wouldn't have met 'Captain Hallsworth'.

Captain Hallsworth was not his real name; he is now no longer with us, but one must assume that while he was, somebody somewhere loved him, and the object of this wander down Memory Lane is to tell the truth, but without deliberate hurt. Therefore, Captain Hallsworth.

Whether he'd been a Naval captain or an Army captain we never discovered. Whether, indeed, he was entitled to carry the rank into civilian life we doubted, but cared little. What we *did* know was that he was the most bumptious, self-opinionated, arrogant, insufferable bag of wind within a moon's march. Had he not made such an infernal nuisance of himself, the sheer magnitude of his conceited pomposity would have been something of a joke. As it was . . .

My first encounter with the insufferable Captain Hallsworth was on a dark, snow-filled evening, not long before my first Christmas at Brighouse. I was reaching the end of an eight-hour stint of Office Reserve duty and had had a long and dreary day picking up the bits and pieces of minor complaints pushed across the public counter, answering unimportant telephone calls, then logging all this garbage knowing that my colleagues wouldn't spare my jottings more than the passing glance they deserved. In short, I was tired of humping crap and looking forward to home and Avis. So maybe I was in the mood to vent a little spleen, given half a chance.

Captain Hallsworth handed me that chance on a plate.

A car drew up at the entrance to the police station and a camel-hair-coated figure bounded out, flashed past the public counter and made for the stairs leading to the upper floor. The impression was that he'd just *bought* the nick, and everything and everyone therein, and couldn't wait to see whether he'd pulled a bargain or not. He'd left his car empty with the engine running.

'Just a minute.' I leaned over the public counter as I called to attract his attention.

'*What!*' He stopped in mid-flight, turned and glared with a mixture of amazement and outrage at this lower-ranker who's had the audacity to speak without permission.

'If you've a minute, please.'

'I'm in a hurry.'

'If you have a minute,' I insisted.

He bounded back to the public counter and snapped, 'Do you know who I am?'

'No, sir.'

'Hallsworth. Captain Hallsworth.'

'Well – *Captain* Hallsworth – you've left the engine of your car running.'

'Of course I have. It's a cold night.'

'It's illegal,' I murmured.

'Don't be such a damn fool.'

'It *is* against the law,' I assured him. 'It's also smack in front of a police station. Do you mind switching your engine off, please?'

'Certainly not.' He turned for the stairs again. 'I have an appointment with your detective sergeant.'

'In that case,' I called towards a disappearing back, 'you might like to reach an agreement with the detective sergeant . . . to pay *his* share of your fine.'

Agreed, it was not the way the Book of Words *said* it should be done. On the other hand, it rarely is. By this time I'd found the 'feel' of bobbying; that inexplicable switch to 'on duty' personality which, while stopping well short of arrogance, ensured that you took slop from *nobody*. While you were right, and knew you were right, you remained polite (more or less) for as long as possible, but beyond a certain point you bared your teeth and started to bite back. Nobody pushed you around . . . and the punchline was *always* yours.

Thus, having nipped outside to take details of the offending vehicle, I returned to the Charge Office and patiently awaited the reappearance of Captain Hallsworth and a careful examination of his driving licence and the certificate of insurance.

The telephone rang and, rather impatiently, I answered the call. It was from Force Headquarters at Wakefield, from the chief constable's office, no less.

What the devil was I playing at?

I didn't know. What the devil *was* I playing at?

Harassing an innocent member of the public.

Who? Me?

Throwing my weight about.

What?

Threatening everybody in sight.

They *must* be ballocking the wrong bloke.

A Captain Hallsworth had just telephoned from Brighouse Police Station. From the CID Office. He was in a towering rage. He had every intention of making a formal complaint.

Big deal.

I allowed the character from the upper atmosphere to clear his chest of dirty water, replaced the receiver and waited with something not far short of murder in my heart.

At shift-change, as I was collecting my bits and pieces before going off duty, Tosh arrived at the nick. He too, it seemed, had been telephonically castrated by some headquarters lunatic.

'Did you book him?' he growled.

'You *bet* I booked him.'

'Good.' Tosh sounded highly delighted. 'Now we're going to tame him. There's only one gaffer in this town . . . and his name *isn't* Captain bloody Hallsworth.'

It wasn't too difficult.

Hallsworth, you see, considered himself above and beyond the normal pin-pricks of legal inconvenience accepted by lesser mortals. The Road Traffic Law didn't apply to *him*. He parked his ancient, but expensive, car where the hell he liked and on four occasions in the past he'd ducked summonses by claiming that the car had been 'stolen' from some perfectly legitimate parking spot and, thereafter, been left abandoned at the place where it *shouldn't* have been.

On the face of it, it was a neat gag. It removed Hallsworth from the hook and left some conscientious copper with egg on his face. The 'ex-service' mentality most of us still retained made for reluctant admiration, but it was being pulled too often.

On four occasions some suffering flatfoot had been obliged to fill in a Crime Complaint, a Crime Report and take a long-winded statement, Fingerprint Section had had to be called out from Wakefield. Fictitious 'enquiries' had had to be made and dutifully recorded in a moderately thick file which we all knew to be no more than a figment of Hallsworth's cunning imagination.

In short, the police officers of Brighouse were being made to look like a collection of not too juicy lemons, Tosh was losing his temper at a rare rate of knots and something drastic was called for.

About a week after the engine-running episode Tosh telephoned the nick from his and Hallsworth's favourite drinking hole, the Constitutional Club.

'Hallsworth's here. His car's outside, without lights. Do something.' Then, after a very pointed pause, '*Drastic!*'

We arrived outside the Constitutional Club at a little after eleven o'clock. There was the car. No lights, and constituting a very obvious traffic hazard. One of us kept look-out, while the other went to work. All it needed was a skilfully operated matchstick and in no time at all every last puff of air had been removed from all four tyres.

We knocked on the door of the club and Hallsworth, accompanied by Tosh, eventually joined us.

'You don't think I'd leave the damn thing without lights, do you?' blustered the slightly tiddly captain.

'Somebody has,' droned a po-faced Tosh.

'It must have been stolen. *I* didn't leave it parked here.'

'Stolen?' We were happy to leave the patter to Tosh.

'Obviously. I didn't . . .'

'What's this? The *fifth* time?'

'If your men aren't capable of . . .'

'Somebody in this town doesn't like you, Hallsworth.'

'I don't give a damn about popularity.'

'Positively *dis*likes you.' Tosh followed the beam of a carefully aimed torch. 'Enough to let your tyres down.'

'*What!*' Hallsworth's neck stretched forward as he received the sudden shock.

Tosh took a quiet stroll around the car, then added, 'All of 'em.'

'What the devil are your men doing, letting somebody . . .'

'They found your car,' Tosh reminded him. 'They "recovered" it, before you even knew it had been nicked.'

'Oh! Ah!'

'You bloody nigh need crystal balls for that sort of bobbying.'

Hallsworth sniffed.

'Put the lights on,' said Tosh, airily.

'Eh?'

'It's not illegal to park your car here with flat tyres. It *is* illegal to park it here without lights, and now that's *your* responsibility.'

'Good God, man. You can't –'

'Two upright and conscientious coppers,' said Tosh solemnly. 'And any minute now, one of them's going to book you for *leaving* this motor car where it is without lights. They've no choice. *I'm their chief inspector, and I'm* watching 'em. Much more hesitation, and I'll book *them* for Neglect of Duty . . . you get the drift?'

Slowly – almost painfully – Hallsworth unlocked the front door of the car and switched on the lights.

'Good.' Tosh nodded heavy approval. 'Now everybody's happy.'

'I need a garage,' choked Hallsworth.

'A garage?'

'To get the tyres inflated, before I can drive it home.'

'Know any all-night garages, Wainwright?'

'Not this side of Huddersfield, sir.'

'Good God, surely you can –'

'It's not our pigeon, Hallsworth.' Then to me, 'Your beat tonight, Wainwright?'

'Yes, sir.'

'Keep an eye on it. Make sure nobody nips along and switches the lights off . . . anything like that.'

'Yes, sir.'

'I – I don't think the battery will take it.' Hallsworth's tone had that hint of a moan that goes with reluctant defeat.

'Hard lines.' Tosh allowed himself a quick and very knowing smile. 'Keep your fingers crossed, eh?'

'Can I . . .' Hallsworth couldn't bring himself to say it at the first attempt.

'What?'

'Can you give me a lift home in your car?'

'Good Lord, no.' Then after a perfectly timed pause, in

64

a very casual voice, 'That would defeat the whole object of the exercise . . . wouldn't it?'

For the rest of my stay at Brighouse, Captain Hallsworth paid due attention to the Road Traffic Law. In the words of that other Yorkshireman, Guy Fawkes, 'Desperate diseases require desperate remedies,' but, as Tosh reminded me, later that night:

'Don't make a habit of it, Wainwright.'

'No, sir.'

*   *   *

I stay with Hallsworth, if only because when Brighouse Town duty was required to be performed, there was *always* Hallsworth. *His* antics were the perpetual trigger to either hassle or black comedy, and sometimes coppers were over-enthusiastic in their efforts to bring the stupid man into line.

None of us could ever claim complete success, but few of us made such a hash of it as the detective inspector.

He was known as the 'Man with the Concave Chest' and for obvious reasons. He wore fancy waistcoats, calculated to inflict mortal injury at ten yards. He favoured cravats, rather than ties, and his weary drawl gave the impression of great agony whenever he had cause to exercise his larynx. In short, he was a joke . . . but he took himself very seriously.

He was stationed at Halifax DHQ but periodically he drove out to Brighouse to check on the hoi polloi. Thus, at a little after ten o'clock one morning, he was at Brighouse Police Station when a lady strolled in and assured us she'd been raped. By Captain Hallsworth.

The DI moved from his normal state of semi-stupor and hurled himself into action. He rushed the lady upstairs and took a statement from her. Not a detailed statement, but a carefully worded one (*his* words) which covered every legal point required in order to sustain a complaint of rape.

The rest of us sighed and waited.

Rape, of course, is a very serious crime. One short step from murder and, in many cases, more foul than murder. The lady claimed she had come straight from the scene of the rape. But she hadn't a hair out of place.

She was in no way dishevelled, showed no sign of distress and, if anything, had *sauntered* through the front door of the nick.

She returned from the CID Office, escorted by an ever-solicitous DI, and agreed to the usual requirement of an examination by a medic. She didn't mind *which* medic. She was, it seemed, quite prepared to submit to pokings and proddings from anybody above the status of vet.

One of us left the station to seek a local GP and came back with a man we all knew. A good doctor, a rugby enthusiast and a man given to calling a spade a spade. The GP trotted the complainant into the privacy of Tosh's office and, a few minutes later, returned to give his verdict.

'Anything?' The languid DI was almost excited in his unaccustomed eagerness.

The GP looked quizzical.

'She's been raped,' explained the DI.

'She tells me. I've taken a swab.'

'Any signs?'

'Signs?' The GP raised mildly surprised eyebrows.

'Scratching? Bruising?'

'No scratches. No bruises.'

'Signs of a struggle?'

'No signs of a struggle.'

'But she *has* been raped?'

'That's what she tells me.'

'And?'

'It's possible.' The GP was a very outspoken man. He was in adult, all-male and shock-proof company. He didn't mince words. As he ran the tap to wash his hands, he added, 'In non-medical terms, I've seen smaller horse-collars.'

Nevertheless, the DI forged ahead and, at the Magistrates' Court, sitting as a court of committal, Captain Hallsworth stood accused of rape. Tosh wasn't the prosecuting officer. He had more sense; he chose that day as his weekly rest day. Instead a sweating and embarrassed County Prosecuting Solicitor stood up and tried not to look *too* foolish.

The case got as far as the cross-examination of the first

witness. The lady who had opened her heart to the DI.

Oh, indeed, she *had* been raped.

She was (she agreed) a Lady of the Streets; a high-class whore with a neat little list of convictions for plying her profession in the borough of Harrogate. She had agreed to accept a lift back to Brighouse and, equally, she had agreed to stay the night at Hallsworth's home. It had, indeed, been a very *long* rape. An *exceptionally* prolonged rape. It had started at ten o'clock one evening and ended at nine o'clock the next morning. Not non-stop, of course. Twice, they'd donned dressing-gowns and descended to the kitchen to seek sustenance – not to say energy – in coffee and chicken sandwiches.

Oh yes, there was a bedside telephone – and, oh yes, Hallsworth had left her alone while he visited the bathroom a couple of times . . . but no, she hadn't even *thought* of telephoning for help.

The defending solicitor sat down. The lady in the case left the witness-box. The County Prosecuting Solicitor rose to his feet, moistened his lips and moved his shoulders in tired resignation.

'Your Worships, I think it advisable at this point, and in order not to waste any more time of the court, that the Prosecution withdraw the charge.'

*   *   *

All of which is not to deny that rape is a most terrifying and terrible crime. The Hallsworth fiasco was a one-off job; sheer pantomime built upon pseudo-solemnity. But the *real* thing is horrifying. Physical injury apart, it can tear the victim's mind to shreds and can never be forgotten. Those who try to excuse it are on a par with the animals who commit the act.

It is said that rape is the easiest accusation to make, and the most difficult crime to disprove. Not so. No copper with a modicum of experience could mistake a genuine rape victim. The degree of mental anguish, along with the stammering terror, can never be faked. Equally, the rapist is the type of man almost *eager* to admit to what he is pleased to look upon as his 'virility'.

It is argued that no woman can be raped against her will; that, so long as she struggles, the offence can never be committed. Rubbish. Mob-handed, *men* can be raped ... and are, with sickening regularity, in HM Prisons. On a one-to-one basis, by the nature of his crime, a rapist is a brute and stronger than the average woman. He doesn't give a damn whether she's conscious or unconscious when he commits the act, or care what other physical injury he inflicts.

This is one reason why coppers tend to work harder than, on the face of things, seems called for when out to catch and convict some pathetic little 'flasher'. The indecent exposure wallah is the butt of smutty jokes made by music hall comedians. He is the yokel of the criminal world. The village idiot of wrong-doers. But let me assure you that indecent exposure is, far too often, that first tentative step made by the pervert. He knows (or hopes) it won't be taken too seriously. If he gets away with it, he gradually becomes bolder and eventually tries indecent assault for size. First on children, then on women. Thereafter, and if he isn't stopped, comes rape. It is a natural progression, and countless records of previous convictions prove that fact to the hilt.

And, after rape ... murder.

So many women – so many kids – have been killed merely to keep them quiet. To silence the one person capable of pointing an accusing finger.

The copper knows this. He knows that, by tracing the pervert at the 'flasher' stage, he just *might* be preventing some as yet uncommitted murder.

* * *

Fortunately, for our sanity, policing wasn't all solemnity or crass stupidity. There was a liberal sprinkling of gentle chuckles; situations that hurt nobody but with which life was endlessly spiced.

One such situation was the 'Dog Rescue'; the first time an amazed reading public saw a photograph of PC718 in their local newspaper.

It was a nice morning. One of those not-yet-spring-but-not-cold-enough-for-winter mornings. The indications were that it was going to be a pleasant day, and I'd been called off Clifton Beat to cover one of the Brighouse Town Beats from 6 a.m. until 2 p.m. My companion was

Lloyd and, because he had a few extra months of service under his belt than any of the rest of us, he was PC i/c. Frank (or was it Percy?) was on Weekly Rest Day and Lloyd was carrying the section throughout the 6 a.m. to 6 p.m. period. He was a pleasant companion, despite the fact that he'd been born south of London. He'd fought his war in Burma and, if pressed, he would admit to having a small piece of shrapnel still buried somewhere in the base of his neck, which the blood-letters had decided was doing no harm and would cause him no inconvenience if left there.

Somebody – some passing pedestrian – mentioned that a dog was stranded on a ledge, halfway up the face of a quarry.

Probably in order to break the boredom, we 'attended the incident'. We didn't rush. The damn dog had obviously found its way to the ledge and could presumably find its way *off* the ledge.

It couldn't.

To this day it remains a mystery how that silly animal managed to reach the ledge without injuring itself. The face of the quarry was as near perpendicular as to make no difference, and the ledge was all of thirty feet from its base. It was almost as far from the top lip of the quarry. The dog had obviously been running around at the top, dropped off the edge and landed on the ledge. It was a mongrel and, to fall that distance without hurting itself, one of its many ancestors must have been a cat.

'I never did like dogs,' grumbled Lloyd.

'They vary.' I remembered my own dog, Snogger, and rushed to the rescue of the canine world. 'Like coppers. Some are barmy, some aren't.'

'What do we do?'

'You're the boss. *You* decide.'

Twice Lloyd took a flier at the face of the quarry. Both times the loose muck and shale brought him slithering down into my arms before he was shoulder-height.

'Think we can knock the stupid hound from its perch?'

As he mused the question, Lloyd stooped, picked up a stone, let fly . . . and missed. He hadn't time for a second shot before rubber-neckers, some of whom were no doubt animal-lovers, began to gather. Meanwhile the dog barked a little, wagged its tail a lot and seemed to quite enjoy being centre-stage while a duo of uniformed coppers made clowns of themselves.

Meanwhile, some well-meaning idiot called the Fire Service, who arrived in a cloud of dust and flashing lights, saw that the Police Service had the matter in hand and left. They wouldn't even *lend* us one of their ladders.

'Sorry, Constable. *We*'d be in trouble if we did.'

'They go up trees for cats,' complained Lloyd.

'It isn't a cat,' I explained, unnecessarily. 'Nor is it up a tree.'

But ladders had been mentioned and ladders seemed to be the answer. Lloyd threw his weight about a little and a couple of youths from the audience went away and came back with two shortish ladders and some scaffold ropes from a nearby builder's yard. Roped together, the ladders *just* reached the ledge.

The PC i/c went up the ladders first. The uniformed dogsbody followed close behind. Which was OK, apart from the terrifying strain on the roped-together ladders and the shale and general bits and pieces of quarry face kicked loose by Lloyd which showered down on my head and shoulders. But, eventually, Lloyd was able to reach gingerly upwards, grab the dog by the nape and hand it to me. And I, with helmet askew and quarry muck cloaking my shoulders, was able to clutch the troublesome little brute to my chest and, very shakily, descend to the safety of the quarry floor . . . which was when some over-enthusiastic camera-clicker pointed his lens and, as a result, Wainwright's heroic deed was immortalised next day in the local rag.

The sequel came almost a year later.

It was Court Day and Frank told me Tosh wanted to see me in his office, before we made our way into court. As always, I wondered what might have caught up with me, and his brusque, 'What the hell's happening *now*, Wainwright?' did little to ease my conscience.

'Happening?'

'After court this morning. This "presentation" thing.'

'What "presentation" thing, sir?'

'From the RSPCA. A framed testimonial. I'm told they're going to perform some sort of presentation ceremony.'

'Who?'

'The magistrates. Who else?'

'No, sir. Who *to*?'

'To *you*, for Christ's sake. Why wasn't I told about this before now?'

I think the look of stunned amazement on my face convinced him.

'You rescued some dog from a quarry face.'

'Oh, my God.'

'Which dog? Whose dog?'

'I don't know, sir. When I let go of it, it ran away.'

'It's the first *I've* heard of it.'

'Yes, sir. There were two of us. We –'

'Don't!' He glared me into silence. '*One* unsung hero is as much as I can take in a day.'

'Yes, sir.'

'Well?'

'I . . .' I swallowed, then muttered, 'It wasn't important, sir. It didn't even merit an official report.'

'Don't tell *them* that. What the hell you think – what the hell *I* think – some idiot thinks you're a hero. Don't go out of your way to disillusion them.'

'No, sir.'

'And bear it in mind, Wainwright,' he growled. 'It's not the *best* way to run a police section. Dropping things like this into the chief inspector's lap. I could have looked a right pillock.'

We had that beautifully framed testimonial from the RSPCA for ages. I don't know to this day who put me up for it – one of the onlookers, presumably – but it made wild use of words like 'courage' and phrases like 'at great personal risk'. It was nice, and Avis viewed it with obedient, wifely pride, but it was phoney and I never had the arrogance to hang it on the wall.

* * *

The 'CID' – the Criminal Investigation Department – brings to mind pictures of 'Fabian of the Yard', 'The Sweeney' and superb manhunters like 'Nipper' Read.

71

Well, not at Brighouse, but because we were a sub–divisional headquarters, we did have a CID Office. (Come to that, it isn't like that at New Scotland Yard, either; some few years after I became a professional author I asked for, and was given, a guided tour of the Yard and recognised it for what it was ... Brighouse, with a lot more rooms and a little more flash.)

The West Riding was a county constabulary and if, like me, you were responsible for a specific beat everything up to and including armed robbery was *your* pigeon. You exchanged the tunic for a civilian jacket and started asking questions. You were your own CID and, if you couldn't bring home the bacon, nobody else was going to handle the pig.

'The CID' meant weirdos with cameras and goofs with dusting powder who manufactured far more fingerprints than they ever found. The system followed (and I *still* remember it) was a Crime Complaint, made out in triplicate, then Statements, followed by a Crime Report and Continuation Sheets. The Report and the Continuation Sheets were of good quality, pale blue paper, with three columns: 'Date', 'Name' and 'Result'. It was a game, and a pretty stupid game at that. After the first two or three days, the 'enquiry' was opened up by the creation of 'Continuation Sheets' and every constable in the section had a nibble. All coppers were required to make entries on these Continuation Sheets; for each crime committed within the section boundary each copper had to make one enquiry per day for a week, thereafter one enquiry per week for a month, thereafter one enquiry per month for a year.

It was all highly mathematical, and utterly useless.

In effect, it meant that some brainless type had figured it out that, say, to approach a complete stranger and out of the blue ask, 'Do you know anything about a pint of milk stolen from Mrs Smith's doorstep four months ago?' would result in something more productive than a very nasty reply.

The Continuation Sheets were universally known as 'The Daily Liar'. And that's exactly what they *were*.

The hours we wasted. The 'Date' column had to be

carefully worked out. The 'Result' column listed a perpetual repeat of 'No useful information obtained.' And the 'Name' column was made up of both factual and fictitious names, names culled from the Electoral Register and names noted from gravestones.

At Brighouse that was Eric's main occupation; counting the dates, tallying the names and making sure that the Continuation Sheets all stacked themselves very neatly and gave an immediate impression of fiendish activity. Eric was a detective sergeant and somebody had the job of making this crazy paper-chase *seem* to work. Thereafter, the garbage was shipped to DHQ at Halifax where, presumably, it was all carefully re-checked prior to it being finally dumped in some dark and damp cellar at Force Headquarters, Wakefield, pending it slowly but surely rotting away into a soggy mess.

Eric was a nice guy. Quiet, almost to the point of shyness. He'd made detective sergeant the easy way – he'd married the daughter of a chief superintendent in one of the neighbouring borough forces – but he never pretended otherwise. He sat in the CID Office, up to the ears in paper, and did what he was paid to do. Make the system *look* as if it worked.

He had an abundance of patience. He *needed* patience. His immediate underling was called Harold; he was the detective constable.

I digress a little in order to remind you that I write of the late 1940s and early '50s. In Europe things were still in an unholy mess. The armies of occupation were busy trying to create order from chaos and, although the fighting had ceased, the pre-war man-hunters and thief-takers were mostly holding rank in the provost-marshal set-up, chasing a thousand and one 'Harry Limes', and had not yet returned to their respective forces.

Meanwhile, people like Eric, and people like 'the Man with the Concave Chest', pottered along and were happy to allow the more enthusiastic uniformed men to detect what crimes they could, while they, the CID, jollied things on, kept their fingers crossed and hoped for the best.

Not that we of the uniformed branch complained. This was bobbying. We, too, wished to catch as many thieves as possible. We therefore brushed up our local knowledge, worked out our own interview techniques and did our best to keep the crime-rate as low as possible.

But back to Harold . . . Harold was a detective constable. Nobody disliked him; he provided far too much unintentional laughter to be unpopular. Indeed, everybody went out of their way to ease what little burden he deigned to lug around, in order that he might have a little more elbow-room for his crazy carryings-on. I suppose he was looked upon as something of a mascot, and this despite his never-ending flow of monumentally bad language.

Basically, he was a very kind-hearted man. But he should never have been allowed within a ten-mile radius of a police station. He was a hundred things . . . but the one thing he *wasn't* was a policeman.

I came to hold my own theory about Harold, and why he was a detective constable. I believed that the plain clothes were there to hide him. To allow Tosh and the rest to pretend he wasn't their responsibility; to pass him in the street, and make-believe that he wasn't *their* fault. It was, when all was said and done, the only reasonable way of disowning him.

Harold's 'crime detection' was a thing of wonder. He knew six names – minor scoundrels who lived in Brighouse and who'd been convicted of crimes in the past – and he never moved from those six names. When a crime was reported he chose one of those six names . . . and that was it! From that moment nothing could dissuade him.

'Bill Sikes is the bugger you're after,' he might say. And a visit to Mr William Sikes would prove that, of all the men walking the face of the earth, he was the one who could *not* have committed the crime.

'Ballocks,' Harold would say.

'Eh?'

'He's having you on. *He* did it.'

And, let the crime be detected; let the culprit stand up in court and plead his guilt in the hope of a lighter sentence; at the back of the court you'd find Harold, with a worried look on his face.

'What the hell's he saying *that* for? He knows bloody well *he* didn't do it. It was *Sikes*.'

I recall once – a fine afternoon, but a miserable task – I was on Coroner's Officer duty at the public morgue. The pathologist had opened the body and the innards were laid out along the side of the slab for examination. As always, the scene was sepulchral with the normal sickly-sweet smell.

The door opened and a pensive Harold strolled into the mortuary. We watched as, hands deep in his pockets and head bent in frowning concentration, he walked slowly around the PM table, then left without saying a word.

The dumbfounded pathologist asked, 'Who on earth was *that*?'

'The – er – a detective constable.'

'A detective constable?'

'*Our* detective constable.'

'Oh, I see. But why – I mean, why . . .?'

'He'll have his reasons, sir.'

'Ah – er – quite. Quite. Shall we continue?'

Later that day I met up with Harold and sought to solve the mystery.

'This afternoon, in the morgue,' I said. 'What were you doing?'

'Eh?'

'The public mortuary. You came in halfway through a post-mortem.'

'Oh, *that*.'

'Why?' I asked, desperately.

'Enquiries. That bugger Sikes. Somebody *must* have seen him nick that bloody bike.'

Poor old Harold – dear old Harold – for all his shortcomings, he was harmless. He always *meant* well. He was always so *sure*. And he was always so wrong.

Whenever he wore his other hat and became Aliens Officer, the angels wept with a perfect mix of joy and despair. The war (always that war) had resulted in the Russian occupation of so many East European countries, and England was a refuge for thousands. From Poland, from Czechoslovakia, from Hungary, from Rumania, from Yugoslavia, from Bulgaria, from Albania. They were terrified of Stalin, and they sought refuge in the United Kingdom even though they couldn't speak our language. A goodly proportion of them sought work in the woollen trade, and not a few lived in the Brighouse police area. A monthly check was necessary to keep tabs on their whereabouts and, because he was the Aliens Officer, Harold did the checking.

I accompanied him a few times, and I grew to know the patter by heart. It never varied.

Harold (as you will have gathered) was a man of fixed and immovable beliefs and one of them was that *everybody* – including the simplest peasant from Outer Mongolia – understood the English language. Merely let it be shouted loudly enough and slowly enough.

Thus, 'What's your name, lad?'

'Please?' That was sometimes the only word they knew, and it was always accompanied by a smile.

'Your name, lad. What's your name?'

'Please?' The smile would become a little fixed.

'Your *name*?'

'Please?' The smile would be replaced by a worried expression.

I'd say, 'I don't think he understands, Harold.'

'Eh? Oh, aye.' Then, after a deep breath, 'What ... is ... your ... name?'

The worried expression would turn to one of near-panic.

'Oh, my Christ! WHAT ... IS ... YOUR ... BLOODY ... NAME?'

At that point, the unfortunate alien gave the impression of wishing he'd stayed with Stalin.

'Harold,' I'd plead. 'He doesn't understand.'

'Oh, sod him.' Harold would blow out his cheeks. His disgust would be absolute. 'Why? I ask you ... *why*? Why do *we* always get lumbered with the thick bastards?'

On paper it means nothing. In cold print it gives the impression of a lout – of an oaf – but Harold was never that. He was the verbal equivalent of Buster Keaton; the deadpan innocence of the Keaton character caused chaos and destruction and, with it, hilarity; Harold's mannerisms, coupled with his language, left a trail of popping eyes and gaping mouths; but get over the shock and the humour was there in abundance. To him they were merely *words*, and not even swear-words. It was *his* form of expression – *his* way of going to war against a world hell-bent on screwing him into the ground – and, if it caused a few chuckles, he didn't mind. At heart, he was a kindly man. His priorities were a little peculiar. No more than that.

Take the case of . . .

Actually, it was a case of petty larceny, and I figured I had it sewn up and ready for delivery. All I needed was a few minutes with the suspect, and the suspect lived at Dewsbury. I didn't own a car in those days, so it meant a bus and then a fairly long walk.

Harold offered to drive me there, and sit in on the interview.

I jumped at the offer. Why not? A few miles ride in a car, a DC to pick up any points I might miss and not having to keep an eye on the time in case I missed the return bus.

What I hadn't taken into account was Cooper Bridge.

Cooper Bridge was part of Clifton Beat; it is on the Leeds side of Huddersfield, and much of it is a traffic roundabout. The Three Nuns hotel and restaurant isn't far from the roundabout but, apart from this rather high-class victualling spot, few people live at Cooper Bridge. It is, you see, the site of a fairly substantial sewage disposal plant, complete with filter-beds.

In short, and at certain times in particular, it pongs.

We left Brighouse on the Wakefield Road, reached Cooper Bridge, then, without warning, Harold spun the wheel and turned into the gates of the sewage plant.

'I've always *wanted* to know how this bloody place works.'

Two hours later, he knew. We both knew. The chap in charge was remarkably proud of his personal, and very smelly, baby. Every pipe, every valve, every cleaning chamber, every filter-bed. We saw it coming in, we saw it being processed and, finally, we saw it going out.

'Purer than drinking water,' insisted the chap in

charge.

'Oh, aye?' Harold was obviously impressed.

'Taste it.' The chap in charge filled a tumbler and handed it to Harold. 'Taste it and see.'

Harold took a good swig. He smiled, then nodded. Then he held the tumbler out to me.

'No thanks.'

'No?'

'I'm not thirsty.'

He finished off the liquid in one gulp. It must have been pure – there were no after-effects – but *I'd* remembered what it had started as.

I took the bus to Dewsbury that evening. It was easy. Five minutes, and the suspect shrugged his resignation and 'coughed'. I didn't mind. The afternoon hadn't been wasted. My old mate Harold had given me another fistful of chuckles to store away in my memory bank.

* * *

Every copper recognises Saturday night as *the* night of the week. If it's going to happen – no matter what it is – the chances are it will happen on a Saturday night. The 'ale-cans' fill their guts with beer. The missing-links air their muscles. The mutton-hawkers waggle their tight-skirted bottoms and egg otherwise normal idiots into an excess of lunacy.

Everything happens on a Saturday night.

Saturday night usually saw me adding what weight I could to the town beats and, to get from Clifton to Brighouse Police Station, I walked down the long, straight Clifton Common. I walked rather than cycled because, come 6 a.m., I had that hill to climb before I reached bed; the bicycle would merely have been something extra to push and the Sunday bus service didn't start until mid-morning.

Harry lived halfway down Clifton Common and if he, too, was on night duty, we usually linked up and strolled to the nick together.

We did so on this particular Saturday night and, as we reached the bottom of the hill, we heard a ding-dong taking place inside the Roundhouse pub. The fun and games were starting early and, as we wheeled into the boozer, we saw the reason. One of the local troublemakers had had a few pints too many, and the landlord was having difficulty bouncing him out on his ear.

Harry and I took over and frog-marched our catch into the Charge Office. There we proudly presented the first arrest of the night to Frank.

Jim was on duty as Office Reserve and, before I continue with this episode, it might be as well to introduce you to Jim.

Some men bust a gut to be popular, but never quite make it. Jim was one of them. He wasn't *un*popular . . . he was merely too *anxious* to be liked.

Let Jim spot you for the first time on any day and he'd hurry up and, in a near-conspiratorial tone, start, 'Jack, I just want to tell you . . .' The same with everybody. Up to and including Tosh. He was the congenital spreader of tit-bits of unimportant information. Not a tell-tale. Not a snitch. Merely that he wanted you to know he was there, and that he was your friend. During the war he'd served in some Scots regiment and, although he was born and brought up a Yorkshireman, when the mood took him – presumably when he remembered his tartan glory – he wound his tongue around a brogue Robert the Bruce himself wouldn't have been able to decipher. This, then, was Jim and Jim was busy on the switchboard when Harry and I delivered the drunk to Frank in the Charge Office.

The drunk was awkward. *Bloody* awkward. He suddenly allowed his leg muscles to turn to jelly, flopped on to the floor of the office and almost dragged Harry and me down with him.

Frank frowned his displeasure, and snapped, 'Up on your feet, lad.'

'Go tie a knot in your knackers.' A remark which was neither witty nor polite.

Frank's frown darkened, and he growled, 'All right. While you're down there, take your boots off.'

'Get screwed.'

'Right, come on, Jack – Harry – let's have him up on his feet. I'll take his bloody boots off.'

So Harry and I hauled the drunk to his feet and held

79

him with his back to a wall of the Charge Office, while Frank approached to remove the footwear. Which was when the drunk lashed out with his boot and landed a full-blooded kick under Frank's kneecap. It was one of Frank's more painful experiences, and I winced in sympathy as he gasped and grabbed his knee.

With some justification, Frank lost control of himself. He brought his clenched fist up from ankle-level and had it landed it would have decapitated the drunk.

This is of course against all the rules. And, despite gory tales to the contrary, it rarely happens. In twenty years of street-level bobbying I only saw a punch swung at a prisoner twice, and this was one of the occasions.

And Frank's punch landed on the wrong target.

Only God in His infinite wisdom knows why, or even how, Jim scuttled from the switchboard and arrived between Frank and the drunk at that precise moment. What is beyond doubt is that Frank's fist bounced from Jim's shoulder, lost much of its steam and landed right on the button. Jim was knocked as cold as a Boxing Day turkey.

Harry and I guided a rather surprised drunk to the nearest cell, and when we returned to the Charge Office Frank had positioned Jim in a sitting position, with his back to the wall, and was gently slapping him back to consciousness.

'What – what . . .' Jim blinked his way back to the land of the living. 'What happened?'

'You don't know?' Frank's question was in the nature of an exploratory probe.

'No. I just – y'know . . . I was answering the telephone.'

'You passed out,' said Frank, confidently.

'Eh?'

'Out cold. Haven't you been feeling too good?'

'I . . .' Jim touched his jaw. 'Jesus Christ!'

'You caught the side of your face against a chair.'

'Oh!'

'You'd better take the night off.' Frank helped a still shaky Jim to his feet. 'Get some sleep. You'll feel better.'

'I've never . . .' Jim frowned worry which wasn't far short of panic. 'I've never fainted in my *life* before.'

'It happens,' soothed Frank. 'It comes to us all, in time.'

*   *   *

And that was Brighouse. Not Clifton – we'll come to Clifton, later – but *my* Brighouse. The Brighouse of the Astoria Ballroom and the weekly Saturday-night punch-up. The Brighouse of much laughter mixed with practical experience in the craft of law-enforcement. The gradual acceptance of policing, not as a job but as a way of life. When I arrived at Brighouse I still had some of the bloom – some of the innocence – of a young copper with little experience. I left Brighouse with an abundance of that mystical 'street knowledge' without which no policeman is complete.

Escort and Accused

There was a story, told by Harold. He told it far too many times, and always with the same amount of detail, for it to be other than true. It held a warning, and I heeded that warning.

The story went like this . . .

Harold stumbled his way through the war wearing police uniform, and on one occasion he was required to travel to a force south of London, pick up a man arrested by them and bring him north to face one of the West Riding courts. In those days – as was still the case when I was a minion in that force – the West Riding Constabulary was very 'cost conscious'. I know of no other force that sends less than two men to collect a prisoner. The West Riding always sent one. *Always*. To my certain knowledge, one unhappy constable had the unenviable job of traipsing off, by rail and sea, to Northern Ireland, linking himself up to a mildly belligerent prisoner, then returning to Brighouse via the route he'd taken out. It was a three-day job, and Joe Heap never quite forgave the force for lumbering him with the responsibility of remaining handcuffed to a fairly dangerous felon for more than half that time.

Harold had to collect a prisoner, make his way through wartime London and then catch a train at King's Cross for the north.

Knowing Harold, I can almost hear his words.

'Bugger the bloody handcuffs. They're a sodding nuisance.' Therefore, no handcuffs, and because Harold was a kindly man at heart, and because they were both hungry, he took the prisoner into a restaurant for a meal. They finished the meal, Harold paid the bill, then followed his prisoner from the restaurant. From good lighting, into the blackness of blacked-out streets.

Find the prisoner!

It must have been rather like suddenly going blind. The poor old boy couldn't see a thing. He toured the area in a mounting rage, but no prisoner. At last he made his way to King's Cross and stood on the platform waiting for a delayed train to arrive and turn round.

'I tell you, lad,' Harold would say. '*Lonely*. You don't know what the bloody word means. 'There was I, standing on this fornicating platform, on my tod when there should have been *two* of us.'

That was the highlight of Harold's story. The point where, feet astraddle, hands deep in the pockets of his trousers and head lowered as he scowled his recollection at a point on the chocolate-coloured lino about two feet away from his shoes, he would pause, allow the fire of the Charge Office to warm his backside in silence while the rest of us tried to understand the panic and hopelessness of the situation. And it must have *been* a terrifying situation. Two hundred miles and more from home base. Alone in one of the world's largest cities, which had been bomb-blasted to hell, and without a prisoner who, by the basic rules of the game, should have been handcuffed to his wrist.

I'm prepared to believe that even Harold felt worried.

But there was a happy ending to the story. As the train drew on to the platform Harold felt a tug at his sleeve. The lost prisoner smiled up at him. The prisoner, too, had been blinded by the switch from the lighted restaurant to the blacked-out street. *He had lost Harold.* They'd been searching for each other in the darkness and, in final desperation, the prisoner had made his own way to King's Cross, in the hope that he might find his missing escort.

'I tell you,' Harold would growl. 'That bloody prisoner could have had anything. Anything! I gave him every fag I had in my possession on the way back. I bloody-near wept when they sent him down for six months.'

It was a good story, and always well told. It had a moral. Never fall soft and unlock the handcuffs. Harold had been lucky – monumentally lucky – but his had been a thousand-to-one shot, and the other nine hundred and ninety-nine prisoners would have jumped at the chance.

* * *

And yet . . .

He was a nice enough chap. In his early forties. Married to a good woman and with a son he just about worshipped. He wasn't a scrounger; indeed, the building firm for which he worked figured him as one of their best employees.

Look at the guy. Look at his 'public' facade. Look at his home and his outward way of life. He seemed to be a decent, ordinary, upright citizen.

The hell he was!

If it wasn't nailed down, he claimed it. Anything. Unless it was either too hot or too heavy, it was tucked under his jacket and deposited in the shed at the bottom of his garden. He was a typical 'habitual criminal'. He hated prison – it broke his heart and after every spell he swore he would go straight – but he couldn't help himself. He was basically a sick man; somewhere between his ears a tiny cog had slipped and he couldn't *not* thieve. At a guess, he'd spent about a quarter of his adult life behind bars, and my job was to escort him the two-hundred yards or so from the police cell to the court of committal; along fairly busy streets and around a couple of corners. As I took the handcuffs from my hip pocket, he pleaded.

'Not *them*, Mr Wainwright.'

'You have to be joking.'

'Please. I'll walk alongside you. We'll make believe we're talking to each other. Like friends.'

'And if you run for it?'

'I won't. I swear I won't.'

'You aren't likely to say you *will*.'

'We pass the school playground.' He had tears in his voice. 'My kid will be there. He'll see me. His pals will see me.'

'So?'

'Look, my missus can spin him a tale. She always *has* done. But if he *sees* me – if his pals see me . . .'

With some hesitation I returned the handcuffs to their

pocket. I gave him a stern warning.

'You walk ahead of me. About two yards in front and to the right. Keep both hands deep in your pockets. *Keep* them there. You can't run too far with your hands in your pockets. If you take 'em out, I'll have you. I'll *drag* you past that school playground by the scruff of your neck.'

He behaved beautifully. Even when he paused at the school railings to chat for a moment with his son, the hands stayed in the pockets of his trousers. While he chatted, I made believe my bootlace needed retying.

In the privacy of the courtroom he nodded and said, 'I owe you, Mr Wainwright.' It was the usual copper–crook remark. To me it was empty. It meant nothing . . . but it did to him.

Back in circulation, he became the best informant I ever had. I didn't lean. I didn't threaten. I certainly didn't pay him. But he knew things, and he told things. Sometimes I knew about jobs before they were even pulled. But whatever *he* knew, *I* knew. Nor was he a general snout. With every other copper he was as dumb as a brick wall. But with *me* . . .

*   *   *

Looking back, I don't think I *minded* barging off into the mid-distance to collect some barmpot for whom an arrest warrant was out. In the main, they were bent and deserved their come-uppance and however far the journey there was never the suggestion of an overnight stay. On to an early train, pick him up and catch the next train back home. Sometimes it was a twenty-four-hour stint, and boring with it, but each copper had his own way of doing things. My way was to always take a raglan mac, whatever the weather; over the arm it hid the handcuffs and, if the weather was bad, each man with a hand in his mac pocket did the same disappearing trick. And the key to the cuffs was *always* left at my home station; even had I *wanted* to – which was very unlikely – I couldn't have unlocked them before delivering His Nibs at his final destination. It made for a certain amount of discomfort and, at times, no small inconvenience, but it was very absolute. Short of sawing me off at the wrist, His Nibs would be lumbered with me until we reached Base Camp, and the key.

One of the advantages of taking trains to all points of the compass in order to collect some wrongdoer was the chance to see how other forces worked. Their methods, their composition, the ways in which they were better than – or fell short of – the West Riding.

For example, a tiny Midland constabulary. In those days boroughs and counties had their own forces; it was well before the curse of 'amalgamation' brought unwieldy and impossible law-enforcement conglomerates; it was a time when many forces only just reached three figures in their authorised establishment.

This was one such force.

It was a beautiful summer's day, and I arrived at the market town wherein was situated the county constabulary headquarters to find that neat little establishment empty, except for a solitary, and very creaky, sergeant. All the other coppers were out, either playing cricket or watching the match. Their priorities were perfect. Bobbying was being left in abeyance, pending the winning or losing of some local shield.

I had an hour or so to wait for my return train, and the sergeant told me of the force establishment. It carried one chief constable, one chief superintendent/acting assistant chief constable and two superintendents. The chief constable, the chief superintendent/acting assistant chief constable and one of the two superintendents were all brothers. The other superintendent was their cousin.

It may have been the most nepotistic constabulary in the United Kingdom, but what matter? It had a feeling of homeliness; a gentle rusticity, far removed from prisons and Charge Sheets and Bail Forms. I conveniently 'missed' my next train back in order to wallow a little longer in the warmth of a genuine 'family' force, with men in charge who had the sense to put cricket before criminals.

Glasgow, on the other hand, was quite a different case. In those days it was a city with a legend attached, and the name of that legend was Sillitoe. Sir Percy Sillitoe, KBE, DL. At Sheffield he'd earned the reputation of being the definitive fighting chief constable by taming the South

Yorkshire race-course gangs. When the Glasgow gang riots were at their height the city fathers were given a straight choice. Either offer the post of chief constable to Sillitoe and give him a free hand, or accept martial law.

They chose Sillitoe and he in turn brought hand-picked men north of the border – his 'Cossacks' – and declared open season on the razor gangs of Protestant and Catholic fraternities alike. These coppers were forbidden to use truncheons but that didn't matter. They didn't *need* truncheons. One of them – 'Big Tom of the Toll' – dumped four gangsters into hospital beds with his right fist while holding a toddler who'd strayed into the battle with his left arm.

That was Sillitoe and the way he worked; the only head of MI5 who publicly acknowledged his taking over of that post when he left the Police Service.

Sillitoe did things *his* way . . . always.

That was the legend, that was the place, and I had to go there to pick up a prisoner one evening in late February. I arrived at about 10 p.m. and the immediate impression was of Hades, thickly coated with ankle-snapping ice. It was a dark bully of a city, and it greeted wandering Sassenachs with a scowl of disapproval.

It was too late to get a decent meal, but the men at city police headquarters knew of a café, beyond the Gorbals, which (they assured me) could serve egg, sausage and chips at any hour of the twenty-four. They offered to take me in a squad car, then collect me when I'd had time to eat.

We never reached the café. A nine–nine–nine call interrupted our journey.

The driver warned, 'Stay in the car,' as he weaved a suicidal route through unlit streets and between canyons of black tenements. I didn't need the advice. I, too, had read *No Mean City*.

We skidded to a heart-stopping halt and, almost before the wheels had stopped sliding, the driver and his colleague were out and in the blaze of the headlights.

'*Freeze!*'

And they did. Seven or eight young bucks became so many statues, and remained so while the two Glasgow coppers moved among them, collecting a fine assortment of weapons. There was a hatchet, and a bayonet, honed to a needle point and a fine cutting edge, and quite a large haul of flick-knives and clubs. The Glasgow officers dumped the weaponry in the boot, then returned to the car.

As we drove away from the scene, I was puzzled enough to ask, 'No arrests?'

'Not serious enough,' murmured the driver. 'We wouldn't have cell-room.'

His companion added, 'Anyway, where the hell do we find a complainant?'

I commiserated, and congratulated them on being in control enough to merely call that single 'Freeze!' and command immediate respect and obedience.

'Sillitoe.' The driver spoke the name in a tone holding justifiable pride, but also strange bitterness. 'They still scare their kids into behaving themselves by threatening them with "Sillitoe's Cossacks".' Then, to his pal, 'How many do you reckon tonight?'

'Six.'

'At least six,' agreed the driver. Then, noting my puzzlement, added, 'Windows. Shop windows. Plate glass. They go for plate glass . . . the bigger the better. Sling a brick, then away before anybody can dial. Retaliation for what we've just done. We can thank Sillitoe for *that*, too.' He sighed. 'The shop-keepers have a rough time. The insurance people demand a hell of a premium before they'll cover shop windows. Especially plate glass.'

'Sillitoe?' I murmured.

'Eventually somebody had to pick up the tab.'

By unspoken, but mutual, agreement I skipped the egg, sausage and chips. I had a train to catch, and a prisoner to escort south of the border. I was also eager to leave that city of inherited hatred and perverted pride.

I am told that Glasgow is now a different place. That the infamous slums have been removed, and that neat, new housing estates occupy much of the land once covered by tenements. I wouldn't know. Nor have I a yen to re-visit and see for myself.

*　　　*　　　*

At a guess there are fringe benefits to most jobs. Not what the on-the-take coppers used to call 'nawpings', but rather surprising and even fascinating bibs and bobs of information. Glimpses of worlds you will never know. And during the boredom of a long train journey, being steel-linked to a talkative type who represents 'the opposition' can, at times, be very edifying.

On one such trip, I'd travelled to the south coast, stood at a police cell door while the chap I'd come to collect had soothed a tearful wife there to bid him a prolonged farewell and now, thanks to the courtesy of the Railway Police, we were alone in a compartment with a Reserved sticker on its window and, as far as handcuffs would allow, we were relaxing.

He bore me no ill-will, nor I him. We were players in a game, albeit a serious one, and, this time, the throw of the dice had gone against him. He knew the rules of the game – he'd played it all his life – and these rules insisted that sometimes he won and sometimes he lost.

Part of my mind was occupied with a problem I was trying to resolve but, nevertheless, as he chatted I was able to listen, and realise that even criminality had its subtle offshoots.

By that time I'd taken many prisoners to HM Prison at Leeds. I'd stood alongside them at the reception desk, and heard a prison officer drone the same liturgy.

'Name? Address? Age? Religion?'

'Always say "Salvationist",' explained my companion. 'The old Sally Gash takes an interest, see? When you come out, they're waiting. There's always a free meal and a hand-out. Usually about a week's wage. All the other sods do is pray for you.'

I shared my cigarettes with him, and that brought up the matter of tobacco.

'Snout, see? Snout . . . tobacco. Inside, it's a sort of legal tender. It's pretty scarce. Not *too* scarce, but scarce enough. What *is* scarce are matches. The screws don't like the cons to have matches. Some con gets moody, he could set the bloody place alight if he has enough matches. But snout's no good if you can't light the stuff. That's why you soon learn how to make every match into four. With a razor blade, see? It's a knack. You soon learn it.'

It can be done. I tried it. It takes care and patience, but a man in prison has all the time in the world.

We moved to booze, and concoctions capable of lifting the top off your skull. Jam, water and boot polish. In the right proportions, of course. 'Let it simmer a bit, see? Then leave it to cool. Skim the wax off the top . . . and that's it. Real panther spit.'

That one I have never tried. Nor the one which he assured me was equally potent but rather less tasty. Run a tube from a gas-jet and allow the gas to gently rise through a bottle of milk for a specific period of time. Town gas, of course. In those days it was only town gas. Whether or not North Sea Gas does the trick I don't know. Nor do I intend to find out.

Less honest pastimes were touched upon.

'Ever made one banknote into two?'

I admitted it was something I'd never tried.

'Dead easy, once you get the hang. That metal strip, see? It can't be *threaded*. There have to be *two* sheets, stuck together. The old razor blade again. Start at one corner. Split 'em. Then roll the top sheet away on a pencil. Practice makes perfect. I know blokes who can do it in a jiffy. Then pass it at a busy shop, face up. It's in the till and away before it's noticed. Who turns a banknote over to check the other side isn't blank?'

I must admit that since then *I* have whenever a note feels particularly thin.

He was a mine of illegal information, and I listened and nodded, while I pondered upon one small point which worried me. Before we reached Waterloo I raised the matter.

'Your wife you've just left,' I murmured.

'Yes?'

I mentioned a village not far from Bradford, then said, 'I was there last night. I was at your home address. Your wife was very worried.'

'Oh, aye. She would be.'

'Not the *same* wife,' I amplified.

'No,' he grinned. 'I have two. It makes a change.'

'*Wives*?' I insisted.

'Oh aye. All legal. I don't mess about with fancy women.'

'A little matter of bigamy,' I reminded him, sadly.'

'Oh, aye. I reckon.'

He was in no way repentant. Marital law was like every other law . . . there to be broken. Neither wife knew of the existence of the other, but both knew he was a crook and his prison sentences were excuse enough for his absences.

At King's Cross the Railway Police put a room at my disposal and, as we waited for the train to take us north, we sipped tea and he cheerfully dictated a detailed statement, which he signed.

Later, when he stood in the dock and pleaded guilty to the charge of bigamy, he seemed almost surprised at it *being* an offence. The two ladies in the case were there. They'd just met for the first time and they too, were both astonished and displeased . . . with me.

They obviously liked each other. Equally obviously, they were very broad-minded and thought the world of the man who'd tried to make them both honest women. Given the chance, they'd have scratched my eyes out.

But if I rather liked my bigamous prisoner, I could have cheerfully strangled the confidence trickster I also lugged up from the south coast to get his just deserts.

In fairness he'd pulled as nice a gag as I ever came across. All it had needed was flash notepaper and visiting cards. He'd used the name of a genuine American motion picture company – one of those small companies that shoot specialised but very high-class films – and his spiel was that the company was making a series of shorts about the lesser-known English mansions and that he was their UK representative.

He chose the suckers with care. The opening shot of the film was always going to be of the drive to the main door, complete with motor car delivering some would-be important personage. The fly in the ointment was the car normally used by the owner of the mansion. A clapped-out banger, a broken down shooting-brake . . . *that* wouldn't do at all. People of distinction – even of local and limited distinction – required aristocratic motor cars if the films were to have any degree of credibility.

But that, too, could be arranged.

An appointment would be made, and the con man and the sucker would visit the local distributor of some make of expensive automobile. The loan of one of his latest models, perhaps? The shooting script could be changed a little . . . the car given slightly more prominence than had at first been envisaged. If necessary, the actual *make* of the car could be mentioned. Think of the free publicity. Merely loan the car to this most respected landowner for two or three days . . .

The trick was pulled six times and six times the loaned car was shuttled off to the Continent to a waiting buyer.

All *we* found was the rented room at the rear of a shop, a typewriter and a box of very fancy notepaper. None of the cars were recovered, and for months suckers, car manufacturers and car distributors swelled the bank balances of solicitors arguing about who should foot the bill.

An arrest warrant was issued, Smartypants was picked up on the south coast and I had the job of collecting him.

I should have known, of course. The bespoke suit, the expensive shoes and the camel-hair overcoat should have warned me; and if not his outward appearance, the golden-tipped tone of his conversation.

But he pulled another one!

Late that evening we changed trains at Doncaster. We had all of an hour to wait, and I suggested a bite to eat.

'Certainly, old man.'

And that was it. He made no attempt to hide the handcuffs. He led the way – indeed, he almost *dragged* me – towards the station restaurant, past gawping station officials and waiting passengers who cowered away as we passed. At the counter, *he* ordered and compounded the offence by asking *me* what I wanted to eat and drink.

Somewhere, therefore, there will be people who think that one miserable evening on Doncaster railway station, they saw a dangerous and vociferous criminal bawling his outrage at a police officer to whom he was handcuffed. It was, no doubt, one of the highlights of their lives. What they will never believe is that the cop was the one in the raglan mac.

Clifton

You could stand at the rear door of the police cottage at Clifton and, across the fields, you had a clear view of the spire of Hartshead church. The first twenty yards were part of the garden surrounding the cottage. Thereafter, it was meadowland all the way.

So many things were special about Clifton Beat, and that was one of them. That clean, uninterrupted view from the rear of the cottage.

Avis was born at Flockton, a tiny, countryfied village between Wakefield and Huddersfield. All her unmarried life she'd lived in semi-rural communities, within touching distance of trees and stiles, of grass and wild flowers.

Me? I'd been born in Leeds. In Hunslet. In a web of grime-covered terraced houses, with cobbles between the pavements. To see a tree it was necessary to take a tram-ride. The only horses I ever encountered on a daily basis belonged to an uncle who ran a haulage firm: a duo of socking great carthorses whose stable was in the back yard of the house and whose manure was heaped high against the rear wall.

That much, at least, the war and marriage had removed from my life. Leeds – Hunslet – was a thing of the past, and Clifton was one more step in the direction I yearned to take. The country. You have to be born and brought up sharing an outside bog with three other houses – to live all day, and almost every day, within the gloom of industrial smog – to know the magic of those two words. And Clifton was my first taste.

Compared with places we've lived in since, it was almost 'built-up' but Clifton *was*, and still is, somewhere very special.

Mind you, you won't find that view from Clifton these days. The Pennine Motorway has taken care of that. Much building has taken place and, like Brighouse itself, the description I give of it no longer holds good. In those days it had a church and a chapel, a village pub and, on its perimeter, a road house, a village school and a village post office; other than just about enough houses to make one Hunslet street, that was all. The rest was farmland, plus Kirklees Estate. It was sandwiched between Brighouse and Hartshead, and Hartshead wasn't even in the same *division*. To the south, at Cooper Bridge, it bumped against Huddersfield Borough boundary, and in the opposite direction it just seemed to peter out into fields and footpaths and woods.

That's how I remember it. That's how it will always be for me.

The police cottage was in fact two cottages knocked into one, and there was a garden all the way around. A large garden, complete with apple trees, a crab-apple tree, a massive cherry tree and enough good soil to merit the name 'smallholding'. Next to the garden there was a field – a whole *field*, for God's sake – and, because the only way into the field was through the police garden, I was expected to rent the field for £1 per year. That was no hardship. Indeed, it was a bonus.

The copper I took over from was a mug – he must have been.

The cottage was rented by the West Riding Constabulary from Sir George Armytage, who was chairman of the Standing Joint Committee. This meant he was, in many ways, the boss of the chief constable and, as such, he expected the Clifton bobby to chase poachers from Kirklees Estate. So what? Poaching was illegal, and coppers are paid to put the kybosh on illegal activities. My predecessor had held certain Bolshevik notions. Sir George paid a gamekeeper to handle poachers. My predecessor hadn't been paid to be a gash gamekeeper.

There'd been a great argument, the copper had been moved and, for months, the cottage stood empty. Superintendent Lambert offered it to me, and I almost snatched his hand off.

*   *   *

'Met him yet?'

'Who?'

'The old man. Sir George.'

'Sir George Armytage?'

'That's who we're talking about. Met him yet?'

'No, sir.'

I was in Tosh's office. Avis and I had arrived at Clifton police cottage the day before, and yesterday and today were the two buckshee days off granted for the purpose of moving house whenever a copper had a transfer. Nevertheless, I'd been told to report to the office, and here I was.

Tosh was playing his own personal game of official footsie; saying one thing but meaning another. I, too, was playing a game. Mine was called 'dumb-bell'. The two games dovetailed, and by this time we both knew each other well enough to make the joint damn near airtight.

'You have some fences to mend, Wainwright.'

'Fences?' I tried to look and sound innocent.

'The man who used to cover Clifton Beat seemed to enjoy making trouble.'

'Oh!'

'The old man was forever complaining.'

'Sir George Armytage?'

'Christ, he should have had some of the awkward buggers *we* had to keep on an even keel when *I* worked a beat.'

'Yes, sir.'

Tosh took out a packet of Players. He held the opened packet and, when we were both smoking cigarettes, he continued.

'Basically, the whole trouble revolved around a key,' he confided, quietly.

'A key?'

'Have you seen the estate yet? Kirklees Estate, where the old man lives?'

'I – er – not yet, sir. I haven't been on patrol yet.'

'It's big.' Tosh sniffed. 'It covers half the bloody beat. The hall. The gardens. The Home Farm. The wood.

96

Robin Hood's grave. It's a hell of an area, and it's surrounded by an eight-foot-high wall.'

I waited and smoked in silence.

'Other than the main gate,' continued Tosh, 'the only way into the estate is through doors. Doors built into this wall. Six or seven of 'em. They're all kept locked, of course.'

'Of course.'

'The old man and his son have keys. The head gamekeeper has a key. And there's a key kept at the estate office.'

'Four keys,' I murmured.

'Five,' grunted Tosh. 'The old man likes the Clifton copper to carry a key round with him. It gives him access to the estate, and he can poke around a little . . . check that all's as it should be.'

Again I waited.

'I can't *order* you to,' grumbled Tosh. 'It's against force rules to accept keys to property. Furthermore, when you're on the estate – *if* you go on to the estate – you're on private land. Strictly speaking, you've no authority there.' We'd reached the nitty-gritty and, again, Tosh sniffed before growling, 'It's bloody ridiculous.'

'There's always a way sir,' I soothed.

'Don't tell *me*. Just get back to Clifton and *find* a way.'

'Yes, sir.'

I left his office. I waited for the next bus to take me back to my new patch, and as I waited an ancient Daimler drew up at the kerb. A chunky, elderly gentleman with the weather-tanned face of an outdoors type was behind the wheel.

'Are you the new Clifton constable?' he called.

I admitted that I was, indeed the new 'Clifton constable'.

'Get in. I'm going past your place.' Then as we drew away from the pavement, 'I'm Sir George Armytage.'

'Oh!'

'How's your wife settling in?'

'Fine, sir. She likes the cottage. So do I.'

'Good.' He kept his gaze on the road ahead. 'There's a key to the doors leading to the estate . . .'

'Yes, sir. I'll collect it tomorrow from the estate office – if that's convenient.'

'Good. Good. I'll arrange for it to be there.'

Then as we turned into the village, 'Any time, y'know, Constable. You and your wife. It's very pleasant walking in the woods. You'll find some nice footpaths across the Home Farm, too. Feel free . . . anywhere on the estate.'

'Thank you, sir.'

Finally as we pulled up outside the police cottage, 'This place. If anything goes wrong. Repairs. Anything. Don't go through the palaver of sending reports to your divisional office. Telephone my man at the estate office. He'll send one of the estate workmen out to it.'

I joined Avis, humping furniture and putting our new home in order, and I knew the fences had already been mended. Nor was I wrong. It was the most friendly beat I ever worked. It had a character peculiar to itself. I was a copper – a fully paid-up member of one of the world's select communities – and for the first time I *felt* like a copper. Until Clifton I'd enjoyed the job, but at heart I was still a flight-sergeant in the RAF, dressed up in the wrong uniform.

At Clifton I became what in effect I still am.

*　　　*　　　*

There are, of course, classics in the operation of confidence tricksters. The Eiffel Tower has twice been sold for scrap metal, both times with ridiculous ease, by French con experts with the gift of the gab and a gullible American in their sights. The 'ring switch' is known to every jeweller; but that doesn't mean it isn't pulled with almost monotonous regularity by men and women who can give the stage conjuror a street start in the art of sleight of hand. The Three Card Trick, Threading the Needle and the Cup and Ball gag can still be found today in out-of-the-way corners of every race-track, and the suckers still queue while the operators make a good and easy living.

All this, but the longest running blinder I ever encountered was pulled by a man who wasn't a criminal and who lived at Clifton. He was an old swaddy from World War I; an ex-cavalryman who'd caught a packet on the Somme and was obliged to wear a six-inch-wide, heavy leather belt around his middle because of destroyed stomach muscles. He lived alone in a tiny, single-decker cottage, and village rumour had it he was 'worth a bit'. Not that he lived in any sort of style, but because of this rumour, plus his disability, a handful of local biddies fetched and carried for him, cooked his meals, did his housework and generally made sure he was as comfortable as possible.

He died suddenly, sitting alone in a well-cushioned armchair before a good fire. I suspect that, had he been given a choice, that's how he would have liked to have gone.

I shooed the fluttering ladies from the cottage and, having firmly locked the door, accompanied the village undertaker to the public mortuary with the corpse. We were undressing the old chap when the pathologist arrived.

I warned him about the World War I wound, and the necessity to wear the heavy belt. About ten minutes later, the pathologist grunted, 'No wound. There never has been. He's lived a remarkably healthy life.'

Nor was that all. The hunt for next-of-kin showed that he hadn't even served in the armed forces. During World War I he'd been a conscientious objector, and by the time World War II had arrived he'd been too old to trouble himself. As for the 'fortune', it became necessary to sell everything he owned to cover the bare expenses of his funeral.

And yet he'd rented that tiny cottage for as long as anybody could remember. He'd *always* worn the six-inch-wide belt, he'd *always* claimed to have been badly wounded on the Somme and he'd *always* had a handful of the village ladies running his errands and generally making sure he was comfortable.

I consider *that* to be just about the most perfect con trick I ever came across.

The death of the old twister led to me meeting and getting to know the local undertaker and his wife, and as time passed David and Betty Marsden became two of our closest friends. It was a friendship that lasted long after

I'd left the force. It lasted until first David, then Betty, died.

We all four holidayed together. We were 'family' and – a thing I wouldn't have thought possible – I rarely remembered that he was an undertaker.

In fairness, I think he was an undertaker because he *had* to be. It was the only way he could earn a living. At heart, he was a worker of wood. An artist, who took too much trouble and reached too near to perfection ever to make the end-product pay. I watched him make things other than coffins. Pieces of furniture. Doors. Picture frames. Shotgun stocks. It always had to be the right sort of wood, properly grained, properly seasoned. His workshop was alongside the house and he would work well into the night and, when I called in, he'd be there teasing the wood into shape, a sliver at a time. Other than for coffins, he didn't use nails or screws; and even his coffins had dovetailed corners. Whatever he made stood there, firm and solid, locked into position by its own tightly fitting joints. Then he used glue. The old-fashioned glue-pot stuff, which simmered on a slow-burning stove in one corner of his workshop. Glue, fine-grained sandpaper, a steel scraping tool and, finally, pure beeswax.

I think if I ever met a genuine artist it was David Marsden.

And if David and I were close friends, Betty and Avis were like sisters. There was always that extra happiness when they were in each other's company. That such a woman should be an undertaker's wife . . . but I think, like me, she saw her husband as a *reluctant* mortician.

She was a huge woman, but in some magical way dainty. Compassion filled every bit of her massive frame. She laughed easily, but never at the wrong things and never to hurt.

David and Betty. They are now long dead, but as long as we smile and say, 'Betty would have enjoyed this,' or 'David would have liked that,' they remain a little alive for us.

* * *

Clerics have always given me trouble. When we married,

the officiating parson was suffering from a monumental hangover; so much so that he allowed the ring to slide from the open Book of Common Prayer and tinkle its way down the aisle. In the RAF the station Holy Joe was always the guy who (or so it seemed) made *my* religion a namby-pamby affair, and not at all like the creed of a man who defied the Caesars and, by his teachings, triggered off the Crusades.

Nevertheless, as much as I am able, I try to be a Christian gentleman.

Despite this, Avis was worried. We went to church about once a month and, because of her upbringing, Avis derived both pleasure and moral courage whenever she went to the altar rail to join in the Eucharist. I couldn't go with her. I hadn't been confirmed. And because it seemed only right that we level-pegged in the Paradise Stakes, we decided that the omission should be rectified. We made enquiries and discovered something rather terrible. I hadn't even been *baptised*.

Enter the Reverend Ashmore.

A small man, a good man, a perpetually 'busy' man and a man with his own cockeyed ideas about his place in the scheme of things. He lorded it over Clifton church, and not for him ecclesiastical harmony. Half the village were chapel folk, and as far as Ashmore was concerned, they were undoubtedly on the wrong bus. *Their* destination was ankle-deep in shovels and pitchforks. He caused no small rumpus when he marched into the tiny village school and, quite unexpectedly, instructed the infant scholars to always call him 'father'. The local Mothers' Union crossed his path and a couple of the ladies spoke their mind. He immediately 'excommunicated' them and refused to allow them into his church.

And this was the ordained gentleman who was suddenly presented with the job of baptising the village bobby. I called at the vicarage one evening when off duty. I told him what I wanted, and within five minutes he'd thought up a full-scale, London Palladium performance.

'Which is your favourite hymn?' he beamed.

'Eh?'

'I'll arrange for the choir to sing it while you're being

101

baptised.'

'No choir,' I rumbled, firmly.

'Constable, the congregation will think it strange if the choir doesn't . . .'

'No congregation.'

'Are you *ashamed*?' The beam turned into a glare.

'I want baptising,' I growled, in a most unChristian tone. 'I need you to do it. I don't need an audience. As long as my wife and I know – as long as *you* know – we can take it as read that the Almighty can make an educated guess. That's it, vicar. No arguments.'

Nevertheless, one evening a few weeks later there was a witness. One of the vergers. To 'represent the congregation'. Avis was there. So was my father-in-law. There wasn't much fuss and, even though Ashmore seemed more than a little disappointed, he did his piece without making me feel too foolish.

I felt something of a berk when later I was confirmed at a church a few miles from Clifton. All the other candidates for confirmation were little girls. Tots who stopped at about waist-level, and all dolled up in white and wearing veils. I was in best bib-and-tucker and, because we were an uneven number, I ambled down the aisle last. But I *was* confirmed. The mites had all approached the bishop in pairs, and he'd rested a hand on each head. He put both his hands on my head . . . maybe he figured I needed a double dose.

Did I feel better? Did I feel more 'complete'? The truth is, I don't know. I'd been brought up in a God-fearing household, but nobody had ever pushed the gentle-Jesus line too heavily. Sunday School had been the accepted thing when I was a kid. Mother was chapel, but Dad and I had gone to church regularly enough, if only to clear our chests with a good, old-fashioned hymn-sing.

Suffice to say that Avis was happy. I could join her at the rail for the wafers and the wine.

The trouble with the Reverend Ashmore was that he quite simply thought that as the village parson he was also the village headman. Clifton was more than his parish. Clifton was his realm and within this realm *his* power was absolute.

Half the village hated him, and the other half laughed at him, but however many times he fell flat on his face the poor guy was blind-folded by a sense of self-importance. He could never understand why.

Take the time his dog raided a chicken-run. The owner of the chickens had seen and recognised the dog. I trotted round to the vicarage, and there it was. A savaged fowl, and a dog with feathers still fast in its fangs.

'My dog wouldn't *do* that,' protested Ashmore.

'Your dog *has* done it,' I pointed out.

'Rubbish.'

'He was seen.'

'He was *not* seen.'

'Dammit, there's the dead chicken.'

'Somebody must have put it there.'

'His mouth's still full of feathers.'

'That's no proof.'

'It's proof enough for me,' I sighed. 'At a guess it will be proof enough for the court.'

The lunacy of it all was that had Ashmore gone to the owner of the dead bird and offered to pay for the fowl that would have been the end of things. Instead, he stormed the village, accusing everybody of near-blasphemy, and at church the next Sunday he delivered a red-hot sermon based upon the sin of bearing false witness.

We were suddenly in the news. Even the nationals sent reporters and photographers along to check on this cleric who counted himself above and beyond the law. I kept well in the background. If Ashmore yearned for notoriety he wasn't going to get it on my time.

'He's round the bend.' Thus the opinion of Tosh.

'He's a little eccentric, sir.'

'Eccentric! He's sixpence to the bloody shilling.'

'Yes, sir.'

'No interviews, Wainwright.'

'Not a chance, sir.'

'Good. If they think a barmy parson's important enough to merit headlines, *we* don't want to encourage it.'

But I, too, had a dog. Like the Reverend and Mrs Ashmore, Avis and I had no family. Our dog and cat were our 'family'. And I would have fought the world for the good name of my dog. One part of me, therefore, sympathised with Ashmore, and in part understood. But I doubt if I'd have made as big a fool of myself.

At court he refused to take the oath, but insisted upon going into the witness-box.

The chairman of the bench suggested that instead of the oath he might care to make a solemn declaration.

'It's what non-believers sometimes do,' explained the chairman.

'I'm not a non-believer.'

'I think you should take the oath then.'

'I don't need to take the oath. I don't *lie*.'

'Vicar, I think you should be a little more co-operative.'

'I don't *have* to be co-operative. My dog did not kill that chicken. I know that for a fact.'

'He was with you at the time?' suggested the chairman.

'No. I asked him, and he assured me he didn't.'

'You – you *asked* him?' The chairman, too, was suddenly well out of his depth.

'My dog is like me. *He* doesn't lie, either.'

From the well of the court Tosh's growled, 'In that case there's not much point in asking *him* to take the oath,' could be heard in all four corners of the room.

In short, it was a farce, but it was a sad farce and I was sorry to be part of it. The law – and especially Criminal Law – is too immense, too absolute, to admit the nuances of gentle fantasy as propounded by the Ashmores of the world. They are like mice, caught in the maze of cogs which go to make up a vast machine; they can't escape and they are powerless to stop the thing once started.

Ashmore got off lightly. He was convicted and a very nominal fine was imposed. Nobody believed his side of things, but out of kindness nobody called him a liar.

And he had his moment of glory in the pages of national newspapers.

* * *

Any fair to moderate social psychologist could find a whole textbook stuffed solid with high-octane phrases with which to describe and explain the behaviour of Family A and Family B. The future peace of the universe insists that I call them Family A and Family B; both families had kids and, when I left Clifton, the kids were set fair to take over from their parents.

They lived next door to each other in a brace of semi-detached cottages at the end of the steep lane. Fortunately for the rest of the village, there wasn't another dwelling within two hundred yards.

They hated each other and, OK, every village is carved into cliques and clans due to a certain amount of inter-marriage, but these two had long ago passed the point of no return. Had any of them had the guts murder would have been committed, but instead they damn near wore a channel in the path of the police cottage, complaining and counter-complaining.

And, in honesty, both had cause for complaint.

Family A cut the clothes line when Family B's washing was out to dry. Family B shunted the ash from their hearth on to Family A's newly scoured front doorstep. Family A encouraged their dog to crap on Family B's path. Family B sprayed Family A's newly planted vegetables with weed-killer. Each had an outside toilet. Family A planted broken glass around the seat of Family B's bog. Family B screwed up Family A's ballcock, then hammered a wooden plug in the overflow pipe.

The impression was that they stayed up nights, figuring out what new nastiness they could get up to. It was all go, and the rest of the village laughed themselves stupid at the antics. I didn't. I was the mug both families ran to with their troubles, and there wasn't much I could do about it because what they were up to boiled down to tort, which isn't crime; therefore, until they edged over into crime, I had to play at peacemaker. And the truth was I soon tired of *that* role. I blew quite a few gaskets, sent Incident Reports in to Divisional Headquarters and (from Tosh) suffered a few roastings.

'You're in charge of that beat, Wainwright.'

'Yes, sir.'

'*You* . . . not those bloody lunatics.'

'They haven't committed a crime, sir,' I explained, patiently. 'They haven't even committed a summary offence. All they've done – in effect – is to make a

105

nuisance of themselves to each other.'

'Wainwright, you're a particularly nebulous prat.'

'If you say so, sir.'

'Stir yourself. *Do* something.'

'Yes, sir.'

So I did something.

I'd taken the catapult from one of the village lads a few days earlier. It was a good catapult – a poacher's catapult – and his mother had called me in to confiscate the weapon before he landed himself in trouble.

It was Sunday afternoon, a bright summer's day and, by skirting alongside a field, I could overlook the two cottages from behind a hedge but out of sight of the road.

I collected a few nice-sized pebbles, in case I missed the first few times, then took careful aim. I needn't have bothered. The first pebble shattered the front window of Family A's cottage.

I watched with some satisfaction while all hell brewed up. Two men, two women, the kids and the dog. Accusation and counter-accusation. They were really having a go.

I pocketed the catapult, skirted the field, strolled down the path and happily booked everybody for Fighting in the Street, Conduct Likely to Cause a Breach of the Peace . . . and anything I could come up with on the spur of the moment.

They were duly fined and bound over to keep the peace, and both Tosh and I were happy little policemen.

'I take it you put a squib up their arse,' he murmured, after the hearing.

'Sir, I wouldn't do a thing like that,' I objected, innocently.

'No, of course you wouldn't.' He grinned, wickedly. 'Just the old "Ways and Means Act".'

As I wallow in memories of that part of my life, the core of my remembrance of Clifton Beat centres around Kirklees Estate. That key – the key I accepted from Sir George Armytage – unlocked hours and hours of sheer delight.

I took him at his word, and he kept his word. A stroll through the woods, or along the footpaths of the Home

Farm, was something both Avis and I enjoyed whenever the weather permitted. A gentle saunter into the estate, as far as Robin Hood's grave and back, gave us absolute privacy from everything but the creatures of the wild.

The grave was deep inside the wood. A slab of crumbling stone was enclosed behind shoulder-high railing, and the stone was engraved with script of antique English which, if you took the trouble to decipher it, read:

> Here underneath this little stone
> Lies Robert Earl of Huntingdon
> No archer was as he so good
> And people called him Robin Hood
> Such outlaws as he and his men
> Will England never see again.

Alongside the buildings of the Home Farm stood the Kirklees Gatehouse, with an upper room in which odds and ends of clothing, reputed to be Robin's, were kept under a glass. The room was said to be where he'd died, after letting fly with his last arrow, and he was supposedly buried where the arrow fell. And it was one hell of a shot – two hundred yards, at least, and all uphill – from the Gatehouse to the grave. But the old English longbow was quite a weapon.

At Cooper Bridge (still part of the beat) stood a high-class roadhouse. The Three Nuns. It was built on the site of an ancient priory and (or so goes the tale) the prioress was Robin's aunt; records suggest that Robin decided to visit Church Lees (Kirklees) to be bled, immediately before his death. That's the story . . . and I'm sticking to it. There is as much documentary evidence for as there is against, and it's rather nice to think that the greatest law-breaker of them all once visited a beat policed by me.

The wood was a true English wood. It had elm, ash, birch and oaks galore. Yew, awkward-looking, with their 'clustered-column' trunks, jostled with willows and pop-lars. Holly bushes grew thick and tall as a first-floor window, and where footpaths and rides criss-crossed the area undergrowth formed a knee-high wall on either side, and beyond the wall was the never-ending sound of wildlife.

Much of that wood has now been cleared for conifer plantations. The last time I saw the estate it boasted a sign advertising its rose bushes. Progress, like murder, will out . . . but whoever polices Clifton these days will never leave with the memories I still hold.

*   *   *

Some slight deviation – a quick explanation – is necessary in order to explain something that started at Clifton and thereafter formed a thread through my whole police career.

The London Metropolitan Police have their own promotion set-up. To my mind their system is simpler, better and fairer. I thought it then and I am convinced of it now.

In the Met an officer passes the promotion examination from constable to sergeant, or from sergeant to inspector. Thereafter, he can count heads. He joins a queue and, if he cares to, he can find the exact length of the queue. As sergeants (or inspectors) retire, are promoted, resign or even die, the queue becomes shorter. He moves nearer to the head of that queue. The day arrives when he *knows* the next stripes (or the next pips) go on *his* tunic.

It makes for sensible, contented bobbying. There is a minimum of hassle. There is no elbowing aside. Buttering-up can't pay dividends.

In the provinces it is an entirely different ball game. The officer sits and passes the promotion examination. Thereafter he sits and waits, knowing he is eligible for 'consideration'. In my day a man could sit and pass promotion examinations for both sergeant and inspector, while still a beat constable . . . I speak from experience – I'd passed them both before I left Clifton. Nothing is certain. Nothing is ordained. But with enough 'pull' – with enough buddies in the right places – it is possible to pass an examination this year, sport chevrons next and start stitching stars to the epaulets the year after.

There is a fine theory behind this cockle-brained promotion system. It stems from a vague belief that the final assessment should be based upon 'leadership potential', and only the 'leaders' themselves can decide who possesses *that*.

In practical terms, it boils down to this. While it is not necessary to have friends in high places before promotion arrives, to have *enemies* in high places means there is a mile-high wall of veto. And that wall remains until the guy who erected it either retires or falls from favour, and there isn't a damn thing anybody can do about it.

There is even a spin-off. Dozens of excellent coppers, who know all about the system, don't even *sit* the examinations. They honestly believe it would be a waste of time.

From generalities, to specifics ... Offhand, I can't remember ever having failed an examination. Pre-war, during the war and post-war. I've sat dozens and always the top half-dozen places have included the name Wainwright.

This is not because I was ever a boy-genius (nor am today a geriatric-genius), but simply because I have a trick mind. Like a dry loofah, it soaks everything that passes its way and holds it. Above my eye-line there is an attic – a lumber room – in which is stored a handful of priceless gems and a monumental amount of useless junk. I see something, I read something, I hear something . . . and it sticks. It is not an effort. Indeed it is often a greater effort *not* to remember. Quite often it is a thumping nuisance. I hear a tune I haven't heard for decades, and immediately I recognise it, if it has words I remember the words and I even remember the name of the singer whom I heard singing the tune. I watch a late-night movie on TV – a movie I saw once in the '30s – and I'm damn near mouthing the dialogue with the screen actors.

All things being equal therefore (and even had they been a little unequal) a promising police career seemed to stretch ahead of me.

To make sure, I decided to earn myself a law degree. LL.B. (*Legum Baccalaureus*). It *can* be done. *I* did it. Other coppers too, of course, but in those days not many. And as far as I know, no other copper made it strictly in his own time; without asking for a single shift-change;

without a request to be taken off street-duty for as much as one hour.

Simple, plain pig-headedness made me choose the hard way. The damn-near-impossible way. The way that was like climbing Everest . . . backwards. In the event it took me seven, never-ending years without a single day when I wasn't head-down cramming knowledge. In order to sit various examinations, I travelled to Middlesbrough, to Huddersfield, to Salford and, finally, to London. Nor did I once enter a lecture room, enjoy personal tuition from somebody able to answer the thousand and one questions that tumbled out at every stage. I had to find my own answers.

I planned it very carefully.

I'd left school at fourteen – being anxious to slap a few more shillings into the purse of a family that wasn't too well heeled – therefore I had to grab certain qualifications before I could even *enrol* as a potential degree candidate. Specifically, seven G.C.E. passes. Two at 'A' level and five at 'O' level.

Thereafter, the LL.B. was in my sights.

I wrote away for as many old examination papers as possible. This was quite above board; they are there to be bought. This seemed (and, indeed, *was*) a wise move. The number of questions that can be asked on any subject, including law, is finite. Certain 'chestnuts' crop up time and again. Then I wrote away and decided upon basic textbooks . . . and spent a small fortune buying them.

The initial shock was the amount of unused law lying around. Unused, that is, other than the necessity of studying it for the purpose of a law degree. Criminal Law, of course. But, after that, Contract Law, the Law of Torts, the Law of Trusts, International Law, Jurisprudence, the English Legal System and the History of English Law, Roman Law, Administrative Law, Constitutional Law, Company Law, Equity, Mercantile Law . . . and a whole bunch I could also mention if I wished to bore you.

So, what did all this lot take, before I reached my goal?

It took a *minimum* of two hours of concentrated study, every day; seven days a week; fifty-two weeks a year, for seven years. Those two hours were often more than doubled, and if not doubled, they had to be fitted into the various courses I was required to attend during this seven-year period. Common gumption insisted that I daren't miss a single day; if I broke the rhythm, I'd never pick it up again. Coughs, colds, flu? Forget they existed. Social life? No way. An evening out? A sick joke.

I policed the beat as conscientiously as ever. I worked overtime, when called upon. I did my full stint of extra duty whenever it was required. When the examinations came, I took annual leave in order to sit them.

The object of the exercise was absurdly simple. I was going to get that infernal LL.B. without owing anybody a damn thing.

But I must put things into perspective before anybody gets any wrong ideas. Other than proof that you can do it, an LL.B. means very little. It gives you no right of audience in any court of law. At a Magistrates' Court you may know far more about law than the combined knowledge of every member of the bench, but you're not allowed to open your mouth. You can't set up shop as a 'lawyer', even though you *are* an academic lawyer. You're certainly not a solicitor; solicitors pass the Law Society Examination, and that little number can make the LL.B. exam look like a cheap crossword puzzle. Nor are you a barrister; although oddly enough the Bar Examination, via which barristers are spawned, is a few notches less hairy than the LL.B. exam.

You are an LL.B. And that's *all* you are.

Assuming somebody is stupid enough to employ you, you can teach law. If you keep abreast of legal trends (which I've tried to do) most solicitors will find a place for you in their office, as a Common Law Clerk or some similar dogsbody.

But if you make it alone, and in your spare time – if you need neither tutor nor classroom – it proves *something*. It proves you can concentrate for long periods of time. It proves you can aim at a goal, and get that goal, whatever the cost. It also proves you are an incredibly mulish clown who, if necessary, is prepared to lower his head and charge an oncoming tank . . . and further proves you might just stop it.

As for myself, who knows? I might have made it without Avis. I *might*, but I have grave doubts.

It takes a singularly special breed of woman to back her man like Avis did for those seven, mind-blowing years. I grew impossible to live with, but for most of the time she understood, compressed her lips and remained silent. I ranted and raved at trivialities, but she gave me freedom to do so and, at the same time and as much as possible, kept the pinpricks of irritation away from me. I think our marriage shuddered slightly – but only slightly – under that prolonged impact. It held, because we are the people we are, and come from the place from where we come . . . Yorkshire. But perhaps more than that, we are both from an age, and a stratum of society, which (rightly or wrongly) place the word 'divorce' alongside such words as 'cancer', 'incest' or 'gonorrhoea'. It is a foul word, describing a foul thing. It isn't done. It does not even deserve mention. You make a promise before an altar and, come hell or high water, you keep that promise, and every part of that promise. The idea of *not* keeping that promise never enters your head. You hit the rough stuff – you garner what comfort you can from the knowledge that every marriage has its bad patches – but you battle your way through, until you once more reach tranquil waters. You *never* throw in the sponge.

Yet in those years the rocks were plentiful and seemed never-ending; rocks which need not have been, had I not reached a certain decision on Clifton Beat. But the marriage held and, after that, it will never fail.

I recall one incident that typifies everything.

Having provided the house, the police force demanded that one room be decorated every year. The local chief inspector's job included a visit to view your efforts and, if he wasn't satisfied, you re-decorated that room until he was.

Except on odd occasions, I had always hated decorating. I'd taken the First Intermediate Exam and the Second Intermediate was rising fast above the horizon. I hadn't time to fanny around with paint and wallpaper. Anyway, the damn room didn't *need* decorating.

112

Nevertheless, I was up to my ears in it, and had been all day. It was well past midnight, and my mood was like a razor. I fought and struggled with paste and paper while, at the foot of the stepladder, Avis read aloud from a textbook on Roman Law. I doubt if she understood one word in every five, but she ploughed on and I fought to concentrate on two things at once.

That sort of thing – not bedroom gymnastics – cements a marriage.

It came to an end. The blinding, head-bursting slog ended, and the day arrived. *The* day – a day when Clifton Beat was a thing of the past – the day when I was able to officially notify the chief constable that I'd just about walked on water; that the bacon had not merely been brought home, it had also been immaculately cured, then grilled to perfection. I could, if I so wished, add 'LL.B.' to my signature.

I have a feeling I was very cocky that day; that I was insufferably sure of myself.

*   *   *

The chronological telling of this tale has had to be put aside for a moment, if only because, looking back, I find that factual coincidence can sometimes make fictional coincidence look almost logical. I made the decision and started the slog on Clifton Beat and within weeks of making that decision I met the one man who eventually made it all worthless.

He was Head of CID. A detective chief superintendent. He had a couple of notches left on his belt before the final showdown. By then he was the deputy chief constable.

His name was George Metcalfe.

I met him – strictly speaking, *saw* him from a distance – on the two murder enquiries in which I was involved while at Brighouse.

I took little notice of him. Why should I?

Not for one moment did I suspect that in time he'd be the 'immovable object' against which the 'irresistible force' of my planned law degree would flounder.

*   *   *

However, the good people of Clifton Beat paid for a bobby – not a law student – and, before I left for a second stint at Elland, I learned that a policeman needs more luck than a gambler.

Her name was Rosemary. I didn't know her, I'd never met her, but I knew her family. Such families are valid arguments for those in favour of compulsory sterilisation. God knows how many kids they had, but the impression was they could give the average rabbit a few lengths' start. The old man didn't work; at a guess, having expended all that energy in fornication he couldn't have found strength to work had somebody offered him a job. The old lady was a flashy, sloppy creature; she gave birth to kids, and that's about *all* she did. Maybe she hadn't time for housework. Maybe she hadn't time to wash herself. On the other hand, maybe she figured that if her husband didn't mind living like a pig, that let her off the hook.

One late summer evening, I was in the kitchen of the police cottage. I was putting a touch of paint around the windows, and from the front room I could hear Avis chatting to a neighbour who'd called in. I was only half-listening, but I caught Rosemary's name.

'It's terrible, isn't it?' said the outraged neighbour.

'What is?'

'Haven't you heard? Rosemary. She's only just fifteen, and she's pregnant.'

I cleaned my brushes, put the paint away and changed into reasonable togs. By this stage in my life I had dismissed all rumours of storks, gooseberry bushes or little black bags, and carnal knowledge of a girl under the age of 16 was no piffling, take-it-or-leave it offence in those days.

Rosemary's mother was alone in the house when I arrived. The kids were all out . . . but then the kids were *always* out. The old man might have been upstairs recovering from his latest conjugal exertions – I wouldn't know – but certainly he didn't join us, and the lady of the house made no move to contact him.

She asked me inside, and thereafter I tried to keep the talk to a minimum and to inhale as little as possible.

'I'm told Rosemary's expecting a baby.'

'Aye.'

114

'She's only fifteen years old.'

'Aye. Fifteen . . . just.'

'It doesn't seem to upset you.'

'No – well – I've thowt she was on the game for a bit.'

'The – er – game?'

'Picking up a bit o' spare brass.'

'You knew about this?'

'I reckon.'

'You didn't mind?'

'Nowt to do wi' me.'

'You're her mother.'

'Bloody kids! Who can control 'em these days?'

'Do you know who the father is?'

'Do I buggery.'

'Does Rosemary know who the father is?'

'I doubt it.'

'Doesn't anybody bloody well *care*?'

I was outraged, and saw no reason to hide my outrage. On the other hand, the woman seemed genuinely surprised at my tone.

'Young man,' she lectured. 'When tha's lived a few years longer, tha'll be a deal wiser. There's nowt anybody can do to stop nature. And it's nobbut *nature*. Tha'll learn that as tha gets older.'

She meant it, too. And when next day Rosemary visited Brighouse Police Station, to have as detailed a statement as possible teased from her by a policewoman, that policewoman expressed *her* surprise when Rosemary had left.

'She sees nothing wrong in what she's done. She's never been *told*. To her it's as natural, as innocent, as a cat having kittens.'

Nevertheless, a serious crime had been committed and, thanks to my own enthusiasm to become 'the complete policeman', it was *my* crime, therefore *I* had to push whatever enquiry seemed necessary. That was the way a county constabulary worked in those days. The CID played perpetual long-stop, and only then for what *they* counted as 'serious crime'.

As Tosh put it, 'The mess seems to be on your doorstep, Wainwright. Get into plain clothes, and clean it up.'

The only real thing I had to go on was the statement, and the statement said very little. The guy I was after answered to the name of 'Norman'. He was between twenty and forty years old. He might have been clean-shaven, but on the other hand he might have worn a moustache. In all other respects he was 'medium' – height, complexion, hair – in fact every alternate chap you met on the street could have fitted the description.

On the fateful day (a day which she thought was a Saturday, but might have been a Friday) Norman had kerb-crawled and netted Rosemary in the morning. He'd taken her all the way to Blackpool, where they'd had fish and chips, visited the Pleasure Beach, generally tooled around on the prom, then driven to his home. One slap-and-tickle episode had taken place on the sofa, and had been interrupted by Norman's cat and dog, who'd had a fight in which the dog had grabbed the cat across the hindquarters and damn near bitten it in two. Then, having had his quota of lust, Norman had turned particularly caddish, had shooed Rosemary from his house and left her to find her own way home. She'd caught a bus (or it may have been a trolley-bus) to Huddersfield. The fare had been a shilling (or was it one shilling and sixpence?) and, having reached Huddersfield, she'd returned to her home in Brighouse by public transport. Norman's car had been an open sports model. She didn't know the number. She didn't know the make. It was (she thought) black.

And that, in essence, was it.

From that information, of course, Hercule Poirot could have named the culprit in ten seconds flat. Sherlock Holmes could have given the colour of his eyes in five. Wainwright had to do things the plodding way.

I began by telephoning Huddersfield Public Transport Department. How far could a passenger travel for one shilling from the centre of Huddersfield, first by bus, then by trolley-bus? How far for one shilling and sixpence? I had a large-scale map. I joined all the destinations together, and ended up with a very battered-looking doughnut. With luck, Norman lived somewhere within that doughnut.

Norman had a car; a convertible. The chances were it was black. It needed petrol and, at a pinch, it sometimes went on the blink and had to be repaired. Ergo . . . garages.

I took a bus to my doughnut, checked a telephone directory in order not to miss any, then began the leg-work around the garages. I was at it for more than a week. It seemed that Huddersfield was surrounded by a wall of open sports cars, all of them black and most of them owned by chaps called Norman.

By this time in my police career I'd grown pretty brass-necked at asking questions. I needed to be. To knock on a door, then ask a complete stranger if he'd picked up a teenage slag in Brighouse, carted her off to Blackpool for the day and, throughout that day, screwed her up hill and down dale, is a little more hairy than trying to sell double-glazing . . . and flashing a warrant card, prior to asking those sort of questions, doesn't help a great deal. Nor could I take the first denial at face value. I needed proof – *some* sort of proof – otherwise that particular Norman stayed on the list of 'probables'.

A week later I was still trying. Very gradually, I was working my way round my doughnut. I was on well-known territory; on the outskirts of Elland. I called at the thousand-and-first garage, and asked the usual questions.

'No. We don't know anybody called Norman who owns a black sports.'

'Makes a change,' I sighed. 'Most garages *do*.'

'There's Norman So-and-So.' This from a mechanic whose overalled trouser-legs protruded from beneath a nearby vehicle. 'He had that clapped-out MG he sold about a month back.'

'Black?' I checked.

'Where it wasn't rusty.'

'Do you have his address?'

'It'll be in the office.'

So I trundled my weary body to the home of one more car-owner named Norman.

The house was cleaner than Rosemary's home . . . but not much. He was in his mid-thirties, lived alone and didn't seem too worried at the questions I asked when he'd invited me inside.

'You have a car?' I said. 'An open MG?'

'It was knackered. I sold it.'

'We're going back a few months,' I explained. I gave him the approximate date. 'Friday. Saturday. You visited Blackpool, I think.'

It was a gag as old as the hills. Get him there – there's nothing wrong about visiting Blackpool – but get him *there*, and you're paring down his options when it comes to making a denial.

'Blackpool?' His look of amused surprise seemed genuine. 'It's *years* since I went to Blackpool. Not since I was a kid.'

'There's a girl, you see,' I explained. 'This chap – this Norman, who drove an open sports car – took her to Blackpool for the day.'

'Not me,' he smiled.

'A black sports car?' I teased. (I wasn't going to tell him of the umpteen other Normans I'd met who owned black sports cars.)

'Sorry, not me.'

'She's in the family way.'

'Not guilty.' He smiled, and that smile made me feel a little warm. Up till then the remark had been met with some degree of hostility by the other Normans. Even outrage. But all this one did was *smile*.

'Married?' I asked, offhandedly.

'Separated.'

'So women aren't out of the question?'

'I'm not celibate.'

'That's what I mean.'

'They can be had.'

'Women?'

'I know one or two willing to oblige.'

'Girls?' I suggested.

'I wouldn't call 'em *girls*.'

'Fifteen-year-olds?'

'You're riding the wrong horse, mate.' The smile remained.

'There are such things as Identification Parades,' I

Rosemary was placed in care, at one of those establishments *not* visited by investigative journalists. She was taught right from wrong, and in time she gave birth to her child . . . and insisted upon keeping it. I never saw it, but I'm told it was a particularly beautiful baby and that Rosemary thought so much of it she wouldn't allow her mother to even *see* it, much less touch it.

* * *

I left Brighouse – and Clifton – a wiser and more complete policeman that I'd been when I arrived. I was quietly conned into returning to Elland . . . but it was a much-changed Elland.

I didn't know it at the time, but I also ended my spell under Tosh. He retired shortly after I left. He was replaced by another, and very fine, chief inspector. But Tosh was a one-off job, and I owe him much I can never repay.

Duty Elsewhere

The letters 'DE' on the roster board meant 'Duty Elsewhere' and that, in turn, meant no questions were asked and, if they *were* asked, they weren't answered. I saw much of the West Riding of Yorkshire during my various stints of DE. I saw much of which the human race should be ashamed; much hole-in-the-corner foulness and much rank stupidity masquerading as 'enjoyment'. But I wouldn't have missed it, if only because it also produced not a few chuckles on the way.

Why me? Well, not just me – but why the very small group of coppers who are earmarked for this peculiar cloak-and-dagger caper? Probably because none of us *looked* like coppers. Nor, by and large, did we act or think like coppers. We never added up to more than half-a-dozen, we were all ex-servicemen and we'd all kept well clear of that 'Hello, hello, hello' ponderosity with which so many coppers can be identified, in or out of uniform. In retrospect I think we all had one other thing in common: we were all 'loners'; we rarely socialised, were not of the back-slapping, all-palls-together fraternity.

But for whatever reason, and whoever made the choice, Tosh called me into his office one afternoon and passed on instructions.

'Force Headquarters tomorrow at ten o'clock, Wainwright.'

'Sir?' I was puzzled. Even worried. The last time I'd seen Wakefield Headquarters had been immediately prior to travelling to Mansfield Police Training College. A trip to Force Headquarters equated with trouble.

'Don't ask *me*.' He may or may not have been bluffing. With hindsight, I don't think he was. On the other hand when necessary Tosh could play his cards very close to his chest. He continued, 'Dective Superintendent King wants to see you.'

'Oh!'

He tapped his desk telephone, and added, 'A call's just come through. And I'm to tell you to keep it to yourself.'

* * *

King was a stocky, broad-shouldered copper. I hadn't heard of him before but, as I later realised, that wasn't too surprising. Among other things, he dealt with some of the less public side of policing.

I'd arrived at the foyer of Headquarters building, told the string-thin cadet on duty at the reception desk of my appointment, and to my surprise had been told to go to the billiard room. The same billiard room, with the same apology for a table and the same knackered cues. A man was idly bouncing one of the ancient balls from the weary cushions as I entered.

'Wainwright?' He dropped the ball into a handy pocket as he asked the question.

'I have an appointment with Detective Superintendent King.'

'That's me.'

'Oh!'

He held out a hand and, having shaken the hand of one of the demi-gods of Headquarters, I waited.

He offered a packet of cigarettes and, when we were smoking, he said, 'D'you know what Duty Elsewhere means?'

'No, sir.'

'Well, now,' he explained, 'it means you work under me. And *only* me. Nobody else knows what you're doing. Where you are. When you're on duty, when you're off duty. Nobody.'

I was intrigued.

'Interested?' he asked.

'Yes, sir.'

'It's not a cushy number. You sometimes work in pairs. Never more than two of you. You often work alone.'

I waited.

'You could get your earhole punched . . . hard.'

'Yes, sir.'

'You work God-awful hours. Basically, the job is to get where coppers shouldn't *be*.'

'Yes, sir.' I was more than intrigued. More than interested. I was fascinated.

'I want a straight "Yes" or a straight "No",' he said. 'It won't count against you if you say "No". But if you say "Yes" I don't want any fancy qualifications. It's "Yes" all the way.'

'Yes, sir.'

'You'll do it?'

'Yes, *sir*.'

'Good.' He smiled at my enthusiasm. 'Starting tomorrow. You don't go near a police station except to collect your monthly pay cheque. Put your uniform in moth balls until further notice. Then get yourself into the Barnoldswick area.'

'Barnoldswick?'

'There's a pub not far from Barnoldswick.' He gave me the name of the pub. 'There's a dog-fighting set-up in the basement. Very messy. Very illegal. We want to raid it, but what we don't want is a cock-up. We want to arrive, complete with RSPCA and photographers, when the blood and snot's eyeball deep.

'Get yourself in there. Get yourself *accepted*. Witness a few sessions, if necessary. Keep in touch with me by telephone. Once a week. No more, unless it's urgent, and don't leave messages. We raid when *you* say we raid, and bear in mind that it's going to be *your* evidence we'll be building the case upon. Understood?'

'Yes, sir.'

'Good. You're on your own.'

And, indeed, I was on my own. Only Avis could be trusted, and she knew everything but didn't breathe a word. I studied each morning, and every afternoon I bussed my way to Barnoldswick guyed up like an out-of-work navvy. I found the pub, identified the dog-fighting crowd and played drunken lout for all I was worth. I spun the fanny about taking hit-and-miss employment in the general area and effed and blinded with the best (or worst) of them.

It took me a month before they allowed me to see the basement.

The pit was in the middle of what was, in effect, two cellars knocked together to make a single, large room. It was circular and had been dug out to a depth of about a yard below the level of the cellar floor. It measured roughly three yards across, and the sides were lined with upright railway sleepers; this gave a strong 'wall' around the pit and made sure a fleeing dog couldn't escape its torture by leaping to safety. The floor of the pit was covered with sand and it was dark and stained in places.

The brickwork of the cellar was painted white, and banks of wooden forms – much like the seating arrangement of a circus – climbed towards the ceiling, giving an audience of almost two hundred a clear view of the interior of the pit.

I was assured that there'd been some 'bloody good fights' witnessed in that pit. Quite often fights to the death. I was acquainted with the subtleties of the so-called 'sport'. Staffs – Staffordshire bull terriers – when evenly matched rarely failed to come up to expectation. Especially bitches; although two dogs, with a bitch on heat waiting outside the pit, could be guaranteed to put up a 'rare show'. English bull terriers were almost as consistent at fighting as Staffs, but they sometimes tended to 'run away a bit smartish'. Terriers of the smaller breeds – especially Jack Russells – were 'little sods' and, periodically, an alsatian gave good account of itself.

I hid my revulsion behind a moronic scowl, and asked what the entrance fee was.

'Nowt, lad. The betting more than pays for it. I've seen thousands of quid change hands here in one night.'

There was more in the same vein, and that night I telephoned King.

'Good lad.' He chuckled his delight. 'You must have spun a good yarn.'

'Do I have to witness a fight?' I asked.

'The County Prosecuting Solicitor thinks you should.'

'Oh!'

'But be careful. Don't do anything – don't even *say* anything – some smart defence lawyer can twist around to make you look like an agent provocateur.'

'I'll stay in the background, sir,' I promised him.

For myself, I still think a raid might have been organised without my having to suffer the agony of witnessing something I can never forget, but I wasn't a policy-maker. And maybe the evidence wouldn't have been strong enough to merit a prosecution if I hadn't. I admit to being biased. I even admit to seriously considering the possibility of refusing to obey the instructions, but they would only have sent another man in, and *he* mightn't have had the luck I'd had.

What I know is that about a week later I watched my first dog-fight. Six, to be precise . . . six fights that made up the programme on that shameful night.

I will not go into specifics. Suffice to say that I stood well back from the pit and watched as little as I could. There was carnage and although on that night no dog was killed outright, two had to be put down due to the extent of their injuries . . . but their relief came much later, when the fighting had ended, and the wounded animals had had to suffer long journeys in the back of a shooting brake and a van.

The cellar was full to capacity; enthusiasts had travelled no small distances for the spectacle. They yelled and screamed, and my informant had been right . . . money changed hands as fast as banknotes could be fingered from wallets and handbags.

Oh, yes . . . handbags. That was one of the offshoot horrifics of the job. About a third of the spectators were women, and they screamed and encouraged the blood-letting every bit as wildly as the men.

That night Avis held me in her arms and nursed me through the nightmares. Less than a month later I organised the raid from inside, and I did it well. I arranged it to perfection, for the sake of the dogs. Even later I gave evidence . . . and never before with such certainty and such a passionate desire to convey a depth of foulness that would have been unbelievable if not personally witnessed.

126

Other than the dog-fighting episode, I rather enjoyed those months I spent on Duty Elsewhere. The consumption of booze invariably formed part of the set-up, and I'm no great drinker. I sought and was given advice. I pass it on, for what it's worth.

The trick is to tame the alcohol. The fumes, in particular. Oil does the necessary. A tablespoonful of olive oil – or, in my case, a tin of brisling in oil – and the oil forms a floating 'cap' over the beer you thereafter pour down your throat. In effect, you become water-logged long before you become drunk.

Nevertheless, booze had to be consumed, and had to be paid for. So, come to that, had bus journeys, meals and other odds and ends. I was always reimbursed, and without question.

I once asked King what the accountants thought when the annual examination of the constabulary books took place. Did they ever question all this expense for undercover work?

'They don't know, Wainwright. We've a very active Horse Section, remember. What you and your pals spend is included under the heading of Horse Fodder.'

*　　　*　　　*

Who in the first instance blows the whistle on these illegal capers requiring the attention of coppers pretending *not* to be coppers? Civil-minded citizens anxious to clamp down on law-breaking? Snouts, who want to butter up to some friendly, neighbourhood jack?

More often than not it is *wives*. Wives who worry about the company their husbands are keeping. Wives whose husbands spend more time leaning against some bar than they do at home. Wives whose housekeeping allowance is restricted because hubby throws his money away on less important things. They complain to the local copper; the local copper can't (or won't) do anything and, in desperation, they write to the chief constable. Thereafter, a few unobtrusive questions are asked and, if the answers come out right, the undercover crowd move in.

*　　　*　　　*

The briefing always took place in that same tatty room. A time and date would be given and, without even calling at the reception desk, I would make my way to the billiard room and Detective Superintendent King would be waiting.

On one occasion King looked worried.

'This will be the third try,' he said. 'We know it's going on, but it's a club and we need a warrant. To *get* the warrant we need firm evidence. They're fly buggers. They tumbled us both times before and booted our men out.'

'Trouble?' asked my companion.

'They were bruised,' admitted King, drily.

It was a two-man job, and my colleague was a fellow-copper called Jim Conboy. I'd never met him before – neither of us even knew, or asked, which division the other was from – but we worked in tandem a few times thereafter, and I grew to know him as a man to be relied upon. Like myself, out of uniform he didn't *look* like a copper. Like myself, he was prepared to take a calculated risk, but wasn't prepared to go bull-headed at things.

At that first meeting we worked out tactics with King.

The club was at Keighley. On the face of it an ordinary, working men's club, but in fact far more than that.

'It's like a bloody thieves' kitchen,' grumbled King. 'We have it on good authority there's more "knock" passed in that damn place than anywhere else in the police area.'

'After hours, of course,' I murmured.

'Most of it after hours,' agreed King. 'A select few. Less than twenty, at a guess . . . and it's a big club.'

'If we get in,' said Jim, 'we'll need to stay late. Long after the last bus leaves.'

King nodded.

'That means transport. That means somebody else has to know *something*.'

King scowled, then said, 'White's the inspector. He wants the place shut down. *He's* the one yelling for action.'

It was agreed that we meet Inspector 'Chalky' White, and that we meet him way and gone to hell in the wastes of Haworth Moors, up in the Brontë country.

Chalky was a thickset, bull-in-a-chinashop type, but he'd caught the cloak-and-dagger bug and, as far as *he* was concerned, Jim and I could have the earth, with the moon as a loss-leader, if we could only crack this infernal club for him. He arrived in an unmarked car, with a young copper sitting in the rear seat.

'*He* knows,' he explained. 'He knows all he needs to know. He's the only one who *will* know, so if there's a leak it's *him*. He knows that, too.' Then to the young copper, 'These are the men. Don't ask questions. Just recognise 'em, take orders from 'em and be there to pick them up and take them home, when and where they say.'

We asked questions, and were told that the club had a concert room. That it had very recently installed a new baby grand piano and that it was looking around for a pianist. But that because of the undercurrent of illegality that was also part of the club's set-up they were being very choosy as to who they took on.

That was it. In effect, that's all we needed.

Chalky and the young copper left, Jim and I visited a nearby café and, over tea and scones, worked out our plan.

I could play the piano. I could play it well; in those days, I could play it better than the average club pianist. My parents had dreamed of a career for me in music, but the jazz bug and the war had kyboshed *those* dreams. Nevertheless, that was our best 'in' . . . but we couldn't do too much asking round.

'Pubs,' said Jim. 'Pubs and pianos. If we work it properly, we'll get them to *invite* us in.'

And that's what we did. As part of the gag, I held my left knee stiff – once underway, I bound the knee tightly in crêpe bandage, in case I forgot – and, if asked, I claimed to be ex-RAF (which I was) and that I'd been injured during the war (which I hadn't) and that I drew a war-disability pension (which I didn't). The theory was that no force would recruit a man with a gammy leg.

Thus, with living proof that we were *not* coppers, we mooched around Keighley, earmarked the target club and then started a round of the pubs in that vicinity. If the pub hadn't a piano, we never visited it again. If it *had* a piano, I ended up at the keyboard. I could play anything any customer requested; I could transpose into any required key; I could 'vamp 'til ready' should anybody wish to perform. In no time at all, I was the golden boy of the ivories. Because of my leg – plus the fanny given out by Jim – I was something of a hero. And, given half a chance, I always complained about the inadequacy of whichever piano I happened to be playing.

We threw the hook out for about three weeks before we got a nibble.

I'd left the piano and joined Jim at a nearby table. He had company. A moderately well-dressed stranger with whom he was in friendly conversation.

'I've just been telling your mate,' said the stranger. 'You should come down to the club and try *our* piano.'

'The club?' I looked innocent, and tasted my beer.

He named the club . . . and it was the one we were after.

'Can't be done,' I said.

'Why not?'

'We aren't members.'

'As my guest, that's what I mean.'

'A club piano,' I murmured with a touch of contempt.

'It's a damn sight better piano than *that* one.'

'That's not saying a lot.'

Between us we reeled him in, and later that evening I was at the baby grand. In fairness, it really was a fine piano and, as always, the better the piano the better the playing.

Meanwhile at the bar of the club Jim played a very subtle blinder. *He complained about the beer.* Not too much, but enough to convince people that, by choice, he wouldn't be visiting the club a second time.

After that we *couldn't* be coppers working a flanker.

We played that particular game for three nights in a row. We visited the pub, the stranger joined us and took us to the club, I performed on the piano and accompanied whoever needed an accompanist, then, when the lights flickered for Time, we obligingly finished our drinks and left.

On the fourth evening the Concert Secretary took me aside.

'We're looking for a club pianist. Regular basis, like.'

I waited.

'There's a nominal salary, of course. Not much, but it's every week.'

'Are you offering me the job?' I asked.

'Aye. It's thine if tha wants it.'

I touched my leg and hedged, 'It's this war disability pension. I don't want to bugger that up.'

'Who'll know?'

'Some civic-minded sod might drop a hint in the wrong place,' I grumbled.

'Too bloody true.' He scowled, as if at past experience.

We 'thought it over' for a few moments, then I said, 'Tell you what. I'll make a few enquiries. Meanwhile – OK – I'll take the job, but put the money into some fund or another, pending an official acceptance.'

'The Children's Holiday Fund?' he suggested.

'Fine,' I nodded. 'It's a good piano, and I enjoy playing it. I'll come in each night. We'll work *something* out.'

'Tha's a good lad,' he grinned, as we shook hands on the deal. 'Tha's no'an a bad pianist, either.'

And that was it. We were 'in' . . . with knobs on.

Next day we met Chalky out in the fastness of Haworth Moors, and he fairly beamed his delight. Indeed, he was over-enthusiastic. He couldn't understand why I hadn't accepted the fee as club pianist.

'That,' I pointed out, 'would have given the defending lawyer one hell of a stick to beat me over the head with.'

Thereafter Jim and I set the pace and built upon what we'd already achieved.

We'd noticed the men who hung around after official drinking ended, and while I was at the keyboard Jim went out of his way to befriend them. Gradually we became part of the hard core of between ten and twenty who always stayed around until anything up to three o'clock in the morning. Because he fancied himself as an Irish tenor, it was decided that *I* take a personal interest in Paddy.

Paddy was the after-hours doorkeeper. He officiated at the main entrance, when all other doors and windows were firmly closed and shuttered. He sat on a stool and vetted all callers via a peephole let into the very solid door and until Paddy was satisfied the door remained shut, locked and bolted. Alongside the stool was a shelf, upon which Paddy rested his beer, and under the shelf was a switch. If the switch was thumbed, a red light came on above the bar where all the illegalities were taking place.

Fort Knox (or, come to that, Humphrey Bogart) would have been proud. Nevertheless, Paddy and that infernal door had to be bypassed if a raid was to succeed.

So I palled up with Paddy, kept him company at the door – which, fortunately, was a long passage-length away from the room where all the activity took place – and occasionally relieved him when he visited the bar to renew his booze.

Eventually, we'd done all we could do and, once more, we met Chalky White out on Haworth Moors.

Jim and I had worked out the final details, and I was the spokesman.

'Saturday night,' I said. 'Any other night is hit-and-miss, but Saturday is as near a cert as we can give you. You'll have the bent boys, you'll have some sort of stolen property you can collect and, for good measure, you'll have after-hours drinking.'

Chalky was delighted.

'One o'clock in the morning,' I insisted. 'Synchronise the watches via the telephone time signal at six o'clock Saturday evening. And be on the button, please. There's a very strick limit to the time we can have that door unlocked.'

'On the button,' promised Chalky.

'You'll have a warrant, of course?'

'Wainwright.' He winked. 'Don't *worry*. You've done a good job. It won't go wrong because of me.'

'*You* aren't risking a few broken bones, sir,' I reminded him, politely.

'*Wainwright*.' He sounded hurt. Offended. 'The warrant. We'll have a warrant. I have a tame JP. He'll sign it, that's all. He won't ask for details. *I'll* fill in the where and the when immediately before the raid.'

'That's one mouth taken care of,' I agreed.

'*All* mouths,' he insisted. 'If it puts your mind at ease. The men will be brought in, one at a time, on Saturday night. They'll be told to report, but won't be told why. When they're all in the canteen . . . *then* they'll be told as much as they need to know. That it's a raid. But not *where*. I'll drive the front car. The man who's been picking you up will drive the second car. A third car will tag on behind. Once they're in the canteen, they'll be incommunicado. Everybody. No telephoning. No slipping out for a quick pee. We'll be there at exactly one o'clock, Sunday morning.'

It was all we could ask for but, by the nature of the job, we worried a little. I know there are men – even policemen – who find the Duty Elsewhere undercover work repulsive. Their argument is that it isn't 'fair'; that at least some degree of provocateur incitement must take place. I can speak only for myself and the colleagues who occasionally worked alongside me. We were always acutely aware of this danger, and of the thin line dividing the on-the-spot witnessing of illegalities and the tacit encouraging of those illegalities. We watched and we listened – which was the reason for our presence – but never once did we offer advice or express an opinion. We were aware – very *much* aware – that, come a successful conclusion to the exercise, we would have to justify everything we did in a court of law, and at the hands of a cross-examining defence lawyer. We were there to be crucified . . . the hell we were going to provide the nails and the hammer.

Saturday arrived, we checked our watches against the telephone time signal, then we went to the club and, for the last time, I sat at the keyboard. I concentrated upon the music, if only to keep my mind from more unpleasant possibilities. As I recall, Jim busied himself at the snooker table but, I have no doubt, the butterflies were performing loops and rolls in *his* stomach, too.

The club shut up official shop and by midnight the usual Saturday night hanky-panky was well under way and Paddy was firmly installed at the peephole.

By 12.30 a.m. I was with Jim, alongside the bar and watching, while pretending *not* to be watching. We'd arranged that Jim should keep Paddy at the bar. Chatting to him and telling an assortment of jokes.

'You've enough dirty stories ready?' I murmured.

'I'll spill beer all over him first,' promised Jim.

At five minutes to one I strolled to the door and, smiling casually, spoke to Paddy.

'There's a pint waiting for you at the bar,' I said. 'I'll take over here till you get back.'

Paddy left, and I took a few deep breaths before quietly unlocking the door, then sliding the top and bottom bolts from their sockets. Then I leaned against the wall alongside the door and waited.

I heard the cars arrive, glanced through the peephole and saw Chalky diving from behind the wheel. I opened the door for them and it was a copybook raid . . . until poor old Chalky got carried away with himself.

The standard pattern in the undercover capers was that the coppers were 'arrested' with everybody else. It should have happened this time. A dozen hairy-chested, uniformed bobbies had charged along the corridor and confronted little more than their number, all doing various things of which the law disapproved. Everybody had been caught with their pants around their knees.

Why, then, should Chalky have risked a riot?

'Right, Wainwright, who was doing what?'

I glanced at Jim and saw that worthy close his eyes in quick and silent prayer. Somebody threw a bottle. It missed, but the thought was there. And having listed all the naughty things everybody was up to, I breathed a little easier when Chalky made amends by, in effect, giving both Jim and me a police escort as we turned to leave the club.

A villain as big as the side of a house pushed his way through the surrounding coppers, and I figured I'd better be ready to guard with my left.

Instead, he grinned, put out a hand, and said, 'You cunning devil. You beat us, fair and square . . . no complaints.'

We shook hands, then we left. Chalky was over the moon. We'd won. But we'd also lost.

Long before the case came to court – long before Jim and I were roasted alive in the witness-box – the club had voluntarily folded. The defending barrister assured the court that it no longer existed and that the officials 'hadn't realised' it had been used for such nefarious goings-on. Not much! By *that* time it had been re-opened under 'new management' and with a new name.

*   *   *

Not every Duty Elsewhere job was as successful as the Keighley episode, and not every colleague was as good a partner as Jim Conboy. As time progressed, I was given some real oddball types to work with. Coppers who obviously thought it was a pushover and who, when the penny dropped that it *wasn't*, developed a sudden attack of cold feet. One clown even assured me that he had to be home by 9 p.m. because he suffered from stomach ulcers, and that was the time he had to swallow pills and potions; that, because of his ulcers, he couldn't possibly drink alcohol or eat anything fried.

Another refused to go within a hundred yards of the dump we were supposedly out to crack.

'What if they think we're coppers?' he wailed.

'We *are* coppers,' I reminded him.

'No – I mean . . . what if they turn nasty?'

'That's their prerogative. *Our* prerogative is to turn nasty back at them . . . that or run like hell.'

'Bugger that for a tale. I'm not paid for *that*.'

We caught the next bus home.

Nevertheless, the success rate slightly outnumbered both the failures and the non-starters and, in the undercover stakes, I became King's blue-eyed boy.

I was also Chalky White's blue-eyed boy after the Keighley job, and he wasn't satisfied until, along with another hopeful, we were detailed to tackle another club, this time at Haworth.

It was a simple, drinking-till-all-hours job and, in honesty, I wasn't too enthusiastic. The licensing laws (then and now) beg to be broken, and every copper knows it. But White said we should, and King said we must, so there wasn't much choice.

Getting in was no problem. We merely walked through the door, signed fictitious names in a dog-eared notebook then ambled to the bar and ordered booze. We hung our macs on a peg, not far from where we were sitting, settled down and waited for time to pass and make what was now quite legal become illegal. In short, it was a doddle.

Except . . . I saw the chap come in, and knew the wicket had suddenly turned very sticky. Haworth is only a few miles from Keighley and club types wander far afield. He was one of the guys Jim and I had clobbered, and I was damn sure he'd spotted me.

'Finish your drink,' I said quietly. 'We're lumbered.'

'Eh?'

'Finish your drink. Don't panic. We collect our macs, then leave.'

'Oh!'

We probably should have panicked. We probably *shouldn't* have finished our drinks.

In fairness, it must be said that it was a superbly organised mock-up. And, without doubt, it *was a* mock-up. The man from the Keighley club said something to the chap behind the bar, he in turn had a whispered conversation with a couple of other blokes, then all hell broke loose. Two groups of wrestling, yelling, heaving club members worked their way towards us in a classic pincer movement. We gulped our beers, stood up and reached for our macs.

That was when the lights went out.

I don't know who hit me. I don't know what he hit me with. All I know is that I returned to the land of the living in the gutter, outside the club, surrounded by police cars and with Chalky White patting my face and looking very worried.

'Who hit you, lad? Who hit you?'

'I don't know.'

'Come on, Wainwright. Who *hit* you?'

'I don't know.'

'We'll book the bloody lot of 'em. Somebody telephoned a triple-niner about the barney. I *guessed* what might have happened. They'll not get away with it, lad. They'll not . . .'

'They've *got* away with it, sir.' I fingered a particularly painful spot at the base of my skull. 'Somebody clobbered me. Retaliation for the Keighley job, at a guess.' I managed a sad smile. 'It had to happen one day.'

Not that I enjoyed being thumped. But at least I was thumped by the opposition. At Todmorden it was a different story.

Strictly speaking – geographically speaking – only half of Todmorden was in Yorkshire. Nevertheless, the West Riding Constabulary accepted the responsibility of policing the whole of the town and, in so doing, nudged its authority over the Lancashire border. It was also (if you recall) the place where I'd first made enquiries about becoming a copper.

And here I was, back again.

A northern villain – a very fly character, wanted for questioning by half a dozen forces – was said to be visiting one of the Todmorden pubs fairly regularly. Usually on a Saturday lunchtime. Coppers, squad cars and even CID wallahs had set traps for this boyo, but he had friends, all of whom knew every policeman within miles, and he *always* received a tip-off.

'Get yourself in there, Wainwright,' instructed King. 'Start being part of the furniture. Then work something out with the local inspector . . . like you did with Inspector White.'

Unfortunately, the Todmorden inspector was a man with a vastly inflated sense of drama. Not for him the quiet tip-off. He required the works . . . Technicolor, wide-screen, all-singing, all-dancing.

'What we'll do, Wainwright, is this. I'll have a word with Superintendent King. Take another man in with you. I'll have men hidden, surrounding the pub. When the chap we're after arrives, let him settle. Let him feel safe. Then tip the wink to your Number Two. He comes to the door of the pub and blows his nose. That's the signal, see? We'll move in from all sides, and make the arrest.'

'It sounds a little complicated, sir.' It was a token objection. He held the rank. I was only the dogsbody.

'Nonsense. You do your bit. I'll make sure the rest goes as smooth as silk.'

Nor did King help matters by lumbering me with a new boy to the Duty Elsewhere lark.

However, on the third Saturday, old Fly Boy duly arrived, bought himself a drink and melted into the gloom at one end of the bar. I figured it wise to let him get a taste of the beer and feel as secure as possible before I sent the new boy outside to blow his nose. Unfortunately, I hadn't the time. A very agitated female rushed into the pub, yelling at the top of her voice.

'Hey, what's up? There's more coppers than Soft Mick outside. One at every corner. And they're all staring across at this place.'

Fly Boy made a dive for the rear exit, I signalled to my pal to have a sudden sneezing fit, he rushed to the door waving a handkerchief as big as a tablecloth, while I dashed off after the quarry.

I saw Fly Boy nip smartly into an outhouse in the rear yard of the pub and, at that moment, a uniformed sergeant, only slightly less than St Paul's Cathedral in width and height, hove into view on overdrive, grabbed me by the scruff of the neck and the seat of the pants and threw me back into the pub. I picked myself up from the scattered tables and chairs and tried again. This time he hit me hard enough to bounce me from one of the room walls.

I'd had enough. I bawled, 'You big, stupid bastard . . . *I'm one of you*,' dodged another side-winder and, as the massive sergeant gave chase, gasped, 'He's in there. In the outhouse. Hit *him*, not me.'

Back at Todmorden Police Station, having slung Fly Boy into a cell, there was much make-believe contrition and empty-phrased apologies. The inspector was highly delighted, the man-mountain with the stripes on his sleeves hadn't the gumption to be anything other than secretly amused and I counted myself fortunate for not having been killed.

What else but to sigh and put it down to experience?

*　　*　　*

There were other Duty Elsewhere details that fell flat on their silly faces, and some which for sheer, brass-faced cheek – plus the fact that the gags may still be being pulled – I prefer to keep to myself. A couple of times I worked alongside Special Branch men and, compared with them, I was a complete amateur, but most of the time I worked either alone or with a partner from the

West Riding.

I had a long spell, and I liked it. It left me all morning and usually most of the afternoon to graft away at textbooks en route to my law degree.

I lived through some spicy moments and, I suppose, I should be carrying scars from the times we came badly unstuck. But I was lucky, and I can't find it in my heart to blame the guys who, during that period, took swipes at me. In their place, I'd have done the same.

Strangely, Avis never worried. As always – as through the far more dangerous war years – she was convinced I'd come out unscathed. But that's Avis. She remains convinced that (even at my present age) I could, if necessary, cross the Polar Ice Cap in jockey shorts and end up with little more than a slight cold.

The pantomime came to an end where it had started. In the billiard room of the West Riding of Yorkshire Constabulary Headquarters.

I'd answered another summons from Detective Superintendent King, and I waited for details of a new job.

'There's a brothel . . .' he began.

'Eh?' I gaped at him.

'One of these country mansion places. It's been turned into a high-class knocking-shop.'

'You want me to go undercover?' I still couldn't quite believe him.

'That's why you're here, lad.'

'Sir.' I chose my words rather carefully. After all, he *was* a detective superintendent. 'I'm a married man. A *happily* married man. Presumably you expect me to go into that place and collect evidence. I take it you'll want the place to be raided. If things go right, there'll be a prosecution, and I'll be required to give evidence . . . as always.'

'As always,' he agreed.

'Sir,' I choked, 'nobody goes into a whore-house merely to read the *Beano*. If it comes off it'll be front-page news, and my wife can *read*.'

'Oh!'

'And if she reads anything like *that* . . . even assuming I did only read the *Beano* . . .'

'So you won't do it?' The penny dropped at last.

'Definitely not, sir.'

I think King was sorry to see me go, but the rules of the game insisted that a single refusal took a man off the Duty Elsewhere list.

As some sort of reward for what I'd done, I was slapped on a Detective Training Course at Wakefield, from 20 November, 1950 until 10 February, 1951. It was meant as a 'thank you' and I appreciated it, if only because it brought me into the company of coppers from other forces, but what it *really* meant was a double-helping of brain-work. The LL.B. slog remained and, on top of it, I had to listen to, and remember, high-powered lectures upon such exotic subjects as 'The Examination of Fibrous and Cellular Matter and Textiles', 'The Pathology of Sexual Offences and Poisons' or 'Bank Accounts, Post Office Enquiries, Companies and the Registration of Business Names Acts'.

Nevertheless, it was a neat close to another entertaining chapter of what I still thought to be an up-and-coming police career.

Elland Mark II

Elland had changed. It had changed considerably. Sam and Ernest had moved to pastures new, Vic had retired, still convinced that he should have made inspector and, indeed, *would* have made insopector had he only found the secret of an entry to the Freemason fraternity. Tommy had gone – but nobody openly mourned *his* loss – and the whole section seemed to be staffed by a miscellany of almost raw recruits.

Vic had been replaced by Colin, and Colin had complained that without a senior constable to carry the load when he was off duty he was being driven up the wall.

Enter Wainwright.

*   *   *

A certain Inspector Barber – a kindly soul, one of the parade of pip-carriers whom Tosh pointedly ignored, and a man I could have happily strangled within three months of accepting the job – conned me into doing that second stint at Elland.

'You'll be in charge when the sergeant's off duty, Wainwright.'

'Yes, sir.'

'You know the town. That's in your favour.'

'Yes, sir.'

'And obviously it's a step in the right direction.'

That was the con. That by showing my mettle as 'acting sergeant' I'd be sporting chevrons in no time at all. And I sucked. I didn't even *ask* about the house.

The house was in Plains Lane and if Plains Lane (as it then was) still remains, somebody, somewhere wants shooting.

It was a terraced house; two-up, two-down, with a main

room that grew fungus on the walls and a kitchen that was long by narrow and in which it was quite impossible to pass without edging sideways. There was a poverty-stricken back garden; the back garden was necessary, because we had to walk the length of it to reach the outside bog.

The bath was in the kitchen. In fact, the bath bloody-near *was* the kitchen. It stood waist-high and was the longest, deepest and widest bath I've ever encountered. Over it was a deal-planked top which during the day was a 'working surface' upon which Avis performed basic culinary experiments, but come evening when we wanted to use the bath this top had to be removed. It weighed a full hundredweight and, having heaved it from its position, there was nowhere in that damn kitchen to put the thing.

Nobody went for a 'quick bath' at that house!

The setting of the house?

Plains Lane was 'unadopted', which meant that it was unsurfaced. In winter we were ankle-deep in mud. In summer we were up to the eyes in dust. In front of us was a partly built crematorium; behind us was the railway goods yard; at the top of the lane was a quarry, visited at ten-minute intervals by large and open lorries; at the bottom of the lane was a ten-storey wool-mill, then a main road, then the canal.

Had somebody taken a street map of Elland, and deliberately searched for the dirtiest, noisiest, most claustrophobic position in the whole of that miserable little township, Plains Lane would have been well placed on the short list.

And this after Clifton police cottage.

*　　　*　　　*

Enter Colin — stage left — and, having entered, he has difficulty in delivering his own lines.

It is hard to describe this newly promoted sergeant who, while working his nuts off to be liked, was utterly incapable of commanding popularity. Some people are like that. Their personality joints seem to have seized up, and they are unable to unbend. When they smile it is a deliberately thought-out facial contortion. When they make a humorous remark, it always seems to have a hint of frost around the edges. Even when they know they're right – and nobody is arguing with them – they give the impression of being unsure.

Towards the end of my second spell at Elland, I think I became as near to being his friend as any man had ever been. It was hard work, but I felt sympathy for the chap. Friendship – the damn-your-eyes, come-hell-or-high-water brand of friendship – was something the poor guy would never understand. It embarrassed him.

Like Vic, he lived alongside and above the police station. Unlike Vic, he allowed his wife free range throughout the building. She was, I think, his second wife and to the rest of us she was a pain in the rump. Colin doted on her and she, while being very much the plain and ordinary type of female, considered herself the *femme fatale* of the Northern Union. Let her hear the main door of the police station being unlocked, opened and closed to admit some member of the section and, within minutes, she'd be in the Charge Office, fluttering her eyelashes, cooing trivialities and generally making an infernal nuisance of herself. That was bad enough, but in addition she tried to be a trouble-maker. Let her meet the wife of one of the Elland coppers in the street and, via innuendo, her imagination would run riot.

'She doesn't half fancy herself.' This from Avis after one such meeting.

'She's cock-happy.' This from Avis's crude husband.

'She says the men can't keep their hands off her.'

'Specifically, her throat.'

'I hope *you* don't encourage her.'

'Darling, a man doesn't mess about with a clapped-out Morris when he has an immaculately tuned Rolls at his disposal.'

'That's not a very nice way of putting it, either.'

Women!

*   *   *

I think the best (or perhaps the worst) case Colin and I worked on in harness was one that started as nothing, then snowballed until, out of sheer desperation, we had to close the file and stop asking questions.

The suspect's name was Noble. His nickname was 'Penguin' because of the way he walked. He was in his mid-sixties, short, and filthy of person. In his dress-sense, his personal hygiene and his general lifestyle he was an abomination to the human race.

I met him for the first time when the gas man reported that Noble's meter had been rifled and the coins stolen.

Noble lived in what we in the wild call a 'low-decker'. One of a terraced row of one-floor pig pens, unfit for human habitation. No 'upstairs', you understand; just the one main room on the ground floor, which did duty as living room and bedroom, plus a poky little kitchenette which held a grimy sink and a gas ring. Two windows. One door. It was about as primitive as you could get and still call it 'home'.

I met Noble, checked that the gas meter had, indeed, been broken open, then waited.

'It happened this morning, while I was out shopping,' he slobbered.

'Shopping?'

'Somebody must have broken in.'

'Broken into *this* place?' And if I was sarcastic I had cause.

'They *must* have. It was like that when I got home.'

Like a well-trained flatfoot, I dutifully examined the two windows and the door.

'How do you think they broke in?' I asked.

'Through the window, maybe.'

'Noble.' I escorted him outside. 'Not a mark. More than that, there's about a dozen years of accumulated paint holding those sash-frames tighter than a miser's fist. Nobody has broken in through either of those two windows.'

'The door then.'

'No marks,' I explained. 'No sign of forced entry. A moderately good Yale lock. Forget the door, Noble. Nobody's forced this door.'

'What then?'

'Who else has a key?'

'Nobody!'

The question was hardly asked before it was answered.

It was answered *too* quickly. That was the first inkling that this was more than a simple gas-meter job. The old nape hairs tingled a little. I chose my questions a bit more carefully.

'Nobody has a key?'

'No. Nobody.'

'On the face of things, this door's been opened with a key,' I explained, patiently.

'I'm the only one who has a key.'

'OK.' I made believe I accepted his assurance. 'But the door hasn't been forced . . . right?'

He nodded, but looked vaguely unhappy.

'So, you must have left somebody in the house when you went shopping.'

'No!'

Again, the reaction was too swift. A lot too swift. Somewhere among this lot a whole bucketful of guilt was hidden.

'No forcible entry,' I said, solemnly. 'Nobody else has a key. Nobody was left in the house.' I paused to let it sink in, then added, 'Get your coat on, Noble.'

'Eh?'

'You're nicked.'

'Eh? Why?' There was real panic there now.

'There's only you left,' I explained. 'It's been done a few hundred times before. Break into your own gas meter, then swear blind it was done while you were out. It has whiskers on . . . and you haven't even tried to be clever.'

'Can we – can we go inside?'

It was patently obvious that I was talking to a very worried man; that there was something here a damn sight more serious than a few bob filched from a gas meter. Among other things, this character was terrified of policemen.

It took me time enough to smoke two cigarettes to tease part of the truth from him and as he talked the sweat ran down the sides of his face. He had, indeed, left somebody in the house when he went shopping. A youngish man; mid-twenties. The young man had flown when Noble had returned home, and with him the cash from the meter.

No, he didn't know the name of the young man; he was the proverbial stranger he'd met in a pub; taken pity on him because he hadn't anywhere to sleep. With a little prodding the name came out. Then the address. Then the worried admission that – witness the still-crumpled and filthy bedclothes on the double-bed in one corner of the only room in the house – they'd shared the same bed.

That was as far as I got when I left Noble.

It must be remembered that in those days (the mid-50s) the word 'gay' still only meant bright and lively. Homosexuality was still known in law as buggery; it was a felony and it carried the penalty of anything up to life imprisonment. The pros and cons of permissiveness are not the province of a mere pavement-basher. As far as I was concerned, I seemed to have stumbled into circumstances that suggested one of the major crimes in the calendar.

That being the case, I visited the young man.

He didn't even hedge his bets.

'Old Penguin?' He grinned lasciviously. 'He's an arsehole hawker. Didn't you know that?'

'Christ!'

'Didn't you *know*?'

I gasped, 'He's one of the most objectionable-looking sods I've met in my life.'

'He knows his business, mate.'

That's how it started. The young man happily dictated a statement, confessing to stealing the cash from the meter, *and* to having regularly humped away for dear life in bed with Noble. More than that, he named names. And when I re-visited Noble he, too, named names.

That was the snowball I'd started. That evening I told Colin what I'd unearthed and he rightly ordered me to visit all the men named. They, in turn, named names. It was never-ending.

In the course of that enquiry I was sickened. Not by the homosexual side of things – I was thick-skinned enough to shrug that off as mere kinkiness – but by the horrendous side-issues I came across.

One miscreant had introduced his unwilling teenage son to the practice, and that son had become so

146

thoroughly disgusted that he pleaded with his doctor to be castrated in an attempt to regain some sort of self-respect. Married men, with attractive wives and fine children, had visited Noble in search of something 'different' in the perversion stakes. Nor were the men we interviewed confined to one stratum of society. From muscle-conscious athletic types to pseudo-academics; from unskilled louts living on the breadline to self-employed businessmen; from teenagers to pensioners.

I began to hate the job; to detest the necessity of knocking at a door and, when somebody answered, dodging and weaving in a vain attempt to allow the man I was after to retain some sort of dignity.

'Why should you want to see me, officer?'

'In private, if you don't mind, sir.'

'I have no secrets from my wife.'

'Nevertheless . . . if you don't mind.'

Then, having got him apart from his wife and family, and told him the purpose of my visit:

'Noble? Who's Noble?'

'He lives at Elland.'

'Really?'

'He insists you've visited his home for the purpose of gross indecency and homosexual practices.'

'That's an outrageous suggestion! That's a disgusting . . .'

'He names you in his statement, sir.'

'I don't give a damn if he —'

'Other men name you in *their* statements.'

'Other – other men?'

'Men we've already interviewed. Men who were present at the time.'

Thereafter would come the pleading. Sometimes the tears. But always the offer of a full confession and, almost always, the names of other men caught up in Noble's foulness. From Elland, of course, but also from Huddersfield, from Bradford, from Halifax and even from Leeds. I couldn't understand it then. I *still* can't understand it. I sought an explanation; I arrested Noble and, while Colin interviewed him for the umpteenth time, I searched the miserable hovel that was such an attrac-

147

tion to so many men. A handful of pornographic photographs – I'd handled far dirtier pictures when searching men brought in for being drunk and disorderly – but beyond that nothing. A filthy bed with grubby sheets. A tiny house that stank of body-dirt and dampness.

Make no mistake, 'love' had no place in this caper. Not even Oscar Wilde's 'love that dare not speak its name'. That I can understand, and could *then* understand; I'd known men who'd lived together as man and 'wife', and I was wise enough to realise that while it was not for me their feelings for each other were both deep and sincere.

But *this*!

Back at the station, Colin had popped Noble back into a cell and in the privacy of the Charge Office I pleaded to call a halt.

'We have more than thirty,' I said. 'God Almighty, the file already makes *War and Peace* look like a short story.'

'There are others,' Colin reminded me.

'We've broken its back, Colin,' I begged. 'Heaven only knows how many marriages we've shattered.'

'That's not *our* fault.'

'I'm starting to feel it's *my* fault. There's a limit . . . and I've reached it.'

Reluctantly, Colin agreed to close the already-too-thick file, and in due course the whole sordid story was told in court. Everybody pleaded guilty, the gutter press had a field day and Noble earned himself seven years behind bars.

At a guess, he had a whale of a time in prison.

* * *

It was not until after Elland that I could afford to buy and run a motor car. That first, clapped-out, pre-war Ford we lovingly coaxed to a top speed of forty and who, as 'Clara', became one of the family. But like every copper I well knew the lethal potential of the internal combustion engine. Not a week went by without its crop of 'Vehicular Accidents' and, because the West Riding was one of a handful of forces from which the Home Office obtained details with which to break down the general statistics into various divisions and sub-divisions, every accident had to be painstakingly tabulated within its own twenty-page booklet.

Nor were the Motor Patrol boys wildly enthusiastic when motor cars collided. Invariably, the pavement-basher was first at the scene and had already made entries in the 'accident booklet'. Thereafter, it remained *his* baby and the wheel merchants were content to put out cones and direct traffic.

Three road accidents occurred during my second spell at Elland. Three very important accidents, in that one affected my whole police career, one showed me up to be an arrogant fool and one gave me more quiet chuckles than I'd ever expected.

Ainley's was a one-in-six climb out of Elland, on the main road to Huddersfield. The trolley-bus took it at a sedate, dowager-like speed. The lorries ground the teeth of their gears as they changed down, then down again as they neared the top of the long haul. Expensive cars took a run at it, and *very* expensive cars seemed not to notice it was there.

Nevertheless, especially in winter, Ainley's averaged us a shunt-up about once a fortnight.

The West Riding County Council had a depot about halfway up Ainley's, on the right hand side. It was strategically placed; a miniature mountain of salted clinker-ash ready for iced-up roads was kept there; various vehicles, lorries and tools were garaged and housed within its confines. And, on this particular afternoon, a county council dumper ground its way up the hill and, without a backward glance and without giving so much as a hint of his intention, the driver swung right for the entrance to the depot.

A *very* expensive automobile was steaming up the hill and, at that moment, was overtaking the council truck. The dumper clobbered the side of the car which spun out of control and we had a fair-to-moderate accident on our hands.

The driver of the car was a Huddersfield doctor, his vehicle was a write-off and, among his other injuries, the driver suffered a broken leg. I was the copper at the scene. An ambulance was sent for and the doctor was carted off to hospital. Five or six council workers who'd been in the depot and who'd seen the accident gave short statements in which they said, very firmly, that the truck driver had been solely to blame . . . and that was that.

I booked the dumper driver for driving without due care and attention and later, at Halifax Magistrates' Court, he was duly convicted and fined.

A nothing. A come-day-go-day traffic accident. One of a thousand. But a couple of years or so later it scuttled all hope I might have had of promotion.

You do not have to be an actuary, nor yet a high-flying insurance broker, to know that a multi-horse-powered solo motorcycle is by far the most dangerous velocipede known to man. Every flatfoot with enough experience to know not to lick his indelible pencil will verify that fact. Marlon Brando showed the world how in *The Wild One* and, since then, the only good news is that the various 'chapters' of Hell's Angels kill or cripple themselves with satisfying regularity.

The two young fools who tried to burn up the lower road leading from Elland to Halifax were of this breed. Subsequent enquiries filled in the details. Earlier that day, in an attempt to coax a few more miles an hour out of it, they'd stripped the machine, then rebuilt it. Having neither the tools nor the know-how, they'd made something of a dog's dinner of this 'souping up' attempt. The bike went fast – as fast as it had previously travelled – but no faster. What they *had* done, although they didn't know it, was screw the rear wheel up.

Thus, in the early hours they were belting along, not a crash-helmet between them, one crouched low over the handlebars and the other riding pillion, with his hands tucked under his upper-shanks in the approved ton-up manner.

That was when the rear wheel suddenly seized solid.

It had nothing to do with the braking system; the brakes hadn't even been applied. Something within the mechanical link between the engine and the rear wheel simply jammed. As firmly and as immediately as if it had hit a brick wall. The rear wheel collapsed, the machine

150

went completely out of control and the fool in front saved his life by the skin of his teeth by hanging on to the handlebars.

The pillion passenger wasn't so fortunate. Still with his hands tucked under his thighs, he took off in a gradually ascending power-climb.

Coming towards them was a milk-lorry; one carrying crates of milk held in position by chains linked to iron stanchions along the sides of the platform. The pillion passenger had just about flattened out, but was still travelling at a ridiculous speed, when the top of his head hit one of the stanchions. He died immediately. A butcher's cleaver couldn't have done a neater job.

That sort of accident brings *everybody* out. Foot Patrol, Motor Patrol, Ambulance, Fire Service and, even at that hour, more rubber-neckers than you can hit with a long stick. There was much measuring, much photographing, much statement-taking from the lorry driver and passing motorists, and the spreading of about a hundredweight of sand in an attempt to disguise the gory mess.

Eventually a Motor Patrol sergeant, who'd taken over the supervision of the activity, suggested that the dead pillion passenger be moved.

'Get the ambulance to drop him off at the morgue, Jack. Take one of the young lads with you. We need to have him stripped for the pathologist before he stiffens.'

It was the same mortuary at which *I* had been initiated into the less pleasant side of sudden death. The same slab, the same poor illumination, the same foul stench. The young copper I'd brought along still had the shine of a police college on his boots. He carried that vague, worried look of somebody afraid that he might not be able to handle the next hour or so of his life. Me? I'd seen it all by this time. I was the senior constable, and there to set an example.

The ambulancemen dumped the corpse on the slab and left. It seemed wise to get the thing done as soon as possible; not to pussyfoot around and, for the sake of my young companion, treat things as nonchalantly as possible.

Undressing a body is not easy, and one of the more

151

difficult jobs is removing the coat. In this case a windcheater.

I vaulted on to the slab, put a foot at each side of the corpse, then gave instructions in as matter-of-fact a tone as I could muster.

'I'll hoist him into a sitting position. You ease his arms out of the windcheater.'

I stooped, grabbed two fistfuls of shirt, then straightened . . . and his glass eye fell out, bounced about six inches on the concrete floor of the morgue, then tinkled and rolled out of sight in a dark corner.

I joined my shattered colleague outside the morgue. He was squatting, with his back to the wall of the mortuary and with his face buried in both hands. He was trembling.

'Don't ask me,' he muttered. '*Please* . . . don't ask me.'

'Don't worry, mate.' I made believe that my shock was less great than his. I took a few deep breaths, then added, 'Stay here. I'll get him stripped and ready for the pathologist.' Then as cold comfort, 'If it's any consolation, you'll never have anything *worse* than that.'

The third accident was also a fatality. Not as gruesome as Accident Number Two, but rather a lesson in pomposity which went very wrong.

Lambert had retired years before and his successor, Lewry, had moved to Doncaster Division and a chief-superintendentship. Verity sat in the superintendent's office at Halifax DHQ. Verity – known as the 'Grey Eminence' – was the ultimate in new brooms. Sweeping clean wasn't good enough for Verity. He wasn't satisfied until the pile had been scrubbed from the original carpet.

It was the first Christmas under Verity – the afternoon of Christmas Eve – and Colin had decided to take some of his annual leave over the Christmas period. Verity had been under my feet all morning. Was I sure I could handle the section during the holiday period? It being Christmas Eve, I must remember to give the seasonal drunks a little elbow room; he didn't want to hear of all the cells being filled with drunken revellers. I mustn't forget that the pubs had an extension; that boozing time was longer than usual. Was I quite sure I knew how to make up the Section Diary? I mustn't lose sight of the fact that policemen always worked harder when everybody else was on holiday. Could I *cope*?

I'd spent most of the morning performing the old yes-sir-no-sir routine while at the same time wishing he'd take a flying leap, and now he'd returned to his gold-plated nest and we, the section, could go about the job of policing Elland.

And now, some fool motorist had opened his offside door without checking his rear-view mirror and knocked a cyclist from his machine.

The cyclist was dead. I'd been ninety-nine per cent sure when they'd loaded him into the ambulance; that steady trickle of blood from the ear after he'd landed on his head was a near-certain sign of a badly fractured skull. I left one of the youngsters at the scene, taking statements and measuring distances, while I rode in the ambulance to Halifax General Infirmary. The doctor pronounced 'Life Extinct' and before they popped the body in the hospital mortuary I went through his clothes. There wasn't a thing to give so much as a hint of the cyclist's identity.

I had a very busy afternoon and evening trying to put a name to the body but when, after midnight, I arrived back at Plains Lane and wished Avis a Merry Christmas, the cyclist was still unidentified.

Christmas Day came and, with it, Verity.

'Have we identified that pedal cyclist yet, Wainwright?'

'Not yet, sir.'

'Have you circulated his description?'

'Yes, sir. To all divisions and neighbouring forces.'

'Missings From Home?'

'Again, all divisions and neighbouring forces. I've asked them to keep the description in mind if anybody's reported missing.'

'What else?'

'I've had the Fingerprint Section out . . . in case he's on file. I've had the Photography Section out. They've taken a morgue shot for circulation if he isn't identified within the next day or two. I managed to get to most of the cycle dealers before they closed shop yesterday. They have a

153

description of the cycle.'

'Nail parings?' quoth Verity, airily.

'Eh?'

'Hair clippings?'

'No. I haven't –'

'Wainwright, you've only half done the job.'

'Sir, I don't think –'

'I don't like sloppy policing, Wainwright. Every avenue . . . right. Get yourself across to Halifax, collect some nail parings and hair clippings, then get them to the Forensic Science Laboratory at Harrogate. *Then* I'll believe you've done all you can do.'

And, with that, he left. And one rather unhappy policeman faced the ghoulish task of taking a bus to Halifax, visiting a hospital morgue and there scraping muck from beneath the fingernails of a corpse and snipping hair from the corpse's head . . . and this, immediately before a lovingly prepared Christmas dinner.

Three days later the cyclist was reported missing from home in a village a few miles away at the other side of Huddersfield; he'd set out for a Christmas cycling holiday in the Pennines and hadn't returned on the day he'd been expected. The body was identified and a Coroner's Inquest was arranged.

For some reason best known to himself, Verity attended the Inquest and, as we strolled from the court to Elland Police Station, he couldn't resist the opportunity.

'Y'know, Wainwright . . . those nail parings and hair clippings.'

'Yes, sir?'

'We didn't have to call one of the forensic scientists to give evidence. With him being reported missing. It wasn't necessary to call the scientist.'

'No, sir.'

'But they had him located.'

'Sir?'

'They knew where he'd come from. To within half a mile. Knew his occupation, knew his age, knew he wasn't married.'

'Oh!'

154

'I gave them a ring this morning. They listed all their findings.' He paused, then added, 'Let it be a lesson, Wainwright. Never underestimate the forensic scientists. They can do wonders.'

I daren't tell him — but if he reads this he'll know — by Verity's yardstick forensic scientists can't do wonders. They can perform miracles.

It was *my* nail parings and *my* hair clippings they'd been tooling around with.

*   *   *

I can name the day and date I first drew and used my truncheon. It was at Elland, at a few minutes to midnight, on Saturday, 10 September, 1955.

I and a colleague had gone to arrest one of the hooligan element. It was a breaking offence, and there wasn't a shadow of doubt about the guy we were after. The only problem was catching him at home. Hence the hour.

We tapped at the door, the young and unhappy wife let us into the house, and there was laddo, sprawling in front of an open fire, having been out consuming more booze than was good for him.

It was my colleague's case, therefore he recited the reason for our visit, followed by the news that the person addressed was under arrest.

Laddo leaned forward, scooped up the poker and dived into action.

In the normal course of events, we would each have grabbed an arm, risked a few bumps and bruises and wrestled the prisoner into enough submission to clip on the handcuffs. But this was no 'normal' episode. The next day (Sunday, 11 September) I was to start annual leave and was due to travel by train to London, there to sit the General Intermediate Examinations in Law. I'd worked long and hard for that moment and a side-swipe from a poker could have made it all a waste of time.

Hence the truncheon. Hence the smart clip above the ear, and the handcuffs in position before laddo recovered from his dizziness.

The next day, having kissed Avis goodbye, I was on my way, complete with suitcase and (I admit) a whole headful of trepidations, to the Big City and the first giant hurdle I had to clear on my self-imposed race for a personal winning post.

I don't know London too well even today. I knew it not at all in those days. I'd crossed it a few times on escort duty, but always via the Underground or in a police vehicle. This time I actually *saw* it, and it frightened the life out of me. As a native of Leeds I'd counted myself something of a city boy, and in truth Leeds *was a* big place when placed alongside most other towns in the North. But compared with London, Leeds was little more than an overgrown village.

My reason for being there, and the sheer size of the place, combined to squeeze me dry of any confidence I might have had.

A taxi from King's Cross took me to the University of London complex and, from there, I was taken to a set of apartments somewhere in the far distance: a bedsitter, with use of the bathroom, and breakfast provided. I was to report back at the university the next day.

God, I was lonely!

I needed an evening meal and I needed to talk to Avis. I found a telephone kiosk; assured her I'd arrived safely, then found a not-too-grimy café and enjoyed a snack. Then I asked the way to the nearest cinema.

I was of the opinion (and still hold that same opinion) that on the evening before an examination, and however important or tough that examination, the time has arrived to relax a little. To hell with swatting and recapitulation. If you don't know it *then*, you won't know it next morning.

The film was Alexander Korda's *Rembrandt*. It wasn't new in those days and today it is very occasionally shown on late-night TV. But the performances of Charles Laughton, Elsa Lanchester and Gertrude Lawrence still stir the memories of that evening; of that dismal room with its none-too-comfortable bed; of a restless night, made more restless by the surfacing of Underground trains directly under my window; of the silent breakfast of smoked haddock, weak tea and wafer thin slices of bread.

I was haunting the neighbourhood of the university long before the ten o'clock start-time. I worried about the ink in my fountain pen and, to be on the safe side, bought a bottle of expensive ink as a long stop. *Mauve*-coloured ink, for God's sake! After that a quick cup of tea in a nearby café and, on the way, the purchase of a paperback to while away the time in my lonely bedsitter that evening. The Penguin edition of *Famous Trials of Marshall Hall*.

We were a mixed bunch; we, the scores of hopefuls who entered that huge examination hall and made our way to our respective, one-man desks. There was a scattering of ladies, but most of us were men, and we ranged through all ages, from early twenties to the past-sixty mark. About a third of us were coloured; from Asia, Africa and the West Indies, with a fair sprinkling of orientals. We were both Internal and External students, and the London University ties identified some of the former. The young chap at the desk on my right was obviously from the Far East; we exchanged timid smiles of encouragement, but they were very fixed smiles. At the desk in front of me sat a tonsured monk, complete with habit . . . we two, at least, were External.

From the front the invigilator carefully explained the dos and don'ts and, at 10 a.m. sharp we uncovered the examination papers and bent our heads to our tasks.

That first paper worried me. If I was going to plough it would be on 'History and Outlines of Roman Private Law'. Nine questions. Six to be answered. Questions like: 'Consider the authority of *senatusconsulta* at different periods of Roman History,' or 'What were the main peculiarities of the *acto injuriarum*?' I chose the six I thought I could answer, and tried to forget everything else in the world. The invigilator strolled between the desks. There was a slight disturbance when he quietly ordered one of the examinees from the room; a folded newspaper was peeping from the chap's jacket pocket, and odds and ends like that were forbidden. I took time off to send a short prayer aloft that the invigilator didn't spot the outline of *Famous Trials of Marshall Hall* in the pocket of *my* jacket.

One o'clock came, and we put down our pens. I hadn't yet had occasion to use my mauve-coloured ink. The truth was I hadn't yet been able to open the damn bottle.

In the university's cafeteria-style restaurant, there was much milling around and a great babble of chatter. Bursts of relieved laughter showed that most of the others had looked upon that first paper as the terror of the intermediate exam. The relief that it was over bonded us together, and the atmosphere of camaraderie was not too far removed from that I'd known in the de-briefing room immediately after the safe return from an operational flight during the war.

At the table at which I sat the talk was of the morning's paper, the questions and the various possible answers. The ever-present wit put good sense in a nutshell.

'Come on, folks. Let's not waste time doing a post-mortem on Roman Law. Let's have a pre-natal on Constitutional Law.'

That was the afternoon paper. This time ten questions, six to be answered, on 'Constitutional Law.' Compared with the morning's stint, it was easy. Such questions as 'Describe the present composition and jurisdiction of the Judicial Committee of the Privy Council,' or 'Discuss fully the procedural advantages of the Crown in litigation' could be taken at a steady trot and by 5.30 p.m. I was satisfied with at least one set of my answers.

Thereafter a reasonably good meal at a café, a telephone call to Avis, then back to my temporary accommodation to read about Marshall Hall before climbing into bed.

The next day there were two more sessions – 10 a.m. until 1 p.m. devoted to questions on 'The English Legal System' and 2.30 p.m. until 5.30 p.m. on 'Elements of the Law of Contract' – and, as I put the top on my pen, I'd had enough; my suitcase was waiting and a taxi saw me to King's Cross ready to take an early evening train north, back to Elland and an anxiously waiting wife.

By mid-October I'd been notified of success; I'd passed the intermediate examination and, already, I was head down mugging away like crazy for the finals. I was buckling a little under the strain and (of course) it had to happen. By Christmas I ached all over. I figured it was a touch of flu, and went on working. I got gradually worse and, eventually, Avis chased me off to the GP. I'd pushed my way through a moderately bad case of shingles. During the 'blister' period I'd kidded myself that it was nothing more serious than a recurrence of the prickly heat bouts we'd all suffered in West Africa during the war; camomile lotion had eased the itching and aspirins had deadened some of the pain.

The GP was a good man. We'd met and liked each other when our respective jobs had crossed paths. He smiled ruefully as he delivered judgement.

'You're pushing yourself too hard. You've worked through the worst part of it. The blisters arrive when the pain's on the way out. Take a month's sick leave . . . it might help you to see sense.'

I have deliberately gone into details of that intermediate exam trip to London, and all it entailed. The pantomime was repeated at the finals, therefore we can take it for granted, and push the slog for that infernal LL.B. aside. Suffice that it was there, for years to come, and that it took its toll.

*   *   *

It might be best to compare Ned with Colin, the sergeant. Colin was just about the most introverted man I'd ever met; he was incapable of relaxing enough to become *really* friendly with anybody; maybe he was unsure of himself, maybe he'd been let down very badly at some time in the past . . . I could never figure it out, and I never pressed. Ned, on the other hand, was a deal *too* sure of himself. Ned was all top-dressing and flash; his humour was snide and at times lavatorial; his whole existence was built upon the firm belief that the world owed him a living . . . and if it didn't he was going to take it anyway.

As a copper he was remarkably unreliable; go with him to an accident, a disturbance, a crime and, while *you* were busy, Ned would have the unpopular knack of disappearing into the far distance, to reappear (probably at the nick) when all the tempers had been soothed and all the crumbs had been swept up. When Colin was off duty, and

I had the wearisome task of being in charge of the section, Ned would duly report for duty at 6 a.m. or 2 p.m. or 10 p.m. Thereafter it was anybody's guess as to his whereabouts. He was certainly rarely where he *should* have been and, for all practical purposes, the section had to be policed with a man short.

I was not too keen on Ned.

I was even less keen when, one evening, while I was off duty sick with the lingering backlash of shingles, he called at our home in Plains Lane and unburdened himself about Colin.

'Something you ought to know,' he said, as he lowered himself into an armchair.

I waited.

'Colin,' he continued. 'He took a five pound Christmas present from one of the mill owners.'

'So?' I was puzzled.

'It's not allowed.'

'It's not allowed,' I agreed. 'That doesn't mean it isn't *done*.'

'I'm reporting him.'

'Go right ahead.' I didn't like the guy, and saw no good reason to hide my distaste. 'If you feel so strongly about it – or if you feel *you* should have had a share of the fiver – go ahead and report him. You don't need *my* permission.'

'No, I'm reporting him to *you*.'

'I'm off duty, sick,' I reminded him.

'You're still senior constable.'

'No way,' I assured him, 'am I going to come "on duty" merely to listen to that sort of unsubstantiated crap. You may be right. You may be wrong. I've no intention of moving an inch to prove things either way. Hawk your spite elsewhere, Ned. I've better things to do.'

And that should have been it, but it wasn't.

I reported back on duty and a couple of days later I was in charge of the section. Ned arrived at the police station at a few minutes to ten, ready for night patrol.

'Right,' he said. 'I'm reporting it now. You aren't off duty sick this time. And you're acting sergeant.'

'You're making trouble,' I warned him.

'I'm doing what I *should* do.'

'That,' I said sarcastically, 'makes a pleasant change.'

'Are you going to accept the complaint or not?'

And at that moment the inspector walked into the station.

Inspector Payne. He wasn't of the calibre of Tosh, but he was a very decent, very understanding man. He didn't know it, but he'd arrived at *exactly* the right moment.

We greeted each other, then I said, 'I think this constable has something he wants to report, sir.'

'Really?'

Ned frowned mild panic and said, 'I was reporting it to Constable Wainwright, sir. I think it's up to *him* . . .'

'And I,' I smiled, 'would have had to pass the report on to *you*. Second-hand. I think it best that you receive the report personally. Then you can ask what questions you think necessary.'

Payne was no mug. He could see I was in some sort of invidious position, so he looked directly at Ned and said, 'Right, Constable. Let's be hearing what you have to say. Wainwright can witness that I duly note whatever you have to report.'

Then it came.

Colin had accepted the five-quid Christmas present from the mill owner. Colin sometimes helped himself to coal for his own fire from the official police station bunker. Colin helped himself to light bulbs meant for use in the police station. Colin took constabulary pencils from the stationery cupboard for use in the house. We even descended as low as toilet paper: provided by a caring constabulary for coppers taken short, but taken by Colin for use in his own living quarters.

Ned went completely overboard. In retrospect, I think the crazy man was gunning for both Colin and me in the hope that I'd sit on the complaint and, in so doing, give him a double target. Why? I truly don't know, other than that he was that sort of a guy; the kind of clown who figures the easy way to the top is to heel as many of the opposition into the mud as possible.

'Is that it then?' growled Payne.

'Yes, sir.' Ned's voice was tight. Maybe it was emotion, maybe it was fear, at what he'd started. 'I thought somebody should know.'

'*I* know,' Payne wasn't enjoying this any more than I was. He snapped, 'Carry on with your patrol, Constable.'

I followed Ned to the door of the police station. Out of earshot of Payne, I gave him good advice.

'The beat tonight. Don't leave it. Be precisely where you should be for the next eight hours. Don't put a foot wrong. So far I've never fizzed anybody, but there's always a first time.'

Back in the office, Payne was waiting for me. He looked a troubled man.

'I can't sweep it under the carpet, Wainwright,' he said, sadly.

'No, sir.'

'With a man like that, having spewed it out, he'd go above me. He's out for blood.'

'I don't know why,' I confessed.

'The sergeant's been foolish,' sighed Payne.

'No more than that.'

'Up top, they'll call it theft. The coal, the light bulbs, the pencils.'

'The toilet paper,' I murmured, in disgust.

'There'll *have* to be an enquiry. A personal ballocking from me wouldn't be enough. It wouldn't satisfy *him*.'

'I don't think it would,' I agreed.

'Did you know anything about any of this?' he asked.

'No, sir,' I said truthfully. 'Only what I've been told . . . which is less than what *you've* just been told. I haven't asked around. Everything's hearsay as far as I'm concerned.'

'Er – don't tell the sergeant.'

'No, sir.'

'I'll get things moving tomorrow morning. I'll keep you informed. Personally informed. You'll know exactly what's happening, what's going to happen and when it's going to happen. But – er – *don't* tell the sergeant.'

Which, as I read the nuance, meant '*Do* tell the sergeant – don't let's smash a man's career on a piddling little thing like this – but don't tell *me* you've told the sergeant.'

And that's how it went.

I stayed late that night and was up and at the station before Colin walked the few yards of corridor which brought him on duty. I spun the fanny a little – if only to guard my own back – and, offhandedly, told him of the 'rumour' I'd heard about County Constabulary Stores organising a clamp-down on pencils, light bulbs, and such, being used other than where they should.

The following afternoon, I noticed the extra pencils in the stationery cupboard and the extra light bulbs in the general store-room. Colin was behaving sensibly.

That evening I was waiting for Detective Sergeant Garnett; I was expecting him because Payne had warned me of his visit. That was OK. Garnett was a nice enough chap. He was doing his job, but he wasn't tearing up any trees.

'Do you know anything about all this, Jack?' he asked.

'No more than you know.'

'He's a right little toe-rag.'

'Ned?'

'What the hell does he hope to gain by it?'

'Ask him,' I suggested.

'All accusations. He's given a statement, but it doesn't mean much. I've checked round Colin's place. There's nothing to substantiate the statement. Just the Christmas present.'

'You've checked that?'

'Oh, yes.' Garnett sounded distinctly unhappy. 'I traced the mill owner. He gave a statement. He didn't *want* to, but what the hell? He hadn't much choice.' He sighed heavily. 'We haven't enough with the bent bastards. We're reduced to playing nasty tricks on each other.'

'Some of us,' I agreed. 'What next?'

'I send a report of my findings to Headquarters. *They* take it from here.'

Meanwhile Ned was behaving impeccably. Never late on duty. Always being exactly where he should be. Never putting a foot wrong. Nor was he as quick off the mark with his tongue as he had been. He was, I think, a little scared at what he'd done.

One day he asked me, 'Does Colin know yet?'

'I haven't told him,' I said, and it was no more than the

truth.

'I was justified,' he insisted.

'If you think so.'

'Well, don't *you*?' he demanded.

'Not too long ago,' I said nastily, 'we fought a war because some prat thought he was "justified".'

It was a harsh thing to say, but I was the miserable pig-in-the-middle. For the last few days I'd had an inkling of how Judas must have felt. Colin counted me as his friend, and I knew he was heading for a cropper, but couldn't warn him without kyboshing my own future in the force. Maybe part of it was self-preservation amounting to near-cowardice on my part. Certainly some of it was my own doubt about how Colin would react if I risked things and told him what was brewing up behind his back. With some men I wouldn't have hesitated. With Colin I hadn't become close enough to make a firm assessment.

I was a very unhappy policeman, and my only hope was Inspector Payne.

Payne didn't let me down.

I was on the late-night shift – 6 p.m. until 2 a.m. – and, as I stood at a telephone kiosk, Payne's car drew up at the kerb. He motioned me into the vehicle and for a few moments the talk was the normal exchange at such times. Had anything happened while I was on duty? Had I checked all the lock-up property? What time did I go off duty? Then there was a silence while Payne lighted a cigarette.

'I saw the report Sergeant Garnett sent to Headquarters,' he remarked.

'Yes, sir?' I was there to say as little as possible.

'Just the money. The five pounds from the mill owner. That's all it boils down to.'

'Yes, sir.'

'Pity he took it. Pity he *kept* it.'

'Yes, sir.'

Tosh himself couldn't have put it better. The emphasis on that one word was slight, but enough to show a let-out . . . if we had the guts to take it.

After another pause he said, 'What's your duty tomorrow, Wainwright?'

'Two-to-ten, sir.'

'Have you any clerical work?'

'The usual. Nobody can ever quite catch up with it.'

'Tomorrow afternoon . . .' He drew on the cigarette. 'I'd like to know. Detective Chief Superintendent Metcalfe is coming in from headquarters tomorrow afternoon to confront the sergeant about the five pounds he received. If you *can* find enough clerical work to keep you in the police station, then let me know the outcome when Mr. Metcalfe's gone.'

Payne had done his best. Garnett had done his best. But Metcalfe was a shark among minnows compared with those two. Metcalfe would chew Colin to shreds, then spit him out and enjoy the process; that was the reputation he had, and he'd worked very hard to earn it.

That night – well after midnight – I took the chance that had to be taken.

Colin and I were alone in Elland Police Station. Colin was putting the finishing touches to the sergeant's paperwork and was just about ready to go off duty.

'Colin.' I spoke his name, to attract his whole attention.

'Yes?'

'One of the local mill owners gave you a five-quid Christmas present.'

'What!' The reaction was as if I'd jabbed him with a needle.

'One of the local mill owners.' It wasn't *too* comfortable for me, either. 'He gave you a Christmas box of five quid. You kept it.'

'Who says so?'

'*I* say so.'

'Why the devil should you think –'

Very deliberately, I interrupted, 'George Metcalfe will be out here to say so tomorrow afternoon.'

'Eh?'

'Complete with a statement from your friend, the mill owner.'

'Oh, Jesus Christ!'

Poor Colin. He virtually collapsed into the desk chair and lowered his head on to his hands. To his credit he never even hinted that *I* might be the person responsible

165

for his sudden misery. But he did ask, and I told him. Then, having given him enough time to start thinking in a straight line, I did what Payne had hinted I should do.

'You didn't give a receipt for the money?' I asked.

'Good God, no. It wasn't the sort of –'

'Make a receipt out.'

'Eh?'

'You have your personal Receipt Book. Make the man a receipt for the five quid, and back-date it.'

'That's not much good.' Damn the man! He wasn't using his gumption enough to meet me even halfway. I was having to spell it out to him in cat-sat-on-the-mat language. He continued, 'We carry our personal Receipt Books around with us. Force Standing Instructions. All I'd be doing –'

'We're *supposed* to carry our Receipt Books. You forgot. You left it in your desk drawer . . . accidentally. When you arrived back here to make out a receipt, intending to drop it off at the first opportunity, you slipped the original copy into your notebook. That leaves the carbon copy in your Receipt Book.'

'Oh!' Bells were starting to ring.

'Do you have a fiver?' I asked.

Colin nodded.

I glanced at the Police Widows and Orphans Benevolence Fund collecting box on one corner of the shelf and said, 'The fiver goes in there. The receipt's made out accordingly.'

'Ah!' The dawning smile was almost beatific.

'You are a very surprised man.' I briefed him very carefully. 'You know *nothing* about Ned's backdoor antics. You don't even ask. A certain amount of outrage might be called for . . . but don't overdo it. Metcalfe's a man-eater. Don't give him the chance to bite. If we're lucky – *very* lucky – the most he can do is carpet you slightly for not carrying your Receipt Book around with you.

That's how we played it, and it came off. It was a little like knitting gossamer and – magnificent copper that he was – Metcalfe obviously didn't believe a word and didn't take kindly to being outflanked. Payne was delighted. I rather think Ned was more than a little relieved.

Within the week a transfer arrived at Elland.

I was on my way to Bentley, and to what was a recognised 'punishment beat'. Everything in life has to be paid for, and Metcalfe wasn't the breed of man to give anybody cheap rate.

Sports and Pastimes

To paraphrase Dr Samuel Johnson, policemen enjoying themselves is like a dog walking on its hind legs: they do not do it well, but the surprise is that they can do it at all.

Yet in those days it was not for the want of trying.

In a city force, one of the highlights of the year was (and still is) the Police Ball. County Constabularies could never organise one function on such a grand scale. Instead we had Section Dances.

The trick was to get *yours* under way, and get the date fixed, before any of the neighbouring sections. Thus it was possible to edge it towards a point as near to the Christmas/New Year period as possible and snatch the initiative from all rivals by having *your* shindig taking place while the holiday spirit was still flowing freely. You had to break even. Headquarters said so. On the other hand, if you *didn't* break even, the safety-net of the Sports Fund would help out . . . but only after a very close scrutiny which invariably found fault all round.

Every year – regardless of the section – the Section Dance was a complete cock-up, yet every year – and in every section – a notice was pinned on the board, usually in the first week of September, announcing the first meeting of the 'dance committee'. It was a self-styled body, comprising as many members of the section as could be coaxed into attending, and it made up its rules as it went along.

Come with me, and play fly-on-the-wall at a typical first meeting. A very normal, very ordinary, 'dance committee' comprised the section sergeant, most of the constables – say, half a dozen – and the visiting inspector.

Sergeant: 'Right, are we all here? Let's get started. Somebody take the telephone off the hook so we aren't

168

interrupted. First, I'll propose Inspector A as chairman. Who'll second that?'

Constable X raises his hand.

Sergeant: 'Any other nominations?'

Nobody says a word.

Sergeant: 'All in favour say "Aye".'

There is a chorus of muttered 'Aye's.'

Inspector: 'Thank you, Sergeant. I can't very well be here all the time, so I suggest we have a deputy chairman. I propose Sergeant B as deputy chairman. Who'll second that proposal?'

Constable X again raises his hand.

Inspector: 'Any other nominations?'

Again nobody says a word.

Inspector: 'All in favour please show.'

There is a second chorus of muttered 'Aye's'.

This comedy continues until Sergeant B and Constable X have gathered to their respective bosoms the jobs of dance treasurer, dance organiser, master of ceremonies, ticket organiser, buffet boss... and everything else deemed necessary to ensure that Sergeant B and Constable X (under the supervision of Inspector A) take over the running of all aspects of the dance.

Then...

Sergeant: 'Right, first things first. Let's decide upon the venue.' (For some God-only-knows reason he always pronounces it 've-an-you'.)

Inspector: 'I think I can help there. I'm sure I can get us the use of the room above the club... like we had last year.'

Those in the know realise he means *his* club – the local Conservative Club or, sometimes, the local Constitutional Club – and they also know he has only to ask. Because of who he is, nobody at the club would risk his displeasure by suggesting payment for the use of the room.

The inspector is dutifully thanked for his generosity, then the date of the dance is agreed.

Sergeant: 'Now. About price of admission. I suggest the same as last year.'

Inspector: 'There was a certain amount of rowdyism last year.'

169

Sergeant: 'I'm sorry about that, sir. Some of the wrong element were allowed entrance.'

Inspector: 'I think we should double the price of the tickets. Keep the hooligans out.'

Sergeant: 'We wouldn't sell enough tickets.'

Thereafter follows mild argument. Constable X agrees with the sergeant. The inspector gives ground reluctantly. Even sulkily. The sergeant smooths things over with the same promise he gave last year. The same promise he gives every year.

Sergeant: 'Tell you what I'll do, sir. I'll arrange for a couple of uniformed Specials to be on duty at the door. They'll nip trouble in the bud before it starts.'

Inspector: 'Are you sure?'

Sergeant: 'Positive, sir. Leave that side of things to me.'

Fiddling, unimportant matters are then discussed at length. The band. What time the dance should start. What time it should end. Which firm should be approached about the buffet. The cloakroom arrangements.

Other than the sergeant and Constable X, few of those present make suggestions and, when they do, the suggestion is swiftly disposed of as ridiculous/outrageous/plain barmy.

On cue, the inspector glances at his watch.

Inspector: 'I'm afraid I have an appointment. However, we've ironed out the kinks, got things under way. I'll leave what remains in your hands, Sergeant.'

Sergeant: 'Leave it to us, sir. I'll keep you informed.'

The inspector leaves, never to be seen again before the evening of the dance and, as deputy chairman, the sergeant comes into his own.

Sergeant: 'Right, now we've got rid of that pillock, we can get down to important matters.'

The most important matter is the booze. Which of the town's publicans should be given the job of providing liquid refreshment. Provide – not necessarily *sell* – it being understood that behind the official bar there will be a 'private bar'; a room, made available to all members of the section (and whichever guest he asks to accompany him) where free wallop is readily available. Wallop of all kinds and in unlimited quantities. In return for which the limited 'extension' granted by the licensing magistrates will be pointedly ignored, and the official bar will be allowed to remain open until both brewery and distillery run dry.

The second most important matter is the 'knife and fork do'. The buffet firm must be made to clearly understand that the tit-bits openly on display don't mean a thing. In the background, and out of sight of the hoi polloi, there is a sit-down job where *real* nosh is served, piping hot, to those in the know. Buckshee, of course . . . they can charge as much as they like for the sandwiches.

Thereafter, less important matters. Who will be given free tickets. From whom must 'donations' be cadged. Which shops will *not* be approached with a view to them providing spot prizes . . . given that, except for this small minority, every other shop in the town *will* be approached.

From all of which it will be apparent that there was much more to organising a Section Dance than met the eye.

I attended no more than four such dance committees in twenty years of service. I attended only two dances. It pained me to see my colleagues enjoying themselves with such ponderous determination. After midnight, on the night of the dance, more people seemed to be arguing than dancing. Rank didn't matter – correction, wasn't *supposed* to matter – at these functions, and things were said and done that lasted well into the new year and even rankled when the *next* Section Dance came round.

They were breeding grounds of future spite and hotbeds of never-ending hatred.

On one occasion a Motor Patrol constable, well in his cups, had a difference of opinion with a uniformed inspector. The Motor Patrol man ended the disagreement by snarling 'Why don't you bloody well drop dead?'

Next day the uniformed inspector did just that.

If, however, you were like Avis and me, non-gregarious and not caring a damn if some of the socially minded coppers muttered the words 'stuck up', you could give both dance committees and Section Dances a very wide berth. We weren't 'against' them – we merely didn't want to be a part of them.

What you couldn't opt out of, however, was gardening.

On the theory that, if you look hard enough and long enough, you can find an advantage in *everything*, that much can be said of the Plains Lane house. It had nil garden in front and a pocket-handkerchief-sized patch of weeds at the rear. it was near-unique. Every other police house I knew had a garden. A large garden. Usually back and front. Indeed, some gardens – the one at Clifton police cottage, for example – amounted to a scaled-down country estate. And, like the interior decorating, the garden was subjected to scrutiny by the inspector, or chief inspector, to make sure it was being kept neat and tidy.

I like gardens, but I loathe gardening. One may, indeed, be 'nearer to God in a garden' but for my money only because you've damn near killed yourself growing things you can buy for a few pence at the nearest greengrocer's shop. Consequently, I kept my gardens neat enough to pass inspection (just) but grew only that which required the minimum of attention. One year, for example, I concentrated upon lettuce; I scattered the seeds and pricked out the young seedlings with great care and precision. We ended up with enough lettuce to feed the whole neighbourhood and, after feeding the neighbourhood, sold the rest to a travelling greengrocer at a penny a head in order that he might flog it farther afield. Another year it was broad beans. Yet another I recalled Dad's skill at planting chrysanthemum cuttings and that autumn we had almost half an acre of chrysanths . . . all the same colour!

That, then, was the general pattern. But on average once a year, I suffered a flush of guilt and for perhaps two weeks I tried to make up for lost time. I became that most demented of men, a spasmodic gardener. I remembered Dad, and his flawless allotment. I remembered my brother-in-law's garden, with not a weed in sight. If they could do it so could I.

I bought and borrowed books on gardening.

There are hundreds of books on the subject – thousands of them – and they're all so infernally high-minded that they add up to a big fat zero.

To illustrate what I mean, take candytuft. Candytuft is a nice, everyday flower. A typical 'country' flower. Nothing flamboyant, nothing exotic, just . . . candytuft. I consulted the books. Not a mention. Not even a hint. There *was a* flower called *Iberis sempervirens*. (And at this moment, I've had to look it up; I can hardly pronounce it, much less spell it.) Candytuft! I swear – that's what the hotshot horticulturalists call candytuft – *Iberis sempervirens*. By the time I'd worked *that* one out I'd gone off the boil.

In a moment of weakness the same book unbent itself enough to mention Michaelmas daisies – by that name! I was interested. Both Avis and I rather like Michaelmas daisies, so I read on.

It didn't take long. The instructions were short and to the point. 'See aster.'

I dutifully saw aster. 'China or Common Callistephus. See annuals.'

That, I think, is when I packed it in for that year, and returned the book to the shelves.

Gardening books no longer interest me. I have long realised that they concern themselves primarily with creepy-crawlies. Their authors adore garden pests, list them carefully and describe them lovingly. They have plenty to go at. Caterpillars; wireworms; cut-worms; millipedes; blackfly; greenfly; leafhoppers; root fly; carrot fly; narcissus fly and many, many more. Every plant, shrub and tree has its own private little fly; its own personal bug. The list is endless. You name it . . . the chances are you've *got* it.

Nor is that all. I have not yet mentioned the *diseases* and, if the pests don't get them first, the plants will certainly succumb to one of the diseases.

All of which proves my own long-held theory. That gardening books are written not by gardeners, but by frustrated undertakers. They explain why and how every plant in the world will die, and concern themselves not at all about what it's likely to look like or taste like, if it lives. All, that is, except twitch . . .

Twitch. Every police garden I ever viewed – every

173

garden I ever owned – grew (and still grows) twitch. It is the toughest grass in creation. It could well be the toughest *plant* in creation. I have no doubt that it has some jaw-cracking name but, up north, it is known as twitch . . . and it has 'em all licked.

I was told by pessimistically inclined experts that it is virtually indestructible, other than by spending every waking moment in a stooped position removing its long, tough roots by hand. It was an exercise I refused to even contemplate. Twitch, as far as I was concerned, was 'grass', and grass could be cut periodically.

That, then, was gardening, and an occupation encouraged by our lords and masters in the force. We were bobbies. Ergo, we were also gardening enthusiasts.

The hell we were.

Or, at least, the hell *one* of us was.

* * *

If I hated, and still hate, gardening, I loved and still love cricket. Nor, be it understood, merely 'White Rose' cricket. I have watched and enjoyed the warm glow of true appreciation when legends have played that greatest of all games. Bradman and Ponsford, Larwood and Hammond, Sutcliffe and Leyland . . . and all the giants between and since.

I have played, and enjoyed playing. More often than not I have played behind the stumps; and neither Duckworth nor Evans were more determined to scoop up that 'loose one' sent down by an erratic and inaccurate fast bowler. I'd played for my school, and in the RAF I'd played for my squadron.

I was, therefore, tempted and fell. I played 'police cricket' . . . but only once.

It was a local knockout tournament. Local firms and local factories had entered teams and the local police subdivision wasn't to be outdone. We won the toss and the chief inspector (who was also the captain) decided to bat. The batting list bore no resemblance to cricketing ability. The chief inspector was in first, with the inspector. Then followed the two sergeants, in order of seniority. Thereafter (also in order of seniority) the lowly constables. The same thing applied with the bowling. The chief inspector opened at one end, with the inspector at the other. When *they'd* used up their quota of overs, the two sergeants took over.

That, however, was only the basics. When the chief inspector walked out to bat, the 'reserve' went with him. The twelfth man was the chief inspector's 'runner'. There was damn-all wrong with the chief inspector, you understand; other than, that is, that he *was* the chief inspector and, as such, there to hit (or miss) the ball, but not to run between the stumps.

Similarly, when he'd ended his bowling stint, he took over on the boundary, as an out-fielder. I, too, covered the out-field. All of it, other than the bit where the chief inspector's feet covered the turf. I ran myself ragged that evening. On more than one occasion I had to race *past* that lunatic chief inspector to save the ball reaching the boundary-line.

One evening of that brand of 'police cricket' was enough for me. We lost the match – of course we did – and, thereafter, the team lost every other match without my assistance.

* * * ,

In a book like this there must be wisdom after the event. Equally, and try as he might, the author cannot remove every slant and every personal bias.

I know men of my own age who looked upon the annual dances as a very special part of their police lives. They weren't twisters, they weren't lickspittlers, they weren't skivers. But they *were* dancers. They enjoyed ballroom dancing at all its levels. Ask them, therefore, and their memories of section dances will vary greatly from mine.

Equally, the sportsmen, the men who played cricket for the County Constabulary. They bowled and batted according to merit, and not because of either rank or length of service. That sub-divisional team was a one-off affair, but that it *could* happen remains a disgrace to a magnificent game as much as it was a disgrace to the men who made up the team.

For myself, I was a copper and, other than being Avis's husband, that's all I was. My world was limited, my interests were pathetically few. And yet I was content. Not once did I feel I was losing out on anything. I had all I needed for complete happiness and, as far as I was concerned, I led as full a life as I wished to lead.

Bentley

By the time I reached Bentley I was – modesty aside – a moderately good copper. Nevertheless, until Colin and I tangled with Metcalfe, all my policing had been done in Halifax Division, one of the 'textile' divisions of the force. Now it was Doncaster Division which, along with Rotherham Division, made up the South Yorkshire 'mining' divisions. One of the 'tough' divisions in which thick-ear policing had been developed into a fine art.

I was also learning, the hard way, about the workings at the top end of the scale. About the weave and counter-weave within the sacrosanct corridors of Force Head-quarters.

The Chief Constable was Sir Henry Studdy. He'd taken over as chief from the rank of captain in the Palestine Police. Outside the Met, he was the boss-man of what was arguably the largest force in the UK, and he was ambitious. His next step up *had* to be one of Her Majesty's Inspectors of Constabulary; there was no other place to go. This, in turn, meant keeping his face to the fore at the Home Office, which meant he spent an uncommon amount of time in London prowling the precincts of Whitehall. The day-to-day running of the force, there-fore, was left to two assistant chief constables.

This was the situation for years; it remained the situation until Studdy retired (without his HMI) and a new chief constable took over and tried to disentangle the skein of intrigues and counter-intrigues which, by that time, had become a near-accepted way of life. It is known as 'police politics' and it still goes on, even though the writers of detective stories either don't know about it or rarely mention it. But rarely was it so open or so destructive as it was in the West Riding Constabulary during the period of which I write.

In that sort of set-up, then, and with a man like Metcalfe – a supreme copper, but also an utterly ruthless man – in a position where he can 'manipulate', he will, in effect, run the force. Metcalfe certainly did. Both Colin and I had been made well aware of that basic fact and, within the next few years, I was to learn (via myself and other coppers) that to cross Metcalfe was to commit professional suicide.

Metcalfe had dumped me at Bentley. Specifically, on Toll Bar Beat.

* * *

Bentley was famous for one of the largest pits in the Yorkshire Coalfield. It sat astride the A19, and the A19 left Doncaster and arrowed its way north – more or less alongside the A1 – until it reached the border of Scotland.

Coal and the railway workshops. At a guess, about half the male population of Bentley worked in one or the other. They were Yorkshiremen, but a different breed of Yorkshiremen from my home town of Leeds, and even more different from the Yorkshiremen of the Dales. Not better, not worse . . . just different.

It was a busy section. It ran to three sergeants, working in eight-hour shifts, plus a live-in inspector. But it only had two outside beats, and Toll Bar was one of them.

To give an illustrative yardstick, in Halifax Division the Magistrates' Court sat once each week and, unless something untoward happened, you could count on everything being wrapped up and finished by 2 p.m. In Doncaster the magistrates sat three times each week – Monday, Wednesday and Friday – and, with luck, you *might* get home by 6 p.m. on any of those days.

And this wasn't counting Doncaster itself. Doncaster, like Halifax, had its own borough force and its own Magistrates' Court but the borough was surrounded by Doncaster *Division* of the West Riding Constabulary, which in turn stretched south to Bawtry and the Yorkshire boundary.

I was back under Lewry, who'd been the chief superintendent of the division for some time. A plump man who, like so many, looked after Number One at all times; a man dependent upon Misconduct Reports rather than his own personality in order to command respect. No better, no worse than the average divisional officer of that period. A man suffering from that 'tin god' syndrome which was prevalent in the force at that time.

There was, of course, corruption. As I settled in at Bentley, I realised that corruption was part of the bricks and mortar of everyday life in that neck of the woods. Nothing big – no fortunes were made – but petty and annoying back-handers, given and received in every direction.

Coal, for example.

We were perched on top of one of the biggest coalfields in the UK. The men who worked at Bentley Colliery were entitled to free coal. Far more coal than they could possibly hope to burn. A nod and a wink and, instead of the coal being delivered to the miner it was meant for, it was delivered to a policeman's house.

Also, ready-money; off-course betting, for example.

At that time it was illegal, but we had at least half a dozen betting shops in the section. They were 'raided' once (and never more than once) every year. The bookie was contacted and a date and time, convenient to all, was arranged. The required 'evidence' was there, neatly arranged at one end of the counter. A group of pensioners, recruited for the purpose, waited to be 'arrested' as 'frequenters' and completed bail forms were taken on the 'raid' in order to save time. The whole pantomime lasted less than five minutes, and was timed to take place between races in order not to interfere with business. The pensioners were given ten bob each by the bookies for their co-operation and, at court, everybody dutifully pleaded 'guilty' knowing already the exact size of the fine to be imposed. In effect, it was an unofficial bookies' licence . . . and treated as such.

And boozing . . . but of course!

South of Wakefield, the licensing laws didn't seem to apply. The doors of pubs were closed in nodding recognition that *something* should be done, but the beer still came from the pumps. There seemed to be a working men's club in every street, and nobody dreamed of even commenting upon the lights and gaiety issuing forth at 2 a.m., 3 a.m. or even 4 a.m. The chances were that a sergeant or a copper (or both) would be included in the merrymakers anyway.

All this, then, plus Holiday Clubs, Tally Clubs, Death and Divide Clubs, Christmas Clubs and a regular fiddling of the takings that was accepted as part of the 'perks' enjoyed by anybody daft enough to take on the job of 'collector', made for a way of life well beyond the understanding of either Avis or me. It was bobbying *à la* Doncaster and, for what credit it's worth, we never became part of it.

* * *

The inspector asked the sergeant, 'What's Wainwright doing in the office?'

The sergeant asked, 'What are you doing in the office, Wainwright?'

'Filling in the Crime Reports, Sergeant.'

'He's filling in Crime Reports, sir.'

The inspector asked the sergeant, 'How long is he likely to be?'

The sergeant asked, 'How long are you likely to be?'

'Ten minutes,' I estimated. 'No more than a quarter of an hour.'

'Ten minutes, sir. No more than a quarter of an hour.'

The inspector asked the sergeant, 'Can't he do it some other time?'

The sergeant asked, 'Can't you do it some other time, Wainwright?'

I stared – even glared – then asked, 'What the bloody hell sort of a circus is *this*?'

'The inspector wants to know –'

'In that case, let the damned inspector *ask*.'

Inspector 'Bomber' Brown had never been spoken to – strictly speaking, spoken *at* – in that tone of voice before. It shattered his image and played hell with his ego.

Bentley Police Station had one room; a room no larger than the average living room. It held three desks: the sergeant's, the inspector's and one used by constables.

And this was my first day at the section . . . I was getting off to a flying start!

Nevertheless, I failed to see why, in hell's name, and in view of the fact that he wasn't a yard from where I was sitting, Bomber had to direct his questions about my activity via the sergeant. It was pure Goon Show stuff, and one copper newly arrived within the orbit of Inspector Brown wasn't going to play 'silly buggers' for the next few years of his service.

There was an almighty row in which Brown and I let fly at each other with both barrels, while the sergeant opened and closed his mouth like a stranded trout . . . and that's how I met Bomber.

He gave the impression of being slightly too short in height for the Police Service, but that didn't matter at all. He was a terrier of a man and never once did I know him back down from an officer senior to himself when he was fighting for a man in Bentley Section. That was his reputation, and he'd earned it; it was, moreover, a reputation that had spread throughout the division and beyond.

He had his own quirks of policing, and at a guess that opening gambit was one of them. To see how a strange copper reacted to what was a crazy situation. Maybe I'd *over*-reacted, but that didn't matter. In no time at all, he and I came to know each other. He was arrow-straight – no fiddles or 'nawpings' for Bomber – and it is possible we recognised kindred spirits in each other. No Misconduct Reports for Bomber; Lewry carried the rank, but Brown carried the charisma. I think he had a slow-burning contempt for most of mankind, and it showed. I saw him pin men who seemed twice his size with those cold blue eyes of his; pin them and make them squirm with discomfort as he quietly stripped them naked of bluff and exposed them for what they were. Coppers as well as crooks.

Bomber Brown. I mention him because he deserves to be mentioned. As long as men like Brown choose the Police Service as a career, corruption – even minor corruption – doesn't stand a chance of survival. He died in harness and I, for one, mourned the loss of a great policeman.

Bomber and I did, however, have one more magnificent set-to before he passed on.

I was on night patrol duty in Bentley, and by this time I'd come to know the town's 'characters'. And one of the characters was a wild bastard by name of Tony Swift.

Tony, be it understood, was built like a barn-side. He'd been a commando during the war, and everybody – but *everybody* – walked on eggs when Tony lost his temper. Sober, Tony was a great, friendly bear of a man. He might crack the bones of your fingers when he shook hands, or knock you flyng if he slapped your back, but he meant no harm. In a back-to-front sort of way I rather liked him. He took slop from no man, and no doubt as a commando he'd been a one-man demolition squad.

On this occasion, at 11 p.m., Mrs Swift rushed into Bentley Police Station in great agitation. Tony was crazy drunk and, for reasons best known to himself, he'd decided to set fire to the house and every stick of furniture it held.

'Wainwright.' Bomber glanced up from the papers he was checking. 'Go sort him out.' Then, almost as an afterthought, 'Take Constable Hawkins along to give you a hand.'

Hawkins was a slim lad, without much weight and even less experience. Nevertheless, we accompanied Mrs Swift back to the homestead and there we were confronted by scores of onlookers, all being kept at bay by a warlike Tony waving a fireman's hatchet.

Hawkins looked scared.

I tried *not* to look scared.

'Grab an arm,' I advised, 'and try not to catch a wallop from the bloody hatchet.'

We both dived in and each concentrated upon an arm. Somewhere Tony dropped the hatchet, and I breathed a little more freely. But Tony Swift didn't need a little thing like a fireman's hatchet. I had a quick glimpse of poor Hawkins being lifted off his feet as Tony waved one arm around, while I clung for dear life to the other arm. For one moment I contemplated using my truncheon, then I had second thoughts. To quieten this lunatic it would have been necessary to kill him . . . and I wasn't prepared to do that. Meanwhile, Hawkins was being jerked all over the place, and the crowd was thoroughly enjoying itself watching two useless limbs of the law being made to look particularly stupid.

I did what no copper should do. I lost my temper.

I bawled to Hawkins: 'Sod him! Let go, and stand back. If he wants it the hard way, he can bloody well *have* it the hard way.'

In a token gesture that I was, temporarily, off duty, I knocked my helmet from my head, then both Tony and I forgot the rest of the world and waded in.

It was some battle. When eventually I left Bentley Section, people still mentioned the night Swift and Wainwright thumped each other to a standstill. No gloves, no 'rounds' and it lasted all of five minutes. No finesse; we merely stood toe-to-toe and traded punches. We didn't even try to defend ourselves, although – and luckily – Tony had recently had a skinful, and his aim wasn't quite all it should have been.

When I looked back on that scrap, I always marvelled. Neither of us fought 'dirty'. No boots, no knees, no heads and, as far as possible, everything above the belt line.

Was it, perhaps, *still* a legacy from the war?

Nevertheless, it seemed to go on forever and, unlike such episodes shown on television and cinema screens, we bled. Both of us. There wasn't much pain. There never is; the pain comes later, when the adrenalin has quietened down.

Tony wasn't fit. That's why I licked him. He was bigger, stronger and tougher than I was . . . but he'd taken on board too much booze over the years. Gradually – very gradually – he gave ground and backed towards the door of his home. He was about a yard from it when he paused, just for a split second, to gain breath. I clenched all my fingers into a tight, double-handed fist and brought up the hardest punch I've ever thrown in my life. It was still gathering speed when it landed flush on Tony's mouth, smashed his upper lip against his teeth, gave him a second 'mouth' and catapulted him backwards through the pane of his glass-fronted door.

'Enough?' I gasped.

He managed to nod.

'Conduct . . .' I could hardly find enough breath to speak the words. 'Conduct Likely to Cause a Breach of the Peace. Understand?'

Again he nodded.

I collected my helmet and, with Constable Hawkins, returned to the nick.

'What the hell?' Bomber gawped at my bloody and battered face. 'Has he assaulted you?'

'You could say that,' I agreed, wearily.

'Why isn't he nicked?'

'Eh?'

'Assault on Police. Let's have him inside.'

'No.' I examined the burst skin on my knuckles. 'I assaulted him back.'

'That's no damn way to police.'

'It's *my* way.' I think I was snarling at him. I'd had enough. I was beginning to ache. I was also beginning to tremble a little. I continued, 'It was the *only* way. If you doubt that, move your backside from that chair, stop pontificating and go to where Swift lives. There're about fifty people who saw the show. Ask them. But if you *do* feel like arresting him, be advised. Take half a dozen squad cars with you.'

'Damnation, he *assaulted* you. He assaulted one of *my* officers.'

'He'll know about it tomorrow morning,' I promised.

And that was it. I wove my way to the tiny washroom, dashed water on to my bruised face, then took up the street patrol I was being paid to perform. I nipped home at 'supper break' and allowed a worried Avis to do what she could for the places that were swollen and discoloured and, like Tony Swift, when morning came I knew I'd been in a meat-grinder.

Tony appeared at court about a fortnight later. We both still carried marks of that punch-up. Tony had required quite a stitching job to his upper lip. In the witness-box I made things as easy for him as I could, and the half-smiles from the bench suggested that word had already reached the magistrates.

184

Later, over a cup of tea, Tony thanked me for not charging him with Assault on Police.

I later learned that anybody valuing his teeth was wise not to make disparaging remarks about 'Bobby Wainwright' while Tony Swift was within earshot. It was nice to know. Had he nursed a grudge, he could have slaughtered me out of hand.

That, then, was Bentley and the very essence of Bentley-style policing. Anything could happen . . . and probably would, when you were least expecting it. The youngsters who didn't yet know their way through the jungle were terrified; they'd arrive still wet behind the ears from police training college, and within a week they'd be near to tears. One lad – a massively framed young chap with a quiet disposition – was so afraid of Bomber he didn't dare come into the police station to sign off duty while the inspector was there. Instead he'd stand – sometimes for an hour, sometimes in the pouring rain – waiting for the coast to clear rather than risk the razor of Bomber's tongue at some fiddling thing he'd done wrong.

And yet laughs galore punctuated the policing.

The time we caught a nine–nine–niner from a panic-stricken woman about her husband, who, she said, had 'committed suicide' by putting his head in the gas oven. The sergeant and I moved into action. The weeping, wailing spouse was waiting for us outside the house, and as we dashed inside the absence of smell was very noticeable. But he *was* there, and he *was* stretched out with his head in the gas oven. His head was resting on the near-obligatory cushion and his eyes were closed.

But he wasn't dead . . . not by a country mile.

He'd forgotten to turn on the gas, and he'd fallen asleep.

And then the dear old lady, who lived alone and was quite ga-ga. She was harmless, but every week, without fail, she would call in at the police station and solemnly make some outrageous complaint. That the local authority was digging up the bridge over the River Don without permission, despite the fact that it was *her* bridge. That she knew Constable Wainwright very well; he'd once been employed by her as her butler and, presumably, she felt he should return to his previous employment.

This time, it was her eyes. She had this strong suspicion that somebody from outer space was dropping some kind of eye-irritant, and couldn't something be done about it?

Bill, one of the older coppers, answered her complaint, and it was a lesson in straight-faced kidology, which at the same time gave no hurt.

'You must have very sensitive eyes, old luv.'

'Oh!'

'Most people don't notice. Only those with sensitive eyes.'

'I see. I'm right, then?'

'Not quite. It's dumpling dust.'

'Is it *really*?'

'It's the weather, you see. Cold. And everybody's busy making dumplings, and not keeping their doors and windows tightly closed. It gets in the atmosphere.'

'The dumpling dust?'

'Aye.' Bill nodded, solemnly.

'Should I visit my doctor?'

'No, I shouldn't bother, luv. There's not much anybody can do about it. Get a good breeze going . . . that'll shift it.'

'Thank you, Constable. That's a great relief.'

She trotted off, happy in her own slightly pixilated way. Funny? Of course it was funny. . . . Give me a good old-fashioned copper rather than some high-brow psychologist any day.

We also enjoyed certain 'in' jokes. Usually as a result of the monumental amount of paperwork required for even the most trivial incident.

The same copper – Bill – took in a cheap suitcase that some pedestrian had found in the street. The Lost and Found Report was duly made out, the appropriate number of 'enquiries' were made and the report was forwarded to Doncaster DHQ. That should have been the end of the matter, pending somebody reporting it lost.

Not a bit of it. Some self-opinionated clown at DHQ sent the report back with the question: 'Could not this property have fallen from a passing motor vehicle?'

Bill's solemn answering minute was 'It could. Or from a low-flying aircraft.'

My own minor contribution to this never-ending snip-ing between DHQ and the sections revolved around a simple gas-meter break-in. A piddling, penny-a-dozen crime which from the first had obviously been committed by the character who should have put money *into* the meter. He was an old hand, he wouldn't break and it was one of those many crimes that were solved but couldn't be marked 'Detected'. I submitted the file with a covering report in which, using somewhat flowery language, I explained that the berk responsible was (to my certain knowledge) 'in a perpetual state of financial embarrass-ment'. Back it came from the detective chief inspector, with those words underlined and the two-word question, 'Who isn't?'. I returned it with the appropriate answer. 'Detective chief inspectors'.

That little sally cost me an extra week of night duty.

* * *

The rummaging about in my memory, plus a determina-tion to stay as close to the truth as possible, brings its own price. Reflection has brought me to the conclusion that at this period I became what might be described as a 'hard-man'. Not, I hope, towards Avis, but rather in my inability to see the world except in stark black and white. If I have an excuse, it must be that the LL.B. slog was still filling all my spare moments, even though it was nearing its end. Off duty, I was surrounded by a jungle of forensic nit-picking which, unless I was to have wasted both time and money, *had* to be fully understood. On duty it was pure crash-bang-wallop bobbying which called for a surfeit of brawn and very little brain. I was indeed burning the candle at both ends – perhaps more than one candle – and it showed in my refusal to either slow down or take advice.

An example will prove my point.

It was a glorious summer's afternoon. A Sunday. Bomber had died and a new, younger inspector had taken his place. I was in the nick, catching up on the normal overflow of paperwork while outside the station was parked our latest acquisition, a Morris 1000 motor car, second-hand, of course.

For weeks we'd been pestered by the activities of some perverted screwball who had indecently assaulted little girls between the ages of seven and nine. We had a moderately good description of him, but beyond that, nothing.

A nine–nine–niner came through from an irate father. His seven-year-old daughter had just run into the house, distraught, having been the latest victim of the man we were after. More than that. The man was still around; somewhere within an area bounded by a wood and fields on the outskirts of the town.

The inspector said, 'Grab a civilian jacket. You take the lane south of the fields. I take the lane north of the wood. With any luck, we've got him.'

That's what we did, and I won the lucky dip.

I'd parked the Morris and was leaning against a post and rail fence when he walked out of the wood and began to cross the field. He answered the description, he was pushing a pedal cycle, which we knew he sometimes used.

The problem was the fence. If I vaulted it, he'd hop on his bike and be away. If I *didn't*, he'd stroll out of the field and on to a footpath along which I couldn't drive the car.

'Hoi!' I shouted. And when he turned his head, I tapped my wristwatch and called, 'What time is it?'

'Eh?'

'The time,' I bawled. 'My watch has stopped.'

He glanced at his own watch, and said, 'Half-past three.'

'You what?'

'Half-past three.'

I cupped a hand to my ear, and yelled, 'Sorry. I can't hear you.'

He swerved in his line of walk, and came nearer. When he was a few yards away, but still beyond reach, I put on a look of mild gormlessness and said, 'I'm a bit deaf. Sorry.'

He came to within a yard of the post and rail fence, and said, 'It's half-past three.'

I lunged forward, grabbed and growled, 'Great. When they ask you, you'll know *exactly* what time you were nicked.'

He wasn't much of a handful, and in no time at all he was in the car, then back at the police station and we were both upstairs in the Interview Room. It was a very short session. I didn't have to threaten or lean. I snapped my disgust at him, and he coughed the lot. He was a weak man; seven-year-old kids were just about his weight. Kinky? Of course he was kinky. He was a married man, with three children of his own . . . and yet he needed little girls to give him kicks.

I bailed him for court the next day then, before he left, I gave him a tongue-lashing. The sort of perverted bastard he was. The fact that had he groped around with *my* daughter – or, indeed, with any of my real-life nieces – he'd be a hospital case, and deservedly so. There was much in a similar vein, and the truth is I overstepped my terms of reference as a police constable by a few light-years. My job – and my *only* job – was to get at the truth and collect evidence. I was no judge. I wasn't there to condemn *anybody* . . . but on that Sunday afternoon I did.

Having seen him off from the police station, I climbed into the car and drove home for an early-evening meal. The meal was interrupted by a telephone call from the nick. The sergeant broke the news.

'The bloke you've just bailed. The child-molester.'

'What about him?'

'What did you say to him?'

'A few home truths. They *needed* saying.'

'Upset him, did you?'

'At a guess.'

'Rather more than a guess. He didn't reach home.'

'No?'

'He put his neck on the railway-line.'

'Oh!'

'Very messy.'

'That way it usually is.'

'Get back here when you've finished your meal. Somebody has to break the news to his wife.'

I admit, with some degree of shame, that I finished my meal. I wasn't *really* upset. It is possible – even highly probable – that I'd talked a man into committing suicide in a particularly nasty manner, but I felt no guilt. Maybe it was *his* guilt that drove him to such extremes. Perhaps, now, I even hope so. But I was a much harder man then than I am today.

*   *   *

'Wainwright, I'm warning you . . . and I keep my promises. Refuse me this and if you stay in the force a hundred years you'll *still* be a village bobby.'

Those were the words that slammed and locked the door on any hope of promotion. I didn't believe them at the time. I was convinced that no man wielded *that* amount of power.

I lived to learn my mistake.

To this day, I don't how the hell he knew I was at Clifton. It was my weekly rest day, and we'd travelled up to Clifton from Bentley, to spend a few hours with David and Betty. It is, of course, possible that I mentioned our intention to visit Clifton to a colleague; that enquiries had come from the top office. and that a few pertinent questions in the Elland area had resulted in it being known that David and Betty were our friends. I merely emphasize that some degree of urgency *must* have been necessary in order to trace my immediate whereabouts.

What I *do* know is that the telephone bell rang, David answered it and returned to the sitting room with a puzzled look on his face.

'Somebody called Metcalfe, Jack,' he said. 'He wants to see you at Elland Police Station, immediately.'

I, too, was mystified, but with David as a willing passenger, I drove to my old police station, wondering what it was all about.

Two men were waiting for me. My one-time superintendent, Verity, and Detective Chief Superintendent Metcalfe. Nobody else . . . and in my innocence I asked David to wait for me in the car.

'Right, Wainwright.' Metcalfe wasn't one to beat about the bush. 'There's an accident you attended while you were stationed here.'

'I attended a lot of accidents, sir.'

'This was on Ainley's. Some doctor or other, and a county council vehicle.'

I thought back and remembered.

'The doctor ended up with a broken leg,' I said.

'That's the one.'

'A county council dumper driver turned right, without giving any signal, clobbered the medic's car, and –'

'He isn't a "dumper driver" any more.'

'Oh.'

'He's moved up the ladder a few rungs.'

I said, 'Oh,' again and waited.

'The damn doctor's making a County Court case out of it. He's suing him for damages.'

That was the point when warning bells started ringing in my brain. Metcalfe's tone of voice and the presence of Verity. Verity wasn't there to *say* anything. Verity was there as a witness . . . but I'd yet to figure out who needed a witness for what.

Metcalfe growled, 'He hasn't a leg to stand on.'

'The dumper driver?' I asked, innocently.

'The bloody doctor.' There was a definite edge to the words. 'The man you call "the dumper driver" gave a good signal that he was turning right.'

'He was booked,' I reminded him. '*I* booked him. His mates witnessed the accident. They all gave statements –'

'They can't remember,' interrupted Metcalfe. 'I've been to see them. None of them can remember what happened. None of them can remember what they told *you*.'

'I can remember,' I said quietly. 'And if I happen to forget, I have it recorded in my notebook. That the dumper driver admitted to *not* having given a signal.'

'Don't be thick, Wainwright.'

And now we were coming out into the open. Rank was being pulled; the rank of a detective chief superintendent, with the added rank of a uniformed superintendent waiting in the wings. I wished David was alongside me. *I* needed a witness, too.

'The doctor's calling you as a witness,' said Metcalfe. 'Witness against one of my friends. I'm here to find out what you're going to say.'

'Exactly what I said at the Magistrates' Court, sir.' I admit to feeling a little dry-mouthed. I was being gunned at by very heavy artillery. I explained what was to me obvious. 'It's recorded in my notebook. Short of committing perjury, I've no option.'

'In this job, Wainwright,' Metcalfe's tone was heavy and measured, as if he was explaining something that didn't *need* to be explained, 'we sometimes do favours for friends.'

'Fellow-policemen, sir,' I mumbled. 'And then only sometimes.'

'You should know.' And now he was turning nasty. 'It's why you're at Toll Bar.'

I look back on that evening in Elland Police Station with very mixed feelings. Should I have agreed? Should I have taken a chance? Or was I right in being pig-headed? Oh, I know the *theoretical* answer. The upright and honest answer. But I didn't *know* the damned Huddersfield doctor, nor do I know him to this day. I didn't owe *him* anything. It was such a *small* perjury, and if I backed away from it I had a hell of a lot to lose.

With all the wisdom of a backward glance, plus the admission that I am no more perfect than the next man, I think I might have agreed had there been a little less intimidation; had Verity not been present, and had Metcalfe not been so damn sure.

Almost offhandedly, he said, 'You'll do as you're told, Wainwright.'

'Commit perjury?'

'It's not a *request*.'

'No, sir?' Now *I* was feeling annoyed.

'It's an *order*.'

'Can I have that order in writing, sir?'

'Don't be such a damn fool!'

'In that case . . .' I paused, and this time it wasn't a question. 'No, sir.'

I suspect we were of a kind, Metcalfe and I. Stubborn as hell, brick-thick and each refusing to budge ground. But the gauntlet had been thrown down and had been picked up.

There was a moment of silence during which we stared at each other and, I suppose, hated each other.

Then, in a voice with hoar frost at its edges, he said, 'Wainwright, I'm warning you . . . and I keep my promises. Refuse me this and if you stay in the force a hundred years you'll *still* be a village bobby.'

'If you say so, sir.' I turned to leave. 'Now – if you'll excuse me – I have a friend waiting outside.'

I kept my promise and Metcalfe kept his. The doctor won his action for damages, and I remained a constable to the day I handed in my uniform.

However . . .

Five years later, we both thought he'd won.

Ten years later, we both knew *I*'d won.

* * *

I do not see sex *per se* as the root cause of any crime, as is popularly believed. Sex, especially in the context of a happy marriage, is at the least fulfilling and at the best nothing less than beautiful. But lust is so often mistaken for sex, and when lust is allied with perversion anything can happen.

Take John Baptiste.

That was his name, but he was neither French nor holy. He was as Yorkshire as Pontefract cakes, and as evil-minded as they come. He lived alone in a housing estate on the outskirts of Bentley. His wife had left him, and personal cleanliness was a luxury he denied himself.

Like so many people of his kind, he was a convinced believer in the promise-and-pay mode of meeting his debts. Even in the matter of food. He collected what he required from the local Co-op, and once a week, the tally-girl – a young lady in her early twenties – called at Baptiste's home to collect whatever cash he was prepared to cough up.

On this particular afternoon he asked her inside, then, when the door was closed, smacked her on the head with a coal hammer. He carted her upstairs, stripped her, then spreadeagled her on the bed by lashing her wrists and ankles to the four bedposts.

She recovered consciousness to find Baptiste mother-naked, with a carving knife in his hand, ready to go about the business of rape. Baptiste held the knife at her throat and, in disgusting language, explained exactly what he intended to do and assured the terrified woman that her throat would be slashed if she made even token protest.

In fact, having realised what was going to happen, the

young woman made far more than *token* protest. She wrenched one of her wrists free, threw out her arm and smashed one of the bedroom windows with her hand; such was the violence of the blow that the jagged edge of the broken glass sliced through flesh *and* bone and took off half her thumb. Then she screamed the place down. Baptiste panicked and, for reasons best known to himself, jumped through the bedroom window (still in his birthday suit), landed in the back garden, hobbled into the kitchen and tried to commit hara-kiri by driving a rusty safety-razor blade into his wrist.

Neighbours heard the screams, rushed to the rescue, broke down the door of Baptiste's house then unfastened the victim and carried her, wrapped in a blanket, to safety. Meanwhile, in the kitchen, Baptiste was still sawing away at his wrist with a blunt razor blade.

That was when somebody figured it might be wise to get the police in on the act.

Sergeant Hornby and I answered the call.

Hornby wasn't a bad chap. He wasn't the best section sergeant I ever worked under, but he was one hell of a way from the worst. He liked his tonsil varnish and he sometimes tended to be a mite moody, but when (as he was now) sober and in good fettle, he was a good guy to have alongside you.

In the house, the stairwell gave the impression of having been sprayed – floor, walls and ceiling – with blood. Pints of the stuff, splashed in all directions. In the kitchen, Baptiste was weeping and still working at a DIY amputation job on his wrist.

Hornby cocked a jaundiced eye at the lunatic responsible for all this mayhem, and growled, 'Let the bugger die. We'll see to the girl first.'

That's what we did. We yelled for an ambulance and dealt with the young woman, then we re-visited the house. Baptiste hadn't died, he'd merely contributed to the general swill of blood. We wrapped a towel around his wrist, called another ambulance and left *him* to be dealt with later.

Being Doncaster Division, there had to be an extra pay-off. During the general kerfuffle some gather-yerosebuds-while-ye-may merchant had quietly nicked the leather satchel in which the tally-money had been carried. We never found *that*.

Meanwhile Baptiste had his wrist stitched up and duly appeared in front of the magistrates for committal. After the hearing I guided him into the cell area to be photographed and fingerprinted.

'Is this necessary?' he asked, with what sounded like genuine outrage in his voice.

'We think so,' I assured him.

'It makes me feel like – y'know – like a *criminal*.'

He looked quite surprised when, about a month later, the Assize Court judge sent him down for five years.

* * *

It was at Bentley that I ended the slog for the LL.B. Seven years before, it had started as a dream, then, after Metcalfe had issued his ultimatum, it had switched to a more personal level. To deny him the right to carry out his threat.

The pleasure I felt at my success was rooted firmly in a belief that I'd licked Detective Chief Superintendent George Metcalfe. That I'd taken all this man could dish out, and not merely twisted his tail, I'd tied a knot in it. Everybody else quaked when Metcalfe raised a finger. Everybody, that is, but Wainwright.

They couldn't *not* promote me now.

In my own defence, I was not chasing rank. I swear I was *not* chasing rank for the sake of rank. Other than a slightly fatter pay packet, it would have meant nothing. Already I was treated as a friend and equal by men who held much higher rank than myself. I knew my job, could do it on my head and, moreover, thoroughly enjoyed doing it. I was respected. Men who theoretically should have been giving *me* orders regularly sought my advice. And it was given for the asking with no strings attached.

That was the situation then and when I signed the official notification and sent it off to the chief constable I knew that it would pass across the desk of the man it was *really* aimed at.

That evening Chief Superintendent Lewry visited Bentley Police Station, and Lewry was one of Metcalfe's buddies. We were alone and we talked; a smooth, gentle conversation which burned its way into my brain like acid.

He took a cigarette from its packet as he murmured, 'I see you've earned yourself an LL.B., Wainwright.'

'Yes, sir.'

'I must get one myself . . .' He paused long enough to touch the end of the cigarette with a lighter flame, then added, 'When I've a few hours to spare.'

It was a gem of a performance. He must have practised that sentence – that immaculately timed pause – for hours. It would have won him an Oscar nomination in any company. It reduced seven years of gut-tearing graft into something akin to nipping out to buy a pound of apples.

Lewry was, of course, passing on a message.

Beaten Metcalfe? I hadn't even *impressed* him . . . that took another five years.

Yet even at that moment, and despite my detestation of the man, I could not deny Metcalfe his magnificence. I was objective enough to recognise him as a fine policeman. A superb policeman. Perhaps even one of that bare handful of truly *great* policemen.

He handled murder enquiries almost offhandedly, and is the only officer I know of who solved *every* killing he was ever called upon to investigate. He solved them and, moreover, stood the guilty party in the dock along with enough evidence to convict.

As a man I wouldn't have allowed him to cross my threshold. As a copper he was head and shoulders above any other policeman I ever met.

The Bomb

This was the period when somebody in the woodshed decided that the Police Service should interest itself in Civil Defence. The twin thunderclaps of Hiroshima and Nagasaki still gave the world goosepimples, gargantuan golf balls had been teed-up on Flylingdales Moor and Roger Bannister's four-minute mile had demonstrated just how far we could run between the whistle-blast and obliteration.

The Home Office, in its wisdom, had set up three 'Civil Defence Schools'. The name was later changed to the more melodramatic title of 'Schools for Survival'. At these establishments men and women were initiated into the mysteries of nuclear warfare and its aftermath; we were – although this aspect was never emphasised – the potential hewers of wood and carriers of water within the complex systems of the (then) top secret Regional Centres of Government. Meanwhile we were fed semi-confidential data – much of its hogwash and consequentially changed every month or so – then sent forth to train Civil Defence Volunteers who, in turn, would educate the man in the street, his wife and kids in the horrors likely to result from a nuclear war.

The three schools were at Taymouth Castle near Aberfeldy in Perthshire, the Hawkhills at Easingwold in Yorkshire, and Eastwood Park at Falfield in Gloucestershire. Each one was a magnificent establishment and between January 1959 and July 1964 I attended courses at all three.

My most vivid recollection of that '59 Civil Defence Course at Taymouth Castle is that of eating in the dining car of a train for the first time in my life. Via that alchemy which seems to be always present at such times, I'd met one of the other men travelling north for the same course. It wasn't *too* unusual, I suppose. The weather was bitterly cold, and the train was far from full. That, plus the fact that we were all coming from every point of the compass to start the course on the same day. We were due to change at Edinburgh for Perth, then on to Pitlochry. Then by chartered bus we were all due to be taken from Pitlochry to Taymouth Castle.

Just to *get* us all there on time was costing a small fortune.

Meanwhile I settled back in unaccustomed luxury, eating what was, for me, an expensive meal, while beyond the window on my right the coastline slid past. I saw Holy Island, then we pulled into Berwick-upon-Tweed. Thereafter the line ran even closer to the sea, past Burnmouth and on to Dunbar until it swung left for Edinburgh.

Other than that we were both on the same course, I can remember little of my travelling companion. Possibly he was as trepidant as I. This was no 'detective' course. It wasn't even a 'police' course, as very few coppers were fed into *this* particular sausage-machine, and those of us who were policemen were from forces scattered throughout the UK and, in the main, carried rank. This was 'Home Office' . . . top class.

Which, I suppose, raises the question? Why Wainwright?

The truth is, I don't know, and have never been able to find out. I'd fought my own war, and had shown no disposition to become a part of any potential World War III. I hadn't even been too aware of the existence of Civil Defence as an organisation.

Perhaps – just *perhaps* – that LL.B. had something to do with it. I base that possibility upon the fact that on the door of the immaculately furnished bedroom-cum-study, which was to be my private sanctum for the next three weeks, a neatly printed notice read 'JOHN W. WAINWRIGHT, ESQ, LL.B.' . . . and *I* hadn't told them!

I like to think that somebody, somewhere, within the mass of administrative machinery that went to make up the county constabulary, had had the simple gumption to realise that, whatever else, I'd proved myself capable of concentrating for long periods; that I could absorb quite complicated data, and even understand most of it.

Had I not started with Taymouth Castle, The Hawk-hills and Eastwood Park would have taken my breath away. They were, indeed, luxurious, but Taymouth Castle was in a class of its own. Since those faraway days I have visited and stayed in a handful of the top hotels of the UK, but I have yet to even enter anywhere remotely comparable with Taymouth Castle.

It was, indeed, what it claimed to be; a castle, complete with battlements and turrets. Its size can be imagined by the simple fact that its grounds included a golf course, but the building dominated the grounds. The library with its fantastically carved ceiling was matched only by the banner hall whose ceiling might also have brought gasps of wonder had it not been for a twelve-foot-high fireplace carved and moulded, like nothing I've seen before or since, from a single piece of black slate. Everything about the place was lush, without an unpolished surface to be seen or a non-Hoovered carpet to be walked across. It took us days to find our way around the place and, as one self-satisfied instructor informed us, it cost £100 a day merely to centrally heat the castle. Money really was no object and, while I recognised Whitehall profligacy when it was hurled in my face, there wasn't much I could do about it, so I sat back and wallowed.

A supremely efficient, moderately middle-aged lady was personally responsible for each trio of us and she awakened us at 7.30 a.m. each morning with a cup of tea. After we'd shaved and dressed within the privacy of our own de luxe bedsit, we'd stroll into the magnificent dining hall for a menu-chosen breakfast, leaving our ladies free to make the beds, vacuum the carpets and polish and tidy everything for our return later in the day. We were served at table; asked how we liked our eggs, whether we preferred tea or coffee, whether we liked our bacon fried or grilled, which marmalade we fancied that morning for our toast. In short, we were pampered. Mollycoddled. We were each issued with a thick, thigh-length duffle-coat; toggle-fastened and complete with hood. These were to ensure we didn't catch a chill moving from classroom to classroom. At mid-morning and mid-afternoon, coffee was served, piping hot. The lunch was as substantial as the average dinner, and the dinner was a gourmet's delight. There was a 'club', of which we all became automatic members and, in the evening, sandwiches and snacks were there for the taking.

And in return, for five hours a day, five days a week, we absorbed highly technical information about dosimeters, radiac survey meters and contamination meters; about radium and radiocobalt; about X-rays, gamma rays and fallout; about CN gas, mustard gas simulants MS and GTM5 and nerve gas simulants DEG and GTM6.

Within the first week those of us who had seen the sharp end of Hitler's War were taking deep breaths. What *we*'d been through had been a mere fist fight by comparison. These Whitehall Warriors were calmly talking about how many megadeaths one nuclear explosion would – not might, but *would* – cause. How many *million* corpses would be lying around. About the fallout plume from that one bomb; a hundred miles wide and a thousand miles long – one hundred thousand square miles of fallout . . . and we wildly calculated the surface area of the whole of the United Kingdom!

I think they have modified their estimates since those days. They have certainly made nuclear bombardment more fine-tuned. But the cynics amongst us, who gathered in some bedsit in the evenings, away from the ears of the instructors at the bar, tended to view the whole scenario as a cheap script for some over-the-top horror movie. We didn't believe it. Probably we *daren't* believe it.

Our job would be to train full-time members of the Warden Section of Civil Defence. To instruct them to 'note the time of the explosion'. To insist that they 'note the time of fallout arrival'.

I will not go into details of the prophesied outcome of the nuclear explosion. Television and cinema screens have shown nightmares enough, but without exaggeration. Suffice to say that those of us with imagination recognised what our training really boiled down to . . . the careful explanation of how to set a trap to catch a mouse, with a sabre-tooth about to crash through the window.

But at Taymouth I awoke to the sharp fragrance of pine and, as I enjoyed my pre-breakfast stroll, I saw mauve-coloured scarves of mist held to the ground along a hillside covered with those same pines. With two companions I walked to the Kirk at nearby Kenmore, sang hymns with unfamiliar tunes and praised our Maker via the Church of Scotland instead of the Church of England; we walked back along the side of Loch Tay and witnessed snow-bound desolation awesome enough to make even nuclear explosions seem puny.

It was very expensive, it was monumentally time-wasting, but I wouldn't have missed the experience of those three packed, but isolated weeks.

The Easingwold course was of a more practical nature. This time we had to learn the techniques to be taught to the Rescue Section and although, in the background, we still waffled along with high-powered subjects like heat radiation, immediate nuclear radiation and fallout; about areas of complete destruction, areas of heavy damage and areas of light damage, the basic object of *this* exercise was the business of getting trapped people from beneath a few hundred tons of collapsed building material.

It was a four-week course, but because it was being held at Easingwold I could spend every weekend – from Friday evening until Sunday evening – at home with Avis. I and three of my fellow course-members lived in Yorkshire, and while we all four made our own way home it was decided – in order to give ourselves those few extra hours with our families – that on the return journey I should detour, via Wakefield, to pick them up, then all make our way to Hawkhills in my car. And every weekend there was fog. Thick, juicy, oily fog. I'd grope my way to Wakefield, and thereafter one of my passengers would travel with his head sticking out of the front passenger-seat window giving a yard-by-yard estimate of the distance between the nearside of the car and the kerb or the grass verge. We'd arrive at Hawkhills in the small hours, wend our weary way to our respective rooms and flop on our beds . . . shattered.

Not that Easingwold was a re-run of Taymouth. The basic featherbedding was the same; the morning cup of tea, the privacy of your own tiny bedsit and the services of an efficient cleaning lady between each three of you. The food was every bit as good and the on-the-spot recreational facilities left little to be desired. But some deepdown, indefinable *luxury* was missing. I rather think the building had something to do with it. Hawkhills was a large house . . . and having said that you'd said it all. Architecturally it resembled something a prosperous, Edwardian stockbroker might have considered an appropriate home, but it wouldn't have merited a position as gatehouse at Taymouth Castle.

But as always it was my fellow course-members who made things worthwhile.

They were a good bunch and, because they were all destined to train Rescue Section types, they were a mite more earthy than the Warden Section experts. Some were from the mining world, some from the building trade, some from industry, some from the planning side of local authority. All held positions of authority, and all had got there the hard way. There was, therefore, no 'airy-fairy' nonsense about this little bunch.

Injury – even serious injury – was par for the course, and rumour had it that somebody had once been killed. It added spice to the heaving and crawling and lifting.

The thing was (and unlike the Warden Course) makebelieve could only go so far this time. In order to learn how to burrow a way under a house-high mountain of loosely held builder's rubble it was necessary to *burrow* under that mountain. Which meant you had to have some confidence in what you'd been taught about shoring and strutting. There was only one way to prove that you'd assimilated what you'd been told about shifting a five-ton girder from a precarious position down to ground level via a hydraulic rescue kit and a pulling and lifting machine, and that was by *doing* it . . . and if you made too many mistakes you might be a finger short.

The trick was to make haste, slowly; to make damn sure that in reaching a point where you could rescue a casualty, *you* didn't become one more casualty.

There was a whole village in the grounds of the estate. Nobody lived there, but the houses and shops had been blown up, or bulldozed down, in order to make a realistic playground where we might practise our newly acquired skills. And, to add to the reality of it all, while we worked and sweated, instructors tossed thunderflashes or smoke canisters amongst us.

Knots and the tying thereof became important. The figure of eight, the reef, the double sheet bend, the clove hitch, the bowline, the chair, the timber hitch and the draw hitch. To say nothing of the square lashing, the diagonal lashing and the round lashing. And be assured that when your own neck depends upon the skill with which rope is thus fastened, the Scout Movement isn't in the same race.

We learned first-aid. *Real* first-aid – none of this billiard-ball-under-the-armpit crap beloved of theorists – and the instructor painted a picture we could readily visualise.

'Forget the fancy bits. Forget all the love-knots you've been taught to tie on freshly laundered triangular bandages. You've a block of flats flattened, and *you*'re in a cavity underneath that lot. There isn't much air, and there's even less room. You know for a fact that ambulances can't get to within a mile of you and that every medical and surgical facility is being pushed beyond its limits. That's when you *have* to turn priorities back to front. The severely injured who *might* make it if they can be rushed to hospital in time – to some waiting operating theatre on stand-by – forget them. If you've morphine enough to spare, give them a shot. Leave them to die. If anybody – relatives, next-of-kin – wants to stay with them, don't argue. Let them stay. Your job is to rescue those who *want* rescuing and those who are *worth* rescuing. Those who having been rescued can be quickly patched up then help what's left of the community to carry on living.'

A lot of scales were removed from eyes during those four weeks at Easingwold. A lot of thoughtful discussion – a lot of 'What if . . .' questions – dominated our evening chats.

Taymouth had, perhaps, produced cynicism. Easing-wold produced apprehension. Even worry.

In July 1964 I attended my third and last course at a Home Office School for Survival. By this time I was no longer in Bentley Section; no longer in Doncaster Division. I had had some years of lecture-room experience, passing on what I'd learned to eager ladies and gentlemen who were anxious to 'know something about' this new-fangled international threat called Nuclear War. I'd explained things to classes of bored fellow-policemen. I'd yammered away in back rooms at clubs and church halls. My audiences had been as large as fifty-plus and as small as half a dozen or less.

I like to think I didn't bore them too much although, as I knew from listening to some of the lectures myself, the subject-matter *could* be made boring. But not, I discovered, if the lecturer took the bull by the horns and told the unvarnished truth. To call Ground Zero 'GZ', or even 'the area of complete destruction', wasn't good enough. It wasn't *honest* enough. Ground Zero was the point immediately below the explosion and if a ten-megaton nuclear bomb exploded (and the ten-megaton bomb was the one we were expected to use as a norm) then, as I pointed out, the immediate effect would equate with the explosion of *ten million tons* of normal, high-explosive chemicals, as used in World War II. Ergo the expression 'complete destruction' meant rather more than knocking a few houses down. It meant a bloody great hole, half a mile from lip-to-lip and a few hundred feet deep. Further, that the mysterious thing the pundits called fallout was, in reality, everything that had *been* in that hole – animal, vegetable and mineral – which had been vaporised, made radioactive – and been sucked high into the atmosphere and was now drifting gently to earth, carried along by prevailing winds.

It was all very horrific in its stark simplicity, of course, and a few purblind loonies who had already hoisted themselves upon the Civil Defence gravy train were complaining that Wainwright was tending to spread gloom and despondency in the ranks.

I had by this time been given a guided tour around one of those underground Regional Centres of Government the CND crowd were getting hot and bothered about. I could have told them not to worry. The overweening, self-important popinjays earmarked as potential boss-men lived in a world of their own; by the time the echoes of the first explosion had died away, *they* would be curled up in some corner terrified out of their pompous little wits. Come Armageddon and, as always, the men would be sorted from the boys and much of the garbage culled from the over-active minds of Whitehall desk-bound ninnies would be recognised for what it was.

This, then, was my state of mind when I arrived at Eastwood Park, Falfield, and I was delighted to discover that I was not alone.

As a building, Eastwood Park was more imposing than Hawkhills. It didn't come up to the Taymouth Castle standards, but nevertheless it was decidedly lush. The course was, again, Warden Section and, as always, the members of the course came from all walks of life.

I found a friend at that first roll call. To my shame, I cannot remember his name. I know he was a chief superintendent from a Welsh force and that at some point in his past he had earned himself the George Cross . . . and there aren't many of *them* about.

We were in the main lecture hall for the obligatory speech of welcome and, as I glanced down my copy of the list of 'students' I felt a little chary. They were all there. 'Sir' this, 'Alderman' the other, a fistful of 'Councillors', the odd 'Captain' and a few 'Inspectors' and 'Chief Inspectors'. The style and title 'Police Constable' looked very lonely and unimpressive among *that* lot and, given a certain type of man, I was likely to be either run ragged or in for a certain amount of argument.

My name was about two-thirds down the list and, before they reached me, the welcoming official called out the name of the Welsh chief superintendent.

There was no answer.

The official looked puzzled, and repeated the chief superintendent's name.

The chief superintendent stood up and, as was

expected, everybody turned to look at him. He stood about two inches above the six foot mark and had what can only be described as 'presence'. When he spoke, the hint of Welsh sing-song added authority to a voice which already had a no-nonsense quality.

'I will not answer to my rank,' he said. 'Nor will I address any other member of this course by rank. The prefix "Mister" is the only one I am prepared to accept, and the only one I am prepared to use.'

'But . . .' The official was a little out of his depth. He tapped his list with a finger. 'Chief Superintendent, common courtesy demands that we –'

'Mister!' interrupted the chief superintendent. 'And "common courtesy" if it means anything, means that while we're here we're all equal.' He glanced at his own list. 'I see we have a police constable here. A Mr Wainwright. From what I gather, he holds the same qualifications I hold as far as this course is concerned. The same qualifications we all hold. I don't expect him to call me "sir". I intend to call *nobody* "sir" . . .' A gentle smile touched his lips as he added, 'Even the baronet who is, apparently, one of our number.'

The baronet rose to his feet. 'I'll second that proposal,' he said, quietly. 'As my friend so rightly puts it, we're all equal while we're here. As I see things, we're all here to understand – to counter – the effects of a nuclear explosion . . . and *that* would eliminate all rank. I think that until we get to know each other well enough to use first names, the title of "Mister" should be used by students and instructors alike.'

And that's how it was. Some of the self-opinionated ones didn't like it too much, but they fell into line.

I owe that unknown chief superintendent – and, indeed, that baronet – a debt of gratitude. If they happen to read these words I would ask that they take them as a small appreciation of what they did at Falfield.

It was glorious weather, and we all knew our subject well enough to breeze through the course. We treated it as a 'refresher', while at the same time slapping questions at our instructors that they found difficult to answer.

'The expression "megadeath". Meaning a million corpses.'

'Yes?'

'What arrangements have been made to *shift* those bodies?'

'Ah!'

'Presumably the Whitehall experts realise that if they aren't shifted – disposed of – the disease from rotting flesh is likely to kill *another* million.'

That one was never answered.

Nor was the one about Ambulance Columns. 'As I understand things, we're talking about hundreds of ambulances.'

'Naturally. The number of casualties will be numbered in thousands.'

'A point of interest. Where do they come from?'

'The – er . . .'

'The ambulances. Hundreds, we're told. The average ambulance depot's lucky if it has *four*. Where are all these *hundreds* we're discussing?'

We were, I fear, a difficult course. None of us were new to the game, and some of us had grown wise to the dreams and fancies of those responsible for the writing and modification of the Book of Words.

Meanwhile, it was glorious weather and in the evenings a trio – sometimes a quartet – of us strolled the lanes and stopped off at various local pubs. For the first time in my life I tasted draught Guinness, and a pint of it was enough, however much I enjoyed it. I even saw fireflies in England; the last time I'd seen them was near Freetown, in West Africa, during the war. The suspension bridge destined to carry the M4 was under construction; the towers were in place and, from a distance, the Severn seemed to be spanned by a mere thread.

Those are the things I remember. The small memories that stay long after what at the time seemed far more important incidents.

After my last weekend at home I took Avis down to Gloucestershire with me, and she stayed at a tiny village called Stone, not too far from Eastwood Park. During the day she visited Bath, Gloucester or Bristol and, after the evening dinner at the college, I drove out to her and we enjoyed trips to places we'd never seen before. To

Weston-super-Mare. To see the Clifton Suspension Bridge after dark, with its bow of lights against a darkening sky. I had to return to my bedsit at the college each night, but the knowledge that Avis was within easy distance made my heart a great deal lighter. After a day spent discussing a special sort of hell it was nice to settle down to a few hours of personal sanity.

It was arranged that on the last evening there'd be a party in the clubroom. The students of the course would be there, plus the instructors and their wives. I asked that Avis might come too, and they bent the rules a little and agreed.

She was treated a little like visiting royalty, especially by the Welsh chief superintendent, who by this time had become a regular companion. I played the piano and the sing-song grew noisier and a mite bawdy, so I excused myself and drove Avis back to Stone. When I got back it was a little like the old wartime mess. The old favourites, the standard dirty ditties and the filthy poems were given a once-again airing. I suddenly realised that we were all of an age, and that at least three-quarters of us had seen war service and were winding up for one more session of old-fashioned tomfoolery before it all slipped away down the plug-hole of nostalgia.

The curtain-line arrived some time after midnight. I'd left the piano for a last half-pint of shandy, while the rest of them wound their way between the chairs and tables doing a rowdy, high-spirited conga.

The only two non-Brit types on the course were at the bar. One was from Nasser's Egypt – some junior Army officer over to glean what information he could about a weapon his country didn't yet possess – and the other was an oriental chap, here for similar reasons. They'd watched the build-up of organised lunacy all evening, and they were obviously quite mystified.

The Egyptian sighed, and said, 'The British. They are quite mad. These men represent their fighting forces. Their Army, their Navy, their Air Force, and look at them. The way they behave. They're quite *mad*.'

The oriental smiled his understanding, then murmured, 'Quite mad . . . but they always *win*!'

I returned to the piano a few inches taller than when I'd left it. It had all been said in two remarks, and what *had* been said brought a lump to my throat.

I am of a particular generation, and make no apologies for it. Generations since have called us foolish. Even gullible. They see war – any war – as an evil thing, with no redeeming features. But they are only half right.

Had *we* been so sure – had we, perhaps, been less foolish or gullible – *they* might not have their present freedom to express an opinion.

Gradually I moved away from Civil Defence lecturing. It brought less and less satisfaction and other men, viewing it as a cushy number, were waiting to take my place.

Slowly I realised I was preaching a lie. I was perpetrating a gigantic confidence trick. Nothing – but *nothing* – would be able to bring order from the chaos, which the explosion of a ten-megaton nuclear bomb would create.

Reluctantly I reached that conclusion.

It remains my conclusion to this day.

Toll Bar

'I'll tell you what's wrong with our Jack. He wants a spell inside, that's what *he* wants. A couple of years in nick would make a man of him.'

Thus the considered opinion of Ma Sheldon, married to an ex-jockey with a fistful of petty crimes to his name, mother of two sons who returned to jail with a regularity that suggested parachute elastic, and expressing her considered opinion of a third son who was busting a gut to keep out of trouble, despite family connections.

Nor were the opinions of Ma Sheldon out of the ordinary on Toll Bar Beat.

Let me start by saying that good people lived at Toll Bar. Good people live everywhere. It is merely that the percentage of bad people – scoundrels, tearaways and general hell-raisers – was higher than on any other beat I policed.

It was a 'punishment beat' and, regardless of any disclaimer made by officialdom, they do exist. They are recognised and earmarked as beats with which to tame stroppy coppers and, having crossed Metcalfe at Elland, I was due to be chopped down to size.

I don't think I blamed Metcalfe, even at the time. With the wisdom of passing years, I certainly don't blame him today. Had I been in his shoes – had *I* held the rank *he* held – I, too, might have lined my sights upon a mere pavement-basher who'd outwitted me. I'd asked for it . . . and I'd got it.

And, whether Metcalfe knew it or not, there was one saving grace. The police house *wasn't* at Toll Bar. It was on the right side of the railway bridge which marked the boundary between comparative civilisation at Bentley and near-outlawry at Toll Bar. It was also a rather nice house. Modern, semi-detached and the sort of place Avis could (and did) turn into a miniature palace.

But Toll Bar . . .

In size it was a nothing. No more than a dozen streets of terraced houses on either side of the A19 and hidden away behind the dark mountains of Bentley Colliery pit stacks. That, plus a car-wrecker's yard, a working men's club and an area of common land on which tinkers pitched their camps and left their garbage.

But it had a reputation, and it worked hard to sustain that reputation.

Like any copper who knows his job the first thing I did when we'd settled into our new house was to check on the convictions of those whom I was there to police. I ran a finger down the names on the Voter's Register and pulled the appropriate yellow cards – the Previous Conviction Cards – from the file. I had a full house! You name it, and short of murder, some bastard at Toll Bar had committed it. The emphasis was on violence, with theft running a close second and, more often than not, going hand-in-hand.

There was, however, one man (for reasons that will become apparent I will call him 'Tom Smith') and this man was something *very* special. His convictions ran into three pages, and they ranged from every major city in the UK to cities in America and Canada. He was a peterman – a safe-breaker – and he was, without a shadow of a doubt, top-strap. His last conviction was dated some ten years previously, and he'd obviously done his time and was now living in Toll Bar.

It seemed a good idea to visit Tom Smith. To start at the top.

His wife asked me in, and she looked worried.

'Just a call,' I assured her. 'I'm new here. I'd like to meet your husband.'

It was a neat little home – which for Toll Bar was unusual – and she brought us tea as we sat facing each other across the hearth, as suspicious as strange dogs sizing each other up.

'Another glory-hunter?' And Tom's voice carried an

equal measure of contempt and dislike.

'No,' I smiled.

'You'll have checked my form, of course.'

'Of course.'

'You'll have asked around.'

'No. I make my own assessments.'

He sipped his tea, then said, 'I'm a shot-firer at the colliery.'

'It follows. You know all about explosives.'

'A lot,' he agreed, 'It would be a waste of time to say I'm straight these days.'

'I claim to be a Christian,' I countered. 'I believe in miracles.'

He grunted, and I thought he relaxed a little.

I added, 'I just don't believe a miracle happens each evening with a matinee every Saturday afternoon.'

'You're a bloody strange copper.'

'I've been told that before.'

'Well, let me tell *you* something, Wainwright.' The tone was grim, but some of the dislike had melted. 'You're going to need something a bloody sight more potent than religion on *this* beat.'

'Could *you* spend forty days and forty nights alone in the Sinai Desert without food, without water? The guy who founded *my* religion did. And that only for starters. He never visited a Mothers' Union meeting in his life.'

'That's *one* way.' Much of the dislike and all of the contempt had gone. He even managed a quick, tight smile.

'People think I can't handle this beat,' I explained.

'Who?'

'Just . . . people.' I paused, then continued, 'I can handle *anything*, if I understand it. That's why I'm here. I need to be told things.'

'I'm no informant.'

'I've yet to ask you a question, Smith. All I want is an opinion. Your opinion.'

He lighted a cigarette, then told me.

'Two gangs. They call themselves "gangs", but that's just a name. Very loose-knit. Sheldon and Blakey. They're cousins – something like that – and they hate each other. Most of the people here are either for or against one or the other.

'There's a third grouping. Smith and Gascoigne. They're gyppos. They've both bought houses, and they're forever being visited by van-people. But they tend to keep themselves apart. Tame Sheldon and Blakey, and you've got the place in the palm of your hand.'

'That easy?'

'I didn't say it was *easy*.'

'They're both hard-men? Is that it?'

'It depends,' he said, slowly, 'what you mean by "hard". *I* wouldn't call them hard. Put them alongside some of the men *I*'ve knocked around with, and they're soft as shit.'

'Do they know that?' I smiled.

'Wainwright.' He returned the smile. 'I'm clean and I'm straight, but I still have a reputation. When *I* walk along the sidewalk both Sheldon and Blakey have sense enough to step aside.'

Over the years I grew to know this Tom Smith character. We never reached first-name terms, but at least we called each other 'Mr Smith' and 'Mr Wainwright', and with a man with *his* background that was good going. He was, indeed, straight, and he once unbent far enough to tell me why.

'I've made money, Mr Wainwright. More money than you're ever likely to see. All in readies and no income tax. It went on whores and horses . . . every cent. The cops never got a penny back.'

'That's what happens, see? The cells are full of mugs who spend it as fast as they lift it. And why? Because it's never "yours". You spend it like crazy because it's always somebody else's dough. All you did was lift it. It's worth sod-all. It's there to give you a good time while it lasts. It's never there to *keep*.'

I remember we were standing at the gate of the tiny garden of his house. It was summer, dusk, and the midges were making spirals above the untrimmed hedge.

Quite suddenly, he lowered his voice, and said, 'You've seen my record.'

I nodded.

'The last time, it included the lash. The cat.'

'I know.'

'That's a terrible thing, Mr Wainwright. Corporal punishment . . . a terrible thing.'

'You inflicted pain,' I argued, gently. 'It's only fair you should receive pain.'

'*Pain!*' He seemed to spit the word very quietly. 'Not pain. Christ, the pain was nothing. Look, I've had an arm broken, inside. Deliberately broken . . . and I still crippled the bastard who did it. One arm useless, and I *still* crippled the sod before I reported my injury to the screws. I'm not talking about *pain*.'

'What then? I admit to being fascinated.'

'The stripes,' he said, simply. 'The marks. They're there, across my back. Always will be. I'm married to a good woman, and we have a kid . . .' He cocked an eye at my look of surprise. 'Sure, we have a kid. He lives with his grandmother. I won't let him live in *this* crap-hole. But we take holidays together, see? The missus, my kid and me. Summer holidays.

'*They* can wear swimsuits. Go swimming. Lie in the sun. Everybody! But not me. Except in the bedroom, or the bathroom, I daren't take my shirt off. They'd *see*, get it? The lash marks. My kid – my own kid – would *know*.' There was a silence filled with terrible misery, then he muttered, 'D'you know what worries me? What keeps me awake at nights?'

'No.'

'The undertaker. The guy who's going to lay me out. *He*'ll see. *He*'ll know. The last bastard to set eyes on me, before they screw down the lid. *He*'ll know.' He gave a deep sigh. 'Not the pain. The *knowledge*. That's what scares you. That's what keeps you straight.'

Tom Smith was a good man. Whatever he'd done before I met him – whatever lawlessness he'd committed before he came to live at Toll Bar – in my book he's ticked off as a good man. That is why I've called him 'Tom Smith' . . . in the unlikely event of him still being alive. And, if he's dead, I hope the undertaker remained silent about what he saw.

Meanwhile, I had Sheldon and Blakey to handle, and I took heed of the advice given by Tom Smith.

There is no easy way with the Sheldons and the Blakeys of this world. There is no 'reasonable' or 'decent' way. Their coinage is terror, and it is the only currency they are prepared to either give or receive.

I admit to being worried. On the face of things, I was on to a hospital bed to nothing, but it had to be done if my life wasn't to become unbearable.

I was lucky in that I came across them both at the same time. Why they'd called a temporary truce I don't know, but there they were, together and alone in a grubby alley between two rows of terraced houses.

I took a deep breath, walked up to them and played red-necked cop for all I was worth.

'Sheldon?'

'Aye.'

'Blakey?'

'Aye. Why? What's –'

'My name's Wainwright. I think we should get to know each other.'

'Oh, aye? Why's that, then?'

'Because next time either of you step out of line, I'm the cop who'll be hauling you from bed before the dew leaves the roses.'

Sheldon contented himself with another, 'Oh, aye?'

Blakey merely glared.

'I'm told,' I said, 'that it's a toss-up which of you is king of this miserable castle.'

This time, Blakey growled, 'Oh, aye?'

'It doesn't matter any more,' I snapped. 'You've both abdicated.'

'What the sodding hell's *that* supposed to . . .'

I pushed Blakey in the chest. Hard. He stumbled backwards and the back of his head bounced off the brickwork of a gable end. I shoved a stiffened forefinger to within an inch of his startled face, and let him have full blast.

'Be warned, ballock-brains. Don't even *start* to get stroppy with me.'

'Oh!'

Sheldon said, 'Look, he was only –'

'You too!' I switched my charmless attention to Shel-

215

don. 'This hick dump. For your information. I was pupped and brought up in Leeds. The rough part of Leeds. Pillocks like you two would have been tagged pansies.'

Blakey moistened his lips, and I knew I had them licked.

He said, 'We – we weren't doing owt.'

'Honest,' added Sheldon.

'Good.' I was home and dry. I had myself a private little ball. 'Pass the word around. I enjoy being a bastard. Don't let the uniform throw you. Any of you. Whatever any previous copper might have done doesn't apply to me. I make it up as I go along. You break the law – any of you – and *I* break the law . . . and the blood on the pavement won't be mine.'

There was more of it, but strictly speaking it wasn't necessary. As of that moment, Toll Bar was all mine.

Of course they committed crimes. They couldn't *not* commit crimes. But they always committed theirs well away from my beat. They and their cronies ran wild in Doncaster. They kicked up hell's delight at Askern. They drove bobbies from surrounding districts up the wall.

But Toll Bar? The municipal cemetery couldn't have been more peaceful.

Comparatively speaking, of course.

They were rowdy, but rowdiness was par for the course in that sort of a community. They were foul-mouthed, but I'd read *Lady Chatterly* without having an attack of the vapours and, at a pinch, I knew words even *they* hadn't come across. They were drunken slobs, but booze was only booze and, when it was fighting-beer, they only knocked spots off their own kind, usually in the privacy of the club.

In short, it was a tough beat, and always would be . . . but it was no longer a punishment beat.

The measure of what I'd done was that every man, woman and child called me 'Mr Wainwright' . . . at least to my face.

*　　*　　*

You have to be an inverted genius to figure out a way of nicking phosphor-bronze bearings from the axles of railway wagons without moving the wagons from the line. The Toll Bar types did it one night.

They 'borrowed' two socking great jacks from the car-wrecker's yard, then after dark visited the colliery, via the back entrance. They were beyond the Toll Bar limits, therefore 'Mr Wainwright's' displeasure didn't apply. They packed the jacks under the edge of the wagon's body and gradually eased all the weight from each axle in turn. Done properly – done carefully – there is a point where the bearing on each wheel can be slid out of its housing with no trouble at all. Then the wagon is lowered, and from the outside nothing looks any different.

They stripped eight wagons of phosphor-bronze bearings before they left the colliery marshalling yard.

A couple of days later the wagons were loaded with coal and hitched to a train leaving the colliery. About half a mile along the line the engine driver glanced back and had the shock of his life. Clouds of smoke were coming from the axles of some of his wagons.

All clever stuff, but as always they screwed it up.

They flogged the bearings to a bent scrap-metal dealer in Doncaster and, when the local jack nosed around and asked questions, he sang the whole operatic aria.

Nevertheless, the Toll Bar crowd remained convinced that Bentley Colliery was their own private annexe to Paradise. Given half a chance they'd have lifted the headgear. As it was, the colliery marshalling yard was their everlasting target. The loaded wagons were carefully picked over for the best coal brought to the surface. Even the empty wagons weren't overlooked; more than once, every splinter of woodwork was removed from the steel frame, and before morning it had been sliced into neat 'logs' via an NCB circular saw.

But all this was the worry of the Transport Police. Within the orbit of the County Constabulary – specifically within the boundaries of Toll Bar Beat – sticky fingers were kept in deep pockets.

*   *   *

But, as I recall, I began this section with a quotation from Ma Sheldon. The context within which those remarks were made should be explained.

Walt and I were sharing night duty at Bentley. Walt was a big lad; it had been touch and go whether he was to earn a crust in rugby league or join the force. It was around 2 a.m., we'd reached the end of what was laughingly called 'supper' and were ready to face the empty streets again, when the telephone bell rang.

It was Jack Sheldon, and he sounded to be in a panic.

'You'd better get here. I've just killed our Eric.'

'Where are you speaking from?'

'Home. I've just belted Eric over the head with the coal hammer.'

I yelled for the assistance of the nearest Motor Patrol unit, then Walt and I hurried along the road, over the bridge and into Toll Bar.

The story (as we later pieced it together) was that Eric, the tough hombre of the family, had arrived home in the small hours in a drunken rage. For no better reason than to amuse himself, he'd set about deliberately needling his younger brother, Jack. Jack, if you remember, was the one member of the Sheldon family who dreamed of living a normal, non-criminal life. Jack had taken a lot, but eventually the elastic had snapped and he'd picked up the nearby coal hammer and crowned Eric on top of the skull. Eric had sprawled across the hearthrug with blood all over his face, and Jack had run to the nearest telephone to make the call to Bentley Police Station.

When Walt and I arrived at the Sheldon homestead *Jack* was within a whisker's width of being measured for a harp. Tough-egg Eric was far from dead. He'd recovered consciousness and, with enough blood streaming down his face and neck to merit top-billing in any horror movie, he was kneeling astride Jack with his fingers round his throat, happily choking the life out of the brother who'd knocked him out.

Ma Sheldon was sitting on a kitchen chair smoking a fag and, obviously, only mildly interested in who killed who. Pa Sheldon had left his bed and, wearing only an under-shift which barely reached his navel, was dancing around like a demented elf, yelling encouragement to his murderous son.

Walt swung an arm as thick as a ham, and sent Pa Sheldon flying.

I grabbed Eric in a neck-lock and gave him a straight and instant choice of either loosening his fingers from his brother's throat or having his neck snapped.

Thus peace descended and gradually Jack coaxed his breathing back to normal.

That was when, almost offhandedly, Ma Sheldon spoke the immortal words.

'I'll tell you what's wrong with our Jack. He wants a spell inside, that's what *he* wants. A couple of years in nick would make a man of him.'

Meanwhile the squad car arrived and, having seen things were under control, did us the great favour of radioing for an ambulance, then disappeared in a cloud of exhaust fumes.

Walt, who was a very reasonable sort of a chap, asked a very reasonable question.

'What the hell do we do with loonies like this?'

'Don't you call *us* loonies!'

This from ex-jockey Pa Sheldon, still wearing his bolero-sized vest.

Jack rubbed his neck and asked, 'Who are you going to nick, then?'

'We have problems,' I explained, patiently. '*You* telephone to say you've murdered Eric, but when we get here Eric's on the point of murdering *you*. And it's all happened in the privacy of your own front room. I'd say "Domestic Disturbance" . . . wouldn't you, Walt?'

'If that,' agreed Walt.

'Sod that for a tale!' Pa Sheldon suddenly became very indignant. 'You've got to nick *somebody*.'

'OK,' said Walt obligingly. 'I'll nick you. We'll decide what for when we reach the station.'

'I'll hang around for the ambulance,' I volunteered.

And on the way to the hospital in the ambulance I saw a sight I'll never forget. Walt had just about reverted to his rugby days; he was virtually dribbling Pa Sheldon, still only wearing his miniature shift, down the road towards Bentley Police Station. It looked as though, had Pa Sheldon made even token protest, Walt would have tucked him under his arm and dived for touch.

Nor was the duty doctor at the hospital delighted at having his slumber interrupted by the blood-soaked Eric.

'What's the cause?' he sighed.

I told him, and it didn't add to his happiness.

'He'll need at least ten stitches.'

'It's what booze does to a man,' I murmured.

'I'll sober him,' promised the doctor. 'I'll find the bluntest needle I can lay my hands on, and shove an extra couple in for luck.'

He did, too. And Sheldon was stone cold sober before the third stitch was inserted. He was sobbing with pain before we left the hospital.

And that, I fear, was policing at that particular time and at that particular place. I do not doubt that it would not – *could* not – happen today. There are too many 'watchdogs', and the men in the force are trained *not* to meet intimidation with counter-intimidation. And perhaps that's right. Perhaps that's how it should be.

I refuse to be judge.

But this I do know, and will take the time to try to explain.

The Toll Bar period was by far the most difficult slice of a twenty-year-long police career. There had been no pretence – no bluff – when I'd told Blakey and Sheldon of my beginnings. I had indeed been born and brought up in Leeds; in the heart of Hunslet, where both those Toll Bar scoundrels *would* have been dismissed as 'pansies'. But thanks to the war and thanks to marrying Avis and thanks to parents who'd hammered the fundamentals of right and wrong into me, I'd turned my back on a lifestyle of which I now no longer wanted a part.

And now I was up to the armpits in tearaways, scoundrels, whores and drink-sodden louts. To stay ahead of them I had to use their language and, while on duty, measure every action I took by their yardstick. To command their respect I had to be harder and more cynical than they were.

I tried to close the door on it all whenever I came off duty, but it wasn't easy. Avis talked to neighbours, and the neighbours knew Toll Bar and the reputation Toll

Bar had earned for itself. And perhaps because she had slight doubts, and because I saw those doubts as unwarranted accusations, I was hurt. If *she* didn't have unqualified faith in me then, indeed, it was a 'punishment beat' and Metcalfe had me licked.

We had rows and misunderstandings. We both began to hate the damn police force, and what it was doing to us. We still loved each other like crazy – were never complete if we weren't in each other's company – but the love was tinged with heartbreak for a time. Avis knew what I'd put into that infernal law degree. She knew – as indeed I knew – that I was a better copper than some men from whom I had to take orders. She couldn't understand, because she'd never met people like Metcalfe before. But *I* could understand – understand and, in a back-to-front sort of way, even admire as, periodically, messages aimed at me filtered down from the big man's office – and, as far as I was concerned, to crawl, or even to make token complaint, would have given him a satisfaction I was determined to deny him.

I couldn't win . . . but the hell I was going to lose!

By this time we owned a car and on rest days we enjoyed a run to the coast and back. To Hornsea, to Withernsea, to Humberston. They were great days; just the two of us, and miles from a beat that was slowly but surely crippling me.

I admit it now.

I'd have died rather than admit it at the time.

At home, apart from the days when we went for a breath of sea air, I couldn't change my ways. Off duty I couldn't relax. Couldn't adapt. After seven years of mental slog, I found that I still reserved two hours each day, every day, for concentrated study. It was a habit I couldn't break, and I could find no other occupation with which to fill those hours.

In effect, I was unique. I was the only man on God's earth whose day consisted of twenty-*six* hours.

The trouble was, I was awash with law, much of it of no earthly use to me as a bobby. I therefore decided to make that confounded LL.B. work for me and pay back some small percentage of what it had cost. I filleted various aspects of law which touched policing, began to write articles and, very tentatively, submitted those articles to *Police Review*.

I wrote and re-wrote – cut and pruned – but they remained 'legal' pieces and as thick and stodgy to plough through as porridge. Masterpieces like 'To Define Crime' or 'Legal Madness', with great wodges of case law and near-forgotten decisions.

At first I submitted them under the initials of my father, 'D.W.' Then, because they were being accepted with a regularity which honestly surprised me, I submitted them under the pseudonym of 'Caecus'. It wasn't until much later that I had the courage – or the audacity – to tag the articles with my own name and qualifications.

Looking back, I think *Police Review* published the pieces because they contained some of my own enthusiasm for law. And I *was* enthusiastic. Still am. Admittedly, I could not put the fine theories into practice, especially at Toll Bar, but the law was and still is the basic essentials upon which personal freedom must be based while, at the same time, the freedom of other people is kept sacrosanct. Look upon life as a highly involved game of three-dimensional chess . . . the law is merely the rules governing the game.

Eventually, some of the pieces were reprinted in other magazines. *Nursing Times*, for example, carried a reprint of an article covering the intricacies of the law and abortion at a time when abortion was very much illegal. Some were even translated and published overseas. The Italian *Notiziario Per l'Arma Dei Carabinieri* carried a reprint of an article that dealt with a presumption of guilt masquerading under the Presumption of Innocence.

I was being paid a small fee which, in turn, helped to offset some of the money I'd spent on law books. I was pushing boredom aside, keeping out of mischief and, at the same time, keeping abreast with changing legal trends. I was doing fine, or so I thought.

* * *

Tommy Gascoigne and Tiny Smith each owned a house at Toll Bar. They described themselves as 'dealers', a generic term meaning whatever you want it to mean.

They bought and sold. At times they no doubt sold things they hadn't previously bought. Nobody cared too much because the Gascoigne family and the Smith family lived lives apart from the rest, and caused little trouble.

To the community in general, they were known as 'gyppos', but this wasn't strictly true. The elder Gascoignes and Smiths had been born in caravans and at some time in the past had decided to become house-dwellers and lead a less mobile life.

Gypsies – true gypsies – are the Romany people. They have their own language and their own customs. They have their own religion and their own law which in no way cuts across the law of the land. They are shy to the point of secrecy. They do not hawk pegs or artificial flowers. They are interested in neither the 'evil eye' nor snatching other people's kids from prams. Their pride is that when *they* camp on a verge or in a coppice, they leave the site cleaner than it was when they arrived.

They are a very rare people.

The Gascoignes and the Smiths were 'didicoys'. Travelling folk. Van people. Where *they* camped they left muck knee-deep. Both were large families, with brothers, uncles, nephews and God only knows what else, and they all made frequent visits to Tommy and Tiny. As a result, the lanes between Toll Bar and Askern were elongated eyesores.

Take Henry Gascoigne.

Henry had a wife, six kids, four dogs, two Galloways, a van and an ex-Army bell-tent. His worldly possessions. Yet he managed to spread them along a verge for a distance of anything up to a hundred yards. Anything within walking distance that was loose and combustible was fuel for his roadside fire. If it grew and was edible, Henry claimed the right to pick it or dig it up and add it to his pot. If it was *alive* and edible, Henry killed it, skinned it, gutted it then roasted it on a spit above his camp-fire.

'I'm a man of the land,' he would say, with the tremble of soul-deep pride in his voice. 'Nature looks after her own, don't you see, sir? I'm a child of nature.'

'You're a bloody nuisance.'

'I wouldn't say that, sir.'

'You would if you were one of the farmers whose fences you're tearing lumps out of.'

'They're in shocking bad repair, sir. Broken all over the place, they are.'

'They are *now*. Now you've been at 'em with a ripping tool.'

'What would a ripping tool be, sir?'

Oddly enough, I rather liked Henry Gascoigne. Despite his wandering ways, he was rarely away from the beat for more than a month. Then, as I cycled along the lane, I'd spot one of his tethered nags. Then the second. Then, rounding a bend, I'd see the bell-tent in which slept his offspring. And farther along, the horse-drawn cart – remarkably like one of the covered wagons beloved of wild west films – with Henry and his missus sitting on boxes near an open fire and the dogs barking and yapping among more junk than you might think it possible for one man to acquire in a single lifetime.

He'd wave a hand and greet me, as if I were a close relative he hadn't seen for years.

'Good-day to you, sir. It's lovely to see you again.'

'How long?' I'd ask the standard question as I dismounted.

'How long what, sir?'

'How long are you staying this time?'

'No more than a week, sir. If I stay in one place more than a week, I get –'

'Tomorrow.'

'What's happening tomorrow, sir?'

'You're on your way.'

'God save us, sir. I only arrived this morning. I've only just –'

'The beds in the tent have been slept in, Henry.'

'Ah, well . . . maybe *yesterday* morning, sir.'

'Or the morning before. Or the morning before that.'

'I'm not one to keep strict track of time, sir. One day's very much like the next to me.'

'Tomorrow.' I'd lean against the crossbar of my cycle, fish pipe and pouch from my tunic pocket, and know that the cross-talk would follow the same pattern. 'The day after tomorrow, I'll be round with the school inspector. You'll answer to *him* why your poor kids aren't being educated.'

'They're being well educated, sir.'

'Not by you. You can't read.'

'I can read pictures, sir.'

'Don't try to convince me, Henry. Try to convince *him*.'

'I'll be away, sir.'

'Good.'

'You're a hard man, sir. A mighty hard man.'

'I know. You told me that the last time.'

'And so you are, sir. Otherwise, you'd let me have a bowl of that fine tobacco you have there.'

Henry and his kind were harmless. The farmers hated them – other, that is, than when they paid them starvation day-wages to help with the potato-picking – but the farmers knew how to look after themselves, and at times were a mite too ready with a twelve bore.

*　　*　　*

Then my world crashed around my ears.

It was a small family party. Not *my* family – other than Avis, I have no family – but some of Avis's family, of which I counted myself a part. It was my rest day, and we were sitting around the table eating and chatting. Avis raised her cup to her lips and, part-way there, it fell from her fingers. For the moment, we all thought it had been an accident. Then we saw the look of shocked surprise on her face and, as she tried to stand up, she toppled sideways and almost fell from her chair.

We helped her to bed and sent for the GP; a man I knew and trusted and a man whose opinion I valued.

'See she stays in bed. Keep her quiet. I'll be along with a specialist tomorrow.'

The specialist confirmed what the GP had suspected. In non-technical language, Avis had suffered a slight stroke. In medical jargon she'd had a mild cerebral haemorrhage.

If it scared her she didn't show it, but it as sure as hell scared me. I was very lucky. Avis's brother, his wife and our niece were staying with us for a few days, and they could keep calm enough to look after her. Me? I was in a continual state of panic. They took her south for a fortnight's holiday at Putney when they left and, although I telephoned every day, I remained in a state of abject terror.

I still look upon that fortnight as the worst fortnight of my whole life. On duty, I was like a zombie. Off duty I went quietly crazy. Meals didn't mean a thing and not once did I go near my bed.

I sought out Inspector Barber; he, too, had moved to the Doncaster Division, and it was he who'd conned me into leaving Clifton police cottage for Plains Lane. He obviously had some sort of 'pull' with the Headquarters boys. Anything! Just get me to a quiet spot, away from this hell-hole I'd been dumped in. This hell-hole which had caused my wife to worry enough to cause *this*. I was licked, I was sorry, I'd apologise to anybody on God's earth . . . just fix me up with a move, before it was too late.

He did it.

A brand new police house at Harrogate. It would be finished and ready to move into when I brought Avis back north.

At that time we owned a Mini, and on the Friday afternoon I drove it to Bentley Police Station, worked a two-to-ten shift, changed from tunic into sports jacket and at ten o'clock sharp set out for London. Straight down the A1, stopping only for petrol. Straight through the centre of London at some time between 2 a.m. and 3 a.m. Across Putney Bridge, then I parked on Putney Heath, opposite the house where Avis was, and waited for some sign of movement.

I expected to have to wait hours. I didn't wait minutes. She was watching and waiting for me. She came to the door. We spent the rest of the night in each other's arms . . . and I returned to life.

Suicide

I think we all have the seed of self-destruction within us. If, as seems the case, we are the only creatures on earth fully aware of our own mortality, then equally we are the only creatures capable of contemplating suicide. It is the final exit; the door beyond which there is no more pain and no more suffering. And the human animal is the only living thing that knows of that door, and knows exactly how that door can be opened and passed through.

Coppers know all about suicides. They know how near to the edge so very many people walk for much of their lives. And how little it takes to drive those people to step over that edge.

One statistic will suffice. The Suez Crisis of 1956. Anthony Eden made a wrong decision and Nasser responded. The bayonets were fixed, and for a few days something which might possibly wind itself up into World War III dominated the headlines.

In those few days the suicide rate in the UK tripled.

People worry. The more a person *can* think, the more that person *does* think. And with thought comes perplexity. Worry about important things and, equally, about unimportant things, and if the worry gets too big to handle . . .

All it needs is a trigger and, as any practical copper will verify, one suicide is trigger enough. Suicides very rarely come singly. Usually in threes – sometimes more than three – but all it apparently needs is one person to show how easy it is.

Almost invariably, some other unhappy soul takes the hint.

I recall one night when Mike Tully and I were on night

patrol. It was mid-winter and we were working the beat together. It was about midnight, bitterly cold and we were strolling along the road parallel with the canal.

A girl scrambled up the banking that led down to the canal. She was obviously in a very distressed state. Her hair was all over the place and, despite the cold, she wasn't wearing a coat.

She babbled, 'He's jumped in. He's committed suicide.'

'Who?'

'I don't know his name. He was taking me home from the dance.'

'In the canal?' I wanted to be sure I had the facts right.

'We were having a kiss and a cuddle, and he wanted to go the whole way, and I wouldn't, so he said if I didn't let him he'd jump in the canal.'

'Oh!'

'And I wouldn't let him, so he jumped up and ran away, along the towpath and said he was going to do himself in.'

Now, I ask you, was there ever such a silly reason for taking your life?

'Did you *see* him jump in?' I asked.

'No. But he swore he would. The last time I saw him, he was running away along the towpath.'

We took the girl's name and address, jotted down details of what she claimed had happened, returned to where she'd left her coat, then Mike and I made a search along the canal bank.

It was solid ice. Not a crack in it. We did a full half mile in both directions from where the girl had left her coat, and there wasn't a sign. The ice was as smooth as glass, from bank to bank.

The episode wasn't worth more than a short Incident Report. I described what had happened and what we'd done. I suggested what I thought to be the truth; that the unknown Romeo had tried a bluff in an attempt to get his own way, that the girl had called his bluff and that, feeling something of a fool, he hadn't returned to her.

So obvious.

Two days later, however, the ice melted, and he floated to the surface.

He was a single man in his early twenties. He had no family and very few friends. He'd lived alone, worked as some sort of clerk in one of the local factories, and nobody had missed him.

This remains one of the many mysteries of my police career. Why in God's name did he do it? And where, in God's name, did he go in?

I will not accept the proposition that a man takes his life in a particularly painful way merely because a girl he's only known for a couple of hours won't let him have his oats. There has to be something more than that. Something that has built up until the thought of self-destruction fills his whole mind. *Then* the girl's refusal might – just *might* – tip the balance and provide a ready-made excuse for doing what he was intent upon doing anyway. That *has* to be the explanation. But my enquiries failed to uncover any other possible reason for him taking to the water of the canal.

As for *where* he went in . . . at least two miles from where he left the girl were lock-gates. Swirling water. The only part of the canal that wasn't iced over that night. He *must* have run (perhaps walked) all that distance. Far enough – long enough – to make the suicide far too deliberate to be a spur-of-the-moment brainstorm.

Coppers are not supposed to get involved with the problems they encounter. Objectivity is the firm rule, laid down in every textbook and at every lecture. But I felt for that poor, unfortunate young man. What sort of mental hell was he going through? What was the *real* reason for his suicide?

These days I earn a living writing fiction. I play with possible cause and effect; make imagined characters jump through hoops for reasons I have invented. All authors play the same game. But that chap, whose name I can't even remember . . . what sort of web of dark fantasy could, with any degree of credibility, make him do *that*?

In those days (and a reminder that I speak of less than three decades ago) suicide was still classified as a felony. Not because anybody was stupid enough to contemplate imposing any sort of punishment upon some unfortunate who had taken his own life, but because the Common Law classified an attempted felony as a misdemeanour; thus a failed suicide attempt had the added stigma of criminality attached.

It seems the law has always had a strange dread of what it calls self-murder. Until 1824 suicides were on a par with vampires; they were buried in the highway – usually at a crossroads – with a stake driven through the heart. At the same time all the victim's goods would be confiscated, leaving his or her family to fend for themselves as best they could. After 1824 the stake and the crossroads were abolished, but the burial had to take place between 9 p.m. and midnight, in unconsecrated ground and without any form of burial service.

If you would have any present-day proof of this, visit any of the old cemeteries. There is *always* some out-of-the-way corner, rarely visited, with few, if any, head-stones. Press for an answer and you'll be told, perhaps with some embarrassment, that suicides were once buried there.

The goods of suicide victims were still confiscated until 1870 and, even in 1882, when all other penalties were abolished, there remained the prohibition of solemnisa-tion of the internment by a burial service in the accepted Anglican form.

There was, however, a legal loophole. The suicide had to be sane before he could be convicted of *felonia de se*. Even if he were only temporarily insane he would not be capable of having felonious guilt.

Ergo the so-called 'pious jury'. The coroner's jury almost always added the words 'but insane', having reached a verdict of guilty.

We still have it but, thanks to the recommendation of a committee in 1937, the impact has been softened to 'while the balance of his mind was disturbed'. Nevertheless, without that addendum, the ecclesiastical penalty is still in force.

In my opinion, civilisation still has a very long way to go.

*   *   *

She was such a gentle lady. She was unmarried and had

reached that time of life known, vaguely, as 'middle-aged'. Like so many suicides, she had few friends and she lived alone. I think she had few friends because she wanted it that way. She had her books and she had her music. In her own quiet, unassuming way she was a happy person.

All her working life she'd been a schoolmistress. It was to her a vocation and I'm sure she never regretted her choice of profession . . . until the end.

Unfortunately, one of her classes became unruly. Not merely mischievous. Not merely boisterous. Basically, they were wicked children and beyond her control. They made her life such a hell that she began to hate the coming of morning and another day of their taunts.

She'd appealed to the headmistress, but that hadn't helped. The headmistress had suggested firmer discipline, but hadn't explained how that firmer discipline might be achieved.

Then one Sunday evening this gentle, harmless lady decided that the Monday-morning torture of standing in front of that class was something she couldn't face.

She bathed. She dressed herself in freshly laundered underclothes, then put on her best nightgown. She took a pillow and an eiderdown, then stretched herself out in front of an unlit gas fire and turned on the tap. She even crossed her hands over her breasts. She left a note, apologising to the policeman who must, eventually, deal with the incident. She was very sorry to have caused him so much inconvenience.

I was that policeman and, had I had a choice in things, every selfish little bitch who went to make up that class would have been made to visit that room to see exactly what they were a part of.

Of course every suicide is insane when he or she makes that final decision. But it is very rarely his or her choice to *be* insane. The insanity is created by external circumstances. Happy people don't commit suicide. Contented people don't commit suicide. Even *sad* people do not commit suicide.

Nor, as is so often and so glibly remarked, is a suicide a 'cry for help'.

Rather it is a last and desperate attempt at communication. This is something I found so many times. As if the suicide had said to himself, 'They don't understand. I can't *make* them understand. Perhaps they don't *want* to understand. But if I kill myself, *then* they'll see how I feel. *Then* they'll be sorry. Then they'll *try* to understand.'

That, I think, is the immaculate state of pure illogicality to which the majority of suicides have been reduced. Their mind stops short of the obvious realisation that, assuming 'they' are thus *made* to 'understand', it will have achieved nothing; the 'understanding' will be too late for the unhappy person wishing to be 'understood'. I am quite convinced that, to the majority of wretched people on the point of taking their own lives, the word 'suicide' does not equate with the word 'death'.

Thus a suicide, to every copper with feelings, is bad news. News almost as bad is the attempted suicide; the guy who botched it up. The one who took a bottle of sleeping pills, but who had the stomach-pump inserted before it was too late. The one who was rescued from a gas-filled room and given oxygen. The one who has hacked at his own throat, or his own wrist, but has only succeeded in scarring himself.

The reaction is one of shame and self-contempt. For a time the disturbed mind is stable; it may become unstable again, when the would-be suicide leaves hospital but now, thanks to modern drugs, the poor guy can think . . . and he thinks too much.

And if he has any doubts about his standing in the community, the fact that there is a copper sitting in the chair alongside his bed clarifies the situation. The plastic dish upon which is served his food. The plastic knife, fork and spoon with which he eats that food. The fact that he is not allowed a razor with which to shave. They all emphasise the official view of 'authority'. He has attempted to commit a felony . . . therefore he is a criminal, and the copper is there for a purpose.

But you see criminals – *real* criminals – rarely commit suicide. Rarely attempt suicide. If that were not so, few people would leave prison alive.

Some of the most miserable hours of my police service

were spent in darkened hospital wards, trying to comfort some unutterably unhappy man. Trying to convince him that I'm only a token. That, most assuredly, he is unlikely to be charged with a crime and that on his release from hospital some near relative will take over and give the affection he thought he was missing out on.

A most unhappy duty, unless, of course, there happens to be a 'George' present. . . .

I was on night watch alongside an attempted suicide. It wasn't my case, but I'd been detailed to take over at 10 p.m. until I was relieved at 6 a.m. It was Men's Medical, and a large ward in a large hospital.

I'd been provided with a moderately comfortable chair, but the only illumination came from two low-powered bulbs, one at each end of the ward. I was, I thought, in for a long and dreary stint.

The night sister stopped for a chat at a little before midnight.

'I'll arrange for a cup of tea and a sandwich to be sent to you, Constable.'

'That's very kind of you.'

'Meanwhile, can I ask a small favour?'

'Of course.'

'George.' She pointed to one of the beds across from where I was sitting. 'He's a little eccentric.' She smiled, then corrected herself. 'Actually, he's something of a nuisance, and we're short-staffed. Could you keep an eye on him for us, please?'

'Of course.'

'Make sure he stays in bed.'

'Certainly.'

'If it gets too bad, call one of the nurses. She'll understand.'

'Leave it with me, Sister.'

I must have dropped off, because I was awakened by the solemn drone of a man's voice.

'. . . as it hath pleased Almighty God of his great mercy to take unto himself the soul of our dear brother here departed . . .'

I pushed myself from the chair, peered down the ward and saw a figure standing near the head of one of the beds.

233

'. . . we therefore commit his body to the ground; earth to earth, ashes to ashes, dust to dust . . .'

I hurried down the ward and hauled George away from the goggle-eyed man staring up from the bed. The poor guy was ill, but not *that* ill! And it wasn't making for a speedy recovery with some loony standing over him intoning the Burial Service.

I guided George back to his own bed and gave him a stern warning to behave himself.

I'd cat-napped off when a whispered call awakened me. George was at it again.

He was sitting at the table in the middle of the ward. He was happily eating his way through a vase-full of chrysanthemums – stalks and all – and swilling each mouthful down with a swig from the water they'd been standing in.

This time I was firmer with him. Blunter. There was much finger-wagging and a threat to tell the night sister if he didn't stay in bed and behave himself.

But the antics of George had brought the man I was sitting with more fully awake. It had also interrupted his thoughts of self-recrimination. Therefore we talked and, although I only half-listened, I encouraged him to ramble on about the past life. His once-upon-a-time ambitions and his escapades as a youth. The hard, gunmetal sheen of dawn was lighting the ward windows when he smiled and nodded to a point down the ward and beyond my shoulder.

He said, 'He's at it again.'

The poor guy in the corner bed had some sort of skin disease. A large jar of ointment stood on top of his bedside locker. George was happily scooping the ointment out of its container and eating it.

I breathed, 'Oh, my Christ!' and rushed to the rescue.

This time I told the nurse.

George, it seemed, was due to be X-rayed shortly after my relief took over at 6 a.m. As I recall, I left that hospital rather hurriedly. What George might do if let loose in the X-ray department scared me a little.

That, then, is suicide. Something every working copper

234

meets with heartbreaking regularity. Some coppers come to terms with it; to them, it is merely one more compartment within the overall division of 'Sudden Death'. I never did. Unlike a road accident, unlike a fatal heart attack, suicide is still tinged with that mediaeval malediction of the Dark Ages. This is wrong, of course. It is illogical. It is as silly as not walking under ladders, or not seeing the new moon through glass. But it remains and to some coppers – and I was one of them – the handling of a suicide will remain a particularly grim duty.

Huby

By the time I arrived at Harrogate I was fast becoming one of the more ancient monuments of the West Riding of Yorkshire Constabulary. I'd served in Halifax Division: the division of wool and shoddy; in Doncaster Division: the division of miners and pitheads; and now I moved north again, into Harrogate Division.

In some respects it was a little like moving from Joe's Caff straight into The Savoy ... a little like that, but not much.

Harrogate claims to be a 'spa town'. A very select watering place. It boasts the fact that, pre-war, Sir Thomas Beecham, while conducting at Leeds, couldn't find a hotel there capable of meeting his needs and therefore stayed at Harrogate. With a slightly superior smirk it reminds all who care to listen that while in exile from his country Haile Selassie, Emperor of Ethiopia, self-styled King of kings and Lion of Judah, preferred Harrogate to London between 1936 and 1941. It must be admitted that I, too, can remember the time when mere buses were allowed to stop but not *stay* within the town limits. And the very idea of a housing estate!

By the time I began to pound the peeling gilt of the pavements, things had changed. It is even worse today. The road leading to Otley is pock-marked with sprawling estates of identical, flung-together houses. Even the centre of Harrogate is losing much of its original Victorian charm. A statue of the monarch it was so difficult to amuse stands awkwardly alongside a railway station any kid with limited imagination and a Lego set could have modelled.

But when I started there, the only housing estate was at Bilton, and even that estate was tucked away behind a

236

façade of long-established, moderately well-to-do houses. It was a fairly big estate and, in fairness, the houses all had a certain 'craftsman' quality and, with so many souls gathered in one spot, the police authority decided to move in on the act. They built five houses – one detached and two pairs of semi-detached. I was offered one of the semis and, on the day of the removal, I plonked a partly recovered Avis at the Fox Hotel in Aberford, pending all the furniture being humped into place and things generally being ready for her to move into a civilised home.

Thereafter, I started bobbying Bilton Section – which in effect was part of Harrogate itself – along with a handful of younger officers and a sergeant of the old school of policing.

There was a marked absence of bloodthirsty hooligans, which made a pleasant change from what I'd been used to in Doncaster Division. Bish-bash-bosh bobbying was definitely out. On the other hand, some of the residents demanded full value (and more) for what they paid in rates and taxes.

Broadly speaking, the community divided itself into four sections. There was an overlap, of course, but very roughly it worked like this.

The Wealthy. There was (perhaps still is) a stratum of Harrogate society which by normal yardsticks had loot. Not too many millionaires, you understand, and by Belgravia standards positively poverty stricken, but they were the left-overs from an age when the 'servants' quarters' were a vital part of every gentleman's residence. And they certainly had money. They were the people who employed gardeners, cleaning ladies and, sometimes, live-out cooks. Some of them still lived in the rambling houses that had been built by their grandparents or great-grandparents. Some had converted those homes into expensive, self-contained flats, in one of which they, themselves, lived. Some had permanent rooms in the hotels of the town.

They provided a steady income to an over-abundance of solicitors, accountants and private nursing homes. And to these people the bobby-on-the-street was almost a part of the domestic staff.

Having said that, it must be emphasised that they carried their wealth, plus whatever power that wealth commanded, with an easy grace. Merely remove the jingling ice-cream cart from their immediate vicinity in summer and prevent the kids from making slides on *their* footpaths in winter, and they were happy.

The Visitors. What a lot of us tended to forget – at least sometimes – was that Harrogate was a 'holiday town'. A very posh holiday town, I may say, but one complete with two cinemas, a live theatre and some of the most beautiful municipal gardens in the country. It hadn't a seashore, but it was the home of the Yorkshire Show. It couldn't very well boast a pier, but it had more than its share of nightclubs.

It had one of the few five-star hotels in Yorkshire, plus more four-stars than you could shake a conference committee at. People came to Harrogate on holiday. Lots of people. Some to laze away a week or two in the comfort of its hostelries. Some to set out, each day, on an exploration of the Yorkshire Dales.

And just occasionally the visitors had a drop too much to drink and became rowdy. (Rowdy, that is, for *Harrogate*. By Doncaster standards they were still in a state of coma.) That was when you politely pointed them in the direction of the nick before tucking them up in a cell for the night.

The Proletariat. The ordinary people, who were neither wealthy nor holidaymakers. Mostly they were employed in what are called 'service industries'. The Ordnance Survey people had a place there. So had Dunlop, the mattress people. After that, start counting shops (of which there were an abundance) and cafés (of which there were too many). At a guess a quarter of the people who lived in Harrogate worked outside Harrogate. In Leeds or Bradford mainly. A handful even worked in London . . . and that's one hell of a distance to commute, even once a week.

Generally speaking, pleasant, well-behaved people who realised their good fortune at living in a town which, while catering for a certain refined pleasure, did not go in for whelk stalls or fancy hats.

The Itinerants. Not all the itinerants, of course, but in a town with as many hotels and restaurants as Harrogate had the necessary backstairs staff employed in the place was quite considerable and, although the employers doubtless tried to weed out the undesirables, some loonies slipped through the net.

These boys caused what trouble there was and were duly dealt with. As always with voluble minorities their protestations were loud and long, but they still went inside, they still ended up at the local court and, although they huffed and puffed about a 'liberty' they had abused, they were duly fined. Very often this caused them to shake the dust of the town from their heels . . . and everybody was happy.

This, then, was Harrogate. A few light years from Bentley and Toll Bar. Totally different from Brighouse and Elland. A more 'gentlemanly', more sedate style of policing. Boring, perhaps, but I was prepared to tolerate a little thing like boredom for the sake of a quiet life. I'd been licked. Metcalfe had won. Avis was gradually fighting her way back to full health. A few more years and I'd draw a pension.

It is known as 'soldiering on'. Eight hours of pavement-bashing a day. Taking charge of the section when the sergeant wasn't on duty. A spot of traffic control now and again. My fair share of court duty.

That's what I figured . . . but I was wrong.

* * *

The two pairs of semi-detached police houses were set close together: the space between the two pairs just about took a motor car. There was a communal gate – a car's width – and a flagged path leading to the rear of the houses. The side door of each house looked directly into the side door of the other house, with only the width of this flagged path between.

The detective constable who lived in the other house had a car. I, too, had a car. There *had* to be a glorified game of draughts if the guy who put his car in first wanted to get out before the guy who put his car in last. There was, therefore, much knocking on doors and perpetual apologising and asking, 'Do you mind . . .?' or 'Will you please . . .?'

The DC was a young chap, a pleasant enough character, and we got along fine at work. But he had a family and, like all kids, they enjoyed playing in the garden. Because there was no fence – no division of any kind between the houses – their garden was also our garden and our doorstep was their doorstep, and they were too young to understand the difference. In fairness, the wife of the DC tried. She shooed them on to their own area whenever she spotted them, but she couldn't stop them leaving toys and tricycles strewn all over the two doorways.

That was the set-up and, in truth, I blame nobody . . . well, maybe the architect who planned the houses.

The only thing I can be certain of is that one day I arrived home after an early shift and found Avis sitting in a chair, crying. Sobbing, without real cause. Heartbroken because – or so it seemed – a simple thing like peaceful living was beyond our grasp. Understand me. That isn't, and wasn't, like Avis. Avis is a fighter. Nobody – but *nobody!* – rides rough-shod over *her* neck without receiving that stare which makes permafrost seem like an electric blanket.

But now, this.

In a clumsy way I could understand. It wasn't the DC or his wife or his kids. It was the cumulative effect of that damned law degree, plus the punishment posting, plus the fact that, although I could honestly count inspectors, chief inspectors and superintendents among my circle of friends – and coppers and sergeants galore – I still hadn't a cat in hell's chance of promotion. It had all been for sod all. All the work, all the grind, all the sacrifice.

In effect, and temporarily, she'd broken. At that moment, Metcalfe lived only because I couldn't get my fingers round his neck.

I comforted her as much as any man can comfort the woman he loves while fighting his own rising panic. Then I drove to Harrogate Divisional Headquarters.

Because I'd only very recently arrived at the division, I didn't know the superintendent. I'd met him once; while I was on the Detective Course, subsequent to the Duty Elsewhere details, he'd been a sergeant instructor, but other than that I knew him only by name. Nevertheless, I asked to see him, and once inside his office I didn't waste words.

'I'm sorry, sir. I have to resign.'

'Why?'

He was the sort of guy who didn't flap. He'd flown in the war, and the DFC held pride of place among the fruit salad on the breast of his tunic. Maybe we were two ex-RAF types talking to each other. What we were *not* was a foot-slogger asking favours from a divisional officer. Neither of us acted *that* part.

'I have to resign,' I repeated.

'First of all, you have to sit down.' He motioned to a chair. 'Then you have to tell me *why* you have to resign.'

So I sat down, but sitting down didn't weaken my determination.

It wasn't a threat. It wasn't a bluff. It was a simple statement of intention and, as I saw things, the only way out.

Nor were his questions nosey. He merely wanted an explanation.

I gave him his explanation, but I didn't mention Detective Chief Superintendent Metcalfe. That would have been far too much of a capitulation. Instead, I told most of what I believed to be the truth: that I'd obviously stretched both myself and my wife to the limit. Obviously too far and beyond the limit.

'Not an easy thing, a law degree,' he murmured.

'You don't have to draw *me* graphs, sir.'

'Why are you still only a beat constable?'

'I don't know,' I lied.

'You must have upset somebody . . . somewhere.'

I didn't answer that one. It is possible – indeed, probable – I didn't *have* to answer. He was a wise bird, as I later learned.

He continued to ask quiet but penetrating questions. Gentle questions, phrased with care in order not to hurt.

Would Avis recover more quickly in the country?

I didn't know. And that was the truth. When your

241

world is tottering around your ears, you are in no condition to make educated guesses.

'But you've been *used* to a rural beat, haven't you?'

'Yes, sir.'

'For most of your career, you've been a village bobby?'

'For most of my career,' I agreed.

'Happy?' he asked, quietly.

'Sir?'

'Were you happy as a village bobby?'

'Oh, yes.'

'And your wife? Was *she* happy?'

'Yes, sir.' I spoke carefully. 'I think the quietness of a rural beat is something she particularly likes.' Then hurriedly, 'But I'm *not* applying for a transfer. I'm not using my wife as an excuse.'

'As an excuse for *what*?' he enquired, with a smile.

Again, I didn't answer.

He offered me a cigarette and, when I'd taken one, he put forward a proposition.

'Try my way first, Constable.' Then, because I obviously didn't understand, 'I'll accept your resignation, if I'm wrong. But first try it my way. Take some annual leave, as from this afternoon.'

'I've no annual leave left for this year, sir.'

'Let's call it compassionate leave.' Without waiting for a reply, he picked up a telephone and spoke to a sergeant clerk. 'Sergeant. Fourteen days' compassionate leave, as from today, for Constable Seven-One-Eight Wainwright. Make out the application, then bring it into my office for immediate signature.' He returned his attention to me. 'There'll be a rural beat waiting for you when you get back.'

'Look, sir – I thank you – but I've no intention of applying for a –'

'An inter-divisional transfer, Wainwright. Nothing to do with Headquarters.

'Oh!'

'You haven't applied for anything. *I've* decided. A divisional officer can shift his men around when and if he thinks it might improve the efficiency of his division.'

I said, 'Oh!' again, then closed my mouth.

'Give her a break,' he advised. 'Take her to a quiet spot on the coast somewhere. Set off this evening and forget you're a policeman for a couple of weeks.'

'Yes, sir. Thank you, sir.'

Then, a little awkwardly, he said, 'Two weeks' holiday. Can your purse stretch to it?'

'I'll manage, sir.'

'Wainwright.' He shook his head gently. 'You have a reputation. You know that, don't you?'

'Sir?'

'Stiff-necked. The man who does it on his own or not at all.'

'No, sir. I didn't know –'

'We're talking about your wife. Remember that. We're talking about an obligation you have to *her*. There's an emergency fund, if you're short of cash. I'm not offering my own money. It's there to be dipped into . . . and it will have to be paid back.'

I didn't need the cash from the Emergency Fund. The holiday did wonders for Avis; first Silverdale, then Lytham, both on the west coast. Nor did it do me any harm and, when we returned, there was a quiet village beat waiting for me. Huby, on the outskirts of Harrogate. It was a little like the old Clifton Beat; the sort of personal, one-man area I'd grown used to covering and, this time, a place of fields and grass and trees.

Of far more importance, it was the sort of environment Avis needed.

The divisonal officer's name was Craven. Superintendent John Craven. He was nobody's lackey and nobody's fool. Some measured him up as a martinet, because he refused to suffer fools either gladly or at all. I didn't. He did his job, didn't give a damn about popularity and was one hell of a man to have alongside you in a tight corner.

God rest his soul.

The good also die.

Years later, in 1982, I tried to give him some small, but belated immortality in *Blayde R.I.P.* John Craven was the deliberate matrix for the character Superintendent John Chapman.

* * *

Huby. You will find it on no road map. You will, however, find Weeton and North Rigton. It was midway between Otley and Harrogate and, indeed, the sign *did* read 'Huby' although the tiny railway station alongside that sign was Weeton station. It was a puzzle I never solved. So many puzzles; tiny, fascinating puzzles which did much to add to the charm and oddity of the place. It was policed from Harrogate Division, but the local court was at Knaresborough, and when you required the Fire Service you called Otley. For an ambulance, however, you called Harrogate.

Craven had said, 'It's gone sloppy. The man who worked it before you had too many friends. Crack down on them a bit.'

I gave myself a couple of weeks to settle in, then one evening in October I pulled the plug.

It was a cul-de-sac of ordinary, semi-detached houses, off the main road. Most of the householders had cars and, indeed, most of the houses had drives on which those cars could be parked. There was no street lighting, and had an ambulance or fire engine required to get at houses at the end of the cul-de-sac there would either have been a shunt-up or a great deal of manoeuvring. About twenty parked cars, and not a light between them.

I patiently called at every house and politely explained the situation. The cars were parked on an unlighted road. They needed parking lights.

I received the usual non-excuses.

'The battery will be flat by morning.'

'I like to get off without having to back the thing out on to the road.'

'We've *always* left 'em there. You'll learn, when you've been here a bit.'

I didn't argue. I wasn't *there* to argue. I explained the law to them all, and told them I'd like to see the road cleared of unlighted vehicles. A week later, I returned. A few of them had taken the hint and moved their cars on to the drives, but the majority obviously figured this new copper they'd been lumbered with wasn't to be taken too seriously. Again, I did the rounds and, again, I was most polite and, for my pains, received more meaningless

244

mouth-music.

'It's all right, lad. We've parked 'em there for years.'

'It's not on the main road. It's not doing any *harm*.'

On 4 November – the day before Bonfire Night – I paid my third visit. This time, I didn't ask. This time I booked them. Eleven – all from the same cul-de-sac – all appearing at court on the same day, and all of them fined £50.

Craven was delighted.

The villagers got the message. Wainwright had arrived and, if pushed too far, Wainwright was quite prepared to be a regular bastard.

I recall that in an unspectacular way I was happy enough. Avis had recovered, which was the main thing. I was left strictly alone; I had a sergeant, an inspector and, of course, Craven himself but, other than a trip out in the country for a breath of fresh air, none of them bothered me. I worked the beat *my* way, and I had no complaints. I'd fought my battle with Metcalfe – who by this time had gone up a peg and become deputy chief constable – and, although I'd lost, I figured it had been an honourable defeat. OK, I'd always be a village copper. I'd do my 'twenty-five', then retire a comparatively young man and draw a decent pension.

And, of course, there was always the Square and Compass.

The Square and Compass was a roadhouse-cum-restaurant, and it was in the Egon Ronay class of eating places. It stood at the top of a side-road at North Rigton, and every Saturday night its popularity as a drinking place and an eating spot drew the crowds. They all had cars and, unfortunately, the hotel car-park wasn't big enough. By 7 p.m. the roads and lanes around the Square and Compass were stiff with vehicles. By 10.30 p.m. and closing time, it was pure chaos. Occasionally a Special Constable would be shunted in to assist, but Special Constables tend towards pomposity. They must be *doing* something, if only to prove their presence. In fact (as any practical copper will confirm) a clown waving his arms around in the middle of a traffic snarl-up usually does more harm than good. The trick was to stand aside, give them room to untangle themselves and only step into the limelight if and when they'd completely knotted themselves.

In the main, it was watching for drunks. Stopping them from getting behind a wheel and killing themselves.

And, even that isn't quite so simple as it may seem . . .

I saw one reveller come out of the pub and get into his car – a small family car. He was away before I could reach him. And he was *drunk*.

I raced for my own car, jumped inside and gave chase. Mine wasn't a police vehicle, therefore I hadn't a radio link. The take-them-for-granted walkie-talkie equipment of today hadn't yet come on the market. Quite simply, it was a one-to-one situation, but the guy was roaring drunk and driving a motor car on my patch.

I belted down the hill after him and turned right on the A658 towards Otley. He was ahead of me – about two hundred yards in front – and every so often he'd leave the road, cannon off one of the dry-stone walls and leave one more piece of his motor car for me to steer around. He was virtually writing the blasted car off, but he was too damn drunk to notice.

We'd left my beat – we'd left the division – and were haring into the Otley area when he reached a double-bend. God must have had His eye on him, because there wasn't another vehicle on the road. This time he hit *both* walls – first the nearside wall, then across the road and a glancing blow on the offside wall – and the poor car gave up the effort. It had no choice. The double-clout had knocked all four wheels off. Not counting two ruined mudguards, a door torn from its hinges and a radiator that had been smashed back into the engine.

I braked to a halt, climbed from my car and hurried to where the wreck had rested. I expected to find blood and broken bones.

Not a bit of it.

As I leaned lower than usual to peer into the wheel-less car he beamed a smile up at me and turned the ignition key in its lock.

'It's quite all right, Officer. I think the engine's stalled. I'll have it going again in a minute.'

I still pumped out articles for *Police Review*, and they were still published. I like to think they were gradually becoming less stodgy, if only because I was now prepared to put my own name to them.

Then on Friday, 12 January, 1962, I hit the national headlines in a big way. Less than 1500 words under the title 'Operation "Digit Extraction."' put my photograph in the *Yorkshire Post*, the *Daily Herald*, the *Daily Express*, the *Daily Mail* and every other newspaper on the stands, under banner headlines like 'Law Degree PC Raps the Force', 'Village PC Tells Force, "Pull Your Finger Out"' and 'PC718 Writes a Shocker'.

Oh, my word!

And all I'd done was express an opinion.

I had, of course, done the unforgivable. I'd criticised the Police Service from *inside* the Police Service. I'd broken ranks, and that my criticism was valid didn't mean a thing.

My criticism came under five headings.

1. *The Parochial Outlook:* 'Some police constables are little concerned with crime other than crime committed on their own beat. With the parochial outlook comes the lack of that little extra enthusiasm concerning "foreign" crimes which might well have resulted in the arrest of the criminal.'

2. *The Localised CID:* 'It must be recognised that the average criminal investigation department is, of necessity, geared to deal with day-to-day criminal activities in its own area. Local crime must take precedence, and in time a more or less stereotyped routine is developed. This is often incapable of effectively coping with the type of major crime with which we are concerned.'

3. *The Departmental Condition:* 'Generally speaking, it can be said that the less efficient the police force, the less co-operation and liaison it offers to other forces or enjoys between its various departments.'

4. *The Mental Approach:* 'The major criminal is nobody's

fool, but there are still some police officers who refuse to credit the criminally minded person with the ability to think and plan intelligently. To such officers the word criminal is synonymous with the name Bill Sikes.'

5. *The Stable-door Theory:* 'If half the energy consumed after the commission of a major crime had been expended before that crime had been committed, the chances are that the major criminal would have had second thoughts about it all in the first place.'

*   *   *

That was the kernel of the article. Not much compared with what I've written since, but it must be examined in the context of the day. At that time we had no Regional Crime Squads, no Task Forces, no Serious Crime experts and nobody had thought of 'targeting' a known top criminal till he was in the bag. It was very horse-and-buggy bobbying in those days, and that article upset quite a few equilibriums.

Force Headquarters put out a very po-faced reaction in response to the media's nudgings. 'There will be no comment on PC Wainwright's article until it has been fully studied.'

There never *was* a 'comment'.

Later that week Superintendent Craven called me into his office and, being the man he was, it went like this.

'I have word from on high to ballock you, Wainwright.'

'Yes, sir.'

'Consider yourself ballocked.'

'Yes, sir.'

'Now . . . do you want a personal opinion?'

'Yes, sir.'

'It needed saying. It should have been said years ago. I'm only sorry *you* decided to say it.'

'Why's that, sir?'

'You seem hell-bent on going out of the way to rub people up the wrong way. People who matter.'

'Do they matter to you?' I asked.

'No. But I hold a rank they can't take away from me.'

'They can't demote *me*, sir.' I think I sounded a little bitter. I could talk to this man, and he understood. Some of the others I didn't give a damn about but, perhaps because of Avis, it hurt more than I was prepared to admit. I said, 'I'm at the bottom of the ladder. To get me any lower, they'd have to dig a hole.'

'And some of them,' he warned, grimly, 'would do just that.'

I like to think some good came from that article. When I'm in the mood I kid myself that as a result of that piece somebody with far more weight than I had made Crime Prevention something more than a spare-time duty pushed in the general direction of any detective constable with nothing else to do; that a ponderous, but very certain, reorganisation took place within the ranks of the CID and that as a result of that reorganisation some big-time crooks had their collars felt in the last two decades.

Stranger things have happened, and it only takes the movement of one stone to start an avalanche.

But for a few days I was big news, and even that provided a sour chuckle.

I received a postcard – a postcard, mind you, which dozens of people must have read – from the London Metropolitan Police District. It arrived, via Wakefield Headquarters, and the writer pleaded with me to do what I could to stop one of the superintendents of the capital from peeping through the curtains and watching his wife undressing. And it was signed. And it carried the address of the sender. *And* it named the kinky superintendent!

*　　*　　*

Meanwhile Huby kept me busy enough, and the smiles arrived with moderate regularity.

One night the telephone bell rang, just before midnight. I was off duty and an obviously worried man reported that his wife had had an accident.

'She isn't hurt. But she left the road, and the car's straddling a low wall on your beat.'

'Can I have your name please, sir?'

'Bowes. William Bowes.'

'And your address?'

He gave the address, and bells began to ring inside my head. I interrupted what he was saying.

'Excuse me, but are you "Big Bill" Bowes? The

249

Yorkshire cricketer?'

'I used to play for Yorkshire,' he admitted, reluctantly.

'You *are* "Big Bill" Bowes?'

'Yes.'

'Can you – er . . .' I hesitated, then took the plunge. 'Can you get the car moved before six o'clock?'

'I think so.' He sounded puzzled. 'I have a friend who's a garage owner.'

'Do that,' I suggested. 'I know the wall you mean. I know the farmer. He's been going to rebuild that wall for years. Get the car shifted . . . then forget it.'

'Look, Constable, I don't want favours.'

'Not a favour, Mr Bowes. A thank you for a lot of pleasure you've given me in the past.'

That's how we worked it and if, in some small degree, I was doing a 'Metcalfe', what of it? I was doing it for one of my boyhood heroes, and I felt no guilt.

And that night the nine–nine–nine call came, just as we were thinking about going to bed.

To get the best from this story, the nine–nine–nine set-up must be explained. A member of the public dials nine–nine–nine. At the exchange it gets priority and the operator asks which service is required. If that service is the police, the call is slammed through – in this case to Harrogate DHQ – and a bloody great bell on the switchboard starts ringing. The man on the switchboard drops everything and takes the call. He gets the location, then contacts the nearest copper and sends him to the scene. When things have been sorted out, that copper has to submit a report, in triplicate, justifying all this hot-shot activity.

On this occasion a timid resident had heard somebody scratching at his back door. Obviously, somebody trying to break into his home.

I grabbed torch, truncheon and jacket and drove to the house. The man was waiting by a partly open front door. He was scared and, when he led me through to the kitchen at the rear, sure enough the scratching sound could be clearly heard.

I opened the door with a rush, shone my torch, and there they were. Two hedgehogs mating!

250

Now, try to put *that* in officialese, in triplicate, and without making yourself, or the man ringing the triple-niner, sound like a fool. . . .

*　　*　　*

This was the period when I had my first piece of fiction published. A very short piece. Little more than a thousand words in length, and published in the ever-faithful *Police Review*. That journal didn't go in for short stories; articles, opinion, case law and news from around the forces filled its pages. Nevertheless, on Friday, 15 March, 1963 it published a short story called *Tergiversation*. As a short story it isn't up to much. It is, supposedly, a 'police procedural' piece of fiction, but I should have known better. Coppers don't talk that way. Coppers don't *act* that way. And, as every agent and editor I ever worked with will happily verify, I started as I meant to go on . . . it was a stinker of a title.

I was still cobbling out the legal bits and pieces but, for a change, my reading began to encompass fiction. Especially crime fiction. I discovered Chandler and Hammett and, at the same time, drooled over Robert Graves's *I Claudius* and *Claudius the God*.

At that time, Avis and I joined Harrogate Writers' Circle. Somebody suggested we drop in on a meeting. We did, and we were hooked.

I now know that, as a general rule, these groups all tend towards po-faced solemnity. They take themselves too seriously and yet, at rock bottom, are abysmally ignorant about what they profess to understand. Since that time I've seen so many, and the vast majority of them refuse to accept the gulf that exists between 'writing' and 'being a writer'.

The Harrogate Circle (at that time) was 'different'. It was a fortnightly gathering of happy people, none of whom claimed to be boss and all of whom didn't mind being laughed at a little.

Miss Rosita Black, the secretary, was a delightful lady who became our friend. She was unmarried, but of 'independent means', and of Scottish ancestry which ensured her level-headedness. The measure of her character can be gauged by the fact that she was a single

251

lady by choice; until her middle years she'd voluntarily nursed a very sick mother and thereafter she'd lived alone, but through it all had retained a gentle, unshockable humour.

Daisy Dennison, the chair-person. Firm without being bossy. Always ready with the right word or phrase to put people at their ease.

Joan Nicholson, the first published novelist we ever met. She was never top-bracket, but had she spent more time learning her craft instead of guiding some of the hopeless ones, she might have made it.

The men merely made up the numbers but, in honesty, none of us swaggered around making believe we were latter-day Byrons. We were a good bunch and, looking back, I think the happy atmosphere triggered off the enthusiasm and stoked the determination. The graft, as far as I was concerned, was done in solitude, away from the circle, and the most that can be said is that if our batteries flagged, the fortnightly recharge stopped them from going completely flat. We learned nothing. We were taught nothing – authorship being one profession that can never be 'taught' – but by stretching the imagination it might be suggested that we occasionally spotted what *not* to do . . . and, if so, some of us saved time. But no more. In effect, we were a club. To our credit we took neither ourselves nor anybody else too seriously.

Occasionally we roped in a 'speaker', and I well remember one poetic lady . . .

She was a full-blooded, honest-to-God poetess. I'd never heard of her but in those days that was no yardstick. I *still* can't remember her name, or from where the committee excavated her, but I know she looked and acted the part. She wasn't old; she was merely odd. She wasn't ugly; she was merely untidy. She wore expensive clothes, but she wore them badly; the impression was that they'd been thrown at her, that she'd caught them awkwardly, then allowed them to remain where they landed.

No matter. I, whose poetic know-how stopped short in the vicinity of the Young Lady of Gloucester, was ready to listen and anxious to learn.

I listened but I did not learn.

Nor did the fifty or so other listeners. We heard some very high-voltage stuff. We witnessed much arm-thrashing and chin-thrusting, accompanying expositions and abstractions which, at a pinch, Wordsworth and Milton would have gawped at.

We understood none of it.

At the end, the poetic lady flung her cloak across her shoulders, glared at her dim-witted audience, then flounced out of the room leaving us all dizzy, but as dumb as ever.

At that meeting, we took a fellow-copper and his wife along with us. Joe and Florence Heap. We'd been close friends for years, and we'd made a foursome on some truly joyous occasions.

Joe was one of the nicest guys I've ever met, but no literary giant. Prior to that evening he'd counted me as an amiable but harmless eccentric. After the poetess had performed her party piece, he was convinced I was a raving lunatic.

But that was my hobby. Policing was still my business, and it still had a few high-spots to offer.

At one o'clock one morning I'd garaged the car after ending another eight hours of patrol duty. Avis was waiting up for me, as always, and as I walked into the house she said, 'There's a man just been to the door – less than half an hour since – and he wants to know if we can get him back to Menston.'

Menston was – and still is – a mental hospital. Pre-war, when I'd lived in Leeds, a 'green ticket to Menston' had been something to be feared. Those days it had been called 'the Asylum'; a terrible and terrifying place of padded cells and straitjackets. Civilisation had taken a few steps away from the Dark Ages since then, but the name Menston still meant only one thing.

'I didn't ask him in,' apologised Avis. 'I didn't know whether he was violent or not.'

'That's OK.' I re-belted my tunic. 'I'll have a hunt around. See if I can come across him.'

I didn't even have to get the car out. I found him less than a hundred yards from the house, crouching in a hedge-bottom, terrified by the night sounds of the countryside. When the beam of my torch touched him he winced, as if he'd been slapped across the face.

His first words were, 'Are you going to thump me?'

He was such a little guy, made to look even smaller by the shapeless jacket and trousers, both of which were a couple of sizes too big. Nor did the heavy boots, the 'union' shirt and the grubby cap enhance his appearance. But, eventually, I convinced him that despite the uniform I was there to help him.

I took him home, Avis brewed hot tea and, in his own whimsical way, he told us what had happened.

There'd been a cinema show at the hospital. A Walt Disney film. This had meant a walk of a few hundred yards from the main hospital to some sort of theatre. The little guy thought he'd seen the film before, therefore he'd decided to take an evening stroll. He'd walked out of the gates, unchallenged, and had kept on walking until he'd seen the light in our window. Now, he wanted to get back to the hospital, and bed.

Very plaintively, he ended, 'They'll thump me when I get back.'

'They won't thump you, old son,' I promised. 'Just enjoy your tea, have a biscuit and sit there till I organise transport.'

I telephoned Menston, told the man on duty who I was and why I was ringing.

'He walked out?' verified the man.

'So it seems.'

'He can bloody well walk back.'

'I'm not letting him out of my house,' I said, grimly. 'I need transport. I need an ambulance.'

'You won't get an ambulance for that one at this time of night.'

'Don't bet on it,' I growled.

I dialled the local ambulance service and explained my problem.

'Sorry. I'm afraid it's not an emergency.'

'As far as I'm concerned, it's very much an emergency. I have an inmate from Menston sitting in my house, and I want to get him back to where he belongs.'

'It's not our problem, Officer.'

'It's *somebody*'s blasted problem.'

'Can't you take him back in your own car?'

'I could,' I agreed. 'But on a point of principle I'm damned if I'm going to.'

It was now well past two o'clock and both Menston and the ambulance service seemed loath to take my visitor off my hands. Something drastic was called for.

I looked up the home number of the local Medical Officer of Health, dialled and waited.

Eventually a sleepy voice answered and I told my tale of woe.

'I'm not sitting up all night with him,' I assured that official.

'Quite. Menston should come out to collect him.'

'They've refused. They suggest I should point him in the general direction, then tell him to walk.'

'In that case –'

'Just a minute, sir,' I interrupted.

'Yes. What is it?'

'I'm getting my notebook out. If *you*'re going to instruct me to tell him to walk back, I'm going to make a careful note of the time, then write down what you say verbatim.'

'Er – why? Why do that?'

'So that, when I do let the man loose, it's on your instructions. That makes it *your* responsibility. Then if he does anything on the way home . . .'

'What? What might he do on the way back to Menston?'

'Kill somebody?' I suggested, cheerfully.

'Is he *dangerous*?' He sounded startled.

'I don't know. I'm not up on these things. But people don't end up in Menston because they have a bad cold.'

'No, of course not. I see your point, Constable. Keep him there, please. I'll arrange for an ambulance to come out from Menston to collect him. Oh, and you'd better go back with him. He'll have grown used to you by this time. It might help to keep him quiet.'

'The ambulance to return me to Huby, of course,' I reminded him.

'Of course. Of course. Leave it to me, Constable. I'll get things moving.'

Whatever he had to move must have been heavy. It was almost four o'clock before the ambulance from Menston arrived. As I climbed into the back with the little guy he voiced his worry.

'They'll thump me,' he said, sadly.

'No, they won't. You'll soon be in bed, old son.'

'They will,' he insisted. 'They'll thump me.'

At the hospital, the creep who'd suggested I make the little guy walk back was waiting.

'He's scared,' I said. 'He's frightened you'll thump him.'

'We'll bloody well thump him,' he promised, grimly.

'You won't.'

'Eh?'

'I'll be round again, maybe tomorrow,' I assured him. 'Maybe the next day. Maybe the day after that. Sometime. He'll tell me, because he trusts me. If anybody lays a glove on him, a report goes in.'

'Eh?'

'A report,' I repeated. 'And just to make sure, a hint dropped to some hotshot investigative journalist. Sit on those hands of yours, sonny, otherwise they'll land you in trouble.'

The truth is, I didn't return to Menston, and that to my shame. But the creep with the muscles had been quietened and, hopefully, he did what he was paid to do rather than what he seemed to *like* doing.

*   *   *

These memories are about policing, not about authorship. I must, therefore, compress what began as a hobby and is now my profession into as few words as possible.

I'd read a batch of particularly badly written crime novels; the authors had missed out on groundwork, didn't know how coppers talked and hadn't a clue about the sheer chaos of a genuine murder enquiry. I figured I could do as well . . . probably better.

At about the same time, I read Norman Lewis's *The Honoured Society* and Estes Kefauver's *Crime in America*. As a copper, the Mafia fascinated me. As a would-be novelist, it was an obvious choice.

The end result was *Death in a Sleeping City*, sent to an agent and accepted by Collins Crime Club within a month of posting.

Metcalfe wanted to see me . . . of course.

'What's all this about you writing a book?'

I told him, and he was displeased.

'It's not allowed,' he snapped. 'Coppers aren't allowed to write books.'

'Where does it say that, sir?'

'Eh?'

'I've checked the Acts of Parliament. I've checked Police Regulations and Force Standing Orders. I can't find anything that prohibits a serving police officer from writing fiction.'

'I'm *ordering* you, Constable. Get that rubbish back before it gets printed.'

'With respect, sir . . .' I trod very carefully. 'I don't think you're entitled to give such an order. And I'd be in trouble if I obeyed it.'

'Eh?' The glare should have terrified me, but it didn't.

'I've signed a contract,' I explained. 'I don't think you can order me to break the law by not honouring the contract.'

I had him by the short and curlies, and I knew it. He didn't like the experience, and I knew that, too . . . but I didn't give a straight-faced damn. I pretended not to be enjoying myself, but he knew I *was*.

'That rubbish' went rather well. Hardback, paperback, a handful of translations, serialisation and, to cap everything, the BBC asked me to turn it into a radio play for Saturday Night Theatre. And by that time, *Ten Steps to the Gallows* had been published and *Evil Intent* was coming up fast.

Then the publishing house of Wheaton's asked me to write a career guide called *Shall I be a Policeman?* They wanted photographs and I approached our own Photography Section for shots of county coppers doing their thing, and Bradford City Police for photographs of their men at work. I couldn't have been given more help.

I was riding the crest of a very nice wave and, because of the co-operation of my own force and that of the Bradford City force, it seemed only right that I donate what royalties *Shall I be a Policeman?* might bring in to the

Police Widows and Orphans Fund. I myself wasn't doing too badly, and the widow of a copper had a thin time.

It meant making a formal application to the chief constable but that, I was assured, meant little more than going through the motions. Word came for me to visit Wakefield Headquarters, but the chief was away on holiday.

Metcalfe was sitting in for him.

His opening remark was heavy with sarcasm, and was deliberately meant to needle me.

'My word, Wainwright, you'll need Pickfords to take your money to the bank these days, won't you?'

'No, sir.' I determined to play it cool.

'I wonder you can bring yourself to speak to ordinary coppers.'

'I force myself, sir.'

'No doubt your duties as a policeman are suffering.'

'I've had no complaints, sir.'

'This application . . .' He touched the form on the desk. 'You're not serious, of course.'

'Yes, sir. I'm very serious.'

'Oh, no.' He shook his head, and hated me with his eyes. 'Go back to your piffling little beat, Wainwright. You're still what you'll always be . . . a village copper. The widows and orphans don't want *your* bloody charity.'

It was a monumentally stupid thing to say. His detestation had blinded him to all caution. He was talking about a registered charity over which he held no authority and, without any reasonable cause, he was refusing a subscription to that charity. Had I wished, I could have turned his hatred back on him, knocked him flying from his perch and smashed him. And, a few years earlier, I'd have had no hesitation.

Why, then, didn't I?

At that moment, I couldn't have answered the question because things were happening inside me I didn't quite understand. I just didn't want the hassle.

Again . . . why this great upsurge of hatred by a man at the top of the constabulary tree for a man at its very base?

I only realised the truth later. In *his* eyes I was gloating, although I swear I wasn't. But in *his* eyes, and by offering to give money to the Widows and Orphans Fund, I was deliberately reminding him of a time, years past, when that same charity had been used as a let-out to deny him the hide of a man he was after.

But at that moment the fight had left me. The man was a louse, so let him *be* a louse . . . just let him also keep off my back. Five years hence (thereabouts) I'd be clear of the damn police force, and my life would be my own.

I returned to Huby; to eight hours of policing a day; to grinding away writing another book – another radio play – and making do with an average of four hours of sleep each night.

Then, quite suddenly, I cracked and had to crawl a way through the first nervous breakdown of my life. It left a terrible aftermath. A thing called manic depression, and I wouldn't wish that on *anybody*.

I was still groggy when, after two months of clearing the Black Imp from my shoulder, I went back to policing Huby Beat. All I wanted was peace for a few years; peace followed by a pension.

But Huby – dear old Huby – still had a last kick for me.

There was a coppice, out in the country between Huby and Harrogate; an area of about twenty acres, with a stream running through it and with fairly close-growing trees about eight inches in diameter. A B-road ran two field-lengths away, and I'd never been in the coppice since taking over the beat. I'd had no cause to. I'd seen it from the road and had thought it looked very pretty.

I ended up having nightmares about what happened in that coppice.

They were triggered off by an RAF jet trainer; single-seater, complete with ejection seat. I don't know which type. I never got round to asking. The only thing I *do* know is that the pilot lost control, skimmed the fields, dropped into that coppice and, whether by accident or far-too-late design, was catapulted from the cockpit by the ejector-seat mechanism.

I was the first copper at the scene, and I had it all to myself for more than thirty minutes.

The plane was all over the place. The wings had been sheared off, the fuselage had been smashed to hell and the tail-piece had gone. The bits and pieces of that poor aeroplane were scattered the length and breadth of that coppice, and only about half of them were identifiable. By some grace of God there wasn't a fire. I could, therefore, search.

I sought the pilot. He'd had less than a million-to-one chance of survival, but it had to be checked. He wasn't in what had once been the cockpit, so I moved farther afield.

I almost passed out when I found one of his legs, then, about fifty yards from the leg, one of his arms. Gradually – reluctantly – the penny dropped. The cockpit-harness with which he'd been strapped into the plane had done its job. Done it too well. It had torn the poor guy's limbs from his trunk. Somewhere in this coppice was another leg, another arm and the rest of him.

That was when the dogs started arriving . . . and I was still on my own.

Dogs, of course, don't know the difference. To them, blood is blood and raw meat is raw meat, and there was plenty of both around. Before anybody came to help, they numbered close to a dozen and I was throwing stones at them, I'd taken off my tunic and was flailing them with it. The truth is, I was in something of a panic and when the damn dogs found the second leg I had the devil of a job keeping them away from it.

And, of course, there were the rubber-neckers. . . .

Cars were collecting on the B-road. Solid citizens eager to view carnage. Nobody offered to help – it was too grisly for that – but necks were being craned and quite a few binoculars were out. One raving maniac lifted his six-year-old son over the wall, before he vaulted into the field, then ambled down the slope with his offspring towards the coppice.

'Where the hell are *you* going?' I think I screamed the question at him.

'Just taking the lad to see what's happened.'

'Get back on that bloody road.' Had I not witnessed it, I might not have believed any man could be so crazy. I ran towards him, and meant every word, when I gasped, 'If you don't get back on that road, so help me, I'll flatten you.'

The British copper *loves* the British public at moments like that.

Other coppers arrived with a rush, and only I know how glad I was to see them. We organised ourselves, and somebody found the pilot's parachute. We placed the shattered limbs into the canopy with as much respect as the job allowed. We found the trunk, and it was knocked to hell, but we couldn't find the head. Then we found it . . . It had been smashed into the chest cavity.

That was about it. That was about all I could take. I wandered around the smashed trees like a drunk unable to find his way home. I figured we'd found everything; that all we had to do now was to stay put and touch nothing, pending the arrival of an RAF investigation team.

I almost trod in a scarlet, squelchy mess at the foot of a tree. It took some recognising but, eventually, I identified it. It was what was left of the poor guy's liver.

I leaned against a trunk, took deep breaths and tried not to puke.

One of my colleagues walked over. He was as rough as they turn them out; known for his obscenities and not-too-pleasant habits.

'What's up, Jack?'

I nodded at the smashed up liver. I daren't open my mouth to speak.

'That's all right, mate.'

He stooped and, carrying it in his bare hands, took it to the parachute. The right man, in the right place, at the right time. He was the only one there who could have *done* that.

Later that evening, having soaked in a hot bath and changed into pyjamas and dressing-gown, I tried not to re-live those few hours in the coppice. I forced myself to write the book I was working on. Tried to concentrate on the programme on TV.

I didn't help. I still had nightmares – that night, and other nights – and Avis had to shake me awake, and hold me while I convinced myself I still had a life worth living.

Murder

I count myself a very lucky man: a crime novelist, the writer of 'police procedural' yarns, who doesn't have to make do with second-hand knowledge. I have *been* there. I have talked with murderers, talked with their next-of-kin, talked with relatives of the victim. More important, they have all talked to me.

I have reached certain very firm conclusions.

Hit men, terrorists and similar exotica apart, the 'habitual murderer' doesn't exist. Until fairly recently – at the time of which I write – habitual *criminals* who committed murder were rare animals. In the vast majority of cases, murder was a very domestic crime; it was committed by one member of the family upon another member of the family. The man-and-wife row that went a little too far. The mother who lashed out at her child. The son who turned on his father. In the main, a very grubby crime, committed on the spur of the moment and, having committed it, the murderer usually did one of two things: run like hell, or stand there, probably still holding the murder weapon, waiting for the police to arrive.

I hold that every man, and every woman, is a potential murderer. All other crimes carry a certain degree of deliberation in their commission. Not so murder. We *all* have a breaking point. We *all* love, or value, somebody or something which we will defend with our life . . . or with the life of whoever puts that person, or that thing, in dire peril.

I do not wonder that crime novels are almost always written around the crime of murder.

I give six examples of which I had personal experience. Not as the investigating officer but, most assuredly, as a working copper who stood on the fringe of the enquiry,

262

watched and listened, saw and heard ... and, in the main, marvelled that even this most serious of crimes could carry overtones of humour.

These then are 'real life' murders. Only one of them hit the national headlines. The others were parochial affairs, although the victim was no less dead, and the enquiry was no less frantic at the outset.

None of them were undetected ... but 'real life' murders rarely are.

I start with a man who was in his mid-fifties. Not too well educated, unskilled, he was nevertheless a good man. He'd been brought up in the 'chapel' tradition of absolute honesty; envying no man, and always giving good value for the wages his employer paid him. Indeed, he'd been employed at the same firm since his late teens.

His hobby was shooting. Not poaching; he diligently asked permission before he carried his twin-barrelled twelve bore over any landowner's property. In the main he went after rabbits, with an occasional pigeon. Partridge and pheasant weren't his targets; they (in his opinion) were the property of whoever owned the land.

He was teetotal. He didn't gamble; not even on the football pools. Every week he handed his unopened wage packet to his wife, and she returned to him enough 'pocket money' to meet his needs of pipe tobacco, bus fares, etc.

He lived in a terraced house in a God-fearing part of the town, and it was a clean house, modestly furnished and with everything paid for. Each Saturday he walked across nearby farmland, with his shotgun tucked under his arm. Each Sunday he went to chapel. To many it would have been a very boring life, but to him it was all he wanted, therefore he was content.

He was on shift-work. Eight hours at a time, and a change of shift every fourth week. It was dirty, heavy and unskilled work and his workmates were not like this man. Their lives were filled with drinking and swearing and, in some cases, violence. But despite the gulf between this man and those he worked alongside, he was respected. He was never laughed at. He was looked upon as somebody rather 'special'; somebody who had quiet but complete control of his own life.

He had married later in life than the average man. He had been in his mid-thirties when he'd taken a wife. She had seemed the ideal mate for such a man. Chapel, a couple of years younger than himself; a lady well versed in the business of sewing, cooking and housekeeping. She had made him a good home and, although there had been no family, that had caused neither of them either pain or disappointment.

In his own uninspired way, the man was more than content. He was happy. He considered himself well-blessed and wished for nothing more than he already had.

Then came the whisperings.

Not many, and never deliberately within his hearing. But he caught snatches of muttered conversation at work. He noticed hurried glances in his direction. Sometimes those glances carried the hint of sympathy. Sometimes a touch of contemptuous disbelief.

At first he couldn't understand why he was being treated in this way. Nobody told him. Nobody *dared* to tell him. And when he slotted the overheard whispered words into some sort of a pattern – like the putting together of a jigsaw – he was angry with himself. Ashamed of himself, and at the disgraceful possibility with which his mind toyed. But the whisperings continued and, one evening, he deliberately left his pipe in its drawer, as an excuse for returning home in the small hours, at meal break.

It was about 2 a.m. when he let himself into the house. Then, having retrieved his pipe, he climbed the stairs and opened the door of the bedroom. They were in bed together. The good double-bed he'd bought when he'd married. His wife and a man who was a complete stranger. The man's clothes were thrown over one of the bedroom chairs. His wife's clothes were, as always, neatly folded and placed on a second chair at her side of the bed.

They were both fast asleep. The sleep, it seemed, of exhaustion.

He stood looking at them for at least five minutes.

Possibly nearer ten minutes. Then, without closing the bedroom door, he returned downstairs, went into the kitchen, took his twelve bore from the kitchen cupboard and fed cartridges into the two chambers. It wasn't a modern gun – it had a hammer-cocking mechanism – and as he climbed the stairs he carefully cocked both triggers.

He shot the man first without awakening him from his sleep. Then he shot his wife before she had time enough to realise what was happening. Both were shot through the head at a range of about six inches.

There was much blood. Blood, brain tissue and splintered bone from the skulls. Where it hadn't been shattered, the bed head was soaked in the stuff. And the wall, and the bedclothes. Even the ceiling was splattered.

Then the man did something which, to him, was the right and proper thing to do.

He leaned the shotgun against the wall of the bedroom, knelt in the blood dripping from the sheets, and prayed. He prayed for *them*. The fornicators. He prayed that their sin of fornication might be forgiven.

Having prayed – but not for himself – he went to the bathroom, bathed, shaved and put on clean under-clothes. He dressed himself in his 'Sunday best' suit, then went downstairs to sit alone and await a more civilised hour.

At about seven o'clock he arrived at the police station.

'Yes?' The constable was alone. He'd come on duty an hour earlier, and was still ploughing his way through the paperwork; checking the list of vehicles stolen in the area that night; noting the various telephone messages which had been logged since he last went off duty.

The man smiled and, almost apologetically, said, 'I'd like to report a murder.'

'Oh, aye?' The copper didn't believe him.

'Two murders, actually.'

'Any advance on two?' The copper grinned. He couldn't quite see the point of the joke, but people didn't just stroll into the nick and report murder in that calm, matter-of-fact tone. In a more serious voice, he asked, 'Now, what can I do for you?'

'I've just told you.'

'No, I mean what do you *really* want to report?'

'I've killed my wife,' sighed the man. 'I've killed the man she was in bed with.'

'Oh, my Christ!' The copper's jaw dropped as he realised the truth.

'I thought you should know.'

'Yes – sure . . . of course.' The copper lifted the flap of the public counter. 'Come inside. Come inside, and sit down. I'd – I'd better telephone DHQ.'

'Do you mind if I smoke my pipe?'

'Eh? No. Not at all. Anything! Just sit down there, and wait until somebody with weight arrives.'

That was the first murder enquiry I was mixed up with, and *that's* how much it needed 'detecting'. I know the details, because it was my job to talk to the man and obtain his 'antecedent history'. I was required to check the facts of that history; to question his neighbours and workmates. I had to visit the scene of the murder at about the same time as the photographers.

That's how it happened, and that's the sort of man it happened to. But, of course, that sort of thing wouldn't do for fiction . . . that sort of thing only happens in real life.

The file was almost three inches thick before the man stood in an Assize Court dock. It was quite unnecessary. He pleaded guilty and offered neither explanation nor excuse. He was sentenced to be hanged, but the death penalty was commuted to life imprisonment.

He'll be out of prison by this time. He'll have been out for years. He will, I am sure, have built a new life for himself. Probably with a new identity. Which is why I've given neither names nor places.

He committed murder . . . that's all.

The crime we are *all* capable of committing.

*   *   *

Some murder enquiries are held up as models of police determination, of dedication and of the not-so-simple art of following every lead into all the cul-de-sacs until, at last, the culprit is caught and convicted. Other murder enquiries are quoted as complete cock-ups.

One such cock-up occurred at Brighouse. I was not part of it, in that I certainly wasn't the one with egg all over his face but, because it happened on the fringe of Clifton Beat, I claim to know the circumstances better than most . . . better than instructors at various police colleges, who smile superior smiles as they tell it third-or fourth-hand.

In those days as you left Brighouse Town Beats for the rarefied atmosphere of Clifton Beat, it was necessary to climb a steep hill, with the unusual name of Clifton Common. And at the foot of this hill, on the right hand side, there was a fairly large, wooden lock-up shop. A sweet and tobacconist's shop, which also sold newspapers, soft drinks, biscuits and, if my memory serves me aright, patent medicines. In short, it was one of those if-you-want-it-I'll-stock-it sort of shops, and the middle-aged lady who ran it made an honest living by keeping her establishment open seven days a week, from dawn until dark.

Two police constables had finished night patrol duty on this particular morning, and were strolling towards their respective beds in company. On their way they had to pass this lock-up shop.

They noticed the scarlet trickle coming from inside the shop under the closed door, across the pavement and into the gutter. It was very obviously blood and, when they opened the shop door, they found the body of the proprietress stretched out on the floor of the premises. It was a blunt-instrument attack and the unfortunate lady was dead.

Thereafter, the balloon went up with the usual fanfare from loud and large-belled trumpets.

They had all day to wind things up, and they cranked the handle like crazy. For about an hour the divisional detective chief inspector lorded it over events; the time lag necessary for the gold braid to arrive from Wakefield County Constabulary Headquarters. The hell with who ended up with a hernia, he was going to make a name for himself.

Men were dragged from their beds, men were brought in from neighbouring divisions and massive house-to-house enquiries got under way. Every garden in the vicinity was searched for the murder weapon; the grate of every gulley was hoicked from its resting place, while hands groped around in the sludge at the base of the trap; he even borrowed ladders and had coppers crawling around on roofs, searching for whatever had been used to hit the victim with.

At Brighouse Police Station the makeshift canteen at the rear of the building had been earmarked as 'The Murder Room', complete with spare typewriters, buckshee tables, notice boards and enough paper to start a print works. He'd even organised make-do-and-mend road blocks on all the major exit roads from the town.

The Big Boys were delighted. This was how a murder enquiry *should* be conducted. Everybody up to the eyeballs in fiendish activity. The mouths of the ratepayers wide with wonder at a police service able to make a three-ring circus look like a hoop-la stall.

The Photography Section flashed their bulbs and took interiors and exteriors; wide-angled and close-ups. The Fingerprint Section dusted every surface with white powder, black powder and grey powder. The Planning Section measured and sketched, calculated and estimated.

The body – the reason for it all – was eventually removed to the public mortuary, and the pathologist, assisted by the coroner's officer, sliced and cut in order to verify what every copper who'd seen the corpse already knew for a fact.

Meanwhile the detective superintendents and the detective chief superintendents stood around in groups, grim-faced and taciturn; superior beings who, with their hands thrust deep into the pockets of their loose-fitting overcoats, scanned the horizon for possible fault when not scowling disapproval at lesser beings employed by mere newspapers.

The Boss Man (not, let me hasten to add, Metcalfe, who wasn't there at the time) condescended to make a statement.

'We expect an arrest in the very near future. We have a good description of the man we're looking for. All neighbouring forces have been put on alert. Meanwhile, we're following up promising lines of enquiry.'

The place was cordoned off, the Big Boys retired to a local hostelry for lunch and, with the hint that the chief constable himself was likely to visit the scene later that day, the divisional detective chief inspector thought up newer and barmier schemes.

That afternoon will go down in the history of Brighouse. Never had the town contained as many coppers; never before had it even dreamed that the force employed as many detectives. They were almost elbowing each other out of the way in order to ask the same set of questions a dozen times over. It was like a Keystone cops comedy, but with funereal overtones.

The chief constable arrived. Accompanied by a detective chief superintendent, a detective superintendent and the divisional detective chief inspector, he was taken into the wooden lock-up shop where the crime had been committed. He asked questions, and received soothing, confident answers. They were in the shop more than an hour. The divisional detective chief inspector even organised tea and sandwiches, in order that the chief constable might feel that little more welcome.

As he left the shop, the detective chief superintendent issued firm instructions.

'Right. I want this place sealed off. No nosey-parkers. No souvenir-hunters. Nobody! I want coppers on duty round the place till further orders.'

The chief constable returned to his gilded office. The detective superintendents and detective chief superintendents melted away into the middle distance. By late evening, even the divisional detective chief inspector had had a long day; he tottered off towards Halifax and left the section sergeant free to re-organise the re-organisation and ensure that Brighouse and its adjacent beats had something approaching normal night patrol cover.

Two humble flatfeet were left to stand guard on the shop. An oldster, fast approaching retiring age, and a new boy fresh from a police college. It started to spit with rain, and the oldster muttered naughty words because, in full view of the passing public, he couldn't enjoy a quiet pipe of tobacco.

Without much hope, he turned the knob of the door, and found the shop still unlocked. By this time, it was well past midnight.

. 'Keep a weather eye open, young 'un. I'm inside for a quick crack of tobacco.'

And with his rump comfortably hoisted on to the edge of the counter, the oldster began to fill the bowl of his pipe.

He heard a noise behind him, turned and shone his torch into the face of a very frightened youth.

'Who the hell . . . ?'

'I'm – I'm . . .'

'Where the hell have *you* been?'

'Under the counter,' muttered the youth. 'Hiding behind the biscuit tins.'

'Eh?'

'I've – y'know – been there all day. Since I did her in. I didn't *mean* to kill her.'

This, then, is one they would rather forget, but one they will never be *allowed* to forget. The murderer, hiding under the counter and within easy touching distance of the chief constable and his three big-time buddies. The shop – the scene of a murder – left unlocked. Even the description (and God knows where it came from) didn't fit the culprit.

This one was a cock-up, with brass band accompaniment.

And this time they hanged the murderer.

*　　*　　*

A murder enquiry, with the addition of Tosh, had to be different . . . and this one was. We started back-to-front, in that we knew the identity of the murderer (actually the *murderess*) before we found the body.

She was a hellcat, and just about everybody in Brighouse knew her, scorned her or was terrified of her. Rumour had it she'd had at least two doses of clap. Rumour had it she'd once been married. What was *not* rumour was her Saturday night booze-up, followed by a fight during which some of the so-called 'tough guys' ducked round the nearest corner.

I had had experience of her, in that I'd once had to arrest her. Not a pleasant experience. She was spitting, fighting drunk at the time and was rampaging up and down the main road. The only sensible thing to do was to tell a passer-by to contact the station and ask for a police car, while I cornered her in one of the shop-doorways, and kept her there while dodging clawing finger-nails. To grab her *anywhere* would have risked an accusation of indecent assault, so I shoulder-charged her into the doorway, then used my folded cape as a battering-ram-cum-flail to keep her where I wanted her.

Mind you, when the squad car arrived we all three made a concerted dive, closed our fists on whatever happened to be handy and virtually threw her into the rear of the car, where one of us sat on her.

That was the sort of cow she was but (God help us) she was also a mother.

A nipper, not quite at toddling age, who was being brought up by his grandmother. Nevertheless, this crazy woman *was* his mother and, during periodic bouts of maudlin maternalism, she was allowed to take him out.

That's when it happened. More than a dozen people saw her stand on the bridge which crossed the canal, hurl the child into the water, then jump in after him. Heroes were at a premium that day, so nobody dived in after them.

A few reminders as a backdrop to what happened. The canal in those days was rarely used; its colour was bitumen black, with a scum of oily muck on its surface; it was moderately deep with more than a yard-thick base of mud and slurry under the water and with the banks reed-heavy for about a yard from the towpath. It was late autumn and bitterly cold. Scuba-diving, the equipment of which would be readily available today, was almost unknown; we had to use boathooks and grappling-irons.

A youth dashed into Brighouse Police Station and broke the news. We, in turn, hared to the scene, gathered as many witnesses as we could . . . and ended up with as many estimated positions as to where the child and the woman went in.

Tosh took over, with the uniformed inspector as his immediate underling and Percy, the section sergeant, as general dogsbody.

No messing around with 'Murder Rooms' for Tosh.

'I want to be at the scene. Check, personally, that nobody's dropping ballocks. Let's have a barge moored to the bank.'

And that's what we did. Tosh stood in the anchored barge, directing operations. Percy rushed hither, thither and yon, doing nothing in particular, but making more fuss than the rest of us put together. The uniformed inspector tutted around, more or less repeating the instructions given by Tosh.

I was put in charge of the rowing boat, in which were three other coppers hurling out grappling-hooks attached to long lengths of rope.

Within the first couple of hours, we had the kiddie out of the canal and on to the mortuary table. He'd been drowned. He'd been alive when he'd been thrown in. It was definitely murder.

Thereafter, Buster Keaton would have felt at home.

Even Tosh went a little gaga. He started using *naval* terms; bawling them from the prow of the barge through a megaphone.

'A bit to starboard, Wainwright. Right, now a few degrees to port. Steady as she goes.'

I called him a complete prat (but under my breath) and wondered what the gawping audience lining the towpath and bridge thought about it all. Meanwhile Tosh had a private ball with his megaphone and I steered the rowing boat to whichever part of the canal took his fancy.

The uniformed inspector was torn between love and duty. He was a member of the local operatic society, and that society was in the last stage of rehearsal for *Iolanthe*. For a couple of hours each evening, therefore, he absented himself in order to sing his heart out. Metcalfe (who, at that time was a mere detective chief superintendent) honoured us with a visit, and Tosh gave him a quick run-down on what we were up to.

'Who's your second-in-command?'

Tosh told him.

'Where is he?'

'They're doing a Gilbert and Sullivan thing. *Iolanthe*. He's nipped off for a spell of rehearsal.'

'Has he?' growled Metcalfe, dangerously.

'We know where he is,' excused Tosh. 'We can get him if we need him in a hurry.'

'We must keep the priorities in order, mustn't we, Chief Inspector?' sneered Metcalfe. 'We mustn't disappoint the bloody fairies.'

'You should know, sir.' Tosh took slop from *nobody*. 'From what I hear, Headquarters is stiff with fairies.'

For almost a week we dragged that infernal canal. We hauled up rusty bedsteads, broken bicycles, old mattresses, ancient tyres, waterlogged branches . . . you name it, we hooked it and dragged it to the surface. But not a sign of the woman who'd thrown her kid into the water.

It was cold work so Percy, the section sergeant, hit upon a brainwave. He called in at one of the nearby factories and arranged for a large urn of hot tea to be brought to the towpath twice a day: once in the morning and once in the afternoon. We in the boat sculled to the shore and joined the lads dragging from the towpath and, for a short time, Percy was a popular man.

After a week of it, we were all open to suggestions.

'She's been taken downstream,' proclaimed Tosh.

'That gives us a fair old scope,' I grumbled.

'Don't be bloody thick, Wainwright. She can't have gone *up*stream.'

'No, sir.' I'd said my piece, and decided to keep quiet.

The uniformed inspector said, 'I read a book about Trafalgar a few months back.'

'Oh, aye?' Tosh cocked a sardonic eyebrow.

'The guns,' explained the uniformed inspector. 'All that gunfire. It brought the corpses to the surface.'

'I've never heard of *that* before.'

'That's what it said in this book.'

'Does he know what he's talking about?' asked Tosh, suspiciously.

'Who?'

'Whoever wrote the book.'

'He wrote a *book*,' said the uniformed inspector,

innocently.

So, as a result of that particularly stupid exchange, the rowing boat was taken downstream out into the country, and we continued dragging, while the uniformed inspector and a couple of delighted flatfeet blasted off from the towpath with twelve bores.

'If she comes up,' propounded the uniformed inspector, 'she'll be floating on her back.'

'Is that a fact?' I was past caring. I was frozen to the bone, and it was becoming increasingly dangerous with all that lead shot flying around.

'She's a woman, you see.'

'I didn't think she'd have changed sex,' I grunted, crossly.

'No – what I mean is this – women come to the surface floating on their backs. Men float on their bellies.'

'You learn something new every day.'

She didn't come up at all, so we were unable to test this enthralling theory.

A fortnight after we'd brought the kiddie to the surface we had a council-of-war on the barge. We still hadn't found the woman. We'd spent a small fortune on twelve-bore cartridges. We'd lost half a dozen grappling-hooks in the weeds. We were all candidates for double-pneumonia and the whole damn thing had lost what little sparkle it might once have had.

'Anybody any ideas?' asked Tosh, 'Short of draining the bloody canal – which I understand we *can't* do – what other brainwaves can we come up with?'

'I don't think she's in there, sir,' I volunteered.

Tosh glared his irritability.

'Oh, she *went* in,' I conceded. 'Too many people saw her *go* in. But what if she swam to the bank?'

'Have you found somebody who saw her swim to the bank, then?'

'No, sir. But she *might* have.'

'It's possible.' It was a very grudging admission. 'If that's what *did* happen . . .'

'We've dragged every inch of that canal, sir,' I reminded him. 'Every damned inch.'

'She's sitting somewhere, laughing at us.' The possibility brought a scowl like thunder to his face. 'Damn the bloody woman. She's sitting somewhere *laughing* at us. I'll give the bitch something to laugh about.' Having reached a decision he nodded grimly. 'Right. Get all the gear ashore, and back to where it belongs. We'll have an all-district Express Message out this evening. Get this bloody barge back to where it came from. I'll have her – by God, I'll *have* her – before another twenty-four hours are out.'

He did, too.

When they moved the barge she floated gently to the surface.

The final pay-off came when Percy received a bill for all the tea we'd consumed. Nobody at DHQ or Head-quarters wanted to know. Nor was anybody interested when he tentatively suggested a whip-round. It was a fitting end to a murder enquiry which had had all the energy of an interspace lift-off and all the polish of a bed of nails.

Murder enquiries come like that, too.

*　　*　　*

Some murders have strange spin-offs. Thanks to media coverage, there is always a slant. Always an emphasis that shouldn't *be* there. Who, for example, knows – or gives a damn about – Donald Neilson, the Black Panther? Who knows the name of his wife? Or indeed whether he had any family? The Kray brothers – Reginald, Charles and Ronald . . . but the Kray family didn't stop at three brothers. Parents, aunts, uncles, cousins. Even in-laws.

These people are like the rest of us. They have next-of-kin. They have relations. They have friends who knew them, and liked them, before they became notorious. Perhaps *still* like them.

They lived somewhere. They worked somewhere. The chances are they had a favourite pub. The ramifications go on and on. The main character in the drama ends up in prison and, thereafter, he (or she) is removed from the spotlight of publicity. But what of the others? The people and places touched by those few weeks of infamy?

They are never the same. They never *can* be.

For example . . .

The incident I have in mind was a particularly mean,

but grisly, killing. The man had visited his unmarried uncle, asked for money and been refused. It ended up a skull-cracking job. Almost twenty vicious blows, delivered with a household hatchet, using both the blade and the butt.

When we shaved the head at the mortuary, even the pathologist was sickened and when in court *we* passed those glossy, black-and-white photographs to the jury, one of the women jurors fainted.

The crime needed no 'detecting'. It didn't even rate a mention in any of the nationals. The defending barrister tried for a reduction to 'Manslaughter', but failed, and the murderer was duly convicted.

End of story . . . but it *wasn't*.

The location of the murder was one of those tight-knit villages which pockmark all industrial areas. Not quite in the country, not quite in the town; the grime from the factories touches what greenery there is, but the bus service suffers every rural inconvenience. There is a gloom about these places – a vague disappointment – which seems to work itself into all who live there. It makes them sour and bitter. They tend to 'call a spade a spade' . . . which is as good an excuse as any for being ill-mannered trouble-makers.

And the house in which the murder had been committed had to be sold.

It was a rambling place. Stone-built and with the minimum of modern requirements. It needed some degree of repair and, even without its recent history, it would never have topped any house agent's list of desirable property. Every time a stranger came to look the place over, the locals damn near formed a queue to tell the details of the murder, which made it a complete liability to whoever was trying to sell it.

It stood empty for some years. As the tale of the murder quietened off the disrepair of the house grew worse until, eventually, the villagers no longer hurried to give morbid details, and the house was there, at a give-away price, for anybody who cared to take it on.

The Police Authority stepped in. They bought the house, did what repairs were needed and dumped a newly married copper and his wife in the place.

He was in – nailed! – long before he learned the truth and, for obvious reasons, he kept his mouth shut.

Which makes me wonder . . .

Is there today some copper in the old West Riding area, living in an old (maybe by this time quite comfortable) house, without being aware of its past infamy?

Or if not a policeman . . . *somebody?*

* * *

On Wednesday, 6 January, 1952, Alfred Moore, of Kirkheaton, near Huddersfield, was hanged. He was a thirty-six-year-old married man; his occupation was given as a poultry farmer but in fact he was one of that small band of men, the professional burglar.

He felt the noose because he shot and killed two policemen: Detective Inspector Fraser and Police Constable Jagger. The killing hit national, even international, headlines, and what happened was this . . .

Fraser was the divisional detective inspector at the Huddersfield Division of the county constabulary. He was the sort of man who hated losing, and the presence of Moore on his patch was like a sore he could never stop picking.

Moore was a pro. Let that be clearly understood. At his own nefarious art he was a highly skilled practitioner. Given the right sort of safe he could – and did more than once – rip the back away with as much ease as the average man opening a tin of sardines. On at least one occasion he performed this neat little trick with a watchman sitting having a midnight snack in the next room. He concentrated his attention upon mills and offices, but was known to have knocked over at least one major post office and earned himself a nice, thick packet of postal orders, etc.

Moore's farm was at Kirkheaton, a village to the east of Huddersfield. It was fairly isolated, and virtually unapproachable during the day without being seen. What it was *not* was cheap. The farmhouse was modern with plenty of expensive gadgetry and not for a moment did anybody believe he could afford *that* lot from what he made as a chicken farmer.

Moore lived on Police Constable Jagger's beat.

That, then, was the set-up, and Fraser was determined to put Moore where the crows couldn't get at him. The informants went to work and, in due time, Fraser received a tip-off that Moore was planning another job. The time and place were given, and Fraser decided to nobble his quarry *after* the break-in.

It was past midnight when Fraser threw a police cordon around Moore's farm. Every lane, every approach to the farm was covered. All it needed was Moore to return to his home and be caught in the net . . . complete with loot.

It worked. Moore *was* nailed. Police Constable Jagger stopped Alfred Moore as he made his way back to the farm via one of the footpaths which cobwebbed the area. Moore was annoyed – which was understandable – but not homicidally annoyed. Jagger then called through the darkness to the man who'd arranged this police cordon, and Fraser joined the beat constable.

There is no doubt that Fraser's presence triggered off what happened next. Because of what each man was, there was deep and reciprocal hatred. Equally (although nobody is alive to deny or verify) there seems very little doubt that Fraser made no effort to hide his satisfaction. And why not? Everything had gone right; the tip-off, the cordon and the capture.

Now everything went very *wrong*.

Moore drew a revolver and shot Fraser dead on the spot. And having shot Fraser, he *had* to shoot Jagger, if only to remove a police witness to the murder of Fraser. He therefore shot Jagger – but without killing him instantly – before racing for the safety of the farmhouse.

The situation, then. A few hours before dawn; an isolated farmhouse a few miles from Huddersfield; a dead detective inspector and a severely wounded police constable; the man responsible for killing one officer and wounding another inside the safety of the farmhouse and still armed; the place surrounded by bobbies.

The obvious Number One Priority was to get Constable Jagger to hospital. This was done, then Huddersfield DHQ and Wakefield Headquarters were informed. The

Head of CID – Detective Chief Superintendent Metcalfe – issued firm instructions; Moore was not to be allowed to leave the farmhouse, but at the same time nobody was to make any immediate attempt to arrest the man.

Would-be wiseacres have criticised this decision of Metcalfe's. Why (it is sometimes asked) was Moore given the opportunity to burn almost all the evidence of his recent thefts? Coppers, standing there like prize berks, watching smoke billowing from the farmhouse chimney and knowing that the man they were after was burning as many documents, postal orders, etc. as he could stuff into the fireplace. Why not rush him? Why not collect shotguns from farms in the neighbourhood in order to counter Moore's own firearm? Why give a man who's shot two policemen so much rope?

In short, why *wait*?

But Metcalfe was right. It is a measure of his absolute objectivity that he refused to be influenced by an immediate, and quite natural, reaction. The object was to arrest Moore . . . not to indulge in some sort of wild west shoot-out. What (for example) if Moore's wife had been shot? What if a third copper had been killed? Added to which, of course, Moore was still technically innocent of any crime.

In the event what happened was that Metcalfe arrived shortly after dawn, gave Moore warning that he (Metcalfe) was coming into the house then, with his hands in his pockets and accompanied by two uniformed marksmen, each carrying a drawn revolver, walked through the front door and personally arrested Moore. No shout, no sweat. An immaculate piece of policing, coupled with sheer nerve . . . which, incidentally, helped to win Metcalfe a well-earned MBE.

Then Metcalfe left the scene, taking Moore with him . . . and an assortment of clowns took over.

Those of us who had been at the scene from the word 'Off' marvelled that one constabulary could produce so many detective chief inspectors and detective inspectors from the woodwork. They outnumbered the lower ranks by about two-to-one; they were all convinced they were in charge of the enquiry once Metcalfe had moved himself out of range; they all had a different idea of what to do and how to do it.

We were, you see, looking for a revolver. The murder weapon.

Moore had rid himself of the gun at some point between shooting Fraser and Jagger and his arrest. It was *very* important that it be found.

This, then, was the conversation as first one, then another, gold-plated jack strolled around giving orders.

'That dry-stone wall, Wainwright. There's a possibility he may have dumped it in there, among the stones, on his way to the house. Let's have it down. Every inch of it.'

Then, less than fifteen minutes later: 'What the hell are you doing there, Wainwright?'

'Searching for the revolver, sir. Pulling this wall down.'

'Don't waste your bloody time there, man. He can't have hidden the gun *there*. Let's have you on top of the farmhouse. He could have thrown it up there as he ran inside.'

Then, again, less than fifteen minutes later: 'What are you doing on the bloody roof, Wainwright?'

'Looking for the gun, sir.'

'Don't be a blasted idiot. He hadn't time to chuck the damn thing on the *roof*. This lot – these raspberry canes – there's a good possibility he tossed it into them, when he ran for it.'

Then only a few minutes later: 'What on earth are *you* doing, Wainwright?'

'Searching for the weapon, sir. Here, among the raspberry canes.'

'Good, but don't arse around pushing them aside. There's a scythe somewhere. Let's have the whole bloody lot down, then we can *really* see.'

Everybody was giving orders, and a handful of us were obeying them. Orders, then counter-orders, then orders countering the counter-orders. Chaos was the name of the game and, in no time at all, the farm was a shambles. The hen-houses had been searched, and the hens were fluttering and clucking under everybody's feet. The pig sty was searched, and a handful of pigs were grubbing and snorting their way through the vegetable garden.

Every wall was a shambles and every hedge had had hell torn out of it. In the search for that gun, official vandalism had no limits.

Then, at mid-morning, a group of us were convinced we were watching the missing weapon leave the scene of the murder.

Mrs Moore decided she wanted to go stay with friends. In the absence of Metcalfe, none of the CID Big Bwanas had the simple guts to say her nay. Nobody had had the gumption to first-guess this move, therefore there wasn't a policewoman at the scene. This meant that Moore's wife couldn't be searched.

She left the farm in a friend's car, and some of us figured we could now search for the murder weapon till hell froze . . . we wouldn't find it, because it was no longer there.

It didn't stop the lunacy.

That afternoon a gang of us were spaced almost shoulder-to-shoulder and, an inch at a time, we worked our way through fields of ripe corn. There was a brickworks not too far away; asbestos suits were conjured up from somewhere and a trio of sweating coppers were instructed to enter the cooling furnaces and see if, by some impossible means, Moore had dropped the gun into the dying fire.

That evening word reached us about Police Constable Jagger. He'd made a Dying Declaration.

It was a very sobering thought. We all knew the impeccable theory behind the admittance of Dying Declarations as evidence. We *knew* it . . . but now I, for one, realised the terrifying requirements. That the person giving that declaration must *know* that he (or she) is dying. Must know – must, in effect be *told* – that there isn't a shred of hope left. Then (and only then) and because the law accepts, without qualification, that with certain death staring him in the face, the victim of a homicidal attack will speak only the truth, a genuine Dying Declaration can be made, will be accepted in court and may not be challenged.

Jagger was going to die. Jagger *knew* he was going to die. And with that knowledge he'd given Metcalfe a weapon Moore could never counter.

It quietened me a little. Made me sad.

Some of us had been there from the beginning, and without food other than the occasional bar of chocolate some kid in the onlooking crowd had bought for us from a nearby shop. We were tired, but from past experience we knew sleep was something we could fight and brush aside for a long time yet. Hunger was a different matter.

We mentioned it to a handful of the self-styled boss-men, each of whom thought he was in charge. We explained that although we were all prepared to carry on until we dropped, fodder would keep the engine going just that bit longer.

From some dark and forgotten depths of County Constabulary Headquarters they unearthed what can only be described as an old-fahsioned NAAFI wagon, painted police blue.

Thereafter, we had sandwiches and tea. Strong, sweet tea and doorstep-sized, pickled beetroot sandwiches.

As it happens, I *like* pickled beetroot sandwiches. I eat them as a quick snack to this day . . . although not as jaw-crampingly big as those we were served with. Nevertheless, I could understand the mutterings and mumblings of my colleagues who watched the various plain clothes wallahs disappearing towards Huddersfield and a civil-ised meal, while they stood around chewing their way through a very makeshift nosh-up they didn't particu-larly enjoy.

I think we stuck it, without too much complaint, because of PC Jagger. We truly wanted him to live. We didn't want to have to *use* that Dying Declaration.

We spent the first night in the farmhouse. Still searching for the missing revolver. Taking every room and every stick of furniture to pieces. We found guns – automatic pistols, rifles, shotguns – but not a single revolver. Somebody had ripped the ledge from the inside of a window and, almost casually, I shone my torch into the wall cavity. Ammunition galore! Hundreds of rounds of the stuff, and of every calibre made. But all *rimless*; the sort of stuff used in pistols. Not a rimmed round amongst them, and a *revolver* will only fire *rimmed* cartridges.

We also found keys. Dozens and dozens of keys; latch-lock type, blanks, skeleton and the best set of craftsman-made pick-locks I've ever seen in my life.

By dawn you could have driven a car through the gap in the front wall of that farmhouse, then out through the gap in the rear wall, and nothing would have stood in your way. Or, had the fancy taken you, in at one side and out of the other. Why in hell we didn't bring the whole building down around our ears I'll never know. We were searching cavity walls, and what we found made Alfred Moore a most unusual 'poultry farmer'.

At the time it didn't seem like vandalism. It didn't *feel* like vandalism. But, in honesty, I can now see that it could be viewed as such.

I think we were driven on by a blind anger; an anger shared by uniformed and plain clothes men alike. Fraser was dead. Jagger was dying – he might already be dead, for all we knew – and the man responsible was tucked away in a cell at Huddersfield DHQ and, eventually, would be given a fair trial.

Neither Fraser nor Jagger had had a fair trial. Moore had taken it upon himself to be judge, jury and executioner.

Maybe some of the men in charge were medal-chasing. Maybe we *all* were. At this distance in time memory can play tricks. Let it merely be stated that we wrecked that farmhouse and, after the trial, the police authority paid for its complete restoration without complaint.

The next day saw one more brainwave.

It was a glorious day and by this time the sightseers were everywhere. Cars were parked nose-to-tail for miles around that Kirkheaton farmhouse. Ice-cream vans were doing a roaring trade.

Quite suddenly we had very firm orders. Every copper had to move away from the immediate area of the building. The Dog Section was on its way. Give these hounds some article of clothing worn by Moore, and they'd back-track to the point where the shooting took place and thus limit the area to be searched to within revolver-throwing distance of where Moore's spoor could be sniffed out.

All clever stuff.

It must be remembered that this was 1951. Dog Sections – especially in the provinces – were a new and relatively untried branch of the force. We hadn't yet decided which breed of dog suited our purpose best; many self-styled 'experts' still clung to the legend of the bloodhound, and an equal number continued to view the alsatian as a beast only once removed from the wolf and, therefore, dangerous and unstable.

We waited. Probably not with bated breath, but we waited.

The Dog Section arrived, complete with shiny new shooting brake. The handlers looked (and no doubt felt) very impressive in jodhpurs and leggings. Three animals – an alsatian and two labradors – jumped from the rear of the shooting brake. Beautiful animals; sleek and smooth muscled; obviously in prime condition. All three were dogs.

'Stand back,' quoth the chap in charge of the doggies. 'Don't get too near to them. Give them room to stretch after the ride. Give them time to get used to the surroundings.'

Something very special was obviously going to happen.

It did.

A tiny mongrel bitch, very much on heat, whipped through the ranks of watching coppers, yapped canine encouragements at the three new arrivals, then scampered off down the road. The alsatian and the two labradors followed in randy pursuit.

It took the members of the Dog Section more than an hour to round up their charges, bundle them back into the shooting brake and, with very red faces, disappear down the road in the direction of Wakefield.

The rest of us continued searching for the gun, continued chewing great wads of pickled beetroot sandwich and wondered when the hell we'd see home again.

That night only about half a dozen of us 'originals' were left at the scene. We'd been topped-up, of course, and those that had returned to their beats had been replaced by other, fresher, coppers. But *we* hadn't seen a bed for three nights. We hadn't even *shaved* since leaving home for this God-awful spot.

And, of course, Sod's Law demanded that, on this night, a complete prat of a uniformed sergeant be placed in charge of the uniformed detail.

I don't know his name, but I'd met his kind. I've met them a few hundred times, since. They are the great obeyers-of-instructions. Human equivalents of the pocket calculator; press the right buttons and an immaculate end-result pops up . . . but for God's sake don't expect it to think for itself. Furthermore until it is switched on it is incapable of functioning.

Somebody had mentioned the possibility of souvenir hunters to this clown and, as of that moment, the exercise ceased to be a murder enquiry and instead we were guarding something far excess in value to the crown jewels. He stationed a ring of coppers, at remote corners of isolated fields, all around the farm.

Moreover, having just jumped from his own bed, this berk pointedly ignored the fact that for some of us this was our third night without sleep.

My own post seemed at least a dozen miles from human habitation, but I dutifully stood there and wished that time might get its skates on and bring relief from this very boring detail.

I filled my pipe. Slowly, in order to waste a little time. Then I carefully touched the tobacco with the flame from a match and enjoyed a first, soothing lungful of smoke.

'What the devil do you think *you're* doing, Wainwright?'

This lunatic three-striper was standing at my elbow and – or so it seemed – was on the point of giving himself a double-hernia.

'Eh?' I gaped at the man.

'Smoking, on duty!'

'For Christ's sake, there isn't a soul within miles.'

'*I*'m here.'

'That was your choice, Sergeant. *I* didn't invite you.'

'Good God, man! Haven't you any sense? Anybody creeping up can see you long before you see them.'

'What the hell are we supposed to be watching for?'

'Souvenir hunters, of course. We don't want any . . .'

'If they *see* me,' I explained, wearily, 'they won't *come*.'

'Put that bloody pipe out, Wainwright. That's an order.'

He had the rank – just – and he was slinging it around . . . so what choice had I? I didn't mind too much. All it needed was another match when he'd returned to the woodwork.

It was late summer – even early autumn – and the nights were starting to be chilly. At about midnight I decided it was time to get the old circulation moving a little. I strolled the width of the field, then returned to my original position.

'Where the hell have *you* been, Wainwright?'

'You must show me how you do it, some time, Sergeant,' I said, nastily.

'What?'

'The genie of the lamp's a non-starter compared with you.'

'Are you being bloody insolent?'

'Can't you work even *that* out?'

'Why have you left your post?'

'I was stiffening up a little,' I sighed. 'Maybe you haven't been out in it long enough, but you have my word for it. It's getting very cold.'

'You stay where you are,' he snapped. 'Where I put you. You don't go wandering off all over the place.'

'You,' I growled, 'must be the life and soul of any party you're asked to.'

Had he fizzed me, there and then, I think I'd have had some small respect for the man. He didn't. He muttered something under his breath and, for the moment, stamped out of my life again.

It was dawn when he did his now-he-isn't-now-he-is act again. I was knackered. I needed sleep, like I'd never needed sleep in my life before. I was where he'd 'put' me. I wasn't smoking my pipe. But I *was* sitting down; I'd found a convenient knoll, by the side of the hedge, and I was resting my aching legs.

'Where the hell *are* you, Wainwright?'

'Right here, Sergeant.'

'You're supposed to be standing up, not sitting down.'

'Sergeant.' I remained seated and did nothing to hide

my disgust. 'If you're going to book me, go ahead. But before you start licking your pencil, check with the duty roster. I've been here since this thing broke – before you bloody well *knew* about it – and by this time my wife must be thinking I've deserted her. Now, as a favour, put up or shut up . . . I've had a gutful.'

He glared petty hatred down at me, and said, 'It's a good job you're not in *my* section.'

'For both of us,' I agreed.

And that, as far as I was concerned, was the somewhat sour ending to my part in the case of R. *v* Moore. To this day, the revolver hasn't been found. Jagger died, and his Dying Declaration did much to send Moore to the hanging shed.

That, then, was it. That was how and why Alfred Moore shot and killed Detective Inspector Fraser and Police Constable Jagger. From the moment it happened until some damn-fool uniformed sergeant figured that a man can still stand upright after a duty lasting three days and three nights.

*　　*　　*

A short digression, while on the subject of murder . . .

The Yorkshire Ripper enquiry is the accepted low spot in the history of the West Yorkshire police – what, in effect, was the old West Riding Constabulary – and when northern coppers talk the question always crops up.

What if Metcalfe had been Head of CID when Sutcliffe committed his atrocities?

I knew Metcalfe. He had few friends, but even his many enemies gave unqualified credit to the man as a copper. The force-wide admiration for his sheer professionalism made him a man apart. On an enquiry, he drove men to breaking point, but he drove nobody as hard as he drove himself.

I knew George Oldfield, the man who *was* in charge of the Ripper equiry. I knew him as a superintendent and, like Metcalfe, he was an unpopular senior policeman, but for different reasons. Metcalfe's way to the top was via a direct route; in there punching, and whoever stood in the way was brushed aside. Oldfield climbed to the top, and some of the stepping-stones were other men's necks.

They were both unpopular – that went with the job – but the difference was the difference between passive unpopularity (mixed with reluctant admiration) and active unpopularity (mixed with an unspoken desire to see failure).

Gregory became chief constable after I'd left the force but, for a man whose reputation included that of being a whizz-kid detective, he made some ghastly mistakes during the Yorkshire Ripper enquiry. Like a handful of other chief constables, he gave the impression of yearning to be a TV personality. Had he been a little less glamorous and a lot more hard nosed things might have been different.

These opinions are firmly based.

Peter William Sutcliffe (for example) was interviewed no less than *nine* times before, by pure chance and in another police area, he was stopped for a minor motoring offence, virtually minutes before he committed what would have been his fourteenth killing.

Nine times! Which meant he was very much shortlisted. And, for the life of me, I can't see Metcalfe having given him freedom enough to kill again once he was on that list.

Oldfield was side-tracked by the false clue of the hoax tape recording. He was blinded by voice analysts and dialect experts who claimed to be able to place the man who made the recording to within a mile or two of his birth. The enquiry was switched into a wrong direction. Bradford (where Sutcliffe lived) was ignored.

Gregory appeared on TV on the evening of Sutcliffe's arrest, and told the world, 'We've arrested the Yorkshire Ripper.' Not so. The man arrested was Peter William Sutcliffe . . . that and nothing more. Technically, he was innocent of any crime, and would remain innocent until he was convicted in a court of law. And a chief constable handed *that* legal defence to counsel who would, eventually, represent Sutcliffe.

All that, then, plus a cross-reference system which broke down under the weight of paperwork. Plus a team that had little faith in either Oldfield or Gregory. Plus members of that team who might secretly wish failure, if only to repay Oldfield for past wrongs.

It was a shambles, overseen by men incapable of sorting out that shambles.

Sutcliffe's last victim was Jacqueline Hill, and the mother of that victim tried, unsuccessfully, to bring the West Yorkshire police to court for failing in their duty.

Nevertheless I hold the view that, morally, Mrs Hill was right. In my considered opinion, had Metcalfe still been in the chair occupied by Oldfield, Sutcliffe's reign of terror would have been very much shortened.

* * *

A last murder. And, had I not witnessed the outcome, I wouldn't have believed it. At the very least, I'd have accused the teller of exaggeration. But it did happen . . . exactly as I put it down.

A market town; population around the 14,000 mark. And these four people – two young men and two young women – had been friends since schooldays. They were now married, but children had not yet arrived. They were from honest, decent, middle-of-the-road families, and their lifelong friendship was such that they were a regular foursome, and happy in each other's company. They went on holidays together. Had anybody been asked, they would have been told; these four were friends for life; they would enter middle-age, then grow elderly as a quartet who, in effect, were closer than many families.

One of the chaps was doing some small alteration to his kitchen, and his electric drill went on the blink. His pal offered the use of his electric drill, and suggested he call for it on his way home from work.

The chap took up the offer, called to pick up the drill, but found his buddy out. No problem. The wife knew where her husband kept his tools and handed over the drill.

Then, he killed her.

He hit her with everything. Hammers, mallets, chisels . . . anything and everything he could get his hands on.

Then he left the house, saturated in the young woman's blood and, still carrying the electric drill,

289

wandered the streets of the town.

People saw him – lots of people saw him – somebody dialled a triple-niner, he was picked up by a squad car and he was brought to the nick. He told us where he *thought* he'd been, and we visited the house. The young wife was still alive . . . just. She didn't regain consciousness. She died on the operating table and the surgeon expressed an off-the-record opinion that her death was a minor blessing; that the brain damage was such that she'd have been little more than a vegetable had she lived.

Thereafter, the enquiries.

Now it may be taken for granted that, in such circumstances, every copper's mind strays in the region of his crotch. Every copper who touched the case, from Metcalfe down, expressed the firm opinion that sex, in some form or another, had been the trigger. We were all wrong and, eventually – having run ourselves ragged to prove we were right – we were forced to accept the fact that we *were* wrong.

It had been a brainstorm. Sudden and savage. The doctors, the psychiatrists, the experts all arrived at the same conclusion. Something in the poor guy's brain had snapped. Just like that. Without warning. His pal's wife – one of the inseparable quartet – had just *happened* to be alongside him at the time. It could have been anybody.

But that wasn't the pay-off and few people, other than myself, knew of the pay-off.

For some weeks the accused had to appear at the local court for a weekly remand in prison custody, and it was my job to produce him in the dock for what was a few minutes of legal formality. I was an old copper by this time. I was prepared to bend the rules a little. I knew the details of the case, and I saw no good reason for keeping the poor guy cooped up in a police cell and, anyway, his solicitor liked to have a talk with him.

No cell, therefore, but instead the comparative comfort of one of the Interview Rooms in which witnesses and such were taken to make statements. It was my risk – my neck – and nobody complained . . . just as long as I was present to keep an eye on things.

And every week the accused's wife visited him. *And* the victim's husband. *And* the victim's parents. Four people, and all four of them tried to comfort the poor guy.

They couldn't.

That man suffered more self-detestation than anybody could measure. He refused forgiveness, even when they pleaded with him to understand that there was no personal blame attached.

That amount of sheer, unqualified compassion could never be included in a novel. That degree of suspension of disbelief would be unacceptable.

And yet it happened.

More than that, even. When the charge was reduced from murder to manslaughter, the victim's father went into the witness-box at the Assize Court and pleaded for leniency for the man who'd killed his daughter.

Murder, you see – in this case, reduced to manslaughter . . . and the permutations are endless.

* * *

I now write about murders. I invent motives and, in so doing, I try to find a way into the mind of a man who kills, even though that man is a creature of my own imagination.

That isn't difficult.

The difficulty is making readers accept what every working copper knows. That what will make a man shrug today, might make him commit murder tomorrow.

Otley and Out

The transfer from Huby to Otley – from John Craven to a superintendent whose name I don't even remember – came as a mild disappointment but not as a surprise. In those days the average stay at one section, or on one beat, was five years. After five years (or so the theory went) you'd made too many friends to police the place efficiently. Nor did the counter-theory that it took all of five years to properly separate the sheep from the goats cut much ice.

Housing Section at Wakefield seemed to be under the day-to-day control of cadets with nothing better to do. Nobody *I* ever met could figure out any sort of system. Just that, after about five years, your name reached the top of the pack and it was time to up sticks and move into a new neighbourhood, and that if you had kids at school or even if you'd chanced your arm and decided to buy a home at wherever you were that was *your* worry.

Not that those things concerned me. We'd no family, I was nearing the end of the slog and in five more years – thereabouts – I could draw a half-pay pension. In ten more years I could draw a two-thirds-pay pension, but I wasn't aiming for that. I was writing and enjoying writing. The BBC were actually commissioning me to write radio plays, and Collins were ready to take police procedural yarns as fast as I turned them out.

I could handle Otley without breaking into a sweat . . . but I *couldn't*.

Somebody with brains, but very little feeling, had figured things out.

I was on a five-and-a-half-day week. I worked office hours from nine in the morning until six each evening, and four hours every Saturday, and every minute of that time I was seated at a typewriter building up other men's files. Incident Reports. Accident Reports. Crime Files. Sudden Death Reports. Summaries of Evidence.

I was being drowned in a sea of paper and it was being dumped in the 'In' tray faster than I could shift it.

I could almost hear some smart-arse saying, 'Get the sod behind a typewriter. Make him type all day. Make him type till his balls ache. He won't feel like typing fiction when he comes off duty.'

Whoever it was, I could almost hear him *saying* it.

But he was wrong. I was far too near the goal I'd set myself ever to allow him to be right.

With the monumental wisdom of hindsight I think the thing that *really* licked me was the fact that I never once saw the streets. I knew what was going on – everything that was going on – but I wasn't a part of it. The biggest decision I was allowed to make was when to change the ribbon in the typewriter.

For a few weeks – for a few months – I was arrogant enough to think myself tough enough, and still young enough, to shrug off anything any damn fool could brew up which might stop me from writing fiction. Therefore, I typed. All day and every day, and far into the night. I prided myself that I was not an easy man to lick – I *still* carry that ridiculous pride in my hip pocket – but I was fooling myself. I was deliberately ignoring my weakness.

That Black Imp of depression dug its claws into my back. The headaches and the anger that was born of an inability to concentrate stretched my nerves to near-screaming point. I suffered but refused to admit I was suffering. I refused to admit it to myself. I had deadlines to keep with the BBC, deadlines to keep with Collins and now even more deadlines to keep with my official typing in the force.

I remembered the firm rule instilled into me by a father I'd just about worshipped. You make a promise, you *keep* a promise . . . regardless of how much it costs.

I figured pills might help, and sought the advice of a doctor.

He was a nice guy, and a very honest guy. He knew me

as a copper, and also knew me as a novelist and radio playwright. He was blunt to the point of rudeness.

'Your trouble? You think you're God, and you're just about crazy enough to try to prove the point. You'll either kill yourself or drive yourself into a madhouse. Make up your mind. You're either a policeman or you're a writer. You can't be both . . . not full-time. Pills won't help you make up your mind. One or the other. Come and see me again when you've made the choice.'

It took me a few more months to appreciate the wisdom of his advice; a few more months of headaches, of bad dreams and of deadline bottlenecks. But, eventually, I made the choice.

I resigned, virtually within touching distance of a pension. In effect, I took my bonnet and flung it over the tallest windmill I could find.

It was one hell of a decision, but I had to make it alone. I couldn't ask Avis to become even a small part of that decision because, had she agreed with the choice and had it been wrong, she would have blamed herself for the rest of her life.

I recall little of those last few weeks. I know we had a month in which to find somewhere to live, and we hunted like crazy until we came across a tiny wooden bungalow on top of the cliffs at North Landing, Flamborough. It was a 'holiday bungalow' and it took the full belt of every gale coming in from the North Sea. Flamborough lighthouse flashed its beam into the bedroom window at night and that was rather romantic, but the foghorn blasting your eardrums when the sea fret lasted days on end was something the guy who sold us the bungalow forgot to mention.

But that was *after* I'd left the force.

I stopped being a copper on Wednesday, 1 July, 1966. The removal van was packed with our worldly goods, stacked in position by professionals, as opposed to muscular coppers with an enthusiasm well short of any sort of expertise. My last task was to hand in my warrant card at Otley DHQ and bid goodbye to the few colleagues I was sorry to leave: the inspector who was too nice a chap to be a policeman and who wished me luck in the privacy